Public Batt~~~~~~~~~~Wars

Public Battles, Private Wars

Laura Wilkinson

W F HOWES LTD

This large print edition published in 2017 by
W F Howes Ltd
Unit 5, St George's House, Rearsby Business Park,
Gaddesby Lane, Rearsby, Leicester LE7 4YH

1 3 5 7 9 10 8 6 4 2

First published in the United Kingdom in 2014
by Accent Press Ltd

ISBN 978 1 51005 770 8

Typeset by Palimpsest Book Production Limited,
Falkirk, Stirlingshire

Printed and bound by
Printforce Nederland b.v. in the Netherlands

*For my mum, Marian Williams. Inspiring woman; lousy cake maker.
And all the women of the strike.*

PROLOGUE

The race is about to begin, gun aimed at the pewter sky. A boy, older than the girls, watches from the sidelines, intent. The girls ignore him. Their eyes are fixed ahead, looking down the white line of the track. Blue sashes quiver against pounding young hearts. Team St Andrew is a winner.

An explosion, a puff of smoke, and they are off, galloping down the course, wind in their ears, blooms on their cheeks. Ruth is small and light; Mandy is solid, tall for her age. They make a good piggy-back team. There is nothing ahead but the finishing tape. The screaming crowd fades to a blur on the edges of vision. They canter on.

But Mandy's legs grow tired; there's heaviness in her thighs, despite the desire for victory. 'Practise, practise, we have to *practise*,' Ruth had said. Mandy hears the panting of another rider approaching. A sharp pain. A kick against her buttocks. The finishing line is within reach. They can win.

Ruth's arms tighten round Mandy's throat. Mandy dips her head and pushes her chest forward.

Everything closes in. She can hear Ruth's bark above the roar of the crowd, 'Giddy up, Horsey, giddy up!' Before Mandy falls she sees the yellow glint of the St David girls' sashes.

When she opens her eyes, Ruth is shrieking. Hysterical. 'You know what happens to old racehorses, don't you? Sent to the knacker's yard. Turned into dog food. Stinky, squishy, lumpy old dog food.' Ruth tears off her sash; throws it to the ground. Mandy crawls to where it lies, and as she picks it up she catches the pin of Ruth's sack race winner's ribbon. A bead of blood gleams at her. She watches Ruth crossing the field, pigtails flouncing. The boy approaches; offers Mandy his hand. He wants to help her up. Mandy shakes her head and stands, throws down the ribbon, and stamps on it again and again, until it is buried in the muddy earth. When she looks up, the boy with the kind grey eyes has gone.

BEFORE

1983

Soufflé

A light cake served as savoury or sweet depending upon the filling. From the French 'to blow, or puff, up', the dish is infamous for its tendency to collapse if removed from the oven too early.

CHAPTER 1

'Mrs Walker! Your fingers are meant to float over the keyboard. Dewdrops landing on grass; a dancer's feet brushing the stage. Not galumphing over it like a carthorse through mud.' Eyes closed, the teacher demonstrated, sweeping her delicate hands across some imaginary typewriter.

'That's all well and good if you've fingers like twigs, mine are like skittles.'

'It's merely a question of relaxing the wrists, Mrs Walker.' She strutted over, heels clickety-clacking on the parquet flooring, the sound fighting with key tapping as the rest of the class continued to wrestle with phrases from the books sitting on the desks. She rapped the back of my chair with her fingernails. 'Back straight, shoulders square, elbows in, knees together.'

'Knees together?'

'Secretarial work is more than typing and taking dictation,' she barked. 'A good secretary will accompany her boss to important meetings, conferences. Appearance is important. How we carry ourselves – vital.'

'And here was me thinking it were all about making cups of tea and knocking out the odd memo.' I turned to a woman on my right whose name I repeatedly forgot; she was as hopeless as me, though she did at least look the part in her tartan skirt and sensible shoes. She giggled and pulled a face, as I knew she would.

Teacher was not best pleased. 'Mrs Walker, you are here of your own volition, are you not? Do you or do you not want a qualification that will open the doors of opportunity? Afford a job for life?'

I lowered my eyes, humbled; a rock formed in my belly. What was the point in playing the class clown? No one had forced me here. Was my path to be the same as my mother's or Ethel Braithwaite's? I stared out of the window at the distant hills; the pithead cast a long shadow. Pulling in my chair, I rolled my shoulders, lifted my chin, and hammered away at the keyboard.

I looked at the sheet poking up behind the ribbon. *The xar sau int e mat. How now broan cowe, The red goc jumpef iver the brown gate. How ow broan cow> The cat sat ont eh mat. The red goc jumped over the browna hagte. The cat asua on the at;, How no brown cow?*

Ruddy hell, is there any hope for me?

The White Lion was heaving, the slap of the beery atmosphere sharp as we pushed open the heavy saloon doors. It was rare for me to come to the pub after class, usually I skittered home double quick to relieve Mum of her babysitting duties, but there was nothing on telly, I fancied a shandy, and there was a darts match on. Rob was playing.

The Boar's Head team perched at the bar; The Lion team sat with old man Braithwaite who looked as if he'd downed several jars already, though it was only shortly after nine. Same old faces everywhere. I shoved my way across to Rob.

'To what do we owe this honour, Mand?' he said, lighting a ciggie.

'Delighted to see you too, love. Get us a drink, will you?'

Rob didn't move. Vince got to his feet and gestured for me to sit. 'I'll get round in. By way of celebration.'

I raised my eyebrows. 'Celebration?'

'My lad's coming home. Back to where he belongs. Bosom of his lovin' family.'

He wandered to the bar, listing occasionally. No one said anything but they were as surprised as I was. Less than three years ago Dan Braithwaite had left for a career in the army. A lifelong career, Vince had boasted.

How is it possible to be discharged so quickly; isn't three years the minimum you can sign up for?

I remembered seeing Dan when he was home on leave during training. He was in uniform, marching down the high street towards his mam's house, looking handsome and proud. He never noticed me; I was six months pregnant, swallowed up in a dress that could have been pegged out as a marquee.

'How is the returning hero?' Rob asked, as Vince plonked the drinks down. I detected a hint of irony in his tone, though thankfully no one else seemed to notice. Vince was well-known for outbursts of violence, like most of the Braithwaites. Rob had never liked Dan; and though I'd not known Dan well, he'd struck me as arrogant. He kept his distance, like he was a cut above everyone else round Fenley Down.

I sipped at my drink but it tasted right funny.

'He's bringing a bride back with him,' Vince said. 'Used to live here, left while at secondary school. Funny family, didn't fit in.' He slurped his bitter, downing the pint in one. 'Break's over. Let's knock seven bells out of this sorry lot.' He slammed the empty glass on the table and pointed to the opposing team, who were hovering by the board, flexing their wrists, replacing feathers in tips.

I sat bolt upright – my typing teacher would have been proud. 'Ruth. Ruth Felix?'

He turned back to me. 'That's the one.'

'When they back?'

'Day after tomorrow.' With that Vince staggered towards the darts board. Heaven knows how he thought they could win; he could barely stand.

Bloody hell, that's quick. Why's he said nowt till now?

My mind swirled with memories. Ruth Felix: the

8

best friend in the whole wide world. At school she gave teachers lip but never got into trouble; she was the first to try a ciggie with the older lads at the back of the slag heap – she was popular and pretty, and I felt blessed that she considered me – plump, red-haired me – her friend. It made sense that Dan had married someone like her, someone different. Bit special. But coming back? Who'd have thought it?

Vince missed the board with his first shot but hit the bull's eye with his next. The pub erupted with jeers and cheers. In the corner was old Jean, unmoved by the commotion. We called her old Jean though she can't have been much older than Mum. Fifty, maybe, bit overweight, with fading red hair and disappointment etched into her features. The missus of one of the team, she looked bored stiff, like she'd been sitting in that spot for most of her life. Stuck. My belly twisted, like a wrung-out rag.

It could be me, thirty years from now.

Our team lost and I left for home soon after, shandy untouched. Rob was pissed and I needed to get some sleep. Johnnie would be up demanding milk in a few hours, though he was way too old for that nonsense. Little blighter.

The day Dan and Ruth came back was sticky and still, grey clouds pressed down on the village; we waited, hoped, for the sound of distant thunder. A storm to break the clammy weather. It was such

9

an ordinary day that I felt their arrival must have been delayed. There was no bunting, or marching band fanfare, sunlight bouncing off brass.

Not as if Braithwaites are royalty, though some of that family act like they are.

As usual, I dropped Mark at school. Through the wire mesh of the fence we watched him limping across the playground, one grey sock crumpled around his ankle. I nattered with the other mums, ignoring David's yelps of boredom and Johnnie's whining. Finally, to shut them up, I suggested we walk to the recreation ground for a play.

The rec was deserted. The climbing frame was wrapped in fraying plastic ribbons, a hand-written sign warning us not to use it. A wasp's nest had been found there. The slide was covered in broken glass, a half empty bottle of cider stood at the base next to a pile of sick and a crushed pack of Embassy Number 6. Johnnie strained against his straps, fighting to get out of the buggy; I stood behind the swing, idly pushing David to and fro. He screamed, 'Higher, higher,' but I ignored his cries and soon he grew tired. Half an hour passed and he was moaning that he was bored. Johnnie had fallen asleep. We headed home.

The boys played in the back garden while I washed the pots. Barely twenty-three with a husband and three kids. What would Ruth make of my life? Perhaps she knew already. The Braithwaites were a gobby lot.

I tried to focus on my day, but it was just another

brick piled on top of the others in the low wall that was my life: tidy the breakfast dishes, make the beds, break up a fight, have a brew, put the laundry on, feed the kids, hang out the washing, break up another fight, go down the shops, fetch Mark from school. Was this it for me? God help me, no. But what could I do? Nothing much.

After filling the paddling pool, I dragged out the old typewriter I'd picked up at the Sally Army and plonked it on the table.

I must practise, I must.

But it was too hot. After ten minutes my fingers and wrists ached and my head thumped. I decided to bake a cake. I loved cooking, especially baking. I took the yellow mixing bowl down from the top shelf. Made from ceramic, it was substantial and satisfying, unlike that expensive Tupperware rubbish. I ran my fingers along the heavily ridged edge, cut a slab of butter, and watched it slide off the knife. The bowl had belonged to my grandmother, four times winner of the 'Best Apple Pie' contest at the three villages' summer fair. With my grandmother's wooden spoon, I blended the caster sugar in the butter and added the eggs, enjoying the ease with which everything fused in the heat. No aching arms and sweating brow that day. I took my time sieving in the flour, folding it over and over and over. The consistency perfect. I took an orange and grated the peel into the mixture, my nose fizzing with the citrusy smell. David pattered in, water slapping on the tiled floor.

Chubby fingers gripped the work surface and he asked if I was making chocolate cake.

'Orange. Orange and lemon, petal.'

'I hate lemon. It's all sucky.'

He pulled his lips together, tight, and scrunched up his nose.

'It's your dad's favourite.'

He pulled another face and tapped my generous bottom. Womanly, Rob called it.

I crouched on my haunches; my thighs gluing themselves to the back of my bare calves beneath my cotton frock. 'I tell you what. How about I forget the lemon and make the buttercream chocolate? Chocolate orange cake?'

He nodded and padded back outside. After I'd prepared the tins, and before turning the oven on, I made the filling. Then I went to join the boys, noting the time first.

It was twenty-five past four but the heat pressed down, relentless. The grey clouds dropped lower and lower. The brittle grass crunched beneath my feet, pricking the soles. Our garden was small, south-facing, narrow without borders or flower-beds, at the bottom was a pear tree so weedy its shade offered little relief. I paddled in the pool with the boys and pretended not to like it when they splashed me with the lukewarm, grassy water. In the end, laughing, drenched, and absolutely not thinking about Ruth and Dan – their exciting life and my really, really boring one – I sat down in the pool and watched water gather in the folds of my dress. A butterfly landed on the side and we stopped and stared. Black wings with dusty orange eyes folded together, its antennae quivering. All four of us silent, wondering what it might do next. It was David who spoke first.

'What's a group of butterflies called?'

'I haven't got a clue. Only butterfly I know is a cake.'

We fell silent again, watching, and it was then that I heard it: a banging, pushing through the sticky air. It sounded like the front door. I stood, gathered my skirt in my fists, wringing out as much water as I could, then stepped over the plastic rim and pushed my sopping feet into my flip-flops.

The hammering at the door grew more and more insistent as I padded through the back room and into the hall, water dripping on the bare concrete floor.

It was Phil Braithwaite, red-faced, a triangular patch of sweat on his t-shirt. He was an odd shade of grey and something in his eyes liquidised my insides. 'There's been an accident, at pit. Chance your Rob's involved. I've come to get yer.' He gestured to the red Ford Escort parked opposite and continued to speak, though I didn't hear the words.

'I'll need to turn oven off,' I said, waving him in. I staggered through the house to the garden, boneless. Mining was dangerous, everyone knew it. Dirty, risky work, even now. If it wasn't the

13

cause of Dad's illness, it finished him off. But I'd never thought it would affect me again. Rob.

There was an invincible quality to Rob, though he wasn't tough. Not in the way that the Braithwaite brothers were. He seemed to have a protective shield, like those children in the Ready Brek adverts; it's what attracted me to him, this glow. I'd never considered, not for one moment, that Rob would ever get hurt. I couldn't believe it; not even now.

The boys knew something was very wrong; they followed me without a protest, cry or word, to Phil's car. 'Chance your Rob's involved.' The words ricocheted round my head.

So there's a chance he might not be.

'Is your mam at bakery? Can we drop lads there?' Phil said, as the car screeched down the road. 'Pit's no place for them.'

'No.' I agreed.

Someone must have brought the news to Mum because she was waiting outside when we pulled up, face fixed with her cheeriest smile. 'Ey up, lovelies. Look what Nana's got for you.' She waved a bag of goodies, crouched down, gathered all three boys in her arms and hugged them, nodding at me over Mark's shoulder, wordlessly telling me not to worry about them, to get myself down to the pit.

Back in Phil's car, with the children dispatched, I found my voice. 'What happened? What about Rob's mum and dad? Have they been told?

14

Are you sure it's him?' The questions poured out of me.

'Steady on, Mandy. I don't know owt meself. Other than there's been an explosion, at coal face, some of men are out already. Me Dad's down there an' all. Was in same shaft as your Rob.'

'Jesus, Phil, I'm sorry.'

We drove the rest of the short journey in silence, the car heavy with the smell of fear.

Outside the pit, a small crowd had gathered, waiting wives, girlfriends, lovers, held at bay by sympathetic policemen. There were even a handful of children running between mounds of coke, faces smeared with sweat and black dust. Medics, firemen, and other rescue workers ferried between the pit head and their vehicles. I saw Ethel, Phil's mum, amongst the crowd, wrapped in a head-scarf, curlers poking out of the front. She walked over to where Phil and I stood, her face set in a mask of grim determination. I expected her to hug Phil, some sign of affection, but she merely nodded.

'The twins?' he said.

'Fine. Different shaft. Michael, Richard, Stephen. All good,' Ethel replied. Before I had a chance to speak, she looked at me and said, 'No sign of Rob yet.' She offered a bag of sweets. 'Humbug?'

I shook my head.

And then we waited. Everyone hoping that their man would be one of those to make it out, even

15

if it meant their neighbours' loved one didn't. Unspoken prayers. Fear making us selfish.

After a time, people began to talk. Hushed whispers from mouths hidden by cupped hands. Cigarettes and boiled sweets shared. One woman, hunched with age, even had a flask. She'd been here before. She offered me a cup of tea and I accepted it gratefully. It was cold and tinny tasting.

The first miner came out; the crowd surged, craning to see who lay on the stretcher. A raised arm, a wave, a cry of relief, moans of disappointment and dread.

By dusk there were only three left trapped in the tunnel: Rob, Vince, and a man I didn't know. We'd watched, hope fading, as the crowd peeled away, one after the other, separated from our neighbours by guilt and terror. No fatalities, so far. Food was delivered and taken away untouched. Blankets draped over our shoulders. Soon I was flanked on all sides by Braithwaites. Everyone else had gone.

'Shall Phil take you home, Mandy?' Ethel said. 'He'll fetch you again as soon as there's news. Nowt you can do here, chicken.'

'Oh, I couldn't, Mrs Braithwaite, thanks all—'

A scream of brakes on tarmac interrupted my scrambled reply. We shielded our eyes from the dazzle of headlights and watched two figures climbing out of the car. A voice came from behind.

'Comes another!'

I swung round towards the mine head as rescue workers emerged with another body. Arms flayed in the gloomy air; gruff cries of 'leave me be' rose above the purr of the still-running car engine.

Ethel roared, 'That's my Vince!' and another voice rang out behind me.

'Thank heavens he's alive! We came as soon as we saw the note. We've only just arrived. The traffic was appalling!' It was a female voice, posh. Not from round here, but it stirred something deep within me. I spun on my heels yet again.

A woman, tall and lean, with long brown hair held back from her face with an Alice band. 'Mandy! You haven't changed a bit!'

Stunned, I stared.

'It's Ruth, Ruth Braithwaite. You knew me as Felix.' Even her voice was different; no trace of an accent.

'You've changed. You look . . .' I stammered, 'amazing.'

'Oh my God. What are you doing here?' And as if realising the stupidity of her question she gasped and clamped her hand over her mouth. It tipped me over the edge. I'd not cried till then. I'd clenched my fear in a grasp so tight, it couldn't breathe, and the look on Ruth's face made me loosen that hold. I howled like a baby, tears and snot streaming. 'I'd forgotten you were coming home today,' I blubbered.

'Of course you did, darling. Who wouldn't? We knew something was wrong as soon as we pulled into the close. There was no one to welcome us.' The shock of such neglect still evident in her tone.

A man approached and stood by Ruth's side. Dan. Tall, poker-straight, his face the colour of ash, well-defined cheekbones illuminated by the overspill of light from the headlamps. His eyes were an extraordinary blue-grey, like metal, and it struck me as odd that I should notice such detail at a time like this.

'You go on and say hello to your dad. He'll need cheering up, I'd say,' I snuffled into my hankie.

'Best not fuss. He's enough round him,' Dan said.

I was about to protest when there were more shouts and there was a burst of activity; emergency workers running from the mine head, yellow jackets flickering in the fading light. The policemen raced towards us, waving their arms. 'Move back! Move back!'

I felt hands grabbing me by the shoulder and pulling me backwards; I stared at the mine. Four rescue workers raced, heads down, one hand clutching a stretcher, the other holding onto their hard hats. Two stretchers; two remaining miners. And the shaft was about to blow again. Rob.

With strength I didn't know I possessed, I freed myself and hurtled towards the stretchers, falling to my knees when I saw Rob's blood-stained face. He smiled at me, teeth gleaming white against his blackened face, and then he closed his eyes, head flopping to one side.

'Rob!' I screamed.

'He's going to be fine, love. Now get down!'

18

I felt the ground rumble beneath me. I looked at the pit head, anticipating an explosion, but none came.

Rob and his colleague were taken away in the only ambulance left. The police offered but Ruth insisted she took me to hospital. Ethel had gone with Phil and the others. 'Dan won't mind a bit. He'd be going anyway.'

Head between folded arms, Dan was leaning on the car roof. He jerked upright as we approached, beads of sweat glistening on his upper lip. Mopping his brow and muttering, he opened the back door for me with a trembling hand, before climbing into the front. He reached across into the glove compartment and a medicine bottle fell onto the passenger seat. He swept it up, glancing round as he did so. I looked away. He offered me a travel sweet.

'You'll need one. For shock,' he said. 'Come on,' he yelled at Ruth who was talking to one of the firemen.

She looked in through the window. 'Oh,' she gasped, 'you've cut your knee.'

Dried blood snaked down my leg. She opened the door, then pulled a silk scarf from her fashionable chain-handled bag and wrapped it round me with care. As she finished I glanced up and saw Dan swallowing hard, throwing the pill bottle back into the glove compartment.

'Thanks, you're a star,' I said. 'Don't know what I'd have done without you.'

Ruth climbed in next to me, leaving Dan alone in the front like some kind of cabbie, and draped her arm across my shoulders. 'What are friends for? Now let's get you to hospital. Rob will be wondering where you are.'

CHAPTER 2

A&E was bonkers; folk milling everywhere; chewing fingernails, snapping at the receptionist. We'd been told that the injuries seemed minor, but no one could be sure. Dazed, I glanced around, catching sight of Rob's mum and dad hovering in the corner. His mum saw me and came over. For one horrible moment I thought she was going to hug me, but she thought better of it. Unsure what to say, we stood there like lemons.

'There's a bit of a backlog. The more serious injuries are being seen first,' Ruth touched my arm, reassuring, 'Close relatives can go through to the cubicles. Rob's in number four, next to Vince.' She led me through the crowd.

Rob lay on a bed, grey-cheeked, hollow-eyed. He'd been wiped clean, though not well. Coal dust mingled with sweat at the edges of his face, small cuts wept across his forehead. One jacket sleeve had been cut away to reveal a blood-soaked dressing near his shoulder. I stared at the wound, my gaze trailing down his arm. I gasped at the shape of his lower arm; below the elbow, maybe two inches, the limb flopped down at a right angle. It looked like rubber tubing, not a limb of flesh, blood, and bone.

'It's a right state,' Rob said. 'Paramedics reckon busted in three, maybe four places.'

'Painful?'

'You what?' he said, though I'd not spoken quietly.

'Painful?' I repeated, louder this time.

'Too fucking right. And I can't have no pain-killers till I've been seen. In case of needing surgery,' he shouted. He rolled his head toward his shoulder and winced.

'Pull that curtain back!' Vince's familiar tones snapped through the flimsy divide; the floral curtain whooshed away to reveal the old man flanked by Ethel, Phil, Michael, Stephen, twins Craig and Paul, Dan, and Ruth. No other patient would have been allowed so many visitors, but this was Fenley's answer to the Godfather. 'Stop your whining, you great nancy. We were lucky. There's them that have seen much, much worse, eh, Dan?' Vince looked at his youngest son, and I wasn't sure if I saw pride or pity on the old man's face. Dan stared at the floor and didn't reply; he was as grey as Rob. Ruth clutched his hand and squeezed; I caught her eye as she did so and smiled.

'Would you like to see your parents, Rob?' Ruth broke the atmosphere. 'I'm sure it can be arranged.'

Rob didn't seem to hear and then a nurse

appeared at the foot of the bed. She read the notes attached to the bed frame and shouted, 'You're next, Mr Walker! Registrar will take a look at you now.'

'See the old man first, please,' Rob said.

'As you wish. Another will be along soon. Right then, you lot. Time to make yourself scarce. Aside from Mrs B, of course.' She pulled the divide across; Ruth's head poked between the gap. 'Coffee, while they're being seen?'

Rob told me to go. 'Doctor'll be along soon enough, love. Nothing you can do here.'

The WI shop was closed so we made do with machine coffee and huddled in the corner of the still jam-packed reception, sitting on the tiled floor, knees to our chests, like we did as girls.

'I'm glad you're still here, Mandy.'

'Not likely to be down pub, am I?'

She laughed. 'No, I mean, here,' she waved her hand around her head, 'in Fenley Down. Thought you might have moved on.'

It was my turn to laugh. 'No chance!'

We sipped our drinks, scalding lips on the boiling liquid. 'Will there be an investigation?' she said.

I shrugged. 'Imagine so.'

'Vince doesn't seem keen. Dan brought it up earlier and Vince got quite heated. Said that it "were dangerous work and we all know risks. Part of job."' She mimicked Vince's gruff tones. Perfectly. I giggled.

We'd not finished our coffees when the nurse reappeared and informed us that the doctor wanted to talk with me. Vince and Rob had been dispatched to different wards. We hugged each other goodbye, promising to see each other soon. I was so glad she was around; delighted that she was back.

Rob had escaped with just cuts, bruises, and an arm broken in three places. He was incredibly lucky, the doctor said. His arm would take months to heal fully, but he would be back in work by autumn. Rob was deaf in one ear, on account of the blast, though this was temporary. I suspected that Rob would use it to his advantage, ignoring the cries of the boys, the doorbell, me, whenever it suited. He was discharged within days. Ruth offered the use of Dan's 'taxi' service to collect Rob from hospital, but Rob refused.

'I want nothing from him. See his face when his old man went on about danger?'

I shook my head; I hadn't the faintest idea what he was shouting his mouth off about.

'Like I were scum. Just 'cos he's been in some poxy little war, don't make him no hero in my book.'

Rob had always resented the top dog status of the Braithwaites – he wasn't unusual in this – but Dan's return challenged his position as probably the best-looking bloke in the village, though Dan wasn't conventionally handsome in the same way Rob was. Men could be right stupid at times.

★   ★   ★

24

Fists clenched, I pummelled the dough, enjoying its stretchiness, its resistance to my pounding. The warm September air was rich with the scent of yeast; I loved the smell of it in its raw, live state, and when it was baking, wafting through our house. My arms began to throb; I picked up a piece of yeast from the work surface, rolling it between my thumb and forefinger. It felt like putty, and I found it hard to believe that the compound was alive, growing, cells dividing and multiplying. Exactly like what was going on inside me.

After a restless night, still not used to the cast on his arm, Rob was in a foul temper but I'd been building myself up to telling him for days and I was determined not to back out.

He was sitting at the kitchen table, cradling his mug of tea and slurping it occasionally. I plonked porridge bowls in the sink, and turned around, looking for the tea towel. There were black lines engrained in the skin around his ears and at the back of his neck, like coal seams; even after weeks at home. My first instinct was to take a cloth and wipe away the dust, kiss him on the ear, how he liked it, and tell him that I fancied him as much as I did the day I first clapped eyes on him. Something stopped me.

I was running the hot tap to wet the rag when he asked me where his toast was.

'In the bread bin, where it always is,' I said, joking. I was about to say, 'And how would you like it this morning, love? With jam, marmalade, or just butter?' when he stood up, waving his plastered arm and said, 'I'll get it myself then, shall I?'

I told him to sit down. I was nervous, and though I'd gone through the words a thousand times in my head, they slipped away in a moment of mild panic.

Toast made, I placed it in front of him and sat down opposite. Elbows resting on the table, he opened his mouth to take a bite and I blurted, 'How do you feel about another baby?'

Still hunched, he lifted his head, those crystal blue eyes staring at me. 'You asking me, or telling me?'

'Telling you.'

He dropped the toast onto the plate. The room was silent, apart from the steady drip from the leaky tap. I expected him to start shouting, ask stupid questions, like how did that happen, but he held his head in his hands and ran the fingers of one through his hair. I watched the thick black tufts sprout between his fingers and waited for him to speak. He took his time.

'We agreed three was enough.'

'I know. Three's enough.'

'Are you wanting to get an abortion?' He looked pained as he spoke.

'Too late for that.'

'Oh, Mand.' He took my fingers in his. 'You said you wanted your life to change. But this?'

I bit my lip, and shrugged. He was right. What

a stupid thing to do. Let happen. I'd denied it was happening for weeks.

'You can get a refund for course?' he said.

'I'm still going. It's typing, not rugby.'

'What's bloody point? You'll have baby to look after soon enough.'

He pushed the chair out behind him, he knew I hated the sound of the metal legs scraping against the tiles, and let his head fall onto the table with a thump. Then he stood, quite suddenly, and announced that he was off to The White Lion. I protested that it was Thursday and there was no money in the tin till sick pay came through and drinking wouldn't solve anything.

'I'll run a tab, Bill won't mind,' he said, slinging his jacket on.

'I mind. We're going to need all the money we can get soon.'

'You should have thought of that.' He slammed the front door behind him so hard I thought the glass would shatter.

Livid, I chased after him but stopped when the front gate fell off its last remaining hinge. I yelled down the street, 'And that's another thing that needs fixing. Put that on a tab, will you?'

I wanted to scream. All those plans of getting a job, working in an office: scuppered. I heard a voice behind me and turned as Johnnie jumped off the step, the front door slamming behind him. In my haste to catch up with Rob I'd forgotten to wedge it open.

'Shit and bloody shit.'

Braving the alley at the back, we stumbled round to the garden, clambering over rusting fridges and old trainers. Bindweed wrapped itself around everything; the stench of cat shit turned my stomach. After crawling on top of an old dustbin, I helped Johnnie over the fence. Then I pushed myself up and swung over, catching my skirt on a nail. As I struggled to free myself, I heard the click of a door opening, the shuffle of slippered feet, and I wondered if I had decent knickers on – my skirt was round my waist. A neighbour was about to get an eye full.

'Morning, Mrs Walker.'

'Morning, Doug.' I lifted my head and smiled, pathetic.

Doug was seventy-two, a widower, and partially sighted. He carried a plastic liner to the bin, lifted the lid, slung it in and slammed the lid back down as if he was knocking out the final note of a symphony. Doug had played the cymbals in the village band till his poor eyesight meant he was a hazard to himself and others in any public parade.

'You alright there?'

'Fine.'

'Champion.' He turned back but before he closed the door he said, 'Nice arse.'

'You dirty old git,' I said, under my breath.

'Nothing wrong with my hearing, Mrs Walker.'

'Eyesight's not so bad either, eh?'

He shook his head, smiling, and closed the door behind him.

The back door was locked and the kitchen window closed. There was an open window upstairs but I was four-and-a-bit months pregnant; scaling a drainpipe was out of the question. So we clambered over the fence again, and went back down the alley.

By the time we got to the pub Johnnie was grumbling that his legs were hurting. I'd kept him going with the promise of a packet of crisps and a dandelion and burdock, and as I pulled open the door to the saloon I hoped that Rob was there, that he'd not gone on elsewhere, or made his way home again. All feelings of embarrassment had disappeared; I wanted to sit down and rest my aching feet.

The stink of alcohol and cigarettes turned my stomach as we stepped into the room. My shoes clung to the beer-sodden carpet making it an effort to put one foot in front of the other. As I approached the short bar and looked around the room, I saw the back of Rob's head. He was sitting in the corner, with Dan and a bloke called Lesley who'd done a spell in the nick.

Dan tipped his chin and raised his pint. Rimmed with dark shadows, his eyes were steel: cold and hard, more grey than the twinkling blue of my Rob's. I glanced at Rob, surprised to find him sitting, drinking, with a man he didn't like. 'Nothing but contempt for that jumped up wanker,' he'd said. He even refused to give Dan any thanks for taking me to hospital after the accident.

'Big, bloody deal. He was on way to see his dad.'

A free pint was evidently enough to change his mind.

I'd not seen Dan since that day; he'd lain low, and not only from us. I'd seen Ruth a few times – I'd dropped a cake off as a thank you – but not as often as I'd have liked. She'd been busy, making house and getting ready for the start of term.

'Nice to see you again, Mrs Walker,' Dan said.

'Call me Mandy.' At the sound of my voice, Rob turned and smiled. He looked surprised, but the beer had softened his mood.

'Hello, love. What you doing here?'

I bent down and swept Johnnie up, onto my hip, and walked over to the table. 'Locked myself out.' I stuck my tongue in front of my teeth, behind my bottom lip and made a "what an idiot" face.

'Sit down.' He tapped the stool beside him.

I plonked myself down. 'Don't mind if I do. I'm knackered. We've been all over.'

'And how are you, young Johnnie? Your dad's been telling me all about your adventures,' Dan said. Johnnie buried his face in my shoulder.

'Love kids, me. Have a house full of them, I would,' Dan said.

'He's always shy with strangers,' I said.

'Now that you're settled, you can get on with it,' Rob interrupted.

'Plenty of time.'

'None like the present,' Rob said.

Dan stared into his glass. How tired he looks.

'Ruth's got her career to consider,' I added.

'That's what she says.' Dan half-smiled and added, 'Feminists, eh? Who'd have them?'

The men all chuckled.

'Nothing against them feminists, but I like my Mandy where she is,' Rob said, wrapping his arm round my shoulder.

'What? In pub?' said Lesley, laughing.

'No, you pillock. At home, with kids.'

'You certainly do,' I said, smiling. But I wondered what it might be like to have a proper job. A career. But there was nothing I could do. I was kidding myself about the typing.

'Would the nipper like something to drink?' Lesley said.

'Please. And I'll have a coke an' all. And some crisps if that's OK?'

'Doesn't ask for much, does she?' Lesley said, pushing himself up. He looked unsteady on his feet as he ambled to the bar.

How many had they had in the hour or so since opening?

'I like a woman who knows what she wants,' Dan said, pulling a couple of cigarettes part way out of a packet of John Player Special and offering them round.

I shook my head; I'd never been a smoker.

'That your Ruth then, eh? Determined?' Rob said, taking a cigarette, nodding his thanks, a hard edge to his voice. He made it sound as if admitting this was tantamount to admitting weakness.

'It is,' Dan said, staring directly at Rob, as he leaned over to offer a light. 'What about you?' he added, jerking his head in my direction. 'You a feminist?'

I didn't know what to say; I'd never really thought about it. But before I could think up a clever answer, Rob jumped in. 'I've nothing against strong-minded women. In principle,' he withdrew his arm from my shoulder, 'though there's one I can think of that I'd like to throttle.' Everyone laughed and it lightened the atmosphere, this reference to the prime minister.

Johnnie and I drank our drinks and ate our crisps. My stomach was growling, those crisps barely touched my hunger, so I was pretty sure Johnnie would be starving too. We went to leave. We were about to step onto the street when I remembered that I'd not collected the keys.

Back inside, Rob handed them over, saying, 'I won't be long, love. I'll collect lads from school later, if you like.'

'Blimey. You have had a few! They can walk themselves.'

'Be nice to spend some time with them. What's point in having kids otherwise?'

Dan stood up, a jerky, sudden movement. He drained his pint and said, 'Time I was off,' and marched out of the pub.

'Almost heard his heels click, then,' said Lesley.

Johnnie and I left, walking as fast as we could down the high street. As we turned at the cross-roads I saw Dan. He took long, straight strides, arms stiff at his sides; he kicked a stone or a can or something, hard, and I wondered what troubled him, for it was obvious that something did.

CHAPTER 3

Parents' Evening was running late; I kept looking at my watch as if that would hurry things along. Rob was on shift later and he'd want a supper before he left. It was warm in the school corridor, and I enjoyed the stinging sensation in my fingers and toes as they came back to life. It was a parky night, and I could no longer fasten the buttons on my coat. Another mum stepped out of the classroom and tipped her head, eyes rolling.

'Says you can go in now,' she said.

I pushed myself up, belly leading, and picked up the pile of exercise books beside me and stepped forward. I felt ever so nervous, like I was going for an interview or something. Not that I'd ever been to an interview, not since the one with the careers adviser at school, when I'd been told to register at dole come July and check out the situations vacant board. 'There'll be all kinds of opportunities. Shop work, bar work. Shame you didn't work for those exams. You might even get the chance to work in an office if you keep up your typing,' she'd said. 'Whoopee-do,' I'd thought then.

As I entered the classroom, Ruth stood, and smoothed down her navy skirt; her stomach was flat, her hips narrow. 'Good evening, Mrs Walker.' She pulled a face; I saw the ten-year-old Ruth. 'We're supposed to call parents by their surnames!'

'This is funny, isn't it?' I said.

'It is. Think I'm getting used to it now. It's amazing how many of the mums remember me. It's so embarrassing. I barely remember any of them.' She smiled, and I relaxed a little. I wasn't surprised they remembered her; she was special.

'How is everything? You like it here?' I said.

'I love it! You know when I left my last school I thought "I'll never find as lovely a school as this, as lovely children, parents, everything". I cried when we left, Mandy, cried, and I thought I'd never be as happy anywhere else. But I was wrong. I love it here. It's perfect. Everyone is so kind and friendly and the children . . . well, lovely. Just lovely.'

'You can't have been long at that first school?'

'Heavens no. Only a year.'

'I bet they miss you.'

She nodded. 'Only yesterday I received a letter from a teacher friend there. She says my replacement is nowhere near as good, despite years and years of experience. But she's a friend, so bound to be biased!' She sounded surprised by this, but I couldn't imagine anyone measuring up to Ruth. Not that I knew much about schools and teaching.

'What have you been up to?'

'Oh, this and that. Work. Mostly. Been terribly, terribly busy. You know how it is.' I hadn't got a clue, but didn't like to say so. I was always busy, with the kids, but not like she must have been busy, with a proper job and all. 'How's the typing coming along?'

'Fine. Still going, though for how much longer . . .' I looked at my belly. 'Probably never use it for years and then I'll be right rubbish again.'

'Not true.' She wagged a finger. 'You can practice when baby sleeps and if you're good enough you might even take in freelance work. Plenty of graduates need dissertations typing up.'

Freelance was a new word to me and though I guessed at its meaning I knew it was way too fancy pants for the likes of Mandy Walker. And as for dissertations . . . I smiled and kept quiet.

She clapped her hands together. 'Look, Mandy. I'm terribly sorry, but you're only supposed to get ten minutes and I'm already running late. Let's have a proper catch-up chat another time.'

'It'd be grand to meet up, have a natter.' I didn't like to say that it was her that had done all the talking.

'Everything alright?' Her tone was business-like.

'Oh yes. How are you settling in to your house?'

'Fine.' She tapped the exercise books. 'We'd best get on. Pop over any time.'

'Will do.'

'So . . . young David. He's bright.'

'Must take after his father then.'

36

'Oh, don't be so modest, you great apeth!' It was what she called me when we were small: an apeth, and we laughed out loud. 'You were so clever. Full of bright ideas, weird facts. God knows where you got them from!'

'Was I?' I couldn't remember ever being considered clever.

''Course!' She drew out the 'or' sound and she sounded like she did as a teenager. Funny, bit melodramatic.

She talked some more, about David's reading and writing, his sums and games. He didn't sound like any son of mine.

'Golly. Look at the time. We've been chatting for almost fifteen minutes.'

'I'll be off then.' I stood.

'Are you seeing Mrs Michaels about Mark?'

'I'll pop over soon.'

She looked puzzled.

'To yours?' I said.

'Oh, yes. Do. That'd be lovely.'

'Any particular time?'

'No, no. Take your chances! Bye for now!'

Mrs Michaels was sitting waiting for me when I turned into Mark's classroom. I apologised but she brushed me aside saying there was no need. 'Mrs Braithwaite likes to talk to all the parents in detail. Here till gone seven last night, we were. Kept some of them talking for twice as long as she should have done.'

★　★　★

37

Rob was sitting in the living room when I got back, *The Sun* folded on his lap. Mark and David were sitting on the floor, legs crossed, watching *Emmerdale Farm*.

'Johnnie in bed?' I said, my head popped round the door. 'He go down alright?'

'No bother. Piece of cake. Don't know what you go on about.' He smiled, but didn't take his eyes off the television.

'Different when you do it every night,' I said, before scurrying to the kitchen, not waiting to hear his retort. He had a gob on him at times, Rob did, and I wasn't sure if he'd been serious or not. There were three plates scattered across the table, the remnants of fish fingers and beans. I chopped some onions, put the kettle on, and heated a drop of oil in a pan before frying some liver I'd bought that afternoon. A packet of Smash lay accusingly on the work surface; to peel and boil and mash some potatoes would take too long. I was starving and could guarantee that Rob's grumpiness was down to his empty belly. I opened a tin of marrowfat peas and slung them in a pan.

The living room door clicked open. The soap opera theme tune floated through to the kitchen and I heard Rob sending the boys up to bed, yelling at them not to forget to clean their teeth.

'Perfect timing. Tea's ready,' I said as he wandered into the kitchen. 'Sit yourself down.' I placed the plate in front of him. 'Your favourite.'

For the first few forkfuls we ate in silence. Then,

38

he put down his cutlery. 'What kind of potato is this, Mand? Tastes funny.'

'Instant. Sorry, love, there was no time. Liver's good, though, eh?'

'Best. And it's alright, this mash. Just different, that's all.' He smiled and cut another piece of meat. I liked to watch him eat, even when it was rubbish grub like the crispy pancakes we had from time to time. 'So how'd it go?' he said, sipping on his lemon pop.

'OK. Mark's a bag of trouble. But we know that,' I said.

'And what about our David? How's that monster getting on?'

'He's bright, according to Mrs Braithwaite.'

'Mrs Braithwaite? She's Ruth to you, isn't she?'

'He must take after you,' I said.'

'Brains as well as beauty, that's me.' He winked as he spoke and I smiled, despite myself. He could be an arrogant so-and-so, even if he was right nice looking. After all this time I still found it hard to believe sometimes that he'd married me. Of all the lovely girls he could have had, me.

'Ruth's a looker, isn't she?' I said.

'Not my type. Far too hoity-toity. And skinny. Needs some meat on her.' And he came over, kissed my forehead, and rubbed my belly before taking my plate as well as his own to the sink.

Later, once Rob had gone on shift, I curled up in bed and read my magazine, determined to investigate Ruth's idea of working from home after the baby was born and I'd done my exams. The baby shifted; my stomach rippled and bulged with each jab of elbow or heel. It was going to be a tricky one, this one. Keeping me awake at night, sleeping all day. Don't forget about me, she seemed to say. I ached for a girl, an ally in this house of men. Even the pets were male: two guinea pigs and a gerbil named Gordy.

All night long, the baby kicked and rolled and hiccupped. As dawn broke I fell asleep only to be woken minutes later by a freshly bathed Rob climbing into bed.

CHAPTER 4

All was quiet as I turned into the cul-de-sac. At the bottom end where I stood the street lights weren't working, so I turned off my torch and looked into the evening sky. The moon was low, big as a pie and so bright it hurt my eyes to look at it for too long. I felt small and insignificant and I almost turned back. But to get here had taken a lot of organising, and I was expected.

Mum had all three boys for tea, and it was her day off from the bakery too, so she was doing me a big favour. Usually, she went to the bingo on Mondays – the jackpot was extra-large and it was her habit to go to her friend Joanne's and have a few Dubonnet and lemonades first. 'To get us in the mood,' she said. She gave up that small treat so that I could go out. In the past she'd invited me to join them, but I felt too young for bingo. It was full of old people and some of the roughest characters in town. Old Mrs Braithwaite graced the place with her presence on Mondays, or so I'd heard.

I checked my watch: five past five. There was plenty of time. I couldn't find the doorbell, so I flipped the letterbox instead. It was stiff and didn't make much of a noise; it was one of those that had black nylon bristles top and bottom, covering the hole, the sort that postmen cursed. I waited. No one answered. I banged on the door with my fist. When the door opened there stood Ruth, in leotard, leggings, and neon-green legwarmers, her hair in a ponytail, a twisted scarf tied around her forehead. Her face glistened. I could hear the drawl of an American accent coming from inside the house, barking out instructions.

'No wonder you've stayed so slim,' I said.

'Come in, come in.' She waved me in to a wide, square hall, with pinkish walls and a pale grey carpet. There were no stains on it. Not one. 'Let me take your coat. Golly, Jane Fonda's a tyrant. I'm exhausted.'

'Feeling the burn?' I smiled, wrestling with my anorak and scarf, though I didn't actually know what 'the burn' was.

'You should try it,' she said, throwing my rags onto a free standing wooden coat stand.

'Oh, I'll be feeling a burn soon enough when I have to push this one out, thanks,' I said, but she didn't get the joke, and I felt as if I'd sullied the place, stepped dog shit into the carpet. Holding out a tin I said, 'I made a cake. Hope you still like Victoria sponge.'

She thanked me and took it to the kitchen while I waited in the hall.

We went through to the living room. It was

42

enormous, with a dining table and French windows at the far end and two settees and a coffee table at the other. I wondered why they wanted two settees and then I noticed the telly. It was smaller than ours, which surprised me, but underneath it was a video recorder. Rob would be mad jealous when I told him. And I'd thought teachers were badly paid. She must have seen me taking it all in because she said, 'Two wages. Hope it won't always be that way!' She looked at my swollen belly. 'May I?' she said, hands outstretched. I nodded and she placed her hands on me. Even through my thick jumper I could feel the warmth of her touch and obviously so did the little lady because she stirred and Ruth gasped, pulling her hands away as if she'd been scalded.

'Does it hurt?' she said. What could I say? 'It's worth it, though?' she added and I nodded. It was. Most of the time.

'Look at me! I haven't even offered you a drink!' Ruth said, slapping her forehead with the heel of her hand. 'Sit down.' It sounded like an order she might give to her class, and for a moment I was tempted to sit on the floor with my legs crossed. I lowered myself onto the cream settee and it folded around me, almost sending me rolling backwards it was so soft and deep. It was quite an effort to sit upright; it reminded me of one of those massive cushions filled with polystyrene balls. Looked good, but bloody uncomfortable.

'Now, what would you like? We've Earl Grey, Peppermint, Darjeeling, Ceylon . . . or if you'd like something a little stronger: Sherry, Martini, Malibu . . .' she was wandering over to what I assumed was a sideboard until she pulled down the front to reveal a large selection of booze and a set of crystal glasses.

'It's a bit early for me,' I said. 'A cup of tea would be smashing if it's no bother?'

'Any old tea?'

'Typhoo's fine.'

'I can manage that!' And she disappeared into the kitchen.

The settee was so uncomfortable I got up; intending to sit down again when I heard her returning. I wandered over to the drinks cabinet and caught sight of picture frames on the long shelf above the fire. As I walked over I could see that they were pictures of Dan and Ruth: on their wedding day, her in an enormous dress with puff sleeves and what looked like the longest train I'd ever seen; at a party, sitting at a table with the remains of a slap-up dinner in front of them, shiny-faced from too much Blue Nun and laughter; on a white beach with red shoulders and noses, arms draped around each other, sunglasses protecting their eyes from the glare of a foreign sun. They looked so glamorous, and young, and beautiful. I saw my reflection in the mirror above the brick fireplace: all blotchy and red. It was warm in there; the pretend flames of the electric fire licked against the smoked glass front. Rob and I never looked that good together.

I picked up the wedding photograph and looked closer. Dan was in a soldier's uniform, stiff-backed, his red beret tucked under his arm. His hands were smooth and white. When Ruth waltzed back into the living room I jumped; I still had the photograph in my hand and I plonked it back onto the mantelpiece. If she saw me do it, she didn't say.

Ruth placed a tray on the glass-topped coffee table. After she'd poured the tea, she pushed a plate of chocolate biscuits towards me.

'I'll spoil my tea,' I said, starving, but embarrassed to eat in front of her.

'Go on. You're eating for two now.' She pushed it further forward.

'Oh all right then,' I said, and took a delicate bite. 'What are they?'

'Hand-baked—'

'They're amazing! Never have had you down as a cook!' I said, unable to conceal my surprise, almost choking on the biscuit in my mouth. She didn't look like anything sweet had passed her lips in twelve months or more. In fact, she didn't look like she'd eaten anything at all.

'By the bakery,' she shrugged.

We laughed. It went quiet. I ate the biscuit and Ruth sipped her tea. We smiled at each other, but nothing was said. The silence was making me uncomfortable, but the cat had got my tongue.

And Ruth's, it seemed. I reached for another biscuit.

'I heard about your dad. How awful for you. I'm so sorry.'

'It's OK,' I said, before biting into the biscuit. I didn't want to talk about my dad; I missed him. It'd been eight years, eight years that I'd filled with babies. Little lives. But I still missed his life.

Ruth filled the silence. 'Your mum still at the bakery? I didn't see her there today.'

'It's her day off.'

'Do you remember when we ate all the Bakewells?'

Mouth full of biscuit, I could only nod and smile with my mouth closed.

'She was furious, wasn't she? How were we to know that they weren't the leftovers from the day's business?' She giggled, but despite chewing like mad my mouth was still full, and I could only continue nodding. I remembered the incident well. 'I can't believe you persuaded me to eat them,' Ruth said, topping up her tea.

'Was it my idea?' I said. I honestly couldn't remember.

'Oh maybe it was mine. Who knows! I'm surprised your mum gave us any of the leftovers ever again. Golly, how much did we eat back then? We should have been the size of houses!'

I was, I thought, but didn't like to say. Perhaps she'd forgotten. I took a sip of tea. It was too strong.

'Do you remember when we ran in second in

46

the piggy-back race?! How proud we were! I've still got my ribbon in an old Tupperware box some-where, along with other childhood trinkets,' she said.

'Wish I'd kept stuff like that,' I said, 'might have remembered things better.'

'I'm like a squirrel, storing up goodies to enjoy on dark winter days.'

We continued in this vein, reminiscing about our schooldays, until all the tea was drunk and the biscuits devoured – by me. Sharing the memories was nice, it reconnected us, but I wasn't interested in our shared history that night; I wanted to find out what she'd been up to in the gap. How she'd filled the years of that empty space between adolescence and adulthood.

'What's it like to be back?' I said, although I really wanted to ask what it was like to go away; to be elsewhere.

'It's a bit strange, but lovely. Lovely.'

'I'm glad you're back.' I hadn't meant to say this, it sounded desperate, and pathetic. It slipped out.

'Thank you, Mandy. You always were the best.'

My cheeks burned with pleasure, though I tried to disguise it as embarrassment and changed the subject. Bring it back to the mundane, the everyday.

'How's Dan getting on?' I regretted the question immediately; another atmosphere descended.

'Getting on?' Her voice sounded brittle.

'At the pit?'

'The pit?' I wondered why she repeated everything I said.

'It's hard work.'

'He's used to hard work.'

In my efforts to peddle back to our earlier warmth I was making things worse. 'I didn't mean . . . it must be different, that's what I meant.'

'Not that different. Both jobs are dangerous, physically demanding. There's a great sense of camaraderie—'

The sound of the front door shutting silenced us. I'd not seen Dan since the day I'd locked myself and Johnnie out of the house. Rob mentioned him a few times, slagging him off mostly; they worked the same shift occasionally, bumped into each other a couple of times in the pub, like on that day. And like so many others in the village, Rob was keener than he let on to find out why Dan had left the army.

'I mean. Why'd he come back? Vince was always prattling on about how well Dan was doing. "Going places," he said, though the only bloody place Dan went was those Falklands and fat lot of good that was. That bloody woman. God help us. "Nowt here but pits," old Braithwaite said. Like they're a bad thing. Seems they're alright for Mr Highandbloodymighty soldier boy now,' Rob'd said, on more than one occasion. When he discovered that I was visiting Ruth, he'd stopped eating his breakfast – scrambled eggs, bacon, and tomatoes on toast – and said: 'Find out what you can.

There's a sweepstake running at White Lion on why he left and I fancy bagging jackpot.'

'I won't snoop for you, Rob. Not for anyone,' I said.

'You're as desperate to know as I am.'

What could I say? He was right.

Ruth leapt from her cross-legged position and jogged over to Dan; I was surprised her legs hadn't gone dead, sitting like that. She took hold of his cheeks and kissed him, full on the lips. I busied myself getting to my feet.

'You remember Mandy, don't you, darling?'

Darling. Not a word we heard much in Fenley. And when we did, it sounded false, or over the top, forced, like the drama teacher at school who fancied herself as something or other. But then Ruth was quite posh; her family had never fitted in and she'd always been theatrical. It sounded natural coming from her.

''Course.' He turned to me. 'Alright?'

'Fine, thanks.'

He threw his jacket on the settee. I hoped there was no coal dust on it; Ruth'd find it impossible to get it off the cream cover.

He walked over to the dining table, sat down, and opened a newspaper, pretended to read. I knew he couldn't be reading; his head flicked from left to right, from over one should to the next, as if someone was behind him; the pages turned too quickly.

'I'll be off then,' I said.

'Don't mind me,' he said.

But how could we? I decided to leave. Come back another time.

I'd wanted to ask her so much: like how she and Dan met; was it weird to discover that he was from the same town she'd left as a kid? Was coming back OK? I remembered her words the day she left: No turning back, that's us.

I'd perched on the kerb outside the large, crumbling house with the 'SOLD' sign creaking in the breeze, watching the removal men piling the Felixes' belongings into the truck – the piano with the missing ivories, the oak dresser, and round dining table, large enough to seat ten. Once-grand items that had followed Ruth's grandpa across a war-torn Europe in search of a better life, now served as reminders of what could have been. Moving from Leeds so that Mrs Felix could be nearer her ageing parents, they'd been in the village just three years, and now they were off again, taking with them the best friend I'd ever had. I didn't cry, my grief too deep for tears. She came over to where I was sitting, frozen, and smiled, revealing her braced teeth. Her nose scrunched to stop her glasses from falling down her face, her long brown hair and deep-set green eyes more beautiful to me then than they'd ever been.

'It's been ace knowing you,' she said. Ace was her new favourite word. She said it all the time. I was in the past tense already.

'You're my best friend.'

'Don't ever forget me.'

How could I?

'No chance. Write, yeah?' I slipped her a piece of paper, torn from my geography book. My address. No telephone then.

'I might. But you know us. The Felixes, the Feldsteins. No turning back, that's us.' And she wiped the corner of her eye and I allowed myself to believe she was crying.

'Never say never,' I replied. An expression I'd heard from an adult.

But Ruth had turned back, she'd returned to Fenley, intentionally or not.

I coughed and, checking my watch, said that I had to get back home.

'Nice seeing you. Looks well doesn't she, Ruth?' Dan said.

'Yes. Blooming.'

'Blooming knackered more like. Thanks for the tea, and the biscuits,' I said.

'How's the typing going?' she asked as we walked out of the sitting room.

'Fine,' I said, though truth was I had no talent; my progress was slow. 'Battling on. It'll be difficult to get under the table soon.' I stretched my arms out, over the mound of the baby.

She showed me to the door and stood in the porch for ages, watching as I waddled down the cul-de-sac. She was still there, waving like fury, every time I turned around, in just that leotard and leggings. She must have been freezing.

With almost an hour before I was due to pick up the kids I took the long route home, through the estate and on to the rec. It was deserted and in the middle of the playing field the light pollution was minimal. I tipped my head to the sky; the stars stared back at me. Disappointment swallowed me up like a black hole. It wasn't how I'd imagined it'd be.

What'd you expect, Mandy Walker, you stupid cow? For things to be exactly as they were? It's been ten years. Her life is so different to yours now.

I was home before I realised that she'd not shared the cake.

CHAPTER 5

'And here's one for you groovesters out there,' the DJ purred in a phoney American accent, as the first bars of 'Billie Jean' blared out of the speakers at the far end of the club.

'Oh, I love this one!' Ruth said, jumping to her feet and taking hold of Dan's arm. The damson silk of her dress shimmered in the disco lights, rippling around her knees, the outline of her thighs visible.

'Who is this tosser?' Rob yelled, pointing towards the disco, and downing his third pint of bitter.

'Michael Jackson,' I shouted, knowing full well who he meant. He was drunk; I didn't want to be there – nearly eight months pregnant and sitting in a smoky hall, flanked on all sides by the Braithwaites, most of whom were also bladdered. I'd only come to keep the peace. Rob had never missed the union Christmas party since he'd started at the pit; the lure of cheap beer too hard to resist.

We were sitting at the Braithwaite table by default. We'd arrived late, Johnnie was being a little sod and refusing to get into his pyjamas for Mum, and by the time we'd grabbed a drink there were no spaces at the table where Rob's mum and dad were sitting, staring into the dance floor, silent. Not that I was upset about this. Scanning the room we stood by the bar for a minute or two before Wendy Price, who was sitting at the table next to the Walkers, stood up and offered me her seat – she was the kindest woman, always giving the lads sweets, squeezing their cheeks too hard. But I'd spotted Ruth across the room, so mouthed my thanks and shook my head. Ruth was on her feet waving both arms in the air, flagging us over. I looked at Rob, who shrugged, as if to say, 'What choice do we have?' He was probably as glad as I was to not have to sit with his family. It was only as we neared the table, and I saw the size of it, that I wondered where the rest of the Braithwaites were. It turned out that they'd been delayed too.

Michael Jackson's high-pitched tones rang out. Dan remained welded to his seat; it looked like Ruth might pull his arm from its socket, but he didn't budge.

'What about you, Mandy? Fancy a boogie?' she implored.

If I was going to get to my feet for anyone it would have been for her, and though I was desperate to change position and move around a little there was no way I was getting onto an empty dance floor. Besides, I had no idea how to move to that song. My usual ploy of crossing one foot in front of the other in time to the music wouldn't work with this rhythm. I shook my head and mouthed, 'Sorry'.

She let go of Dan's arm and said, 'Rob? You'll dance with me, won't you?'

'He never dances. Waste of good drinking time!' I laughed. But he pushed himself up from the velvet seated chair and, turning to Ruth, said, 'I'll break the habit of a lifetime.'

Rob and Ruth started a trend; soon the dance floor was heaving. Small children imitated the hip-thrusting gestures of the pop stars, elderly couples held each other around the waist, backs straight, chins high, dancing the only way they knew how, regardless of the music thrashing from the speakers. The Braithwaites arrived in a noisy bundle as Kajagoogoo trilled 'Too Shy'.

The evening rolled on. Vince wandered over to the bar to get another round in, his missus drifted away to speak to a friend, Dan's brothers and their wives disappeared, and as the Belle Stars started up Dan and I were alone at the table. I shrugged and half smiled at him, unsure what to say. I took a sip of my cream soda, rolled my feet in circles under the table to stop my ankles swelling, and stared into the gyrating crowd.

'I don't know how you can drink that stuff,' he said, shouting over the racket, nodding at my pop, lighting another cigarette. He'd been chain-smoking since we arrived.

'It's a right funny colour, that's for sure,' I said. 'Have you tried it?'

'Not since I was a kid.'

'Would you like to?' I pushed the glass of bright green pop across.

He smiled; I'd not seen him smile before. Not properly. His teeth were straight and even. He took hold of the glass and even in the changing multi-coloured glow of the lights I could see that his hands were no longer white as sugar. After taking a sip he pulled a face. 'Lager spoils it perhaps.'

'It takes some getting used to, I think.'

'The best things do,' he said.

We were silent for the rest of the song, awkward, waiting for the others to return. They didn't.

'When's baby due?' he said at last. 'Can't be long, judging by size of you.'

'Four, six week. Something like that.'

'Didn't mean to sound rude.'

I was about to say he didn't when he continued. 'You look lovely. I mean, pregnant, having a babbie.'

Blushing, I thanked him, and stared at my hands. He wasn't at all how I remembered him. The youngest of seven, as a child he was spoilt rotten; he'd grown up arrogant and hard, or so it had seemed to me, two or three years his junior. When I saw him about town, in the playing fields and that, with his surly, mean-eyed friends I was scared. Most people were glad to see the back of him when he left for the army, apart from his mum and dad who missed him like crazy. He reached for his lager and I noticed that his hands shook a little.

With a flourish, the back of her hand resting across her forehead, Ruth collapsed into her seat. 'I need a drink!'

'I'll get a round in,' Rob said, leaning against the back of her chair. His brow glistened and his breath was short.

'Vince is at the bar. Take a seat,' Dan said.

How odd that he calls his dad 'Vince'. There was something bitter in the way he said it.

Rob sat next to Ruth; she leant over and placed her hand on his shoulder. It was a strangely familiar gesture, and I saw him stiffen, shrugging her hand away. Rob wasn't a touchy-feely kind of man. She didn't mean anything by it; it was her way. She'd always been dramatic, full of the grand gesture.

'Your man is a fine mover, Mandy. He's worn me out.'

'You'll not give me a dance then?' Dan said. 'I like this one.' David Bowie's 'China Girl' was playing.

'For you, darling. Anything.' Ruth was on her feet again, pulling Dan towards the dance floor.

I thought I heard him replying, 'Anything?' but Vince and four of Dan's brothers pitched up again at that point, hands curved round pints of ale, which sloshed onto the tablecloth as they pushed empties and plates of half-eaten sausage rolls and vol-au-vents aside.

'Been talking to your dad over at the bar,' Vince said, looking at Rob.

'Right,' Rob said, as if he couldn't give a monkey's.

'That American git was on news again. About the pit.'

Rob lifted his chin. There'd been talk and threats of pit closures all year – ever since the Tories had been re-elected, the country swept away in a tide of nationalism after the war.

'Your dad says we've nowt to worry about,' Vince said.

'He should know. He's union,' Phil said, slapping Rob on the back.

'We'd better not have anything to worry about,' Vince said. It sounded like a threat. 'Only just got over accident. Bastards.' The coal board had tried to pin the accident on the men, Vince and Rob in particular, negligence they'd alleged, but the union and the men had stuck together.

I left before the party finished, before Rob. The barman phoned for a taxi; I was too tired to walk, and feeling queer all of a sudden. It was no fun being sober, surrounded by drunks. They made less and less sense as the evening wore on. Ruth spent most of the time on the dance floor. The men were queuing up to dance with her. She was the belle of the ball. Periodically, she flitted over to check that I was alright, though it wasn't as if I was alone. There was always someone at the table, even if they were talking gibberish.

As I staggered to the exit I glanced back at the disco. Ruth was draped over Dan, her head resting on his shoulders, eyes closed, swaying to the voices of The Flying Pickets and 'Only You'. They turned, and Dan looked at me and mouthed, 'Merry Christmas.'

Smiling, I continued towards the door. As I reached for the handle the baby shuffled inside of me. It was such a strange and unexpected sensation it took my breath away, and I bent over, clutching my stomach. It wasn't exactly painful, but it felt like nothing I'd experienced before. But it was over quickly, and I stood upright again and walked outside.

No taxi. Stamping my feet a little I wandered a few paces down the road, but not so far that the taxi might miss me. I stopped and stared up at the sky as another, pricklier, sensation swept across my lower abdomen. I bent double, my shocked exclamation sending a puff of smoke into the air. It wasn't a contraction; I'd had enough of those in the past to recognise one when it came. The twisting inside of me didn't stop, and I fell to my knees, groaning. The pavement was dusted with ice. Freezing cold water bit its way through my fingertips and palms, giving me something to focus on other than the constant searing pain in my belly.

I prayed that the taxi would pitch up soon; I

needed help, but I couldn't move. I thought about the baby inside of me and prayed she wouldn't be harmed, that whatever was going on wouldn't damage her in any way. I thumped the ground with my fists. Vomit rose in my throat, and through the sounds of my retching I heard a voice, calling.

'Mandy?'

I didn't recognise it.

'You alright?' The sound of running footsteps. Thank God I'd not walked far from the club house entrance. Strong hands slipped under my armpits and hauled me upright. I bent double again immediately, and he lowered me to the ground, gentle. His hand rested on my back.

'Christ! You having the baby?'

This time I recognised the voice: Dan's.

Between another howl I said, 'I think my appendix has burst or something.'

'We need help.' He sounded frightened, panicked, and I wondered what had happened to his training. Pressure under fire and all that.

'I'm going to fetch your Rob. Can you wave your arm?'

I hadn't a clue what he was burbling about but managed to nod.

'If you hear a taxi, you wave. Wave.' And he ran off.

I started to cry, fear and pain ripping me to shreds. My mind swarmed with pictures of all my babies. Fish-belly blue, slimy, newly born. I screamed into the air: 'Don't you hurt her! Don't you hurt her!' My cries swallowed up by the growls coming from deep inside of me.

I closed my eyes and shut everything out, coming round with a wail when the pain raced down my legs, burning me like a flame and a soft liquid seeped through my tights, puddling on the ground at my knees. This was a sensation I recognised – my waters had broken. I wasn't ill; this baby was in a rush to get out into the world. I lifted my head as the sound of clattering feet neared, friendly voices shouting my name. It was going to be alright.

DURING

MARCH 1984 – MARCH 1985

Parkin

A traditional Yorkshire cake made with black treacle and oatmeal, it is sticky when fresh; well-known for its ability to last, connoisseurs consider it at its best when left to harden.

CHAPTER 6

'I'm sorry there's not more, love. He's not baking so much these days. Can't shift it, can't compete with Kwik Save 'n' that.' Mum handed over a bag as she stepped into the kitchen; she often popped round for a bite to eat on her half-days. I struggled to hold the bag with one hand; in the other I held the little girl that had given us all such a shock that cold December evening, no one more so than me, other than perhaps Dan Braithwaite.

'Here, give her to me,' Mum said, reaching over, taking the baby. 'How's Mummy's little surprise; my gorgeous lass?'

Becky gurgled, before returning to gnash on a plastic ring. She clutched her nana's shoulder. I opened the plastic bag: a loaf, a bloomer, and two custard tarts.

'Better than nowt, Mum. I'm ever so grateful.' I followed her through the kitchen.

'So you should be. I've nicked this lot. Be the last you'll get.' I was about to ask her what she meant, when she kicked off her shoes and waltzed down the hall, stopping at Gordy's cage. 'Needs cleaning. That rodent's rotten.'

'Does it?' I said, immune to the smell now that buckets of nappies littered the place.

'It's very quiet. Where are the lads?'

'At a party.'

'That's nice.'

'Johnnie wasn't invited, but he kicked off something rotten,' I pulled a face; Mum knew I was soft on the lad, 'so I asked Sue if she'd mind him coming along. She's ever so good like that.'

Ignoring me, Mum padded into the front room. I followed, turning away from the old typewriter gathering dust on the sideboard. A reminder of thwarted ambition. I never found time to practise these days.

Who were you kidding, Mandy Walker?

'Not on duty, today, Rob?' Mum sounded surprised.

'Even pickets get a day off, you know, Doreen.' He stood and threw the newspaper he'd been reading on the chair behind him. 'Don't know why I buy that bloody rag. I'm off to the Institute. See you later, love.' I knew he was heading for the pub.

No money for my evening class but he finds beer money.

Mum sighed.

'Can I get you a cup of tea, Mum?'

'I'm not stopping. Only came to give this little lass a squeeze and to tell you that I've lost my job,

66

so there'll be no more free cakes.' She could have been announcing that she'd lost a sock at the launderette, not her job. I sank into the settee.

'You're joking.'

'Do I look like I'm joking? Is that ring tasty? Is that ring very, very tasty?' she was nuzzling into Becky's cheeks, kissing them and blowing raspberries. The baby laughed.

'How? Why? Did he catch you?'

'Did he hell! It's been on the cards for a while. Even before strike. People don't want to pay prices for stuff. Cheaper in supermarkets. Oh no, they don't, lassie!' She addressed the last bit to Becky, who chuckled again.

This was bad news. Not only for Mum, and not only because we'd no longer profit from the free-bies, but also because Mum had helped out over the past few weeks, bought the odd bit of shopping, treated Mark and David to the pictures, and now she'd not be able to do that. And the social was threatening to cut our benefits.

'When?'

'A month.'

'Will you get redundancy?'

'Couple of weeks' pay, that's all. He's broke. God knows how I'll get another job. I might have to travel. Anyway, I don't want to worry you. Thought you should know, that's all. Now take care of this lovely.' She handed Becky back to me and pulled a lighter and cigarette from her handbag.

'Mum, I'd prefer it if you didn't . . .'

She flicked off the flame and lowered the cigarette. 'Sorry. I forget you don't like it.'

'It's not good for the kids, especially with Mark's asthma.' I bounced Becky on my knees. Mum sat down on Rob's chair, lifting the discarded newspaper and slapping it on her lap as she did so. An ashtray lay on the window ledge to the left of the chair, three or four butts sticking up in it. Defiant. I blushed on Rob's behalf.

Mum glanced down at the paper. 'Says you lot don't support your men. I'd like to knock their blocks off. Why he wastes money on this I'll never know.' She tossed the paper onto the floor.

'Says he likes to keep up. "Keep your friends close, and your enemies closer, Mand." That's what he says.'

'Talks a lot of shite. Be better off buying a decent paper. Like those your dad used to read.'

I remembered how Dad used to sit in his shed at the bottom of the garden, with his Calor gas fire, pipe, and a copy of *The Times*. Friends and colleagues used to take the mick out of him for reading a posh paper, but I loved him for his individuality. He didn't go down to the pub, or the betting shop. He liked gardening and pipes. He had quite a collection, a clay one with a long handle was my favourite, and I loved the rich smell of his tobacco, the way he tapped the side of the barrel with his fingers as he puffed. He looked so content. On spring afternoons once school was out I'd sit in the shed with him, reading bits of the paper out to him while he planted bizzie lizzies and sweet pea in black potting trays. I learned more about the world during those afternoons than I ever did at school.

'Right. I'll be off then,' Mum said, as if she'd forgotten that she wasn't supposed to be staying long.

I showed her to the door, Becky latched on my hip. She gave us both a kiss before stepping onto the path. 'Make sure you don't eat all the custards. You need to shift that baby weight. Ta-ra.'

I watched Mum walk down the short path, then struggle with the latch on the rusting gate. Rob still hadn't fixed it. She looked tired, but as lovely as ever. Her dark auburn hair, centre parted and tucked behind her ears, fell to the middle of her back. It was unfashionably long, in contrast to her skintight stone-washed jeans. Despite the gentle warmth of a spring sun I shivered. My waist felt sticky and damp; Becky's nappy needed changing. I'd not adjusted to using towelling nappies again or the frequency with which they needed changing. She'd been in the same nappy for hours. Prizing her from my hip, and lifting her in the air, her right fist clutching a clump of my hair, I kissed her nose and was about to shut the door when I heard Ruth's voice.

'Hi,' she called, waving.

My surprise must have been written all over my face, because she stopped dead and said, 'Have I come at a bad time?' An air of vulnerability hung around her; even though she was her usual chirpy self. She'd never called on me before; I always called on her, so my imagination ran riot. But I didn't want to let her in. Mum'd said the place stank, and I'd not tidied since the boys went out.

'It's just that I so need to chat with someone.' She stood opposite me on the doorstep. 'Well, not any old someone – you. I need to talk to you.' She reached out and stroked Becky's cheek. 'Hello, darling. Brrr.' She crossed her arms and rubbed her hands up and down her biceps. 'Not exactly warm is it?' It was warm enough; she was underdressed.

There was no way out of it without appearing rude. I had to let her in. 'Excuse the state of the place. Sorry about the smell.' I stepped aside.

'What smell?' She disappeared down the hall and dived into the lounge. She took in the tatty furniture and the walls that needed a lick of paint, the toy cars dotted about on the floor, under the telly. I noticed the milk stains on the settee for the first time.

'This is cosy,' she said.

I asked her if she'd like a cup of tea, if she'd like to sit down. She refused the tea but lowered herself onto Rob's chair in front of the telly, which was still blaring, her legs crossed, interlocked hands over one knee, arms straight, like you'd see the models in magazines sitting. I hoped she didn't notice the tabloid spilt open on the floor. A busty blonde smiled up at her.

'And how are things? Are you managing OK?' she said.

Nodding, I turned the television off and parked myself on the chair opposite, plonking Becky on my knee.

'I'm so sorry I've not visited before. Now's your chance, Ruth, I said to myself. Easter holidays. More time than usual. You know how it is. Busy, busy, busy! And you always seem to get to me first!'

I must have looked guilty or apologetic, because she added, 'Not that you're not welcome! You are. My door's always open to you, Mandy.' Her eyes flitted round the room, as if looking for something to settle on. 'Oh, she's wearing the dress I bought her! How lovely, she looks like a little angel.'

'Looks can be deceiving,' I said.

Did Ruth want to talk babies with me? Her eyes shone and softened, like glycerine, when she looked at Becky. Did she long for a child of her own?

'You can hold her if you like,' I said.

She jumped, unlocking her hands, uncrossing her legs, both feet planted on the carpet. 'She wouldn't cry?'

I shook my head; Becky was the easiest going baby, a real crowd pleaser. Ruth reached out her hands and I passed Becky over. 'She's a bit damp. Could do with changing her nappy. Watch your trousers.'

'Oh, don't mind these old things. A bit of wee

never hurt anyone, least of all me. Still find puddles in some of the classrooms.'

How silly of me. Ruth was probably more used to kids than me. She kissed Becky's cheek and was rewarded with a gummy smile.

'I'll turn you to face Mummy, so you know where she is,' she said, sitting Becky so that the baby's back rested against her stomach; she offered her index fingers for Becky to grip. 'She's simply adorable. Lucky you.'

I couldn't disagree.

'Mandy, I want to ask you something. Something important.'

I nodded, wondering what on earth it could be.

'And although I'm asking as a favour, I think you'll enjoy it. I really do. It'll be a nice change and you have lots to offer. You'll get something out of it. You can cook and organise the kitchen, the shopping, the preparation . . .'

I had no idea what she was talking about and was only half listening. Becky clutched Ruth's fingers but she'd stopped smiling; her eyes glazed over and her bottom lip tightened. Please God, no, not now, not there.

I asked Ruth if she could explain in more detail, that I wasn't getting what she was driving at. I was interrupted by a loud and explosive sounding fart.

'Good grief. Was that you?' Ruth exclaimed, bending forwards.

Becky continued to strain; a putrid smell filled the room.

'I think she's filling her nappy,' she said.

I stared at my fourth child and watched in horror as a stream of yellow shit poured from her sodden nappy onto Ruth's trousers. I leaped up, apologising profusely, and wrenched Becky from an astonished Ruth who rose, open mouthed, arms held up in surrender, the watery shit sinking into the pale cotton of her pedal-pushers. Hands outstretched I clutched Becky as she continued to expel a seemingly never-ending flow of shit. It would stain, be nigh-on impossible to clean. Ruth's beautiful clothes.

'Dear God, what has she eaten?' Ruth said, and in one smooth movement she picked up the newspaper at her feet and wrapped the sheet with the busty blonde on it around my daughter like a sarong, stemming the flow, before taking hold of her again and kissing her cheek.

'I'm so sorry.' My hand covered my mouth and I wanted to cry, she'd never visit again. Ruth began to laugh and pointed at my body. I glanced down at my t-shirt and jeans; they were splattered with shitty dots.

'Reconsidering having children?' I said, and we burst out laughing

Upstairs we stripped Becky and ran a shallow bath. She was baby-powder fresh before we peeled off our clothes. 'Her lovely frock,' I said as I tossed it into the bath along with ours.

'There'll be others,' Ruth said, sponging herself down. 'Now, I'll need to borrow some clothes?'

73

Considering she was three, maybe four sizes smaller than me, my jeans didn't look half bad on Ruth. She held them up with an old belt and dug out one of Rob's shirts; she tied the tails in a knot at her waist. She could smell him on it, she said, and I wondered if he'd put a dirty one back in the wardrobe.

'Let me find another,' I said.

'No, smells in a nice way. Manly.'

'Is that what you call it. Better than baby poo at least.' And we burst out laughing again.

'Remember when we dressed as tramps for the end of year one show?' she said.

How could I forget? Dad's old suits, his work boots. Listening to 'We're a Couple of Swells' over and over on the Bakelite turntable he kept in his shed, him directing us prancing around the garden, showing us the moves from the film. They were fab days, fab. And things were no different now. Forget her fancy clothes and posh accent, my Ruth wasn't adverse to a bit of muck and dodgy clobber.

Downstairs in the living room I asked again if she fancied a cup of tea.

'Have you heard of WAPC?'

'I heard some of the mums talking about it outside the school. Is it a virus?'

She uncrossed her legs and slapped her thighs. 'Oh, Mandy! You're a hoot.'

I'd been called many things, but never a hoot.

'Women Against Pit Closures,' she said, quietening down at last, patting underneath her eyes

74

with her ring finger. 'You'll make my mascara run.'

'I think so.'

'Well, Ethel—'

'Who?'

'Old Mrs Braithwaite. She's set up an action group in the village.'

'Action group?'

'Yes, action group. We meet as often as we can—'

'Sorry. Mind's gone to mush. Sleep deprivation. You know how it is.'

'Actually I don't. But to get back to the point . . .'

Ethel had been visiting a friend, Lottie, in a neighbouring town. They'd popped into the shopping centre for a drink and a bun at a popular tea shop where they passed a group of young women, students Ethel later discovered, standing beside a trestle table covered in leaflets. Ethel assumed they were WI, or collecting for the Spastics at first. As they walked past, chests out, eyes straight ahead – Ethel never gave to charity, on principle, she said. She believed charities let government off the hook – one of the girls shook a red bucket at them and shouted, 'Support the Miners!' Ethel turned, hawk-like, marched over, and grabbed the bucket off the astonished girl. 'Ta very much,' she said, 'That'll support a few of us for a while.'

Well, the student was flabbergasted, and said in a hoity-toity voice, but all apologetic, that she'd no idea they were miners' wives and if she had she'd never have asked blah, blah, blah. She admired what they were doing and wished them all the luck in the world. 'Come the revolution, sister,' she said, finally, shaking a delicate fist in the air. Handing the bucket back, Ethel'd said, 'Come the revolution, love, you'll be tucked up in your nice house, with your nice job, in London or wherever it is you're from, and we'll still be shovelling shit, but thanks for your kind words all the same.'

Apparently, the poor girl's eyes filled with tears. I reckoned she thought she was going to get her head kicked in – Ethel was one of the hardest-looking women I'd ever seen. Anyway, Ethel and Lottie left with a copy of the newspaper the students were distributing, *Socialist Revolutionary* or something, and despite thinking that it was full of nonsense, she knew that there was no way she wanted 'the likes of them' hijacking the strike. She knew of miners wives in South Yorkshire getting together and resolved to do something similar here in Fenley Down.

The movement was well organised. T-shirts and all sorts.

I interrupted Ruth's story. 'I have heard of them,' I said. 'I listen to the radio.'

'Ethel's got lots of the wives involved,' Ruth said.

'I'm sure she has,' I replied, unable to imagine any poor sod saying no to Ethel.

Ruth went on to explain that the action group was organising a fundraising event at the Institute to raise money to support the families, especially the children.

'That's nice, they'll appreciate that,' I said.

'There's so much to do. We need as many hands to the deck as possible. Especially those hands that are good in the kitchen . . .' She smiled expectantly.

'You're doing this?'

'Ethel asked me to . . .'

'So what do you think?' Ruth said.

I wasn't sure what to say. She'd not exactly asked me to do anything, and I could see all sorts of problems with this fundraiser.

'Who'll spend at this event? Everyone works down the pit here,' I said after a pause. My voice trailed off towards the end; it felt odd criticising Ruth, and that's how it felt.

'Not everyone! I don't, for one,' her mouth formed a smile, but her eyes said something different. I felt uncomfortable. Perhaps they'd all thought of this. 'So, you'll help?' she said.

Becky was starting to get restless, and I realised with horror that I'd not given her a dinnertime bottle. 'I think the baby needs feeding. Will you hold her while I get a bottle?'

In the kitchen I stuffed a couple of Jammie Dodgers in my mouth; it was almost two o'clock and I was starving. I wondered if I should invite Ruth to stay for dinner. There was a pot of corned beef stew on the cooker. I couldn't imagine offering Ruth anything like that, and then I caught sight of my mum's bag of goodies.

I brought Becky's bottle through on a tray with a pot of tea and a plate of two custard tarts.

'Help yourself,' I said, and to my surprise she did. The first tart went down in seconds. I gave Becky her bottle. 'Do have the other one.'

'You're such a fabulous cook. You sure?' She gestured at the remaining tart. I nodded. 'Lucky man who has you to prepare his meals, eh?'

I was about to say that the tarts came from Mum's bakery, Mum's former bakery, but she didn't give me chance. 'Skills like yours are hard to find. Think how many will benefit. The budget's tight, but I know that you'll make them taste like they came from the Savoy kitchens! You'll be the goddess of the tea and cake stall!'

How could I say no? And something inside me stirred. A fluttering of excitement. It would mean getting out of the house, spending more time with Ruth. We'd always made a good team.

'You're on!' I said and we chinked our mugs together, resolved to make it the best fair the village had ever seen.

CHAPTER 7

Rain lashed against the windows of the Miners' Institute the day of the fair, and despite the warm temperatures of the past week there was a bitterly cold wind rattling around the Edwardian building. It sneaked through the gaps in the sash windows, under the heavy swing doors and skirted round ankles and knees. The heating had been turned off weeks ago, and there was no point in switching it back on: it took days to generate any real heat. Despite the miserable weather, spirits were high.

Ethel marched through, all chest and thick ankles. She stopped every now and again to inspect a stall, dipping her chin when she approved. The relief from the women concerned was palpable. She headed my way and I felt sick.

Two crisp white tablecloths – on loan from the tea shop in town – covered the table tennis table, lending it an air of respectability, and as I placed a coffee and walnut cake in the centre, I remembered Ruth's words. Perhaps it would be a 'high tea' fit for the Savoy. Not that I'd ever been there.

I cast my eyes around the spread: the golden

sponges, resplendent on their glass stands, complete with doilies; the towering scones, pots of lush red jam and clotted cream; the date and banana cakes, not long out of the oven, filling the air with their rich sticky scent. There were chocolate cakes, and carrot cakes (very cosmopolitan, and a new recipe for me, taken from Delia's latest TV show) upside down puddings, and pavlovas. I'd made a plate of cucumber sandwiches too – Ruth's idea – though I wasn't convinced anyone would buy them. They looked so small, cut into triangles, minus their crusts (also Ruth's idea. 'It's the only way to serve cucumber sandwiches!' she'd said). As I surveyed my work I felt a pride that I'd not felt in, oh, such a long time. Ruth had been right. It had been hard work, choosing, planning, preparing, and baking. Everything had been left up to me, right down to the choice of teas we offered. Ruth had advised, but that's all it was: advice. She said so herself. Hard work and all, I'd loved every minute of it, and now all that was left to complete my achievement was for people to come and spend. That was the bit I wasn't so sure about, though I kept my opinions to myself.

'Ruddy marvellous spread that is.' Ethel made the compliment sound like an accusation. 'Surprised your Rob isn't fatter. Assuming he gets a look in.' She stared at my stomach and I was tempted to say she must be a bloody good cook too judging by the size of her legs. Like an elephant's they were. Some said that she had some kind of a disease; Dad said she came from peasant stock and those legs were evidence. 'Keep up the good work, Walker,' she shouted as she stomped off. She sounded like a general.

At noon the Fenley Action Group May Day Fair was declared officially open and we waited for the hordes to arrive. The kettles stood ready to boil, the wheel of fortune to spin. 'We' being the members of the Action Group. There were five on the committee. As founder and driving force, Ethel had announced that by rights she should be leader, and therefore Chairperson (not Lady Chairman, or Chairwoman, Ruth reliably informed us. 'So politically incorrect,' she'd said), but it wasn't a role that appealed. She opted to be Treasurer. 'And let's face it, ladies. There's nowt more important than dosh!'

'Can we agree that we won't address each other by such derogatory terms as "ladies"?' Ruth had said.

Everyone around the table looked baffled by this, until Ethel broke the ice with: 'Well, there's none of them ladies round here, so I can agree to that!' and everyone howled with laughter.

Nice, busy-body Paula was Secretary (her typing skills were excellent), Ruth Chairperson (she'd been bullied into it by Ethel), an elderly woman I barely knew was in charge of publicity, and a middle-aged woman called Ann who was heavily involved in the local Labour Party was head of liaison, whatever that was. Ann had stood for the town council on several occasions and had never been elected. I wondered why she bothered; some people never know when to give up. The rest of us were roped in for the fair. I wasn't sure why the Down of Fenley Down was dropped and wondered if it had occurred to any member of the committee that as a result the group name abbreviated to FAG.

Rob arrived early, as instructed. The lads raced over to the tombola, not bothering to say hello to me; they'd heard there were some Mr T figures going as prizes. Rob made his way over to the cake stall, struggling to steer the buggy between the tightly packed tables. Becky was watery-eyed, red-faced, and under-dressed, her shawl was nowhere to be seen.

'Where's her blanket? She never goes anywhere without it,' I said, raising my voice above the din coming from the speakers that were right next to my patch. I'd meant to thank him for coming.

'She does now. Stop fretting and get us a cup of tea, love. I'll have one of those scones an' all. Jam, no cream.'

'That'll be fifty pence,' I said, holding out my palm.

'Get away with you.'

I smiled. 'You're my first customer. Thanks for coming.'

'Might be your only customer. Who's gonna spend?'

I wanted to slap him. It didn't matter that I

agreed with him, that I thought it was a daft idea too, that no one from the surrounding towns would come, that there weren't enough non-mining families to make it worthwhile. What mattered was that I was here, now, giving it a go. I gave Rob his tea and scone, and some home-made biscuits for the boys, and told him to go and have a look around.

'Try the roll-a-penny, guess the weight of the sweet jar,' I shouted, pointing in the right direction. 'You never know, you might win, and for a couple of pennies you'll have the largest tub of sweets I've ever seen.'

They didn't stay long. I was glad it was raining; I could be sure that he wouldn't sneak into The White Lion on the way home, leaving the kids sitting outside with bags of crisps and lemonades.

It was busier than I expected. The publicity woman had done a good job of advertising the event, though I still had plenty of leftovers at four o'clock. Afraid that the sponge was starting to harden I was busy wrapping tin foil over a Battenburg when I heard a voice. I glanced up.

'Hello, Dan. Are you here for some light refreshment?' I put on my best posh voice, as a joke, but he didn't smile.

Instead he studied the table, pointing at the various goodies. I gave him the sales spiel for every item: all homemade, baked with the finest ingredients in the whole of Yorkshire, nay, the world. He smiled a bit then.

'I'd like a slice of date and walnut and a brew please, Mrs Walker.'

'And what kind of tea would sir like?' I've no idea what possessed me to be so familiar. Perhaps it was giddiness brought on by a sugar rush – I'd scoffed two large slices of cake moments before – perhaps it was because of our shared experience the night Becky arrived unexpectedly. I regretted my comment. But he looked at me directly and smiled. And as I watched the folds appear across his cheeks and around his eyes I thought that his legendary aloofness, his arrogance, was possibly only shyness.

'I'll have whatever's in the pot. Don't go to any trouble on my account.' His voice was soft, and while not exactly cultured it didn't have the brusqueness of so many from the area. He offered a pound note and I shook my head. 'You've got to take the money. This is a fundraiser, remember?'

'You're a miner, you daft beggar!'

At it again, that ridiculous familiarity. He'll turn on me in a minute.

'I've a working wife.'

My stupidity silenced me, my cheeks burned. I took the money and began to cut the cake. Neither of us spoke. Then he said, 'I didn't mean to make you feel bad.'

'You didn't.'

'Good.'

I handed him the cake and tea.

'Hello, darling. How lovely to see you. Where've

you been all this time? I thought you'd forgotten all about me.' Ruth was by Dan's side, arms wrapped around his shoulders, leaning in to his face, plonking a kiss on his cheek. She lifted one leg, bent at the knee; her yellow high heels gleaming under the florescent lighting.

He shrugged, his shyness coming to the fore again. 'Mind you don't spill the tea, love,' he said.

Dan went to sit down at the tables and chairs laid out for my little cafe and I made Ruth a cup of Earl Grey. Lemon, no milk or sugar. I cleared up while they ate and whenever they weren't looking I watched them.

Dan sipped at his tea, hunched over, as if he was trying to disappear, barely lifting the cup from its saucer, a fringe of brown hair obscuring his face. It had grown long in the time that he'd been back. Most of the men kept their hair short, but not Dan. It fell to his shoulders; a reaction to the regulation short back and sides he'd had in the army I guessed. I remembered the wedding photos on the mantelpiece in their living room: his hair cropped so close to his scalp he could have been bald. I pondered on their meeting, the story Ruth told of how they got together and how different it was to mine and Rob's.

She'd not wanted to go out, she'd said. A cold threatened, she'd been sneezing all day, and she had first year exams in a couple of weeks' time. They were important. But her flatmate was tired of revising, and truth be told so was Ruth. What she wanted to do was curl up in bed with a glossy magazine, but this was a good friend and what are friends for?

I chased after Rob for months and months. Thinking I wasn't the kind of girl he'd ever admit to being seen with, I worked on being his mate. I joined The White Lion darts team. No one cared that I was too young to be served; I threw three one hundred and eighties in a row; I'd been practising for weeks, and with my shot putter's arms and twenty-twenty vision it was easy.

There weren't many decent nightclubs in Winchester and Ruth didn't look her best. A group of squaddies, paratroopers as they found out later, came over as the girls were sitting at the bar, sipping their Pernod and blacks. The men had travelled from Aldershot for a night out (a change from London, they'd said); one of them was Dan. Tall and straight and handsome in his uniform, he was different to the rest. His voice reminded her of her childhood.

When Rob was dumped by Lucy Stapleton he limped around like a kicked dog. This was my chance, my only chance. As well as helping his team to the top of the local league, I made him laugh. 'You're a tonic, Mand. A right tonic!' he said.

'Take me to the pictures, then,' I said, tipsy on the dregs of beer I'd been supping all night behind the publican's back.

'Alright, then. Why not?' he said; he was drunk too.

Dan romanced Ruth; took her out to dinner, bought her flowers and chocolates; told her she was beautiful. They couldn't see each other as often as they would have liked on account of his leave not being all that regular, and her studies, but 'absence and all that,' she'd laughed. He proposed on Valentine's Day, down on one knee with a diamond ring sitting on his palm.

Trips to the pictures, sharing Kia-Ora and strawberry Mivvies, slipped in to meeting in town after I'd finished school for a frothy coffee and Chelsea bun at the milk bar. I felt ever so grown up sitting there with him, a working man, me still in my school uniform. If she'd not been so swallowed up in grief, Mum might have disapproved. What with him being three years older and me being only fifteen. The first time we had sex was on my sixteenth birthday, in the bushes at the back of the rec, where dogs pissed and kids built dens. Rob brought a blanket, a bottle of fizzy white wine, and a small cake. I was pregnant within weeks.

I'd given Ruth a souped-up version of the truth, and as I watched them sitting together, Dan finishing his cake, I wondered if she'd done the same. Perhaps it hadn't been as she'd described it. She leaned over the table, brushed his fringe away from his face and said, 'Why don't you get your hair cut, darling?'

'I like it like this,' he said, pulling away from her touch. His sharpness surprised me. Perhaps she wanted it short as a reminder of the soldier she first met? No one was any nearer to finding out the truth behind his sudden departure from the army.

Ethel trooped over, jolting me from my eavesdropping, and asked me for the afternoon's takings. She told Ruth she needed a hand totting up the cash – she'd have no one accusing her of dipping her hand in the till.

Once everything was cleared away, I turned my attention to what to do with the leftovers. As Dan had finished I went over to collect his plate, fork, cup, and saucer.

'That was fantastic. Thank you. Nothing like home cooking.'

I stared at the floor, unsure what to say. I blurted, 'Expect your mum and dad are glad you're back.' It was him saying 'home' that did it. I only said it to make conversation, but his reply baffled me.

He said: 'Maybe.'

My reply was drowned out by the sound of a balloon popping. We both jumped, and I laughed, then stopped when I noticed that Dan was on his feet, fists clenched. He stuffed his hands into his pockets. There was a kind of blankness behind his eyes that suggested he'd retreated elsewhere.

'You OK, Dan?'

He snapped back, as if he was standing to attention. 'Fine. Better be off then. Tell Ruth I've gone. Thanks for the tea.'

'Bye.' I watched him cross the near-empty hall, oblivious to the discarded raffle tickets, sweet wrappers, and other rubbish piled in his way. His back was rigid, his path was straight and true. Plastic cups cracked beneath his boots.

I turned to finish the clearing up, heart full; the end of a successful day.

CHAPTER 8

The end-of-terrace house I grew up in and still referred to as home despite having left almost eight years ago looked pretty in the sunshine. Wisteria draped around the front door, the soft mauve of the flowers accentuating the dark grey of the chunky stone walls. Although the garden had not been properly attended to in almost a decade – Dad was the gardener, not Mum – the lilies and budding roses still gave an impression of picture postcard pretty. To an untrained eye it could have passed as a cottage in the Dales; we even called it the cottage amongst ourselves.

This exterior was deceiving; once inside the brutal truth behind the picturesque façade was revealed. The small windows didn't allow much light in; the rooms were dark and damp. The heavy stone absorbed a winter's ice and rain, then took all summer to dry out just in time for the onset of autumn. There was no central heating, and the kitchen was so cramped that even if we'd had the money for all mod cons there wasn't the space, electrics, or plumbing. Little wonder Dad spent all his time in the shed.

I banged on the door before twisting the latch and pushing my way in. The door stuck half way and I bashed against it with my right shoulder. Johnnie charged in. I lifted Becky from her pram and placed her over my shoulder.

'Mum? Mum?'

The house was quiet. I shouted up the stairs, then walked through the back room into the kitchen and out into the garden. Johnnie was running towards the top end. I hadn't checked the front room. There was no point. It was a room reserved for 'best'; it was only ever used on birthdays and Christmas mornings, when we'd sit together, the three of us: me, Mum and Dad, opening our presents and sipping Snowballs. As a child I was never sure which I enjoyed most, the Snowball or the presents.

Mum was at the back of the garden, Johnnie crouched beside her, playing in the dirt. It took me a while to spot them, craning my neck, clambering between the overgrown damson bushes and crab apple trees, shielding my eyes from the sun, not easy with a bonny lass in my other arm. The garden was narrow but almost one hundred feet long. Mum was bent over, on her knees, wearing gardening gloves, a trowel in one hand. She looked awkward holding it, like she wasn't sure what to do with it. Mum was more comfortable with hair dryers and nail files. There were clumps of dark soil stuck on the trowel, mind, so she'd evidently poked it in the earth.

'Ay up, love. Grab that fork, will you?'

I laid Becky in the shade of a gnarly rosemary bush and picked up the gardening fork and prodded at the ground. Johnnie had found a worm and had hold of it by its tail, or head. I couldn't tell which. I'd no idea what Mum thought she was doing. Weeding seemed a rather pointless exercise; the ground was covered in greenery and I was pretty sure that, like me, she couldn't tell weed from plant. It wasn't only Mum and me who missed Dad's tender care; the garden bore witness to his absence too.

We stabbed at the hard earth, passing pleasantries and small news. Johnnie was quiet, absorbed with the wildlife. I didn't know how to begin my request. Only minutes had gone by when Mum said, 'Let's have a cup of tea shall we? I'm parched. And I'm dying for a cuddle.'

Inside, I sat at the fold-away table in the back room bouncing Becky on my knee, while Mum boiled a kettle. With my free hand I played with the green plastic salt cellar as Mum wittered on about this and that, and thought about how much salt Dad used to pour on his food.

'You'll die of heart disease,' I used to say, having read about the dangers of cooking with too much salt in a cookery book I'd borrowed from the library.

'My lungs'll get me first,' he'd wheezed, 'and don't be so impertinent, madam.' His smile told me that he was pleased I cared.

92

'Why don't I make the tea, Mum? You have a squeeze of Becky.' I needed something to do, but it was no good, chucking a couple of tea bags in the pot took no time at all. Stumbling over my words was a familiar sensation. I placed the tea pot and cups on the table, ummed and ahhed, and just as I was about to come out with it my eyes alighted on a pile of paper sitting in the middle of the table, pushed against the wall. Forms, not paper. Forms I recognised.

I leaned over and picked them up. 'What's this?' I said.

'I was hoping you'd give me a hand with the bloody things,' she said, cupping her hands over Becky's ears. Why, I'll never know. Becky wasn't quite five months old and the language she was exposed to at home was far fruitier.

Johnnie looked up from the toy soldiers he'd lined up on the hearth and said, 'Bloody things. Bloody things.'

'Like a parrot, that one,' she said.

'Only not as exotic. You've gone to the Social?' It was a daft thing to say; the forms were proof she had. 'What about compensation?'

'Been gone for years.'

'But it was supposed to last a lifetime. Dad's lifetime and some. I thought you did bakery to keep yourself busy . . .'

'Oh, Mandy. How did you think I paid for those trips to Magaluf? To Corfu? Your wedding?'

'You've paid for the house?'

She nodded.

'I had no idea. I thought it would last forever.'

She raised her eyebrows and gave me the look that reduced me to a ten-year-old. There was no way I could ask her now; there was no point. I'd only hoped for a little something, to tide us over, till Rob and the others went back to work. I picked up the pot and poured the tea.

'Were you hoping for some, duck? Oh God, I'm so sorry. If I'd known then what I know now . . .'

'Mum, you've been so generous. Please don't worry. We'll manage.'

She reached over and squeezed my hand. 'There are things we can do. Your Dad planned on having a vegetable garden.'

'Was that what you were trying to do out there?' I tipped my head towards the garden. 'Start a vegetable patch?'

She nodded, pulled a face and we both laughed.

'No redundancy payment?'

'No. A couple of weeks' wage packets and that were generous.'

The woman behind the screen looked over her glasses at us, scowled, and ticked some box or other on the form.

'He was bankrupt, not tight.' Mum said, lips tight. She was frustrated, ashamed, and increasingly angry. Throughout her adult life, she'd never asked for a penny from the state or anyone else for that matter, and it hurt that she had to now and the snotty-nosed cow sitting behind the desk was only making matters worse. It was alright for Mrs Fancypants, she had a job, had a wage.

As promised I'd helped Mum complete the form from the Social. After all I'd done ours not so very long ago. I didn't find it easy; the chuffing things were designed to put people off. But Mum was nervous about going down to the DHSS alone, officialdom frightened her, so I agreed to go too. It was boiling hot in there, the large windows intensifying the sun's rays. There were no seats; a queue wormed its way round the scuffed linoleum floor before stopping in front of a barricade of plastic glass-fronted numbered hatches. It was as I imagined speaking with someone in prison might be, except that you had a seat to park your bum on in prisons, if the shows on the telly were anything to go by.

We'd queued for over an hour and had been speaking to Mrs Fancypants for almost twenty minutes. Becky was asleep in the buggy, Johnnie lolled on the filthy floor. He'd been rolling round on it pretending to be a slug and was as grubby as hell. He'd nothing to play with other than the pink-haired gonk that was his favourite toy.

The woman had checked the form for us, asked all manner of stupid questions, and written on endless bits of paper. Finally, she pushed a piece of card through the narrow gap and said, 'You'll need to sign on every other Wednesday at 3.05 p.m. Don't forget, and don't be late.'

'What about job opportunities?' Mum said. 'Can't you offer any advice?'

'Try vacancy board. But you'll be lucky.' And with that we were dismissed. She pulled down a blind and several people in the queue swore. As we walked out Johnnie whispered, 'Frigging heck.'

Outside, red-faced and longing for a drink I checked my watch and realised with horror that I was late picking up the boys from school.

They were sitting in reception on the chairs meant for parents, swinging their legs, when I arrived. They were so bored they couldn't even be bothered to get up when I said, 'Let's go.' My throat was parched; I squinted down the corridor looking for a water fountain. Spotting one I took hold of Becky's bottle and Johnnie's beaker and filled them. I was taking a drink myself when I heard Ruth's voice.

'Hi! What are you lot still doing here?'

I banged my teeth on the metal spout as I jerked up, wiping water from my chin. She lolled against the doorframe of a classroom. She wore a cotton frock that skirted her knees. It was crisp and floral and pretty. Her long, slim legs hinted at summers spent on faraway beaches and her cherry red nails matched her lipstick. She looked more like the backing singer of a pop group than a teacher.

David, Mark, and Johnnie appeared at my side. I spluttered my apologies for being late, for drinking the water, for the state of my youngest son – with black-grey smudges all over his face, arms, and knees he looked like a member of Fagin's gang from *Oliver!*

Ruth laughed. 'Oh, you poor things! All of you!'

Mark leaned against me and whined. 'Wanna go home.'

'We'll be off,' I said, wiping my brow and brushing my hands down my skirt as if to flatten creases. My front tooth throbbed.

'Wait, I'll walk with you.'

Surprise must have been written all over my face because Ruth added, 'I'm leaving early today. There's an action group meeting.'

'FAG,' I said without thinking.

'FAG?' She was lost for a moment, then she clapped her hands together and burst out laughing. 'Brilliant! Trust you to think of that! To tell you the truth, I'd much rather carry on with my plans, or, heaven forbid, actually do some marking.' She bent down to place herself at eye level with the boys. 'Don't tell anyone I said that,' and she put her finger over her mouth. All three of them giggled and did the same, fingers over lips, saying, 'Sssshhhhh.'

'Must be nice to love your job,' I said.

'I'm lucky, I know that. I really do appreciate it.' She looked down the corridor, a pinched look on her face.

'No need to feel guilty. You deserve it; you worked hard for it,' I said.

She shrugged. 'There are harder jobs.' Then she

smiled. 'And it's not all great. Part of me would like to be at home, like you.'

'Really?' I couldn't hide my surprise.

'Greener grass and all that, perhaps? Come on. I need to go.'

The journey down the hill towards the high street and FAG headquarters – Vince and Ethel's house for that particular gathering – was considerably easier than the journey up, what with Ruth's easy conversation, and the retreating sun. Dark clouds swept across the village from the hills bringing with them a welcome, cooling breeze. A storm was brewing.

As we reached the top of the street, Ruth stopped and turned to me. 'Why don't you come? It's as important for you as it is for me. If not more so.' I knew what she meant. After all, she had a good job. They weren't desperate, not like most of us.

'What about the kids?'

'Can't we drop them at your mum's? She's not working now, is she? Or at home? Rob could look after them for a couple of hours. Or is he on the picket line?'

I shook my head. 'It's nearly tea time. He won't know what to cook.'

'We could take them with us. Ethel won't mind. She loves children. She must do; she had seven!' She laughed and I tried to join in, but couldn't. The rate Rob and I were going we'd have as many by the time I hit thirty. 'Please come, Mandy. I could do with a friend. I'm terrified of most of them, yet they look to me for ideas, to do the talking for them.'

'It's because you sound like the newsreaders on the telly. I know what you mean; Ethel could put the fear of God into Genghis Khan.'

She stared at me, eyes pleading, and I felt like I did when I was thirteen years old and she persuaded me to come to the rec with her to meet Steve Heppington. I sat on the swings, feeling like a right lemon, for over an hour while they necked and groped each other underneath the slide. But I wanted to go to the meeting; I was intrigued. 'What could I do?' I said.

She hesitated a moment, then said, 'You can make the tea and biscuits. Moral support. Please.' She pressed her hands together as in prayer. I said OK, though I was disappointed; I wanted to do more than make tea. 'So long as I'm back for five. I'll need to have grub on the table by six at latest.'

We stopped at the newsagents on the corner of the Braithwaites' road. Ruth bought sausage rolls in plastic wrappers, sweets, and chocolate digestives for the boys, and a pint of milk for Becky. The boys' eyes were saucers. It was all I could do not to gasp at the carelessness with which she dropped items into the wire basket slung over her arm. At the till she pulled a ten-pound note from her purse, loosening it from a bundle. For the kids it was an adventure, but my guts felt like concrete. Rob wasn't likely to question my absence until his stomach reminded him of it, but he mightn't whole-heartedly approve of me being there. After the fair he'd made it clear that my first duty was to him and the kids.

'All very well these women getting involved 'n' all that. Not that I'm not grateful. They're doing a grand job. But those that's involved have not got three lads 'n' a babbie to look after.'

Besides, he couldn't stand the Braithwaites. Didn't like their attitude. And yet he was creepy around Vince, always sucking up to him. Rumours were still rife about Dan, the most popular that he had been awarded a medal for bravery in the Falklands and given an honourable discharge, though the medal hadn't been seen by anyone. Rob thought it was all talk. 'Crap!' he'd said, and I'd wondered if he was jealous.

Vince and Ethel's four-bedroomed detached house stood at the top of the cul-de-sac, flanked on either side by the homes of their two eldest sons, Phil and Michael. The others also lived on the crescent; the twins remained at home. No one had ever been able to work out how they managed to get so many houses in such close proximity. There was either some kind of corruption at the council or people moved out willingly to get away from them. It was a very well-ordered, perfectly mowed lawns and colourful beds of petunias type of ghetto.

Inside the usual FAG suspects gathered in the front room. The storm had yet to break so we put the boys outside in the garden with their little picnic. I buzzed with excitement; something different, pastures new and all.

It was quarter to six when we got home. Rob was slumped in front of the early evening news, clutching a tin of lager. I kept my mouth shut; I was probably in enough trouble as it was.

He was quiet as I prepared tea. When he came into the kitchen he went to the stove, lifted up the pot lid, and remarked that we'd all look like corned beef stew soon. 'It's cheap,' I offered, unnecessarily. I told him that Mum had no more money and that further cuts would have to be made.

'Like where?' he said.

I was tempted to say, 'From your chuffing beer and fag money, that's where,' but I kept my mouth shut. They were his only luxuries, after all. And he'd clipped me round the ear last time I'd suggested he try to give up. It didn't hurt and he was so apologetic afterwards, I actually felt sorry for him, but I wasn't going to take the risk that evening.

We ate supper in silence. The boys babbled about the treats they'd had from Ruth. They didn't mention where we were; it was of no importance to them, and Rob didn't ask and this made me nervous. After we'd all finished I shooed the boys upstairs and put Becky in her bouncer.

'I'd like to go on a demo,' I said, as casually as I could, running the tap to fill the washing up bowl.

'That Ruth putting ideas in your head again? It's alright for her; nowt else to do.' He slammed his fist on the table.

Momentarily, I wondered how he knew. And then I realised: he'd been in the boozer, talking with the other blokes who weren't on the picket line that day. My heart pumped a little faster. Here we were, eating corned beef stew and tinned peas again, while he was supping in The White Lion. My anger made me bold.

'It's for all of us.'

'There's kids to consider.'

'Lots of women are taking their kids.'

'You're not taking the baby.'

'Mum'll have her. Or perhaps you might look after her for a change. She is your daughter after all.'

'You're one that wanted another.'

'You're the one that won't use a rubber johnny!' I waved a wooden spoon as I spoke, spraying washing up liquid bubbles all over the floor.

He stood up, pushing the table forward and his chair backwards; the legs screeched on the tiles. He staggered towards the kitchen door, catching his head on an iron pan that dangled from a hook on the ceiling. 'Keep your voice down,' he muttered.

As he rubbed his head, confused by the new positioning of the pan, I saw vulnerability in him, and regretted my words. 'Rob, I'm sorry. I didn't mean that. I know you love her as much as I do.'

He continued to rub his skull. 'It's only one day. What harm can it do?'

'You're not going. End of.' He walked out of the kitchen.

No matter what he said, I was going. He'd never know.

CHAPTER 9

The day of the demo arrived. When I called it a rally – a word I'd heard on the radio – Ethel put me straight, though she'd been unable to explain the difference. I found out for myself.

I dragged Dad's old dictionary down from the shelf where it was kept along with his *Complete Works of Shakespeare*, a gardening manual, and a set of *Encyclopaedia Britannica* which I'd been conned into buying from some good-looking, silver-tongued salesman a few years back. The gardening book and plays were the only things of Dad's I'd wanted to keep. I'd never read them, but it was a comfort to know they were there. Gardening wasn't my thing, and I couldn't understand all that old-fashioned language in the plays and poems. Dad used to quote bits, often at the weirdest times, and they always sounded so great and significant coming from him, but when we did *A Midsummer Night's Dream* at school it was the most boring thing I'd ever had to endure in my life. Not that I was present at secondary school that much. I did that much wagging after Dad died that my English teacher said I was more elusive than the Scarlet Pimpernel.

The dictionary took a while to find; it was buried amongst a pile of magazines: *Darts Today, Woman's Weekly*, and the *Beano*. The magazines were all out of date and covered in dust. I discovered that rally meant much the same as demo, and mostly connected to protest. Protest. That was my favourite word out of all three. It seemed to have more force, more power.

I was apprehensive about going and not only because Rob had said I couldn't. I'd never been on anything like this, and although I'd seen pictures on the news of the picket lines and demos in various towns in the county, and in Wales and the North East, they were mostly full of understandably angry men.

The weather forecast had predicted a fine day. Just in case, I stuffed lightweight rainproofs into the rucksack along with a packed lunch for the three of us and plenty to drink. I hid it under the stairs. Mum had offered to have Johnnie as well as Becky, as it wasn't practical to take a buggy and he'd not manage the walking. Not without moaning and making everyone's life a misery.

We left the house at eight thirty ready to meet the coach for nine o' clock. Rob had left with flying pickets at dawn. Given that we lived less than ten minutes' walk away this was ridiculously early, but I'd been ready for almost two hours and was fed up of sitting in the kitchen, afraid to drink any more tea for fear of needing the toilet on the journey.

I couldn't believe the size of the crowd standing outside the pub. I'd never seen so many women gathered in one place other than at the annual WI jumble sale in a nearby village (posh folk lived there so the pickings were fantastic) or Weight Watchers the week after Christmas. I looked at the crowd and the solitary coach; there was no way we were all going to fit on.

It took ages to find anyone I knew from FAG. Ruth, Ethel, Ann, and the others were nowhere to be seen. I pushed my way through the throng, shouting, 'Excuse me, excuse me.' Everyone I knew was there, everyone. My stomach churned 'cos Rob was bound to find out, but it was too late now. I was committed. Finally, Ethel's bass roar rose, as if from the paving slabs themselves, into the air.

'Ladies! Ladies! Do not panic. I have managed to secure a second coach which will be with us forthwith!' she bellowed. She reminded me of a shop steward, one of those from that Carry On film set in the toilet factory. Relief settled on the crowd and conversation turned to mundane subjects, like who'd seen *Coronation Street* the night before.

Ruth appeared at my side. 'We must make sure we're on the same coach. It'd be lovely to sit next to each other,' she said. 'The boys will enjoy sitting by themselves.'

The journey took an hour and a half, mostly because the traffic on the motorway was rubbish. I didn't mind one bit. The scenery was beautiful before we got to the main roads and Ruth and I chatted about everything and nothing. The atmosphere on the coach was like a party, a massive hen party. People shared sweets and drinks; there was laughter every other minute. We played games with our fellow coach, overtaking one another on the motorway, all of us noses up against the windows, sticking out our tongues and waving two fingers up; we were like a great big bunch of kids, and it was brilliant. The carriage smelt of hairspray and deodorant and egg and cress sandwiches and Benson and Hedges.

When we passed the first blue sign for Sheffield, Ethel stood at the front of the coach, microphone in hand. She went to begin then paused as if she'd forgotten something. She rummaged in her bag, pulled out her false teeth (top set), put the plate in, and began. She thanked everyone for turning up. It meant a lot to FAG and it meant a lot to their men. Not all of them, I thought to myself. Then she went on to say, 'Now let's show those Tory rags and those Tory bastards what supporting our men MEANS,' – she belted out the last bit so hard she nearly lost her teeth, the microphone whistled and I had to put my fingers in my ears. Everyone roared their approval and something deep inside of me turned over. She hushed the crowd again. 'Save your voices, ladies. You'll need them for later.'

The driver dropped us off in a side road, it was too busy to get any closer, and we walked the half mile to the meeting point. Flags and banners were unrolled and manned the moment we stepped off the bus. There were homemade affairs, lettering hand-stitched on cheap satin, others were professionally printed onto plastic boards, stapled onto plywood handles. They read 'Coal not Dole' and 'Victory to the Miners'. As we walked down the street strangers leaped out and slapped stickers onto the boys, and us. There were even badges going free, Mark and David were delighted and pinned them to their T-shirts, wearing them with pride.

Nothing prepared me for the sight and sound of the throng outside the NUM headquarters. A multitude of flags and banners rippled in the breeze, like a shimmering sea of, mostly, red and yellow. Thousands of female voices hovered in the air.

'Here we go! Here we go! Here we go!'

The singing faded into angry chants: 'Maggie! Maggie! Maggie! Out! Out! Out!'

A woman with a megaphone stood at the top of the building steps and announced that the march was about to begin. It was a battle cry, a call to arms and people around me responded accordingly. I wasn't at all sure what to do, and must have looked like a right pillock, standing there, looking around me, mouth wide open. I held fast on to the boys' sticky hands. Ruth took hold of David's other arm and said, 'Let's get ourselves to the front; it'll be less claustrophobic than here and we might get our pictures in the paper, boys!' Mark and David smiled, polite, not altogether sure, and she led us through the crowd.

At the front we formed a human wall, all holding hands and set off down the street to follow the path round the city. What was strange was that the men, important men like Arthur Scargill, walked behind us. I couldn't believe it.

We shouted and smiled as we marched along and I began to relax, to enjoy myself. I worried that this wasn't the right way to feel. Weren't we supposed to be indignant, furious, venting our frustration and rage at the government for the wrong they were doing our men, our communities? It felt like a brisk stroll with friends after a night down the pub (minus the booze). Hundreds and hundreds of friends.

The traffic halted; we dominated the road. People stood on the pavement as we went by, cheering us on, clapping, waving, and shouting their encouragement. For a moment I felt like a pop star; I tasted something which, at the time, I would never have been able to identify, but which I later saw with such clarity, such transparency, that it almost made me weep: pride. I felt proud. And there wasn't a cake in sight.

At the park where the march ended David asked me something. I stopped and bent down to catch his words and when I stood upright again Ruth had disappeared. We found ourselves amongst strangers, waiting for the speakers to begin.

The women were young, younger than me, and had tattoos and short hair. Shorter than my Rob's, as short as Dan's when he was in army. One of the girls had rings all the way up her ears, right round the cartilage. It made me feel squeamish, but I couldn't stop staring. It was only when I realised that the boys were staring too that I dragged my eyes away. It felt ever so funny, standing there with trendy girls in ripped T-shirts, dungarees, and torn jeans, me in my cotton skirt and clumpy sandals, but they didn't seem to mind. One of them turned to me after the first speaker had finished and lowering the placard she'd been waving said: 'My arms are absolutely killing me!' Although her voice wasn't exactly posh – I'd have guessed she came from Manchester way – she had a confidence, an air of expectancy, about her which reminded me of Ruth. Her arms were like sticks; no wonder they ached.

'You students?' I said.

'Yes. You?'

I nearly wet myself laughing. 'I'm at the university of life!'

'I mean what's your faction? Your affiliation?' She sounded more well-to-do all of a sudden.

110

'Nothing. I'm a miner's wife. These are my boys.'

'Oh, you're so brave. I do so admire you,' she replied, revealing a beautiful set of white, even teeth.

I'd no idea why she thought I was brave or admired me. 'Thanks for your support. It's brilliant you're doing this. Not really your battle is it?' I wondered why she was here, instead of looking at her books, or going out dancing or whatever else students did with their time.

'Oh but it's everyone's battle. Everyone on the Left. This strike is symbolic of the struggle against the capitalist machine, individualism, and the quashing of the re-emergence of the socialist movement.'

And there was me thinking it was about jobs. I lifted my chin in silent agreement as she turned towards the stage where a man in a dog collar was approaching the microphone. Perhaps he was going to pray for us.

The boys were growing restless and my stomach was beginning to growl so we pulled ourselves away from the group, and pushed back through the crowds till we found some open space at the park's edge. Leaning against ornate black railings we opened our packs of fish paste sandwiches. They were flattened and misshapen, the doughy white bread squashed into almost nothing. We didn't care; we were starving, and devoured them in minutes. We washed them

111

down with a bottle of dandelion and burdock and a couple of Kit-Kats – my way of saying thank you to the lads for coming without complaint, doing all that walking, and being all-round good boys.

After dinner I thought we ought to make our way back to the coach; find some of the other lasses from Fenley. I'd lost my bearings and never having been to Sheffield before hadn't a clue where we were. At the park exit there was a board with a map of the surrounding area. I studied it carefully, but NUM headquarters wasn't labelled. The boys were starting to whinge.

'Come on, we're going this way,' I said, pointing up the street as if I knew where I was heading, and off we went. We walked and walked; David was crying; there were hundreds of women with hundreds of banners, none of which I recognised. In my excitement I'd not even taken note of the name of the street on which the bus had parked. It was approaching half past two; the coach was due to leave at three o' clock. Panic descended. Moisture gathered in the hollow of my spine and soaked into the polyester of my blouse. I could feel my thighs rubbing against each other as we walked faster and faster, the quickening pace of my heart, the dragging feeling in my belly. Faces that only an hour had felt friendly and inclusive became aggressive and soulless. Everyone seemed to know where they were going; no one seemed to notice or care about a mother and her children struggling to find their way home. I felt the anonymity and hostility of the city looming, closing in, trapping us in its grey, concrete gullies. I longed for Fenley Down nestled in the hills, surrounded by miles and miles of open space, where everyone was connected in one way or another, where there was always someone to turn to, no matter what the situation. Bile rose in my throat. David and Mark trudged wordlessly alongside me, their silence troubling me more than their whining ever had.

When I was a girl the Institute organised day trips for the families. Dad had wanted to go to Scarborough, but the vote went to Blackpool and Mum just wanted a day out so off we went. The beach was wide and sandy, the famous metal tower stood watching over everything, trams flew back and forth. The tide was so far out we couldn't see the sea so we walked to the funfair instead. Crowds swarmed between the rides. Distracted by the Wurlitzer, I stopped and stared, my hand slipping from Dad's. Later, when the music stopped, I looked about me and realised I was alone. I thought I would never see Dad and Mum again.

In Sheffield city centre that afternoon I was nine years old: abandoned, frightened and trying desperately not to cry. I paused for breath outside a Chinese restaurant, the sticky smell of fried duck hanging in the air. Feeling as if I was drowning, I slid down the glass front till I rested on my haunches and hung my head between my knees. I must have looked a right state, crouched there on the pavement, but I didn't care.

Mark spoke first. His small voice. 'We're not lost, are we, Mum?'

'Don't be daft, petal,' I said without lifting my head, afraid he might see the fear in my face if he hadn't heard it in my voice. Then David piped up.

'We're lost! We're lost! You're lying. Lying.' He was crying again, sobs rasping at his throat. It set Mark off and he started too. I stood up.

'Will you shut up! We are not lost, we're not.' My voice quivered. Tears came and I looked up at the sky. It was cloudless, a blinding blue. I staggered forward, clutching the boys, tears obscuring my vision. I stopped, wiped my eyes and looked ahead, willing the sight of a familiar face.

Ruth, I saw Ruth, jogging towards us. At first, I thought it might be a mirage, like characters stuck in the desert I was beginning to hallucinate. Then she was right there in front of me, flinging her arms around first me, and then David and Mark.

'Golly, where have you been? We've been looking all over for you. I was so worried. I thought you were going to miss the coach. I persuaded the driver to wait a while. Ethel was sure you would find your way home, but I wasn't. "Why, she might not have any money on her," I said.' Her words came out in a rush, tumbling over one another, and I was so relieved and so grateful I burst into tears again.

'Chuffing heck, am I glad to see you! I thought we were going to be stuck here forever.'

She laughed, all breathy. 'You are funny. Stuck here forever? It's Sheffield, not the Congo!'

I felt stupid then; she was right. We were only down the road from Fenley, though it felt like another world to me. 'How far are we?'

'To the bus?'

I nodded.

'That's the funniest thing. It's just round that corner.' She pointed. And the boys cheered and jumped up and down. I picked up David and slung him across my hip; Ruth picked up Mark – God knows how, she was a wisp of a thing and he was a thumping lad – and we staggered back to the bus. Everyone cheered as we clambered on and my cheeks flared with relief and embarrassment.

Rob was home when we arrived back, slumped in front of the telly. The kids had been sworn to secrecy. Rob didn't look up. My mind raced with excuses. My belly fisted. He knew. I was sure.

'How was it?' I asked, acting all normal.

'Usual. Police, reporters, miners. No scabs today.'

The biscuit tin sat on the floor at his feet with a half empty cup of tea.

'Where'd you get these?' I said, pointing at the custard creams.

'Food parcel on line.'

'That's nice.'

'We had Kit-Kat,' David said.

I shot him a look. Wrong child.

'And we saw women with tattoos and rings in their noses,' Mark piped up.

'There were some right funny—'

'Don't bother lyin'. I know where you've been.' He still wouldn't look at me.

'Rob . . .' What could I say? That I wasn't going to lie? That would have been another lie and we'd always been honest with each other.

'They're all lezzers,' he said, standing.

I don't know where my courage came from; I felt offended on their behalf.

'They're supporting us. How'd you know they were lezzers? You weren't even there.'

'What's a lezzer?' David said.

'Cos they're all same. See 'em on picket line too. Bunch of lezzers, all of them. I'm off to pub. What they need . . .'

But I was no longer listening to him. I stopped thinking about why he wasn't bothered that I'd ignored his order. On the picket line? These girls joined the picket with the men and our women? I was amazed. I'd heard horror stories about the police targeting the women to break the lines, calling them names, spitting and ripping T-shirts to expose their breasts. These girls, who probably all came from good homes, with parents with decent, clean jobs in law and accountancy, or businessmen like Ruth's father, were risking injury and humiliation to support us. These women were taking on the men, the policemen. It was all I could think about for the rest of the evening.

CHAPTER 10

In the early evening sunlight Mum's house took on a mauve hue, the smell of jasmine filled the air as we walked down her path. Johnnie rushed on ahead, pushed open the door with ease and disappeared. I wondered where he got the strength; it wasn't as if he was eating tons of spinach. Too expensive.

Mum appeared in the doorway, arms round Johnnie. 'I've had door fixed!'

'And where'd you get money for luxuries?' I said, only half joking.

'Dean Smithton fixed it up for me.'

Dean was a good-looking publican – he ran The Boar's Head – and had split from his wife a few years back. The brewery had been reluctant to keep him on, they liked couples running places, but he'd managed to talk them round. I wondered if there was anything going on between him and Mum. I thought about making a joke of it, but realising Mum might see this as judgment or disapproval, I kept silent. She'd tell me when she was good and ready, and I would be pleased for her. I really would. She'd been on her own too long. Assuming there was something to tell.

'Thought we'd eat outside as it's so nice and all,' Mum said, ushering us through.

Laid out on the table was the best spread we'd seen in months: pork pies cut into quarters, sausage rolls, crisps, cold meats, cheese and pine-apple on sticks, fresh bread rolls, and salad. Salad. Fresh green salad and a bowl of summer fruits. I almost wept. The boys hovered round the tea like flies, picking at the crisps, and breaking off pieces of ham, stuffing cheese squares into their little faces. Becky gurgled her approval. I gave her a piece of apple, her first.

'There's trifle in fridge and some biscuits, but don't tell 'em till they've eaten some fruit,' Mum whispered in my ear.

'How've you afforded all this?'

She waved her finger at me, curbing my protest.

'Thanks, Mum. This is champion.'

'For the little ones.'

After tea the boys rolled on the ill-kept lawn, scrambling between the unruly plants and bushes. It was a perfect garden for children and foxes: messy, overgrown, with all sorts of hiding places, nooks, and crannies. Becky slept in a Moses basket that had been mine. Her toes scratched at the base she was so long now. Mum and I drank tea and stared into the distance, saying nothing. Peaceful.

There was nothing beyond Mum's garden,

nothing but the hills, and I was gripped with a desire to walk, just walk, without aim or purpose over those craggy moors. I asked if she'd mind watching the children a while.

''Course not, love. Go. I'll put them to bed here. Walk home afterwards, spend some time with that man of yours.'

I couldn't remember the last time Rob and I spent an evening together. 'Thanks. I will.'

I gathered up my things, a light jacket and my handbag, and waved from the back door, promising to be over early the next morning.

'Take your time. Not like any of us has to get up for work or nothing!' The following day was Saturday, so no school for the boys either.

From Mum's garden gate I turned left, following the bramble lined path to the bridleway and the open space beyond. Standing in the first field, I cast my eyes about, trying to decide which direction to head in. It was hard, making that first decision. I was unaccustomed to such freedom, small though it was; I'd forgotten what it tasted like.

The broom was out, great bushes flanked the dirt track, yellow and bright in the evening sun; the scent beautiful. At the top of the first incline I paused, my thighs stinging with the exertion of the climb and the chill that the air now held. I span three hundred and sixty degrees, hand shielding my eyes, searching for hikers or casual ramblers. There was no one in sight, not for miles and miles. And despite the throbbing in my legs I span round again, arms outstretched, and skipped a little further before collapsing in a heap on the grass, flat on my back staring at the milky sky. Wisps of red cloud drifted by, like cochineal poured into icing. I tried to find animal shapes in them as I'd done as a girl with Dad, but couldn't. Minutes later I heaved myself up, and walked on, and on and on.

Dusk was falling; it wouldn't be long before I'd be plunged into darkness; I had no torch. Down in the valley was the faint outline of Fenley, street lights popping on, glowing pink. I turned onto another path, hoping I could drop into the village on the west side nearest to our house, but I couldn't make out any of the buildings to be sure this was the right direction. The path veered left towards a cluster of trees. I became aware of the sound of my feet hitting the dry earth, aware of the steady thump of my heart, the bouncing of breasts against my ribcage. I slowed down, almost tiptoeing, before stopping.

There was a strange noise, faint. It was coming from the clump of trees. Definitely not animal. Definitely not human. I walked closer, ears alert. And then I knew. It was a trumpet, notes rising and falling on the breeze. I recognised the tune; it was one of Dad's favourites: 'Nimrod', from Elgar's *Enigma Variations*. I stopped and listened. It was beautiful, the playing a little ropey – the trumpeter was no virtuoso – but it raised such emotion in me that I stepped closer, lay down on the damp grass and listened, lost in memories.

Dad didn't play an instrument himself, but he appreciated music, and being a Yorkshireman and a miner he loved brass and the colliery bands in the region. Every summer he'd take me to the concerts, and the competitions – they were cut-throat, more like a blood sport than art, Dad would laugh, and he bought the records and played them on his turntable with the Bakelite needle arm. I was ashamed of that thing. It looked more like a vanity case than a record player and it had a funny smell. I wanted turntables like those my mates had, all black and silver with flashing lights like an aeroplane deck.

On the still air, with no one around it felt like 'Nimrod' was being played for me alone and I succumbed to it, allowing it to surround me. The music rose to a crescendo, the notes expanding, pulling deep inside me, lifting me, carrying me into myself and my past and I found myself crying. With happiness or sadness I couldn't be sure. When the piece came to an end silence hovered on the air, like the birds and the animals and the wind itself were afraid of breaking the spell cast by the tune. Then came a cough, followed by a spit and I was reminded that the instrument had a player, a player unaware that he or she had an audience. An audience that might be unwelcome.

After I'd wiped the tears from my face, I rose and looking about, realised there was no other obvious route back – I had to walk past the trees where the trumpeter played. I thought about coughing, or humming some stupid pop song to announce my arrival, but this would look ridiculous and false. I hoped the musician might start another tune, something a bit louder and bigger and well, brassier. Something that might disguise the thudding of my feet.

I took a deep, silent, breath and walked, as normally as I could, determined not to turn my head. But I was overcome with nerves. It had dawned on me that this musician might be some kind of a mad, murdering axe-man. A fondness for beautiful music does not exclude the criminally insane. Hitler was a fan of Wagner, Dad had reliably informed me. A dedicated socialist, Dad had refused to applaud after an aria of the unfortunate composer's at a concert in a neighbouring village.

I pulled my jacket around me, my heart rate increasing, my pace quickening. Torn between irrational anxiety and inquisitiveness, I wanted to run but couldn't because I had to know who the player was.

As I approached the trees, the trumpeter struck up another tune. It wasn't one I recognised, definitely not classical or anything the colliery band would play; it felt modern, and the playing was more confident, more assured. The sound came from behind an oak. It was set back from the path a touch and though I'd meant to keep my eyes fixed ahead I couldn't help myself; I turned. I couldn't see anyone, but the tune played on. I kept my head turned as I walked, craning my neck to see around the tree. In the shadows I saw a silhouette, leaning against the trunk, one leg outstretched, the other bent up. I stopped, listened; it was a man, oblivious to my presence. He played on. And as he finished, my fear evaporated and I applauded. The man leaped upright, but remained in the shadows.

'Didn't mean to make you jump. That were beautiful,' I said.

There was something familiar about his outline, but I couldn't place it. He said nothing, just stood there, stock still. The fear returned. Perhaps I was mistaken, perhaps he was a crazy after all. I wiped my forehead. My voice shook. 'Especially "Nimrod". It's one of my favourites.'

'You know Elgar?' he mumbled. He sounded surprised, and the sense that I knew him grew. I relaxed a little.

'Never was much good at school, bit daft, but I learnt it from my dad; he liked music.' My tongue ran away with me. What on earth was I doing spilling my guts to this solitary trumpeter out on the moors in near darkness? It was that chuffing music; it had disturbed something.

'You're not stupid, Mandy.' Dan stepped forward.

I couldn't tally the beauty of the music, the tenderness of the playing, with a man with a reputation for aggression. He'd been a soldier; he was a Braithwaite. Then I remembered his kindness the night Becky was born, his gentle concern, the way he ate his cake at the May Fair, all hunched like a wounded bear.

'What are you doing out here?' I said.

'I'd have thought that was obvious. What are you doing here? It's almost dark. Could be anyone about.'

'Like an axe-murderer?' I smiled, mocking him and myself, though he couldn't have known that.

He looked at the ground, kicked it with his trainer.

'You're not a bad player.'

He tapped the trumpet against his leg. 'Nice of you to say. But I've a long way to go.'

'You should practise more.'

He nodded, shrugged.

'Play something else.'

'Now?'

'Why not? You've got an appreciative, if small, audience.'

He laughed, rich and infectious, and asked if I'd any requests. I didn't, but said that I'd like to sit down. He gestured to the oak and lifted the trumpet to his mouth, his fingers hovering above the buttons, teasing, waiting for the right moment, composing himself.

I listened to three numbers. He played 'Nimrod' again, better this time, but it didn't move me in the same way. I was conscious of him standing there only feet away, cheeks puffed out, the movement of his long, slender fingers. He said nothing

125

between each piece, didn't even introduce them, but when he lifted his head and lowered the trumpet I knew that he'd finished for good and clapped till my hands hurt and he told me to stop. He took a bow, and I laughed, taken aback by this small gesture of theatricality. Something he'd picked up from Ruth, no doubt.

We walked back to the village together, and I was glad of his company. Night had fallen and I'd never have found the fastest way home by myself. He didn't say much, but as we drew near to the outskirts of town he asked me not to mention that I'd heard him play.

'Not even to Ruth?' I said.

'She doesn't know I'm playing again; she'd talk. Accidentally, of course, she wouldn't be able to help herself.'

'Why'd you keep it secret? Isn't it difficult with that?' I pointed at the black case.

'I don't want anyone to know right now, OK?' he said, and his tone silenced the stream of questions I had spinning in my head.

A few yards on, as we nudged town, Dan said, 'I'm dying for a ciggie.'

'Haven't got any, I'm afraid.'

'Don't be. I'm trying to give up. Been two month now.'

'Why now?'

'My small contribution to saving money.'

I wished Rob would do the same. There was a heavier price to pay than a financial one.

'I was sorry to hear about your dad. He was a good man,' Dan said.

Not wanting to talk about Dad I changed the subject. 'Where do you keep that?' I said, pointing at the case. 'Doesn't Ruth notice?' I knew where Rob kept everything, even his porn collection; he could hide nothing from me.

'In the garage. Ruth never comes in there. It's my domain. Everyone needs their own private space.'

I nodded, wondering if I needed my own space. I'd not noticed a lack of one, but I thought about Dad again and his shed and the time he spent there. 'Putting the world to rights – in my head,' he'd said.

'You'll tell no one?' Dan said.

'Cross my heart and hope to die,' I replied, licking my finger and touching my forehead, chest, both shoulders.

We walked in silence. When we reached the bottom end of town, near the high street I asked how long he'd been playing the trumpet.

'It's a flugelhorn.'

'A what?'

'Flugelhorn. Most people can't tell difference.'

'Bet you get sick of saying that!'

He laughed. 'I did.'

'So how long?'

'I started as a lad. Was in school band, then colliery, for a time. Thought about playing professional like, but that's not for likes of us.'

'Says who?'

'My dad.'

'I see.' And I did. Vince was fierce; he'd not tolerate disobedience and what my mum would call 'uppertiness'.

'I took it up again a while back.'

'When you were in army?'

'I took it with me. Kept it at the . . .' He paused, took a deep breath, as if saying the word needed extra strength, 'barracks.'

But he was a grown man now, able to make his own decisions. Why'd he let his dad's opinions get in the way? Why couldn't he follow his dream?

'So now you're back it's a guilty pleasure.'

'If you like.' He stopped, as if he wanted to say something else; he rubbed his jawline with his free hand and sighed.

I couldn't bear the silence. 'Lucky for you Ruth's not nosy. I know every corner of our house!'

He moved on.

'Why don't you join colliery band again? Your dad can't disapprove of that. Forget what he thinks. You've got the time, and it's a way of keeping your spirits up, not spending all your time in pub.'

'I might . . .'

'You should.'

I tried to picture him in the band from years back. I must have seen him play; we watched many times, Rob and me, and the kids too, but I couldn't picture him.

At the high street we stopped and I felt awkward; I didn't know how to say goodbye.

I looked up at him. 'Makes no sense to me why you keep it a secret, but it's safe with me all the same,' I said, hugging myself. My thin jacket no longer held out the chill; my bare toes were half frozen.

'Thank you.'

In the glow of the street lights he looked different again, his fringe falling softly over his forehead, his generous lips curved into a half smile, the sadness I noticed at the fair still present in his eyes. Gentle, kind eyes, full of longing. For what?

I lifted my hand in a red Indian 'How' gesture, shrugged, and turned, hurrying down the street as fast as my frozen trotters would take me. Rob would be worried; I'd lost all track of time.

I'd not even got the key in the lock when the door was flung open and he stood there, blue eyes scratched red, beer can in hand.

'Where the bloody hell have you been?'

I shook my head. 'I went for a w–'

'And where the hell are the kids?'

'Mum's.'

I expected him to ask why, but he said, 'Thank crap for that!' and turned back into the house.

Following him through to the kitchen and expecting him to ask me why I'd stayed so long, I slipped my arms round his middle and said, 'Smashing, isn't it? We've the evening to ourselves.'

He slumped into a chair, head in his hands, groaning.

'What's up?' Something terrible must have happened while I was out walking on the hills. Guilt drenched me.

'The gerbil's dead.'

'Gordy? Are you sure?'

'He's on his back in cage. Oh, Mand, what are we going to tell kids? They'll be heartbroken.'

I fell into the chair opposite and took hold of his hands. 'We'll get another. Tomorrow. Before I fetch them.'

'They'll know. We've no money till Social comes. Poor little sod. I'll miss him.'

Rob's eyes misted over and I went to him and sat on his lap. He put his arms around me; I felt his heat seeping through my clothes and it felt good. 'I'll tell them.'

He kissed me. I could taste beer. I'd almost forgotten the shape of his mouth, tongue, teeth, the feel of his hands on my breasts. It felt good, and reassuring. He pulled me, his willing victim, by the hand, to bed.

Rob had no condoms and though I'd thought about it I'd not gone to the doctor's to get the pill.

'Come on, love. It'll be alright. Just this once.' He kissed my ear, but I was having none of it.

'What if we have another accident?'

'It'll be fine.' On top of me again, he pushed my thighs apart with his knee.

My body responded, melting at his touch. I wanted him badly, but my mind took control. The thought of another child filled me with dread. Something had shifted for me. Once upon a time I'd dreamt of five, six kids. Not anymore. We were struggling to feed four, I was exhausted and my body didn't feel like it could take another pregnancy, let alone birth. I pushed him off. 'It won't.'

'I'll go down pub and get some from toilets.'

While Rob was out I threw on my dressing gown, dug out an old shoe box, took Gordy, now quite stiff, from his cage and placed him in it. I cleaned out the cage, emptied the water dispenser and food bowl, and put the box on the window ledge. We'd bury him tomorrow; the kids could make a cross with a couple of used lolly sticks. I made a cup of tea and returned to bed. And waited.

Rob had been gone half an hour. The walk to The Boar's Head was ten minutes. I finished my tea and closed my eyes. I woke to the sound of chinking glass, the milkman's van humming down the road shortly after eight.

CHAPTER 11

'So we were thinking that you'd be perfect. Just perfect!' Ruth clasped her hands in front of her chest. She wore an enormous grin on her sun-kissed face. Everyone was staring at me, wide-eyed, expectant. Even Ethel had a trace of pleading about her. My mouth dropped open, and I kept moving my bottom lip, hoping words would come out, but none did. The silence was embarrassing.

Members of the FAG committee and other hangers-on stood in a semi-circle to my right, Ethel with her hands on her hips, Ann and Daisy with their hands clenched to their mostly not-inconsiderable chests, old Jean with her arms folded and a wait-till-I-tell-your-Mum look on her face.

'Well?' Ruth said at last.

'What about kids?' I muttered.

'I've thought of that. I've spoken with your mother, who is only too happy to help out. "I'd be absolutely delighted to look after the little darlings," she said, "especially now I've no job. It will give me a focus." So you see, you've nothing,

132

absolutely nothing, to worry about. I've—' Ethel coughed and Ruth corrected herself, '*we've* thought of everything.'

Mum was a fantastic grandmother (though she refused to answer to Grandma. 'Too blooming young for that!' It baffled me why Nana was OK), but there was no way she'd call the kids 'little darlings', little monsters more like. The inaccuracies in the account made me doubt Ruth, but she was persuasive and I was flattered.

'Come on, you'll enjoy it,' Ruth said.

'Okaaaay,' I said, and they all cheered, apart from Ethel who only nodded, lips folded together, her mouth a thin red line.

'Let me show you the kitchen.' Ruth linked her arm in mine and led us, behind Ethel, to the back of the community centre. The centre was a former Methodist chapel, and functional, if not pretty. The pews had been removed to create the large open space across which we stomped, used variously for discos, baby and toddler groups, and coffee and cake mornings; a plaster board dividing wall in front of what would have been the altar created the kitchen. As a worshipper of food I appreciated that.

I pushed open the door and stepped inside. It reminded me of the kitchens at secondary school. All new and white and gleaming chrome. When Mum and I visited the school before I went we were shocked. Mum went quiet and I knew she was thinking about the kitchen at home. The state of it. The brown stains on the cooker that wouldn't shift no matter how hard you scrubbed, the knackered wall cupboards with flat, circular handles, and pipes that shuddered when you turned on the tap.

Whenever I thought about school a heavy, griping feeling, like undercooked tatties, ate away at my belly. I'd been hopeless at sport, and art, and drama. Cooking was an area I'd hoped to shine in, along with English, Geography and History. It hadn't worked out that way. A missed opportunity.

'So what do you think?' Ruth said.

'It's beautiful,' I said, taking it all in. 'But there's only one cooker and fridge won't be anywhere near big enough.'

'All sorted, lass,' said Ethel, barging past. 'Ruth here has secured another oven from local Labour Party, and is organising a fundraiser at the school to purchase a fridge freezer.' As if reading my mind, Ruth continued, 'And we have permission to rip out a couple of units to fit the cooker and a new fridge can stand here.' She pointed to a space on my left.

'You've thought of everything,' I said, gob-smacked.

'Too bloody right we have!' Ethel bellowed. 'Now that you've seen place, put kettle on and make us all a brew. Others'll be arriving soon.'

'Others?' I stammered.

'You didn't think we were going to feed hundreds

134

of hungry mouths single-handed, did you?' Ethel looked incredulous and I felt like a fool.

'No . . .'

'Get on with it then.' And with that she left the kitchen, the other FAGs trotting after her. Ruth and I were alone.

'I'll help,' she said, crossing to the sink, kettle already in her hand.

Anxiety rose. Ruth wouldn't always be here to help me; I'd be on my own soon enough. Searching for mugs, I rifled through the cupboards.

'You'll be fine,' Ruth said, sensing my unease. 'Now, where is the tea? I've found some instant.'

'How can you be so sure?'

'Because you're capable. Good at practical things.' She touched me on the shoulder, reassuring.

'Except typing, and . . .'

She asked if I practised. I admitted I didn't.

'Is it time?'

I snorted. 'Hardly. Lack of motivation more like. I dunno—'

'Perhaps you need the classes. A spur, a way to force you to make time. An incentive. Isn't that what business types talk about?' She threw tea bags into the enormous metal pot.

'You'll need a couple more.' I pointed at the box, stared at my hands. 'Maybe, but—'

'Is it money?'

'Not really.' A lie.

'I'll pay.'

'No way. Rob'd go mad. I couldn't let you waste your money.'

'It wouldn't be a waste. An investment in your future. You can pay me back when you start earning.'

I explained there was no way I could borrow from her. It was lovely that she had so much confidence in me, but it was misplaced and anyway, I couldn't be in debt to anyone. It wasn't right.

She shrugged, poured the milk, and said, 'But we're all indebted to someone, one way or another.'

I was about to ask her what she meant when Ethel popped her head round the door. 'Are we nearly there yet? We're gasping in here.'

All in all there were about thirty women present at the meeting. All miners' wives, girlfriends, and sisters. Others would help out as and when they could. Here, in this community centre in a town a few miles down the road from Fenley, we planned to provide hot meals for pickets working in the area. Meals and food parcels for families would be prepared in local church halls. The Miners' Institute in Fenley would be our family base. I was in charge of planning all the menus, drawing up the recipes and instructions for others to follow. We'd work on a rota, cooking locally and here, and I was to be in charge of the kitchen whenever I was on duty. I came out in a rash just thinking about it, excitement and nerves all bundled up together but everyone seemed to think I could do it, and I was too afraid to say that I wasn't sure I could.

The journey back to Fenley was uncomfortable; all six of us crammed into Ruth's hatchback. I'd not spoken to Rob since he'd stayed at the pub two nights ago, the stink of ale and fags on his clothes, in his hair, still strong the next morning. We'd not got money to replace Gordy, but we had it to piss up the wall, apparently.

There was an almighty row. Doug next door banged on the walls we were so loud, and when Rob raised his fist to me I took hold of the rolling pin resting on the draining board. He lowered his arm and said, 'I wouldn't have hit you.' But he looked ashamed, and I felt like I'd won.

They were all watching a Sunday afternoon film when I got back. A western: *Butch Cassidy and the Sundance Kid.* When we first met Rob reminded me of a dark-haired Paul Newman, all twinkling blue eyes, roguish and glamorous. I'd been so naïve, so messed up. Becky was asleep on Rob's lap, David and Mark curled either side of him, Johnnie tumbled in front of the telly, spoiling everyone's view. Rob yelled at him for what was obviously the hundredth time and Johnnie crawled over to the far wall, bent over, and kicked his legs up into a headstand.

I said hello and turned to leave.

'What's coven plotting now?' Rob said.

I'd not meant to speak to him, and though clearly

he meant it in jest, I was so angry the words spilled out. 'We're feeding you lot, when you get back from duty, if you must know.'

'Let's hope you're in charge of stirring pot and nowt else then,' he said, laughing.

'For your information I'm head of the kitchens. In charge.'

'God help us. I'll give you two weeks.'

'Just you watch me, Rob Walker. Just you blinking watch me.'

'That's my girl!' he said, blowing me a kiss.

The menu of the day was blue-tacked onto the back of the door, two of the cupboards, and pinned to the fridge with a magnet. In a folder on the side were the meals for the next ten days, all printed out on A4 white paper in my best handwriting.

It had taken ages to draw up the menus. After the meeting when I took on the position of what everyone now referred to as Head of Kitchen (Ruth's idea; she was Director of Fundraising, and Ethel was self-appointed Boss of Everything Else) I'd dragged every single cookery book I owned (three) down from the shelf above the boiler, along with numerous scraps of paper on which I'd scribbled recipes and ideas from radio and television. Selecting the dishes alone was hard work; my choices were limited, because the budget was severely limited, and, frankly, the palate of your average local miner was also somewhat limited.

I'd not wanted to involve Rob at all, but I had no choice in the end. He was my guinea pig.

'What about chilli con carne?' The Milk Marketing Board cook book described this as "a very fiery dish!". I wasn't sure the children would like it.

'What the bloody hell's that?' he said.

'Will you stop swearing, kids'll hear.'

Johnnie wandered through the kitchen chewing on the foot of a naked action man in a nappy so full it skimmed his knees and said, 'Hear what?'

'Never you mind. How about this: pasta carbonara?'

'Don't like eye-ties. Too greasy. Lad should be using potty.'

'He's only in them at night. Can't cope with washing wet sheets night after night.'

'What about one of them lovely cobblers you used to do for us? Lamb? That'd go down a treat.'

I could almost smell the freshly clipped rosemary in the air, the melt-in-the-mouth greasiness of the meat dissolving on my tongue.

'Good idea. If we could afford a decent joint.' I'd moved onto the offal section. 'Devilled Kidneys?'

'I'm full of 'em.'

I ignored his last comment. In the end I took the safe option menu-wise and opted for the staples: cottage pie, bacon and liver hotpot, meat and potato pie (or as it was later nick-named 'find the meat pie'), sausage, beans, and baked potatoes, floddies. Potatoes were a recurring theme; a woman from another village had an allotment and said she could grow them.

It was the third time I'd overseen the day at the pickets' soup kitchen, and despite how well things had gone those first days – no major disasters, only burnt roly-poly and lumpy custard – I was nervous. My voice raised an octave every time I opened my mouth and the July heat didn't instil a feeling of calm. Though I'd not had chance to look in a mirror, I knew that my cheeks were tomato red and my hair as frizzy as Worzel Gummidge's.

Eleven forty-five and we were ready for the dinnertime rush. A Sunday roast awaited the men. Chicken and potatoes fizzed on the hot plate, the sprouts had been boiled to a comforting mush (at Ethel's insistence), the carrots brushed with orange juice (my touch, I'd seen Delia do it and fancied giving it a whirl) and the heady aroma of onion gravy filled the hall. The army of servers stood to attention: spoons, forks, and ladles at the ready. As commander, I wiped my hands down my floral apron, touched the top of my paper bonnet, and nodded at my platoon.

'Ready for it, ladies?'

All five tipped their chins in silent deference. I pushed up my sleeves and braced myself.

The men arrived: hungry, thirsty, and grateful. I knew many of them, their faces at least. Smiling, I handed out plate after plate. Men shuffled down the counter, food piling higher and higher.

'Afternoon, Mandy, petal!'

'You're a bloomin' angel, you are!'

'Sight for sore eyes. Not you, lass, the other bird!'

'Blimmin' gorgeous, Mrs Walker. Bless you.'

In between the meet and greet I'd rush through to the kitchen, checking that supplies were plentiful, that the next lot of poultry was browning nicely, the treacle ready to pour over the sponge.

Handing a plate over, without looking, cheeks aching from all the grinning, I heard a familiar voice.

'Thank you. This smells delicious.'

Dan. I glanced up. He held onto the plate; I hadn't let go. His hands were shaking. I smiled at him and pushed the empty plate towards him gently. He almost jumped. 'You're early. Ruth said you'd be in with the next crew. Same as my Rob.'

'I, I . . . started earlier. Where's Ruth?' He glanced over his shoulder, sharply, like someone on high alert.

'She's at back. On left. Serving drinks. G and T, Martinis, Malibu . . .'

He wrinkled his nose.

'Beer. Bitter. Whatever you fancy.'

He still looked flummoxed.

'Only joking! Water or pop, I'm afraid.'

He forced out a smile. 'Water's fine by me.'

I watched him move to where Ruth mingled amongst the tables, metal jugs in both her hands. They spoke. She didn't smile, but gestured to an empty space. He ate his dinner alone, lifting his eyes from his food every few minutes to look over both shoulders, towards the doors.

We were clearing up after this first onslaught when a woman with brown hair, fringe flicked and lacquered, holding a spiral-bound notebook, flounced into the centre. Behind her an overweight bloke in baggy jeans and Hawaiian shirt trudged. He held a camera. One of those fancy ones with a large lens.

'Who's in charge?' she said, in a southern accent.

Ethel was over in a shot and I marvelled at how quickly a woman of her proportions could move when the occasion demanded it. 'I am. But we'll not be talking to no reporters. Bugger off.'

'You could do with some favourable reports,' the journalist replied. I had to admire her. She was either brave or stupid.

'Bugger off, or you'll get this.' Ethel raised a clenched fist and shook it.

'What you women are doing is marvellous. Simply marvellous. The country needs to know about the hard working, spirited, plucky . . .'

'I'll pluck you in a minute.'

'Ethel,' Ruth had stepped between the reporter and her mother-in-law, 'perhaps we should give her a chance? Think of the publicity. The fund-raising opportunities.' Ruth turned and addressed the journalist. 'Ruth Braithwaite, Director of Fundraising. We get final copy approval. And a fee if you've a budget.'

'No fee. Approval: yes.' She offered Ruth her hand, but Ruth nodded towards Ethel who said, 'I'll not shake no bloody reporter's hands.'

'Very well, then,' Ruth said, hand outstretched, 'I will. Deal.' Then, gesturing to the corner, 'Let's sit down.'

But the journalist, a senior reporter for the *Post*, wanted to speak with someone on the front line. 'Someone like her,' she said, pointing at me.

Ruth's face tightened, but then she smiled, holding the grin a fraction too long. 'As you wish. I'm here when you need me.'

I didn't want to talk to this woman. Not because of any anti-journalist principles, because I didn't know what to say. What if I couldn't answer her questions? I didn't have any opinions as such. Ruth must have seen my hesitation.

'Would you like me to be present, Mandy?'

I nodded.

Once we got started it was fine. The reporter was lovely; she put me at my ease and she didn't ask any tricky questions. She wanted to know where I lived, how long I'd been there, how many kids I had, and how we were managing on so little. She asked about the food, how I found cooking for so many, whether or not everyone enjoyed it. 'Though I can see quite clearly that they do, Mrs Walker!'

'Call me Mandy.'

Ruth interjected a number of times, but the reporter brushed her aside and I noticed that she didn't do any of that squiggly writing in her note-book when Ruth spoke about fundraising and difficulties of finding skilled women in the region. This last comment made me wince. She was wrong, for one thing.

'Your shorthand is peculiar,' I said at one point.

'It's Teeline – a special kind for those in the media. I'm impressed you spotted the difference.'

'I did shorthand at school. And typing. I'm thinking of picking it up again, after strike.'

'So you have many different skills.' She looked at Ruth as she said this. Afterwards, she waved at the bloke in the horrible shirt, who was tucking in to roast dinner. They wanted a picture. 'Photos help draw the eye to a piece.'

I excused myself and went to the bathroom. I didn't need the toilet. I stared at my reflection in the mirror above the basin, sun streaming in through the window behind me. Shiny cheeks, no make-up, a bonnet perched on top of a halo of ginger curls. Ruth appeared beside me. She offered me her lipstick: a pearly pink-purple from Miss Selfridge called Iron Maiden. I said the name out loud.

'Inspired by Mrs T? Blimey. Union wouldn't approve!' I slicked it over my mouth.

'To tell you the truth, darling, I rather admire the woman. Ambitious—'

'Ruthless—'

'Succeeding in a man's world—'

'At any cost?' I wiped off the lipstick.

'Oh, I'm not saying I like her or anything. Just that, you know . . .' she sighed and applied more lipstick, though there was plenty still on. 'You don't like it?'

'It's not that. It looks good on you. Oh flipping heck, Ruth, I hate having my picture taken.'

'I have an idea,' Ruth said, as she flicked her hair over her shoulders.

Back in the hall the photographer was organising the serving women, bunching them together behind the counter.

'Right, Mandy, lovely. I'd like you right here.' He pointed to a spot in front of the counter. 'Hold this in front of your chest.' He handed over a clipboard. 'To make you look more official.'

Ruth came over from where she'd been standing, talking to the reporter. 'I'll take that,' she said, and positioned herself where the photographer had instructed. 'Mandy, you join the others. Look busy with the custard.'

The photographs only took a couple of minutes. There was giggling from everyone as he said, 'Cheese!' I kept my head down and Ruth seemed very pleased. 'It'll appear on Wednesday. Not just a news item either, a feature. I'll be famous!' she said.

As the photographer was packing up Rob and a small gang rolled in. They looked dusty and hot and at least two of them had bloody noses. There'd been clashes with the police, their truncheons, shields, dogs, and not everyone had managed to escape. The reporter made notes while the men recounted the story.

'What's going on here?' Rob said, rubbing his knuckles, noticing the photographer and journalist at last.

'I've been interviewed. They took a photo,' I mumbled.

'You?' He glanced from me to Ruth as if to check that he'd heard it correctly.

'We wanted a proper miner's wife,' the journalist said.

Rob turned to the gaggle of men behind him and muttered, 'Even these ponces can see he's not one of us!'

'What do you mean?' Ruth's voice was brittle.

'Where is he?' one of others said, and they turned and scoured the hall.

'Shifty bastard's there,' said another, pointing. Dan was still sitting in the corner, head down, eyes flitting from left to right and back again.

'You might want to ask your man there why he legged it at first sign of trouble?' Rob shouted.

'Dan abhors violence,' Ruth said. Her tone was apologetic, but defiant. As if sensing the danger Ruth was in, Dan rose from his seat and came towards the huddle.

'What was he doing in army then, eh?' Rob spat the words, blood trickling from the corners of his mouth. I felt faint. It was hot, I'd not eaten. I hated violence too. The air dripped with testosterone, with frustrated, hate-filled resentment, and Dan was about to become the focus of that rage. He stopped outside the cluster. They turned.

'Why'd you run off? You broke the fucking line!' someone shouted. The journalist and the photographer had scuttled back, towards the exit, and I noticed the camera was out once again.

Dan stared straight ahead, mumbling, as if to himself, not addressing anyone. 'Couldn't do nothing. Must act. Fight or—'

'Dan?' Ruth's voice was faint.

'They were blue. Blue,' Dan continued. Ruth moved to his side; the men turned towards her; he snapped back into the room.

'You leave my wife out of this.' Dan's voice was calm, but his eyes were blacker than coal dust, his lips drained of colour.

'I'm going to break your fuckin' nose,' Rob screamed. 'I'm going to fuckin' kill you.'

'Kill? You have no idea,' Dan said.

'Think you know it all, soldier boy . . .' Rob lurched forward, fist clenched. 'You're all trouble; even your old man—'

Two men grabbed Rob's arms and held him back. I wasn't sure why. I knew them; they liked a fight more than most. I saw the silhouettes of Paul and Craig Braithwaite in the doorway. The twins. The mentalists. Done time for ABH before their twenty-first birthday. Noses in the air, they could smell blood. I knew what Rob alluded to and hoped the twins hadn't heard. Rob had hinted that the explosion in the pit shaft, all those months ago, had been Vince's fault. Before the enquiry, Vince had spoken to Rob about loyalty and sticking together. It was men versus management. Rob would never betray another working man, no matter what.

Rob struggled against the two men, and freed one arm, swinging it back and forth. The twins quickened their pace, but before they crossed the hall, Ethel flung aside another man, twice her height, and positioned herself between Rob and Dan. She lifted her index finger, jabbing it at Rob, and said, 'You lay a finger on him and you'll have me to answer to. I'll knock seven bells out of you, Rob Walker. Now go and get something to eat. You've been drinking.' Waving her arm, she added, 'The lot of you. Skit!' She turned to Dan. 'You and me'll be having a little chat later.'

Dan stepped back, the others fell away, including the twins. I reached out to Ruth and said, 'You OK?' She nodded.

'Thank you, Ethel,' she said.

'Think nothing of it. What's family for? Stick together. Go home, both of you. We can manage. Can't we, Mandy?'

Dan reached out his hand, but Ruth didn't take it, walking straight past him towards the cloak-room. I felt the slight, the pain this would inflict on top of all that hate channelled his way. No one deserved that. He needed someone to hold on to. But Ruth had done her bit, it seemed. I watched him stagger after her, like a man in shock, longing to step in and offer him my arm instead. I could not believe the man I'd met on the hills was a coward; a man incapable of sticking by his fellow men. What had happened out there on the picket line? What had happened to Dan?

CHAPTER 12

I slipped out of the house before anyone else was up. It was the first day of the school holidays. The boys had been to bed late, and now that she was on solids Becky rarely woke before seven.

The dew was heavy on the scrubby grass of our front garden; the air loaded with the promise of another sultry day. The extended song of a skylark filled the air and I marvelled at the bird's tenacity. Dad would have approved.

The main road was quiet, bar the rattle of a coal cart sitting at the traffic lights on the crossroads, impatient. As if revving the engine would turn red to green. Why was it in such a hurry? The weather had been warm for months and no one round here could afford to buy fuel. I scurried along, head down (who I'd meet I've no idea), purse gripped in my left hand, towards Smith & Sons on the other side of the crossroads. Bundles of newspapers tied with string lay strewn on the pavement. I checked the top copies to see which paper they were and stepped inside.

'By the 'eck! You're up early.' Rodney Smith,

the proprietor, coughed, bent down behind the counter swiftly, hiding the cigarette he'd clearly been puffing, before standing upright and affecting an innocent smile. Oily blue swirls lingered around his head. Who he was trying to fool was anybody's guess. I'd known Rodney for ten years and during that time he'd tried to give up on no less than twenty occasions. He managed a few days, a few weeks and, once, almost six months before caving in to temptation. He didn't do it for himself, for his health, or the health of his wallet. He loved smoking. He did it for his wife, Betty. Betty's brother died of lung cancer at forty-eight and she lived in a permanent state of fear that Rodney would go the same way. He kept a flimsy tin ashtray and a can of *Glade* hidden behind the counter and snuck in a fag whenever Betty wasn't around. Betty must have been the only person in the village who didn't know that Rodney was partial to the odd Woodbine or ten. Rodney had been a good friend to Dad and gave me my first proper job: a paper round. Rodney had hoped to bestow such an honour on a son of his own, but the sons in Smith & Sons eluded him, as did any daughters. Rodney and Betty had tried for children for years and were at an age when extremely unlikely had finally sunk to impossible. In the absence of Smith children I'd delivered the morning paper to the residents of Fenley for two years, rising, resentfully, at five-thirty to do so. I hated it most in the summer when the warm air blew up my school skirt, exposing my dappled thighs and navy blue knickers. Shortly after Dad died I chucked the job in; there didn't seem to be any point anymore. Not in anything. Until I met Rob.

'Not seen you this early in donkey's years, love,' Rodney said, wafting his hands about, sweeping the smoke from him to me.

'Couldn't sleep. First time in yonks I can lie in and I go and get myself a spot of insomnia.'

'Lod's saw.' He muddled his letters up, Rodney did. It was one of his most endearing qualities and he had many. He continued to smile, and I hesitated.

I was a fool. Leaping out of bed, racing into town, hair loose, unbrushed. I must have looked like I'd escaped from the local mental institution. And for what? To get my mitts on a stupid newspaper article that may or may not include a few choice quotes from yours truly? What was I thinking? I should have been at home, preparing breakfast for my family, not chasing after reading about myself. I felt ashamed.

The butcher's strips behind Rodney rippled and Betty appeared. A small, round woman with what should have been child-bearing hips, a broad smile, and warm eyes. 'Morning! What is that smell?'

'Someone's burning wood down road,' I said. Rodney looked at me over his glasses and thanked me with his eyes.

152

'This early?' She pecked her husband's cheek and patted his back with her plump hands, a small gesture, born of habit and care. They reminded me of my mum and dad. A solid couple. Respectful, loving, caring. I tried to picture me and Rob in twenty, thirty years' time, but couldn't. Perhaps they couldn't in the early days of their marriages.

I steered the conversation away from the lingering smell lingering and went to leave.

'Did you just pop in for a chat, then?' Rodney asked.

I muttered something about running out of milk, having changed the delivery to every other day, and scuttled out, a bottle in my hand, straight from the fridge, slippery and cold.

Later, I bumped into Ruth. I noticed a copy of the *Post* poking out of her handbag and wouldn't have said anything but she must have followed the line of my eyes.

'Nothing in it. No article, no photo, nothing,' she said, almost cheerfully. 'Shame. It was our big moment, wasn't it?'

'Oh, I'm not bothered. Would have been good publicity, that's all.'

'Well, I'm disappointed on your behalf. After all, you gave up your time to speak with the woman, and God knows you're busy.' She touched my shoulder, squeezing it. 'Look, I've gotta dash. Let's catch up properly soon, yes? Ciao, ciao!' And with that she was gone, leaving me standing on the pavement wondering what on earth she meant by 'chow', and if she'd really forgiven me for Rob's behaviour. She left so abruptly.

'You spend more time with that lot than you do with me and lads.' Rob was parked in his second favourite place: in front of the telly, Golden Virginia and papers on his lap. His one concession to the increasingly desperate state of our finances – a switch from straights to roll-ups.

'You're OK with me going?'

''Course, I'm proud of you. You're doing a grand job. All lads say same. Hurry up, you'll be late.' My heart sank. Rob had reminded me there was a FAG meeting; I'd considered 'forgetting' all about it, pretending to the crew that Rob didn't like me spending so much time on it.

I wanted him to say, 'Stay at home tonight, love. Spend some time with me. They can manage without you for one night.' But he didn't.

'Meeting's at Ruth's tonight,' I added, half hoping this would get him to ask me stay home. After the fisticuffs with Dan, he'd said, 'He's dead as far as you're concerned. Got it.'

But attending the meeting at Dan's house didn't bother him. He replied, 'Bastard won't be there. He's out tonight; with rest of scumbags, down Boar's Head. There's a match.'

For Rob, the cost of the fall-out was high. The Braithwaite twins, Paul and Craig were, like Rob, members of The White Lion Darts' team. After the fight, Rob had resigned, or been pushed, it was never clear which, and no longer drank in the pub. He'd defected to The Boar's Head. At least Mum's friend, Dean, was pleased with the extra custom. But if the Braithwaites were at The Boar's Head, Rob couldn't go in.

I trudged up the hill to Ruth's house, a sense of dread building, hot even before I left. Ethel and I had continued at the soup kitchen in virtual silence after Rob tried to take a pop at Dan. We'd exchanged perfunctory details to ensure the smooth running of the clear up and said our goodbyes without warmth. As I crossed the playing field I contemplated sitting on the swings all evening, but as I approached the play area I heard Ann's 'you-hooo.' She half jigged, half jogged to catch up. She linked her arm in mine, like a chaperone, and burbled for the remainder of the journey though I couldn't have recalled one word if my life depended on it. My belly griped; my T-shirt clung to my skin.

The front door was ajar. Ann knocked regardless and we stood outside and waited. And waited. Ann knocked again, and pushed at the door. We stepped inside as Ethel appeared in the hall. She barked, 'Don't stand on ceremony, you great wazzocks. Come in. Ruth's got kettle on.' Ann trotted along behind Ethel into the living room, but I popped my head round the kitchen door instead.

Ruth stood at the sink, leaning on her elbows,

gazing out onto the garden. Steam rose from the kettle; a teapot and several cups and saucers sat on a tray.

'Anything I can do?' I wanted to see Ruth before anyone else, alone.

She jumped, spinning to see who it was. 'Sorry, miles away. No! No! All under control.' She turned to the kettle immediately, busying herself.

'Sorry about what happened and all. I'm so embarrassed about it.'

'Me too.' Her voice trembled, her eyes liquid. She poured the hot water into the pot; I was afraid she might spill it and scald herself.

Footsteps thudded across the ceiling; I looked up, wondering who it could be; the bathroom was at the front of the house not the back.

'Only Dan.'

'Not at match then?' Would he come down to say hello? Probably not.

'He doesn't go down to the pub much anymore.'

'Lucky you. Chance to spend more time together.' I tried to make light, but her hands shook as she poured sugar from the bag into a bowl. A sprinkling scattered on the surface.

'Is everything alright?' I thought about how she walked right past him after the kerfuffle at the kitchen. 'Things are pretty tense with me and Rob. It's not working, it affects them. Moaned about pit when he was there; grumpy bastard now he's not.' I laughed, though it was hollow.

She looked at me, properly this time. 'I don't

know how to help him. Don't know if I can. He doesn't seem to fit in, but it's his home.'

Unsure what to say, I placed my hand over hers and squeezed.

'He won't talk to me.'

'Bloody hell, Rob never talks to me. Not properly. I've no idea what goes on in his head half time. Probably nowt!' I laughed again, and this time she joined me.

'Men have so many secrets, don't they?' She smiled and her face regained some of its usual brightness. 'Not like us women. We share every-thing. Don't we?'

'Couldn't keep me gob shut if I tried! Whatever happens with men, we won't let it come between us, yeah?'

'Yeah.'

'Let me take this.' I took hold of the tray.

'I've forgotten all about that nasty business already.' But there was still an edge to her voice.

I didn't like to say that Rob hadn't forgotten and nor was he likely to, not any time soon, but no way was it going to come between us, our friendship.

'I'll take this through?' I said.

'No. Let me.'

'Everything's alright then?'

'Why wouldn't it be?' She turned. 'Hold the door for me.'

I followed her into the lounge. A heady mixture of perfume assaulted my nose: Lily of the Valley and something expensive-smelling – Ruth's perfume. Paula, our secretary, clapped her hands together and said, 'Well, if it isn't the star of the show.'

She sounded sarcastic and I must have looked confused, because she held up a newspaper and tapped it twice, so violently I thought it must rip. I had no notion of what she was on about and shook my head. Sally, the publicity woman, snatched the paper from Paula and read.

'"Amanda, or Mandy as she prefers to be known, is self-effacing and modest when asked about her, not inconsiderable, achievements in the struggle against pit closures. "I'm only doing what any other wife would do in my position. We need to show Mrs Thatcher that she's not the only woman ready for a fight. You can tell her from me that gloves are off. We're as tough as pit ponies round these parts and we're not for turning neither.'

Everyone stared at me. I looked for signs of a practical joke. I caught Ruth's eye, but she only smiled, knowingly. The perfume was making me feel sick. The silence seemed to stretch indefinitely, the rhythmic clacking of Mrs Ellis Page's knitting needles rattling in my ears. I opened my mouth to speak; to apologise for saying the wrong thing, for making us all look daft, when Ethel slapped her knees and roared. 'Flipping marvellous. Never thought you had it in you.'

'I don't understand . . .' I stammered.

'You've not seen article?' Ethel said, flabbergasted.

I shook my head, unable to speak. There was no article; I'd checked a copy of the second edition of the *Post* on Wednesday afternoon. Passing Rodney's shop later that day my curiosity and vanity had got the better of me, and I dashed in and asked if I might check tomorrow's weather. 'Have it,' Rodney had said. 'Won't sell it now.' There was no report, no photograph. I'd been disappointed.

Ethel came over and held the report in front of me. I was stunned. A whole page. On one side a picture of the Prime Minister, all bouffant hair and pearls, on the other a massive photo of me stirring a jug of custard, head tilted down, little hat ridiculous on top of frizzy curls. Thank God the picture wasn't in colour. At least you couldn't see the flame red of my hair too. The headline ran: 'Maggie v Mandy, miners' wives stand by their men'.

'Turns out editor liked piece so much he wanted to give it full page spread. No space Wednesday, so today it is. It's all over Institute. Vince says union's delighted with positive publicity. "Just what we need after flipping disaster last month. Press's got knives out for us." But what we all want to know is: are these your words, or has reporter put them into your mouth?' Ethel was pointing at a paragraph further down the page, reading snippets from it. But I wasn't listening.

For mingling with shock and fear was pride. Me, in the paper. Blimey.

'Well, are they?' Ethel nudged me on the shoulder with her shoulder.

'What?'

Ethel repeated her question, but only after much tutting.

'They're my words, mostly. I wasn't thinking, I just said what I felt, she was ever so nice . . .'

Sally piped up. 'Stop apologising, woman. This is right good. We've been talking while you've taken your time getting here—'

Ethel interrupted her. 'We've had invitation from a women's group in Leeds, attached to university, wanting one of us to go and give talk in the autumn. About what we're up to and all that, and we think, *most* of us think,' she looked over in what looked like Ruth's direction, though Ruth was pouring the tea and didn't notice, 'that you would be perfect lass for the job.'

I flinched. Ethel continued. 'Now I know what you're thinking. It should be me. But, truth is, it would be better to hear from someone closer to their own age. More relatable.' That wasn't what I was thinking at all. I was thinking I'd rather stick my head in a bucket of semolina.

'What Mandy needs right now is a nice cup of tea. She's had a bit of a shock,' Paula said. 'Sit down, love.'

Ethel steered me towards a chair, wooden and hard-backed – the settees were full – and I flopped

160

down. Ruth heaped a teaspoon of sugar into a cup. 'Would you like another? For the shock,' she said, and I nodded, unable to speak. As she stirred she whispered, 'Don't look so worried. I've an idea.'

I sipped the tea; it was too sweet, but I gulped it down regardless. 'I can't do it,' I said at last.

There was a hubbub from the small crowd, full of, ''Course you can,' and 'Don't be daft, you'll be great,' and from Ethel, 'Where's your gumption, woman?'

Ruth stood and raised her hands, sermon-like. 'If Mandy doesn't feel up to it, who are we to judge, to push her into something she'd rather not do.'

Thank you, Ruth. Always there when I need you.

She looked down at me and winked. 'I've a solution.'

Tea cups rattled as they were replaced on saucers.

'Given Mandy's obvious, and hitherto undiscovered, flair for rhetoric I suggest she pens a speech for someone else to deliver.'

Murmuring bubbled beneath the clacking of the needles. The word rhetoric echoed in my head. I knew the meaning, Dad again. I wondered if Ruth meant it as insult or compliment. Ruth was trying to help me out, and brilliant it was too.

'And that someone would be?' Ethel said, though

it was clear who Ruth meant. Everyone turned to her.

'I talk in front of people,' she said, 'little people, all day long. It would be my pleasure. What you do think, Mandy? I'll be your mouthpiece?'

I smiled. 'It's a great idea. Great. We'll be a team.'

She winked again. 'A team.' And she held out her hand. We high-fived, as we did as kids.

Ethel coughed. 'Well, how about this little "team" supporting the men, collecting, in London? Some kind of carnival. It's a job for young legs.'

Ruth clapped her hands and squealed. 'A chance to get out of Fenley! Are you kidding me? Of course, we'll go.'

Numb, I could only nod. The women talked on, but I had little to contribute. My head was full. London. There were plans to work even more closely with the men, direct fundraising across the country, like the trip to the capital and, after that, the student union in Leeds.

The rest of the meeting passed without major incident. There were no disagreements, no back-stabbing, everyone worked together, towards our common goal. It amazed me. There were women from families who'd been bickering for generations. Petty stuff like garden border disputes, the selling of a dodgy motor. As the meeting rumbled on I tuned out and took in the room. The walls had been painted – Dan with time on his hands and no shortage of money – new curtains hung to match the primrose hue and the shelf across the fire place was bare.

All the photographs of Ruth and Dan had gone, replaced with enamel decorated boxes and a small vase containing a solitary white carnation.

CHAPTER 13

The smell of cheese and onion sandwiches filled my nostrils as I opened the car door. I plonked the cushion on the denim upholstered front seat, asked Mark to make sure there was no dirt on his shoes, and fastened his seat belt. It seemed odd putting him in the front, but there was no other way if Becky was to be held firm and we weren't to break the law.

'We'll have to leave windows open a while before we hand this back to Dean,' I said, clambering into the back, squashing myself between Johnnie and David, Becky on my lap.

The car, a VW Jeans Beetle, belonged to Dean, now Mum's official boyfriend, and it was his pride and joy. Cars were his passion and, according to Mum, he made quite a lot of extra cash from his hobby. He'd buy old bangers – rare, unusual ones – do them up, and sell them on at a great profit. I've no idea how he found the time, what with running the pub, though I'd heard Rob complaining that The Boar's Head didn't do lock-ins and the legal opening hours were strictly adhered to, unlike The White Lion

164

and other boozers he was banned from in the village.

The boys had been beside themselves with excitement at the prospect of a ride in the custard yellow car, the day out itself paled into insignificance. The chug of the engine was so distinct, tank heavy, that whenever we heard it around the village the boys would stop, leap up and down, and wave as Dean rumbled past.

'Are you sure he doesn't mind us borrowing it?' I said.

'He loves me,' Mum replied. 'Do anything for me. He's a good man.'

I didn't doubt it. He was a good man: kind-hearted, gentle, straightforward. Simple, in the best possible way. I wondered what made Dean special in Mum's eyes, how he measured up to Dad, with his intelligence, his quirks, his wicked sense of humour. Was she settling for second best? Tired of being alone, searching for another special someone? Her money had run out; she was no longer a woman 'of independent means' as she used to say, winking as she did so. She was forty-four with almost half a lifetime in front of her. I remembered something Dad said to me, shortly before he died. I'd not thought about it in years.

'Don't rely on anyone else for your happiness, Mandy. You are responsible for that. No one else. Not a husband in years to come, not any future children, or grandchildren. You and you alone. You are the key,' he'd said, tipping the barrel of his pipe towards his lighter, the brown curls of tobacco poking out the top, smouldering before catching alight.

Mum turned the ignition, the engine caught, and we all began to judder.

'Right! Ready for off then?' she yelled.

'Yeeeeees!' We all roared back.

The journey was shaky, and it wasn't solely because of the bone-rattling nature of the VW. Mum hadn't driven in months, not since the Citroen Dyane we'd had as a family finally died on her. Even Dean couldn't resuscitate that old girl. But the roads were quiet as we headed north, towards the posh part of the area, and nothing could quash the children's enthusiasm – nor mine. We waved at passing cars, startled pedestrians in the genteel villages we rumbled through, enjoying our celebrity status, as passengers in this special car. I named the car Herbie after the film I'd seen down at the Coronet in a neighbouring village when I was a girl, and promised to take the lads if it was ever shown again. Saturday matinees were reserved for old films and tickets were cheap, though the boys would have to wait till the strike was over before any such trip. Assuming the cinema was open. There'd been talk of closure recently; we'd wondered what else they wanted to shut down round these parts.

Overcast and grey when we left Fenley, as we

166

approached our first port of call the clouds broke and blue sky appeared in the fissures.

'Enough to make a pair of sailor's knickers?' Mum shouted, head bent so far forward her chin almost rested on the steering wheel, her nose on the windscreen.

The boys' stared out of the windows, Mark craning to see over the dashboard, the cushion hadn't helped raise him up much, but the thrill of riding in front silenced any complaints he might have had.

'Definitely,' I said.

'Then it'll be fine all day,' Mum replied, and the children cheered.

It was only ten past eleven when we pulled into the scrubby car park, but the children were carping and so we dragged the picnic bags out into the open. Becky was strapped to my back, in a rucksack-type thing Mum had borrowed from a customer of Dean's. It meant I could walk, hands free, over a landscape inhospitable to pushchairs.

Our principle destination had been a wood due east, but when we were choosing where to go I realised that the limestone pavement I'd visited on a school field trip in the days before I lost interest was close by. I'd begged Mum to take us there first.

'Why?' she'd said.

'I don't right know. Can't explain. Please?'

She agreed, of course.

The boys didn't want to get out of the car; they'd have been happy sitting in there all day, but the prospect of dinner did the trick. We scrambled up the grassy bank towards the open space, boys' dragging their bags along the stony ground.

'Mind grub. You'll ruin it,' Mum shouted.

I didn't care, not about anything. It felt glorious to be so free, to be surrounded by nothing but sky and air and birds. I so rarely escaped the confines of Fenley, other than my now-regular trips to the soup kitchen. Perhaps these trips had given me a taste for more. I stopped and closed my eyes momentarily, before striding on.

Even the boys were silenced by the sight of the pavement. Mark and David at least. Johnnie screamed, 'Wow!' and ran and jumped from slab to slab, a crazed kind of hopscotch.

'Be careful!' Mum yelled.

We laid out our spread, wedging drinks in the grykes between the stones, and it wasn't long before an army of ants appeared, ready to nab any leftovers. Fat chance with us lot. A starling flew above, followed by another, then another.

'A chattering of starlings,' I said.

A frown appeared between Mum's brows. 'A chattering, really? How funny. They are noisy, mind, so it's a good fit.'

I smiled. 'Yeah.'

'Dad's favourites were the birds. A parliament of owls, nightingale watch. Can't remember any others,' Mum said.

'A congregation of magpies, a charm of gold-finches,' David said.

'Who's a clever boy,' said Mum, squeezing his cheeks. And to me, 'It's nice you've passed that on, love.'

I told the boys how the pavement was formed, millions of years ago, when glaciers ruled the earth. They weren't really interested, but I enjoyed sharing what little knowledge I had. Mark humoured me, like the good boy he was, asking all sorts of questions and not for the first time I wished I'd paid more attention at school.

'I do know that where we live is very important. The geology, you see. That's the land, the earth. Great seams of rock, pressed down and down on each other for thousands and thousands of years. Millions. How coal was made, and we all know how important that is,' I said. They'd glazed over, and were inspecting a crack where the ants emerged, pressing down on some of the poor creatures with their fingers.

'They'll bite,' I said. They wandered off and I wiped the crust crumbs from round Becky's mouth, held her in my arms, and gave her a bottle.

'Dean says they'll never win. This woman is different.'

I looked at Mum. 'And what do you say?' I was surprised Dean had an opinion.

'It'll be long and hard. The world's changing.'

'It's always changing. We'll fight on. What choice do we have?'

'I don't know, love, I don't know.'

Becky continued to slurp at her bottle.

'Heard you've been asked to do more than cook after that newspaper piece?' Mum said.

'Group have asked me to go down to London at the end of the month.'

'Well, I never. You pleased?'

'Think so. Bit scared, excited too.'

The bottle slipped from Becky's mouth; she was asleep, and my arm ached with the weight of her head. I tipped my face to sun, enjoying the warmth on my cheeks, my eyelids, till I remembered I'd regret it later, when my skin would feel like it had been rubbed with sandpaper. I grabbed my wide-brimmed hat from the bag at my side, and asked Mum for the sun cream.

'Dean says your Rob's quite the regular,' she said, rubbing the cream into my legs and exposed arm.

'He does get some money from strike fund, for the picketing.'

'That why he took it up?' She was slathering herself in cream, her pale skin already tinged pink.

I wanted Becky to wake; I jigged my arm a little. I didn't want to argue; I wanted a perfect day.

'I remember now why the geography trip stuck with me. Ruth. It was the last trip she came on, before they left. She sneaked off from group with a lad from year above. I covered for her!'

'She was a one. And you always made excuses for her.'

'She'd do same for me. She was my best friend, is my best friend.'

'Is she?'

Mum knew Ruth was my best friend. 'She's doing ever so well. At the school and that.'

'Your dad and me, we had high hopes for you.'

'Am I such a disappointment?'

Everything seemed to have soured, and I didn't understand why. Had Mum suggested the day only to be critical of my life?

''Course not, love. You're doing just fine,' she reached over and touched my shoulder. 'You're young. Plenty of time.'

Becky groaned, her arms jolted, and she woke with a yell. The sound of her cries bouncing off the stones, filling the air.

By contrast the woods were busy; tourists swarmed everywhere, the early afternoon air buzzing with the sound of different accents. In the car park, while Mum sorted out the remaining food from the boot and I bounced Becky on my hip, the boys skittered about in the dust, throwing stones at trees, looking like ragamuffins. I noticed a family a few rows along, accents like Ruth's, all 'grarse' with a long R, glossy hair, and swanky walking boots, even on the kids. Ruth's children won't look like this, I thought, looking at my lads in their hand-me-down shorts and T-shirts donated from

171

the FAG Clothes for Striking Miners' Children collection. Even Becky, a baby, no longer had new stuff. I tickled her tummy and pulled on the egg-yolk stained dress. 'But you don't care what you wear, do you, petal?'

We didn't walk far; stopping and starting every few minutes. It was hot, even in the dappled shade of the wood, and there were so many trees for the boys to climb. At a clearing Mum threw a tartan blanket over the scorched grass and we lifted Becky out of her carrier. All three of us lay flat on our backs while the boys made mischief. I was on the verge of sleep when Becky rolled over and smacked me on the nose. I sat her upright and she grabbed at her small collection of toys: the wooden rattle, a fabric cube, and a battered orangutan with super long arms, even for a monkey. When the boys returned we laid out the remains of the spread – pork pies, crisps, apples, and some biscuits.

'You didn't make any cake?' Mum said.

'I don't get time, and there's that much cooking to do in soup kitchen I don't feel like doing much more than basics at home.'

'Shame, I was looking forward to a nice sponge.' She meant it kindly, but I felt guilty without quite understanding why.

'I'll make us a coffee and walnut cake next time you pop in,' I offered.

'Nuts are dear, Mandy. Don't you worry. Better for our waistlines this way, at least!'

Johnnie bounced over. 'We're bored.'

'Hide and seek?' I suggested.

There were squabbles deciding who was on and so I offered.

Mum jumped up from the rug. 'I'll play too.' The boys cheered.

I knelt on the blanket and buried my face in my hands, counting to fifty. Becky slapped my head.

'Forty-nine, fifty! Coming, ready or not!'

I circled round the clearing and within minutes saw Johnnie as he popped his head round the trunk of a silver birch. Johnnie sat with Becky, both within eyeshot. Next to be caught was Mum, followed by David. Delving deeper and deeper into the woods, Mark was nowhere to be found. Mum and Johnnie joined the search; we asked David to stay with Becky, ordering him to yell loudly (not difficult for him) if they needed us.

'Now we must stay within reach of each other. We don't want to be losing anyone else,' I said.

'Mark's not lost, is he?' whispered Johnnie, clutching Mum's hand.

'Don't be daft. 'Course he's not,' I said. 'Come on. You two go that way, I'll go this.'

Twigs cracked underfoot as we plodded through the undergrowth, sunlight playing tricks, creating the illusion of movement as it shimmered and blinded. Time rolled on, panic began to set in.

Mark was quietly stubborn, 'unwavering' his teacher called it, but he'd been gone too long. I started calling out, 'I give up. Come out, come out, wherever you are,' struggling to keep my tone jocular. Mum and Johnnie called out too.

In front of me, a little to my left, maybe ten yards, was a dead tree, thick trunked, bare branched, a dry gold colour. When Ruth and I were nine years old we had a den in the hollowed out trunk of an oak at the bottom of the Felix's garden. I called Mark's name, gently this time. Nothing. I nearly turned back, but thinking of that old oak den, I stepped forward, peering round the tree trunk. And there in the decayed, rotten centre crouched Mark, scraggy knees under his chin, eyes like a bush baby's.

Fury swamped my relief. 'What the chuffing heck are you doing! Get out! We've been looking for you everywhere!' I grabbed Mark's wrist and as he crawled out I yanked him to his feet. He was floppy, like a rag doll, and while I was screaming and shouting the other two gathered round.

'I didn't want to get caught,' he whispered, cowering from my words.

'I said, "I give up!"'

'You might have been tricking,' he said.

'You needed the loo,' I said, pointing to the dark stain in the crotch of his shorts.

'I couldn't come out otherwise you'd have got

me . . .' He hung his head, and I began to smile, then laugh, finally seeing the funny side.

'Oh, am I glad to see you! Where'd you get that stubborn streak?' I said, hugging him.

'From you,' said Mum. 'You were like that as a kid. Single-minded, determined to be great. You didn't shout about it, like some. You just got on with it.'

Holding hands, all except Johnnie who marched on ahead like the squadron leader, we made our way back to the clearing. As we neared, Johnnie stopped abruptly and pointed, without words – unusual for him.

There, in the centre of the rug, stood Becky. Stood. David was standing next to her, eyes wide, pointing with both hands at his sister. We all froze, hands no longer linked but dangling limp by our sides, and watched. She wobbled, placed her hands on the floor, as if she was touching her toes, steadied herself, then stood upright again and put one foot in front of the other before toppling to her knees.

We ran, all four of us ran.

I got to her first, or was allowed to reach her first, and swept her off her feet and into my arms. 'You clever, clever lass! Did you see that?' I said, spinning round, talking to the other picnickers. 'Did you see her? Eight months old, eight months old and she can walk!'

Mum came to my side. 'You walked at nine

months. Right across the lawn. "Look at her go," said your Dad, "see how far she can go. That's my girl.'"

What happened? When did I change? When did I decide to stay put, to settle for ordinary like everyone else? But I already knew.

CHAPTER 14

The dirty brick walls on either side of the train closed in, blocking out the sun; the tracks split apart like a zip as we slid into the station.

I staggered onto the platform, stiff from the confines of the narrow seat I'd been wedged into for the two hours and ten minutes it had taken to travel from Leeds to London. When Sydney Turner, campaign co-ordinator for the Fenley Miners' Institute, had told me the journey time I hadn't believed him. A dour man in his late forties, he was well known for pedantry and tenacity. He was a pillar of the community; one many would have liked to let their dogs piss against – until the strike made those hitherto undesirable qualities an asset.

'Them's new trains, Mrs Walker. 125s they're called, and that is because they travel at 125 miles per hour, not that they travel at speed for whole journey, like . . .' He'd carried on for some time, explaining the intricacies of the engine, but I'd stopped listening. All I could think about was London. London. I'd never been and the prospect was exciting and terrifying.

Once we were through the ticket barriers we stood in the station concourse, people weaving round us, oblivious. Everyone seemed to know where they were going, except for us. From her handbag Ruth pulled out an A to Z and studied the underground map on the back cover.

'We need to get to Barons Court,' she said, pointing at the navy blue line that bisected the page. 'Luckily for us it's really straightforward. All the way on the Piccadilly line. Dump our bags at Jane's, grab a coffee, and a few hops round to Notting Hill Gate. Easy-peasy!'

'Lemon squeezy,' I replied, without conviction.

Ruth knew what she was doing; I'd have been a gibbering wreck alone, or with someone as clueless as me. I trotted after her as she dived between the hordes towards the tube entrance. People bounced off me like pinballs as I stumbled after her. In the ticket hall we fumbled with machines that eventually spat out tickets, men and women in smart suits tutting and cussing behind us, tapping their leather soled shoes on the tiled floor as if to say: 'hurry, hurry, hurry'. The thin wooden slats of the escalator down to the trains were hypnotic and dizzying. It was the steepest staircase I'd ever seen; we were descending into the bowels of the earth and I thought about Rob and Dad who'd made similar journeys underground every day of their working lives. It gave me the creeps; all that earth and rock right above our heads, pressing down on us. It was suffocating; like being buried alive. And the tube was brightly lit, unlike a mine shaft.

The train was crowded; the smell of curry and perfume and body odour mingling to create a fetid cocktail. Pressed up against complete strangers, back to belly, nose to armpit, I murmured apologies, though none were returned. My fellow passengers remained detached, clinging onto their dignity as well as the spiral handles dangling from the train ceiling. Those sitting behaved as if they travelled alone, comfortable in a spacious surrounding, flicking out their newspapers, turning unread pages of novels, others tried to disappear entirely, staring straight ahead, faces blank. No one made eye contact, or smiled, or spoke. The whir and rattle of wheels on track filled the carriage, punctured occasionally by a high-pitched whistle, like the mating call of a mechanical bird. I thought I might faint.

The tube spewed us out into the blinding light of a late August morning. Following the A to Z Ruth led us through the back streets of a west London suburb, though 'back streets' gives the wrong impression. Elegant terraced houses, red-bricked beauties with steep eaves and bay windows, black and white tiled paths leading to wide front doors inlaid with stained glass.

'And this is Queen's Tennis Club, don't you know!' Ruth said in a royalty-posh voice, sweeping an arm across the air.

'Well, bugger me,' I said, bobbing a curtsey and

nearly falling over with the weight of my overnight bag. We started to laugh.

'Oh, we're going to have such fun, Mandy. What a gas! It'll be just like old times.'

And it felt wonderful to hear the joy in her voice, to pretend that we were thirteen again and the world was ours for the taking.

Jane's home wasn't how I'd imagined it. A one-bedroomed ground floor flat in a converted Victorian terrace with a pay phone in the communal hall. Jane was away on holiday, Corfu, Ruth said, with a boyfriend, another teacher at the Hammersmith secondary school where she worked.

'Blinking 'eck. Blokes'll have more room in camper van,' I said, broadening my accent in jest. 'Where'll we sleep? There's only one bed.'

'Sofa bed,' Ruth replied, blasé.

Although the flat was small, '*bijou*' Ruth corrected me, the high ceilings and ornate cornicing lent it an aura of opulence. Wine-coloured velvet curtains hung in drapes, floor to ceiling, oak shelves bowed with the weight of hardback books, rugs were scattered across bare floorboards.

'I've heard teachers aren't well paid, but surely they can afford carpet!' I laughed, uncomfortable. I felt like a burglar, or intruder, creeping around while the owners were out.

'Splendid, isn't it? Absolutely gorgeous. Of course, I'd have liked a house with more character. One of the cottages like your Mum's—'

'Character? That what you call it? Damp's bloody spiteful, creaking's noisy—'

'You know what I mean. More like the old place. Do you remember it?'

'How could I forget! How are your folks?'

'Fine. Good, I think.' She moved towards the kitchen. 'Look, you do fancy a cuppa before we head off?' It was more like a corridor than a kitchen, though the units were lovely.

'Why didn't you?'

'What?'

'Get a place with "character".'

'There wasn't time. We took what came up.' She opened several cupboards before finding the mugs.

I searched for the fridge. No luck. 'Why the rush? Was it to do with Dan leaving army and all that?' Like everyone, I'd never asked about, or even mentioned, Dan's departure from the forces. Being away from the village made me bold, or cheeky. 'Can't see a fridge.'

'Here,' she said, opening another cupboard door, 'integrated kitchen. All the rage. We'll be having one as soon as this blasted strike's over.'

She sniffed the milk. 'Look, I've heard the rumours about Dan.'

I had too, but I kept quiet. 'Rumours?'

'We don't like to say because it sounds boastful.' She looked at me and I didn't know what to say, so said nothing. She blinked, looked away, and then carried on, filling the silence. 'He was very brave, I mean, over and above the call of duty.'

The words sounded odd on her tongue. 'He received a medal, for valour, but he was injured.' So it was true, what Rob had reported, and scoffed at.

'Injured?' Dan showed no signs of obvious injury.

'He saw terrible things. Terrible things.' Her voice trembled, she placed the back of her hand against her forehead, as if she might collapse, or weep, but her eyes remained dry. I remembered his bowed head, like a snowdrop, as he ate his cake at the May Fair, the look in his eyes as he played the trumpet that night on the moor, the accusations he'd broken the picket line at the first sign of violence.

'Where'd it happen?'

'The Falklands.' She stirred the tea vigorously. She began to cry. 'Oh, Mandy, I can't talk about it. It was so awful. Poor, poor Dan.'

'You don't need to say another thing. I'm too bloody nosy for me own good. Forgive me?' I went over and gave her a hug.

'Of course, I do, darling. It's not easy to talk about. You won't tell anyone, will you? It dredges it all up and Dan doesn't like to talk about the medal, the war, what happened . . . You understand, don't you?'

'I do. Mum's the word.' I didn't like to say that most people knew already. At least some of the story.

She brightened up instantly. 'Look, no more of this. We're here to have a good time, and a good time we will have!'

In my recently appointed role as Fundraising Assistant to Ruth's Fundraising Manager I said we were here to fundraise, but, giggling, admitted there was scope for some fun too. 'Right. Sup up and let's be off then!' I said, chinking my mug against hers.

Before we left Ruth reapplied her make-up and persuaded me to wear some lipstick and eye-shadow. I looked better than I thought I would; nice even, and resolved to buy some make-up as soon as there were a few spare coppers. Then she backcombed her hair, and dived into the bedroom to change. When she emerged she wore a day-glo green T-shirt and a very short skirt.

'Wow! Look at you!' I said.

She winked, shook out a lean, tanned leg and said, 'All part of the fundraising effort!'

'I'll make 'em laugh,' I said, lifting my skirt.

'Or sorry for us!' she howled, and though I laughed and told myself she was only kidding my heart contracted, shrivelled.

The tube was heaving again and everyone in the world and his brother seemed to be going to Notting Hill. Ruth had hold of the A to Z, but there was no need; we were swept along with the crowd. But finding Kensington Park Gardens was hard, and when we did Sydney and Roger looked less than pleased.

'Ladies, you is late. The appointed rendezvous time was thirteen hundred hours. It is precisely twenty-eight minutes beyond that. We have been collecting for over two hours.'

'And flipping hard work it is too,' Roger chipped in, sweating and decidedly pissed off.

It was difficult to take Sydney seriously. Not least because he was dressed in a raffia skirt, a garland of plastic flowers round his neck, a handkerchief tied at all four corners on his head. He wore white mid-calf length socks with Jesus sandals. Both him and Roger were covered in Dig Deep for the Miners and Coal not Dole stickers.

Handing me the bucket, Sydney said that he and Roger were off to meet a fundraising crew in another part of the capital. 'You'll need to get yourselves to Portobello Road.'

Ruth peered into the bucket. 'Not much in here, gentlemen. I'm sure Mrs Walker and I will fare much better.'

Sydney harrumphed and said they'd be back by seven to collect the day's takings.

Standing there, shaking the bucket whenever I remembered (which wasn't often), I was overtaken by the beauty of the city and its people. Exotic smells wafted on the breeze; I recognised only a few: pineapple, banana, coconut. Strutting flocks of costumed revellers paraded by, the tinkling of steel bands filled the air.

'It sounds like music from fairyland, another world,' I shouted.

'It is from another world! The Caribbean!' yelled Ruth, and for the first time I didn't care that I sounded gauche. I was part of this other world; this world where the sun always shone, where people danced in the streets, wore feathers on their head, sat on door steps drinking and smoking and laughing.

After a couple of hours we took a break and drifted towards the food stalls lining the streets. There was so much to choose from. Foods that I had never even heard of, let alone tasted: plantains, goat curry, green curry, satay, and noodles, dishes from the west and the east. I gobbled the sights and smells, like a glutton, finally plumping for roasted plantains and curry. Ruth didn't want anything, it was too hot she said, sipping on a Diet Coke as I tucked in. I finished off with a tropical juice served in a hollowed-out pineapple, complete with paper umbrellas.

By seven my feet throbbed and I was glad that Sydney and Roger were punctual. We handed over the bucket; it was richer than it had been at lunchtime, though I was disappointed with the takings. We'd had too much of a good time.

'Do not fret, ladies. Richer pickings tomorrow. Rendezvous at HQ oh-nine hundred hours,' Sydney said.

We limped back to the flat, picking up a pint of milk and a loaf of bread on the way. Ruth dived into the shower first and I mooched around the front room, enjoying the cooling sensation of the stripped floorboards on my trotter-like feet. I ran my fingers along the books, collecting dust on the way. Clearly Jane wasn't much of a cleaner. No wonder. She wouldn't have the time with all these books to read. There were lots of novels by women. I pulled one out at random: *The Golden Notebook* by Doris Lessing, and flipped it over to read the back page: 'A powerful account of one woman's search for personal, political and professional identity.'

'A classic, that one.'

I jumped, nearly dropping the book. Ruth stood wrapped in a towel, water pooling at her feet.

'Sounds a bit heavy-going.'

'I wouldn't know, haven't read it myself to be honest. I prefer a damn good thriller, or something racy. Do you remember those Jilly Coopers we used to leaf through in the library?' She hooted with laughter. 'You knew where all the dirty bits were 'cos the pages were always dog-eared and torn! Golly, I got most of my sex education from those books. Mum would rather have died than talk about *that!* Bathroom's free.' And she padded into the bedroom, laughing all the way.

It surprised me, that Ruth didn't read books like the one in my hand. Clever, thought-provoking works. I wondered if Jane was anything like Ruth and looked around for photographs; I couldn't see any. I turned the book over and opened it, reading some of the reviews and foreword.

'Says here that Doris Lessing left her kids. Toddlers. Didn't think she was the right person to bring them up,' I shouted. 'Imagine that.'

'Can't,' Ruth yelled back.

I returned the book, walked to the bedroom, and leaned against the doorframe, watching Ruth, who was bent double, brushing her hair, droplets of water flying through the air, illuminated by the setting sun pouring through the floor to ceiling windows.

'I'm missing my lot already,' I said, taken aback by the physical pain that skewered me as I said the words. It was eight thirty. Becky would be tucked up in bed, fair eyelashes grazing her shiny cheeks, sleep heavy and warm in her cot; Johnnie too would be drifting into oblivion; on the bottom bunk Mark would be lying patiently, watching the metal springs above him contract and expand, as David bounced up and down, up and down. I hoped Rob had remembered to heat the cottage pie I'd prepared the day before, not skimping on the ingredients like I usually did these days. I wanted them to enjoy decent, hearty meals while I was away, transmitting my love for them through the food. Cottage pie, chocolate cake, suet pudding, hotpot. 'I've never spent a night away from them. Apart from when Becky was born.'

Ruth stood upright, throwing her hair over her head. 'That's amazing. Mum was always away when I was little.'

'She was ill.'

'Yes, but, still.' She sat on the edge of the bed. 'Didn't do me any harm.'

I wondered if that was true. For sure, Ruth grew

up quickly. When we were kids, she was independent in a way that no one else of our age was. She cooked and cleaned and got herself off to school most days, though she was absent more than most. Forever poorly. And when puberty hit, just before she left, she had a strange attitude towards it. I didn't see that at the time; it was only afterwards I realised that she swung from six to sixteen and back again. Maybe we all did, but despite her self-sufficiency she was more reluctant than most to growing up.

'You missed her though?' I said.

'Honestly? I don't really know. What you've never had and all that. I loved her, of course.'

She had missed her mum; she must have done. As a girl, she craved attention, forming bizarre attachments and fixations on certain teachers. She longed for affection; she competed with everyone for it. If I played with other children in the yard she'd march over and say, 'I love you, Mandy. You're my bestest ever friend.' The other girls would look confused because no one said things like 'I love you' in Fenley Down. Not in public at any rate.

'It won't hurt yours to do without their mum for a night. It might even be good for them. It'll certainly be good for Rob. See what you do for him.'

'You sound like those feminists.'

'They're not the enemy. Though I do wish some of them would use a little make-up, stop wearing such ugly clothes.' She laughed. What did she make of my clothes, lack of makeup?

'Will you and Dan have children?' I asked.

'Most definitely. Though not for a while. I think thirty is a good age, or thereabouts. I plan to be deputy head before I have children, and then I shall give up work and bake cakes all day like you.' She threw her legs onto the bed and lay down, hands cradling her head, confident and youthful. I envied her; I wanted to be like her. I hated myself for it. The damp from her hair seeped onto the pale bedspread.

'You don't sound much like a feminist now.'

She giggled and wiggled her toes. Her nails were painted bright red, like glazed cherries. 'I know! Jane would never approve!'

'What's she like, Jane? It's ever so nice of her to let us use her flat.'

'She's terribly clever and terribly ambitious. She could have gone to Oxbridge but chose instead to go to our second-rate teacher training college. Don't ask me why!' She glanced over and raised her eyebrows, as if I should understand her implication. 'She's a dedicated teacher – English Literature – hence the books. She has short hair and wears thick-rimmed glasses. Boyfriend Graeme teaches chemistry and wears tweed jackets with leather patches on the elbows!' Ruth was almost screaming with laughter and though I was ashamed to admit it I was enjoying her swipe at Jane, this competitor of mine for Ruth's affections.

189

Mr Markham, our geography teacher at Fenley Down High, wore patches on his jackets. Ruth larked about no end in lessons. 'What's the point?' she'd say in her high-pitched squeal. 'Who cares about rocks and rivers and shit like that?' And I wanted to say that I did, but was too afraid of looking stupid. After she left I hated going to school and then all the stuff with Dad exploded, and Mum didn't seem to care what I did, so nor did I. Mr Markham became the butt of my jokes, and then I near enough stopped going to lessons altogether.

'Why did *you* go to a "second-rate" teacher training college? You were so clever,' I asked.

'Didn't get the grades. Didn't work hard enough. Too interested in the fellas!' She rolled her eyes and smiled.

'You wouldn't have met Dan if you'd gone somewhere else.'

'Absolutely right. Gosh, he looked so handsome, so sexy in his uniform.' She looked wistful and I wondered how she felt about Dan now that he wore miners' overalls and a hard hat with a lamp on it. Was it a sexy look? I couldn't say; I'd grown up with it.

She sighed and continued, 'Still, there's a reason for everything. We get what we deserve. Look, why don't you jump in the shower and we'll go out? There's a pub, not far from here. Ever so trendy.'

'I've no money, and our expenses budget won't stretch to drinks.'

'My treat.'

'I've nothing to wear.' The word trendy was a punch in the stomach. Me, in a fashionable London pub? I'd stick out like steak and kidney pudding on a *nouvelle cuisine* menu.

'You're fine just as you are. It's so cosmopolitan round here. Takes all sorts.'

I paused, my brain scrambling for another excuse, and with that pause I lost the argument.

'It'll take your mind off the children. What else are you going to do? Sit round moping all evening?'

A nice cup of tea and bed would have suited.

'Mandy, you're twenty-four. Live a little! And you're so pretty when you smile.' She jumped from the bed, sleek and fresh in her button-through summer frock.

I nodded, stumbled to the bathroom, and stared into the mirror. You're young and free, if only for one night, Mandy Walker. Enjoy.

CHAPTER 15

By the time we tumbled into bed it was gone midnight. Drunk on white wine spritzers – it'd tasted bitter at first, but the third and fourth went down like pop – and without the A to Z we took a wrong turn on the way back to Jane's flat and wandered round some of the less salubrious streets of Fulham, or Flarm, as the locals called it. Ruth was apologetic, explaining that she'd only visited once before with Jane. 'Everything looks so different in the dark,' she'd wailed, clutching her high-heeled sandals.

'And when you've had a skin-full,' I'd replied. 'Mind that dog dirt!'

Back at the flat, I offered to make us a mug of tea, but by the time I brought it through Ruth was sprawled across the double bed, fast asleep, breathing heavily. Snoring really. The room was still warm but the heat wouldn't last. She might wake in the night shivering and disorientated; I pulled the bedspread from underneath her, she weighed almost nothing, and draped it over her. In the kitchen I filled a glass with water and placed it on her bedside table, then I took both mugs of tea through to the lounge, and unable to find the light switch, sat in the near-dark drinking them, the room spinning if I moved my head too quickly.

The sofa-bed was impossible to fathom; I couldn't get it to open. Exhausted, desperately needing to lie down, I gave up. With a cushion for a pillow and a velour throw as a blanket I curled up on the sofa. It wasn't long enough for me to lie flat; it was narrow so that curled foetus-like my knees hovered over the edge. There was no room to toss and turn. I shut my eyes, determined to rest. Acutely aware of the sounds of the city leaching through the walls I found it difficult to sleep, but must have dozed off because I woke hours later, stiff and desperately thirsty, to the sound of a child. A baby, my baby.

Opening my eyes with difficulty – the lids were glued together with the mascara Ruth'd insisted I wore, which I'd liked so much I'd not removed it – the room appeared oppressive and gloomy. The bookshelf loomed like a giant, the tiled fireplace gaped and I realised that the child's cry could not have been real; I was hundreds of miles away from my babies. My head throbbed, my stomach whirled. I pushed myself upright, startled to hear scrabbling. Was there a mouse in the room? Then it came again, a strangled crying, a heaving.

Tentatively, I forced myself upright and listened again. The sound was coming from inside the flat; I was sure of it. I tiptoed towards the door and squeezed through the narrow gap, careful to avoid the creaking noise it made when fully opened. The bedroom door was shut; I crept down the narrow hall, the smell of toast filling my nostrils, reminding my body that I'd not eaten since the feast at the carnival, which was over twelve hours ago. My belly griped.

Even before I opened the kitchen door I recognised the sound of someone vomiting. Ruth must be in the bathroom. I went into the kitchen and pressed the light switch. The glare of the strip lighting blinded me momentarily. I'd intended to go straight through to check that Ruth was alright but I stopped, stunned by the sight that greeted me. The kitchen looked as if it had been attacked by a dray of famished squirrels. Cupboard doors hung open, scattered across the worktop was the remains of the cupboard's contents, the non-perishables like spaghetti, dried fruit, and cornflakes, interspersed with empty packets: the milk bottle and carton, the plastic loaf bag, open jars of jam, honey, and treacle, a butter pat with finger marks gouged out of it, a hunk of cheese with a bite mark, a squashed tube of tomato puree, a can of beans with a fork poking out of it. What had gone on here? And even as I asked the question, I knew.

Pencil-thin Ruth hadn't always been that way. Not that she'd ever been fat. As a girl she was all elbows and knees, knobby and sharp, but as adolescence knocked Ruth swelled, her shape shifted, became comfortable around the hips, full in the breast. Her beauty emerged at full throttle too, but Ruth couldn't see beyond the fleshiness. In the six months before she left she was forever on a diet; starving herself. I'd erased that memory, until now. How often did she do this to herself? Binge, make herself sick. Did Dan know? Did anyone? And why? Everything I knew about this kind of behaviour I'd read in those cheap magazines I bought when we had spare cash to blow on fripperies. They claimed it was symptomatic of deep unhappiness; it was an attempt to claw back control, any kind of warped control, in a life marked by an absence of it. Why did Ruth feel her life was hampered?

My thoughts were punctured by hollow retching and a long, low moan that reminded me of cries made during childbirth. I moved on towards the bathroom, knocking at the door, waiting to be invited in.

'Ruth? It's Mandy.' What a stupid thing to say. Who else was it likely to be? 'Everything alright?' I marvelled at my predictability.

The toilet flushed and I heard, 'Yes. Super. Just had a bit too much to drink.'

'Me too. Me head's spinning.' I waited, listening to the sound of running water, cupboard doors opening and closing, the scrubbing of teeth. Finally, I turned away and began to tidy, methodically, quietly. Ruth remained in the bathroom and once I'd done in the kitchen I returned to my bed without seeing her.

In the morning I woke early – that sofa didn't get any more comfortable as the night progressed; and at seven o' clock I got up and went looking for a corner shop or newsagent. There was no way I'd be able to face the day without a cup of tea and I couldn't drink it black. She'd polished off the milk we bought. I snatched the A to Z from the coffee table before I left.

Half an hour later I brought Ruth breakfast: two slices of buttered toast. 'Oh, thank you, darling. But you know, I don't think I could eat a thing. What a corker of a hangover! How are *you* feeling?' She sounded bright, brighter than I felt by a long chalk and I wanted to shake her, tell her she must eat, tell her to get a grip. Her life was good; what could she possibly grumble about? How dare she be unhappy? Instead I plonked my behind on the sofa and ate her toast as well as my own.

Dab hands at the tube in under forty-eight hours we rumbled up to Finsbury Park. The area was evidently less prosperous than Notting Hill, with boarded-up shops and beggars sitting underneath the railway arch, surrounded by piles of pigeon crap. Crowds built as we neared the park, and I clutched my handbag against my stomach.

The festival-goers were generous and our takings grew quickly. We wandered round, rattling our buckets, while Sydney and Roger manned the stall, the table top strewn with leaflets for the grown-ups and stickers for the kids. After a couple of

196

hours, feet aching, we swapped places with the men, crumpling into the chairs laid out for us. Folding chairs never felt so comfortable. My ankles were swollen, the skin on my feet pink. Sticking my legs out I twizzled my ankles round and round; Ruth did the same though it had to be said that hers didn't look like they'd suffered from the walking. It was only then I noticed another stall had sprung up a short distance from ours. A woman was spreading leaflets out. She looked tired, middle-aged, slightly grubby. She saw me staring; I smiled and turned away.

'Don't mind a little healthy competition, do you?' an upper-class voice said.

I turned to the shabby woman. She grinned. 'Though competition's a dirty word in our circles. Don't tell anyone I suggested that, will you?' And she laughed to reveal a set of astonishingly yellowed, filthy teeth. Even at a distance I could tell that she'd not visited a dentist in years, that her teeth hadn't made contact with a toothbrush in months. On a rare visit to Betty's in Harrogate, my boys togged up in their Sunday best, I remembered Mum scanning the tea room and commenting that you could spot the posh kids a mile off because they were the ones with snotty noses, mucky clothes, and nits; no respectable ordinary family would have the nerve to present their children, or themselves, so poorly.

At the woman's laughter Ruth leaped up. 'Greenham Common?' she said, crossing to shake hands with the woman. It flitted through my mind whether or not to go over myself, but the chair was so comfy I stayed put.

'Shall I man the stall?' I said.

Without turning to me, Ruth said, 'Language! It's a slippery devil, isn't it? "Woman the stall" sounds crazy. What can we say? I'll come back to you on that, Mandy.'

The Greenham woman laughed again, and I didn't understand what was so funny. I watched them talking, fanning myself with a leaflet, sipping on my bottle of pop. My head thumped, the effects of the aspirin I'd taken earlier wearing off by the second. Ruth seemed so comfortable talking to the woman. I didn't understand why, but a southern or aristocratic (or even just well-spoken, non-accented English) voice sent me into a spin, transforming me into the shy, unsure of herself young girl I'd been at junior school, before I got mouthy and wild and 'totally out of control', according to Mr Stanton, the Headmaster of Fenley High. I watched Ruth smiling, and talking, her hands flapping about, emphasising her words; she looked so beautiful, confident, in control. Only seconds earlier she had been complaining of the mother of all headaches, that she would rather shove her head in a barrel of snakes than make polite conversation with strangers, all to squeeze a few pennies out of them.

I'd always seen her as theatrical, but she was a good actress. Really good. The image of Jane's ransacked kitchen flashed in my head. My thoughts drifted to Dan and his medals and her version of their meeting and I pondered whether or not their marriage was as happy as she cracked it up to be. Momentarily, I felt disloyal, but I couldn't help myself, and all the rumours about Dan echoed in my ears, the cruel words she'd spoken as a teenager: 'You're not wearing that are you?' 'Mandy's the funny one.' 'Only certain people are destined for great things.' I recalled my mum's warning and I saw the way Rob looked at her, the way all the men did, and envy smouldered in my heart as the throbbing in my head closed in. I closed my eyes, dropped my head to my knees, and let myself feel the pain.

'Not only is Mandy an absolute marvel in the kitchen and the best mummy ever to four, yes, four! beautiful children, but she's a whizz at raising money. Mandy, meet Gretta.'

I jolted upright, the flimsy aluminium legs of the chair lifting off the ground, almost sending me flying. I opened my eyes and shut them immediately, the imprint of the sun flickering on my eyelids, stinging. I shielded them, before squinting at the two silhouettes. 'Nice to meet you.' I took her offered hand. Her greeting was firm and sure of itself.

'And I forgot to mention that she's got a magnificent way with words too. She's going to write my speech for the Leeds gig!' Ruth chirruped.

Leeds gig? What is she blathering about?

'Gretta is also addressing the meeting in Leeds this autumn.'

I must have still looked blank because Ruth added, 'On behalf of the Greenham women.'

They talked on, but I wasn't listening. I felt bad. I let myself believe that my aching joints, tumbling stomach, and raging head were punishment for thinking so ill of Ruth, for my envy, rather than because of the skin-full I'd had the night before. I felt overwhelmed by a sadness I didn't understand, a kind of longing.

One of the best things about going away is coming home. And this was never truer than after my first visit to London. Ruth and I were due to travel on the morning following the festival in Finsbury Park, but at the end of that gruelling day the pull on my heart was so strong I persuaded her we could make the nine-ten from Euston and be back in Fenley shortly after midnight.

'Darling, what's the deal? You'll be back by midday and we won't have to bust a gut. The children will be asleep!'

'I'll be there when they wake, cooking them breakfast. Egg-bread, beans, bacon if we've got it, as a treat.'

At the station Ruth called Dan. 'Why pay for a taxi when I've got a driver at home?' she said, her voice thick with sleep. She'd nodded off on the train, while I sat wide awake watching my fellow travellers, wondering where they'd been or where they were going, and why. So many people travelling. Did they do this often? Or was it a rare adventure, like mine?

I pushed my face against the glass as we rolled through cities, towns, and villages. Places I'd never been to, nor was I likely to. So many lives. I thought about all that I'd seen and done over the past two days, the people I'd met. It was a big world out there.

'Darling! Couldn't bear to be away from you for one more night . . . too expensive, we don't have the cash . . . yes, yes, Mandy's here too. She so wants to be there for the children in the morning . . . you're an angel. Quick as you can.' She replaced the receiver and a couple of coins clunked into the change tray. 'All sorted.'

'You woke him up?'

She pulled a face. 'He'll do anything for me.'

'Didn't sound like he was too chuffed. I feel right bad now.'

'Don't.' She flicked her wrist, dismissive. 'It was you and the mention of the children that swung it.'

Dan didn't look crumpled, or puffy-eyed, as I'd expected when he climbed from the car; he smelt of aftershave. He opened the boot before greeting Ruth with a peck on the cheek, then took her bag and threw it in. I lumbered over with mine, but before I could chuck it in he took hold of the handle, brushing my hand as he did so, and said, 'Let me, you must be exhausted.' His eyes shone as he smiled.

201

'Sorry if you were sleeping. Thanks ever so much for this, I really appreciate it,' I said.

'I know you do.' He looked straight at me; Ruth was already sitting in the front. 'And I was up, don't sleep so well anyway.'

It was gone one o' clock when I turned the key in the lock, the house as silent, familiar and comforting as the night sky. I tiptoed to the boys' room, then into Becky's, the scent of sugar and sticky farts fulfilling a primal maternal need in me – at least for the time being. Rob didn't stir when I slipped in next to him, not even when I rolled him over to stop the snoring. The smell of hops rose from the sheets like mist.

CHAPTER 16

The evening sun drenched the landscape, golden and shiny. It poured across the moor, sweetening everything in its path. I turned around to look at the outskirts of town; trees red and gold and yellow. It was my favourite time of year: autumn, before the clocks went back, before the leaves fell and turned to mulch, before the dank smell of rotting vegetation filled the air, before it was so parky you needed to wear a heavy coat. This year, more than ever, I was dreading the winter. How on earth were we to heat the house, feed the kids? Everything felt more bearable when the days were long and the sun shone.

I'd taken to walking on the moor whenever I could, ever since that night when I'd bumped into Dan, and though I listened out I'd not happened upon him again. Had he stopped playing? Had his flugelhorn been discovered?

Rob seemed to like me going out. I thought he'd object, want me shackled to the kitchen, but so long as the kids were sorted out first he didn't mind. 'Only fair, Mand,' he'd said, hoofing it to the front door. 'Your turn, then mine. See you later. Don't wait up.' No matter how short of cash we were, he always found enough for a pint or two a couple of times a week. He hinted that Dean gave him the odd pint for nothing, for collecting the empties at the end of the evening, but when I asked Mum to pass on my thanks, she said Rob didn't drink in The Boar's Head any more, not according to Dean. I meant to ask Rob where he was drinking nowadays – God knows there was enough choice in Fenley even ruling out The Boar's Head and The White Lion – but he'd never been a man to take kindly to too many questions and I never found the right moment. I was busier and busier.

The days were drawing in, and though my jaunts began during daylight hours – I'd go as soon as I'd given the kids their tea – they ended in the dark. Soon it would be impractical to go out at all. My heart sank at the prospect, but I shook off the feeling.

Enjoy it while you can.

I walked on, losing myself in the action of putting one foot in front of the other. It was a creative time; I'd often come up with new fundraising ideas as I stomped across those hills, new ways to save a bit of cash for the soup kitchens, inspiring words for speeches.

The school uniform swap-shop was the result of one of these hikes and everyone agreed it had been a great success. I even managed to get Mark a new pair of shoes. New to him, that is. No mean feat with his clodhoppers: size three, and he was only eight. Lack of green vegetables wasn't slowing down his growth rate, though all four kids were looking pasty. They weren't the only ones. The faces of all the little children when they lined up to go into class reminded me of those photos taken on the streets of London and Glasgow during the thirties. Dad had a book of them from the library once that he took with him when canvassing during some election. 'To remind people what we never want to go back to, before the Welfare State, before socialism,' he'd said. His fellow party workers thought he was bonkers, eccentric said the polite ones, lugging that book door to door, but it did the trick. Fenley was red through and through.

What would Dad make of it all now, what would he do?

Night had descended before I turned back and though the path was as familiar as the shape of my own hands, I wished I'd brought a torch. The moon was almost full, but a wind came up, sweeping clouds across her periodically, thrusting me into blackness. The wind whistled as it arched over the rocks, eerie and unnerving.

I thought I'd imagined it at first, but as I approached the last cluster of rocks, before the tumbledown stone wall and the home straight, I heard it. I knew it was him. He was playing 'Nimrod' and my heart lightened. I almost ran into the rocks. At the sound of my heavy footsteps, the music stopped.

'Please carry on. It's gorgeous.'

'What you doing out? It's pitch.'

I shrugged and sat on a low rock. 'Please?'

As Dan put the flugelhorn to his mouth, a cloud cleared and moonlight fell on him like a super trouper light at a concert. He played the piece from start to finish.

'You're getting better and better,' I said, clapping.

'Been practising.'

'You'll be a professional yet.'

He shrugged.

'Not seen you up here in ages. Have you got a new hide out?'

He shook his head, wiped the mouthpiece with a hanky. The only sound was the howl of the wind.

'I'll leave you to it then. Thanks for that.' I stood, wiped down the front of my jeans and started to walk away, disappointment rising in me.

'Shall I play another?' he shouted after me.

I turned immediately.

The next piece wasn't anything I recognised and nowhere near as polished as 'Nimrod', but I applauded regardless.

'Needs work,' he said. 'A Dizzy Gillespie piece. That man is incredible,' he said. 'Needs work.'

'Doesn't everything? I don't know how you do it at all.'

'It's easy. To start, I mean. To become like the

greats, Gillespie, Davis . . . that takes work. A lifetime, maybe.'

I laughed. 'Easy?'

'Have a go?' he offered me the instrument. He didn't wipe the mouthpiece.

I shook my head. 'I can't do it.'

'Bet you said that about public speaking before you had a go.'

'I didn't have a go; I was forced.'

The gig at Leeds had gone well enough, though it was odd hearing my words spoken by Ruth. Invitations to address meetings flooded in. I'd been thrust into the limelight at Manchester University after Ruth came down with a nasty bout of 'flu. The hall was rammed and despite the almost paralysing nerves, after a few minutes I relaxed, and when I got into my stride there was virtually no shutting me up. Once I finally ran out of steam, people stood to applaud. As I answered questions, I saw Ethel scowling in the wings, tapping her wrist so vigorously I thought she must surely smash the watch face. Turns out, we'd collected more money than any other speaker in the history of benefit gigs, according to the president of the students' union.

'Students. Bloody loaded, the lot of 'em,' Ethel had commented on the way home. Ann had hesitantly suggested we'd best keep our expectations low; it was the start of term and grant cheques had only recently been cashed. Ethel ignored her.

'You'll be doing more of these. You mark my

words.' It wasn't a request, but I didn't care. I'd wanted to do more, to feel the surge in my chest when the crowd roared.

Dan pushed the flugelhorn towards me again.

'My fingers are numb.'

'Don't need your fingers first off. Just put your lips together and blow. Pretend you're spitting a hair out of your mouth.'

I thought about wiping the mouthpiece with my T-shirt; it was strange to think that his mouth had been pressed against it only minutes before, his spit wetting the metal. I should have felt disgusted, but didn't. Breathing in deeply first, I blew. A pathetic noise, like a fart, came out. I tried again. I felt light-headed, my lips tingled.

'See,' I said. 'Rubbish.'

'Mam says you're good, at the speaking. Right good. "Between you and me, Daniel," she said, "she's a whole lot better than your Ruth. They listen to her, really listen. There's fire and passion in her . . ."'

I could feel myself blushing and was glad he wouldn't be able to see this.

He continued, '"She does all talking now. I'd never have had her down as capable, but full of surprises that one is."' His impersonation of his mother was spot on and although I tried to conceal my laughter I soon gave up. I asked if Ethel knew about his mimicking skills and he shook his head. Another secret.

'Do you enjoy it?' he said.

'I'm still seeing stars.'

'I mean the lectures, talks, whatever you call it. To the students.'

'First time, I was so nervous, I was actually sick. In toilets.' I put the flugelhorn to my mouth again. This time the sound was stronger, more sustained. I pressed down on two of the buttons to create a different note. I wasn't altogether successful.

'Ruth loved it at Leeds, when she'd done the speech,' Dan said, as I paused, lightheaded again with the effort.

'She was great. A natural,' I lied. She'd sounded as if she was reading from a script, which she was, and afterwards, when the students were asking questions, Ruth said things I didn't agree with, didn't make sense given the content of the talk. The audience looked confused. I butted in once, but didn't do it again after the look she shot me. That was the thing about Ruth; it was the same at school; you really didn't want to get on the wrong side of her.

'But not as much of a natural as you,' he said, then added, 'according to my mam.'

'Perhaps it's because they're my own words. Got to be easier, hasn't it?' I tried again on the flugel-horn. 'This is hard work,' I said.

'Is your mouth humming?'

'Yeah. Feels weird.' But I liked the sensation. It reminded me of the tingling I used to get in the roof of my mouth when Rob and I kissed after he picked me up from school. How that feeling travelled from my mouth, down my spine, to a place I didn't even know the name of back then. A point below my stomach, lower than my guts. The point that sent shivers up and down my whole body and made me melt like butter in sunlight. My head span to think on it, my legs weakened, and I hoped that Dan couldn't see the change in me. Those magazines that Ruth read, *Cosmopolitan* and that, said it all happens in the clitoris, but it doesn't. There's somewhere else too. A place you can reach with your mind, but not your hands. I'd forgotten how that felt; how good it felt, and I struggled to remember when Rob had touched me last.

'Try this,' Dan said, manoeuvring my fingers into position over the buttons. He was so close I could smell him: the scent of his aftershave mingling with the sour, musky smell of masculinity. I could feel the heat from his body. When my finger position was correct, he let go and stepped back. I almost moved a finger so that I could feel his touch again, sense his body close to mine.

I closed my eyes, feeling the cool of the metal against my throbbing lips, like a kiss.

'Now press here, then here,' he said. 'Ruth says she's very busy anyway, what with the school and all that.'

My eyes snapped open; the fantasy over.

'Is she OK? I've not seen her for weeks. Didn't see her at the last meeting.' Handing over the brass,

I said, 'Here, you'd best have this back, don't think I'm cut out for it.'

Dan took the flugelhorn, twisted it apart, stroked the metal with a chamois leather until it gleamed. He treated the instrument with love, and respect. He lowered it into the velvet-lined case like a new-born baby; the brass catches made a satisfying thud as he flipped them shut.

'I'll be off then,' I said, stuffing my hands into the front pockets of my jeans.

'I'll walk with you,' he said, before adding hurriedly, 'if that's all right with you?'

''Course.'

We walked in silence until I asked if Ruth ever wondered where he went, what he did when he disappeared at night.

'She knows I'm wandering on the moor.'

'Does she never want to come? It's lovely up here.'

'Never said. She's got exercise class, and school work, and friends to visit. Always busy.'

'Friends?' My voice sounded high and strained. I hadn't realised Ruth had other friends in the village; she was popular with folk, but she'd not spoken about friends that you'd pop in on.

He stared at me.

'She must have loads of them. I bet they're queuing up outside your place,' I quipped, hoping he'd not heard the surprise, the jealousy in my tone.

We stopped at the top of the path that ran down

alongside Mum's house. It was narrow; the brambles old and bitter, plucked of their fruit after a long summer, stretching into the path at eye height, they wanted their revenge. Dan gestured for me to walk ahead. Neither of us moved, as if we didn't want to begin the final leg of the journey.

'Will you be coming up here much, now winter's on its way?' he said.

'Will you?'

'If I'm to perfect that piece of music . . . you could do with some practise too.'

I smiled, but said nothing. He was joking, I was sure of it. 'Have you thought any more about joining the colliery band?'

'I've been to a few gigs. Watched the pros in action.'

'Learning tricks of the trade?'

'Maybe. I'm thinking of going to an open mic night. Seeing how I get on.'

I told him how fantastic that was, how I admired his guts, that if things worked out they could survive on a teacher's wage while he built a career. After all, they were getting by on one wage right now. What better time to go for it? My mouth ran away with me, in my excitement.

'What about you? Your dreams?' he said.

His question startled me. I'd never thought about dreams of my own. 'I'm not sure,' I said, half laughing, half sighing. 'Never really thought.'

'I suppose you're far too busy travelling all over, preaching to the masses.'

I laughed properly then. 'Let's hope it's all over soon and people'll be spared me droning and on and on at them.'

'Don't put yourself down. And make time for your dreams.'

'Aye-aye, captain.' I raised my hand to my forehead in a salute and clicked my shoes together. Mouth in gear before my brain again. The shift in the atmosphere was instant.

I apologised profusely, said that I didn't mean to . . . to what? I fell silent again.

'See you.'

He walked ahead; I jogged after him. 'Ruth told me. She said not to tell anyone and I haven't. No one. I don't know why you feel embarrassed, you should feel proud, but I respect that you want to keep it quiet—'

'Like you respect Ruth? She asked you not to blather. You just can't shut up, can you? Found your voice and there's no stopping you.'

I froze. 'I've told no one. Not about that or about the trumpet.'

'Flugelhorn.'

'Sorry.'

He stopped; he knew I was telling the truth. 'Ruth needs to keep her gob shut. It's none of your business.'

'I never said it was. I'll never tell. Promise.'

He turned and walked off, I stood still, the distance between us increasing until the dark swallowed him up.

I could almost feel myself shrinking, diminishing, back to how I'd felt months ago. But I'd grown to enjoy feeling valued, I wasn't going back to being a nobody, and something within me lashed out. How dare he make me feel this way? I'd not done anything wrong, had I? I wanted to shout after him: you and your bloody pride! Your stupid secrets. Medal for valour. Dreams of becoming a professional musician. Ha! They're nothing, not really. Not when you think about what's happening here, now. That's what really matters. Men losing their livelihoods, families without food on the table, warmth in the fire. And worse . . . You're part of this, Dan Braithwaite; you came back; you're as connected to Fenley Down as anyone else. You need the community, the pit, as much as the next man. A voice within screamed: you need *me*.

Ethel and Vince and the rest of them, they'd tried to set him apart, make him seem bigger than he was, more important. I'd fallen for it. But he couldn't even tell his dad about his dreams. Hadn't told his wife. He might have been brave on the battlefield, but he was a coward. I hated him for making me feel small again, and the strength of my rage surprised me. Why was I getting so het up? He was a friend's husband; nothing more.

Walking on, heart still thumping, I got to thinking about what might happen if we didn't win. What would happen to us? To me? What would I do? And if we won? What would I do? Go back to being just a wife and a mother? At least Dan had ambition. That was something worth guarding. The temperature seemed to drop a few degrees, and I quickened my pace towards home.

CHAPTER 17

'Morning, Mrs Walker.'

'Morning, Doug.'

'See you've been in papers again. Quite the little hero, aren't we?' He was brandishing a pair of secateurs and hacking ineffectually at a cluster of twigs that had sprouted from the hedge in much the same manner as the hairs protruding from his eyebrows. Doug was a meticulous, bordering on the obsessive, gardener.

'I think you mean heroine, don't you, Doug?'

He cleared his throat and continued to snap at the twigs, missing every time. He couldn't see well enough to clip them. 'Would you like me to have a bash at that hedge later? We've a pair of shears somewhere; they'd make job easier. And it'll be done till spring then.'

'I can manage, thanks all same.'

He was a stubborn, proud old man. I took hold of the gate, lifted it with both hands and turned it ninety degrees, before resting it against the wall running alongside the path. I made a mental note to ask the postman to leave it where it was and not attempt to close it, and another to ask Rob to fix it, yet again.

'I hope it's all worth it.'

I paused to answer him, buttoning my coat. I was late; Becky had a heavy cold and Johnnie had only just got over chickenpox. I was about to say of course it was all worth it, when another button came off, taking with it a chunk of worn out fabric; there was nothing to stitch the button back onto now.

'Not sure what you mean,' I said, dismayed the winter had barely started and my only warm coat was falling to bits.

The secateurs clipped and a twig bent over, felled but not severed. 'That it's something worth saving. Want your boys going down pit like their father, do you?'

I glanced down at Johnnie who hung limply by my side. Bush-baby eyes and pallid skin, he looked like he already spent most of the time underground. I ruffled his curls and replied, 'I'd like him to have a job,' and stomped off down the road. Doug's words troubled me.

'He's got a point, hasn't he? Dangerous, filthy. Wouldn't wish it on an animal myself. I hated your dad going down there. He used to say there was something Victorian about it. A bygone age.' Mum was drying the dishes when I arrived to drop off Becky and Johnnie; it was my day on at the kitchen and I was making oxtail soup and Lancashire hotpot. A winter warmer.

'But he also used to say that you take away a man's right to earn a living and you take away his dignity.' I was cross with Mum. I'd been looking for reassurance.

Her tone softened. 'Mandy, love, you're doing a grand job. You and the others. Everyone thinks you're a marvel. I think you're a marvel.'

I almost gasped; Mum was not one to dish out compliments, not to me. She folded the tea towel and placed it over the plate rack. 'I remember your dad saying that too many folk dread change, are frightened of the future. But if you're prepared for it, there's nothing to fear, nothing at all. Change is good and there's nothing worse than standing still. It's human nature to strive for better.' She touched my shoulder. 'We wanted a better life for you, like all parents.'

I wanted to ask her exactly what she meant: did she think my life was no better than theirs? What was wrong with theirs? Had I let her down? What were her hopes for me? She'd never said and I only remember Dad talking in the loosest of terms. He told me to be honest, fair, and true to myself. To remember that the whole is greater than the individual but the whole was measured by its individuals. Emotion rose in my breast, thinking about Dad. Along with sadness came anger.

'Do you think my life's worse than yours then?' I dropped Becky into the high chair, offered her a rusk and turned to Johnnie. 'Go and play in the front room, petal.' I shooed him out.

'I didn't say that, love.'

'But you meant it.'

'I—'

'What?' I glared at her. Her eyes brimmed with tears. 'Dad wanted more for me. You didn't. You weren't there when I needed you most, Mum.' They were harsh words; my cruelty surprised me.

'I let you down, and I'm sorry.' Her voice caught in her throat; she looked at the floor. We'd never spoken like this. There'd been unkind words when I told her I was pregnant, that I was going to keep the baby and marry Rob. She'd shouted and screamed and said thank God Dad wasn't here because it would have broken his heart. Then she'd cried, said sorry, she didn't mean it, if it was what I really wanted then that was all that mattered. I said it was what I wanted. I'd thought it was. We'd never spoken of it again. Until now.

Becky squealed, jolting me out of my reverie. In that moment the fog of confused thoughts surrounding Doug's earlier comment about whether or not it was worth it cleared; I realised something. I looked over at Mum; I couldn't move from where I stood. It made sense why Vince and Ethel had been so pleased and proud when the army accepted Dan. Yes, there were dangers, but there was choice too. A chance to train, travel, rise up the ranks. I'd not understood before. 'I don't want my boys going down pit. But I do want there to be a choice, for them and others, for there to be a community here, industry. I can't imagine what it would be like without, and that's what we're fighting for. It's what I'm fighting for.'

She came towards me and put her arms around me. I felt her grip tighten. 'You're your father's daughter; you always were. It's been buried a while, but it's out again.' She pulled away, still holding onto my shoulders, studying me. 'I'm proud of you. I always was. Now go and do what you do best.'

She glanced at the wall clock and my gaze followed. 'Flipping 'eck, I'll be late.' I leaped away, placed a kiss on Becky's cheek, grabbed my bag from the floor, and scurried out, shouting my goodbyes to Johnnie as I darted down the hall. Mum tripped along after me. From the path I yelled, 'Be back round sixish. Don't worry about their tea. I'll fix it when I'm back.'

'Don't be ridiculous. You'll have had enough of kitchens. I'll do it.'

I legged it back down the path and threw my arms around her. 'Thanks, Mum. I couldn't do it without you.'

'I know. Now clear off or you'll miss bus.'

The bus was pulling up at the stop as I turned into the high street, breathless and hot despite the chill. I ran the last few yards, my coat flapping out behind me like a cape. When Ruth and I were little we'd put our hoods up, leaving our duffel coat arms free and run down the hill from primary school, pretending to be super heroes, Wonder Woman or Bat Girl.

Ann was sitting on the back seats and waved as I paid the driver. She reminded me of a robin with her rosy red cheeks and sharp beak. She was aggressive when the need arose too, just like the bird.

'That were a close call. Next bus isn't for another hour.' Her nod was disapproving.

The bus juddered and pulled away, fumes pouring from the exhaust, the stink filling the lower deck.

'Got talking with Mum.' I stared straight ahead. The bus was almost empty.

'Your Rob not got kiddies?'

I turned to her, confused. What was she blathering about? Rob was on picket duty, and Ann would know this. Her husband organised the flying pickets and Rob and the others reported to him daily.

'He's on duty,' I said.

'Good. There's been a drop off since money's run out, and temperature's dropping.' She snorted as she spoke, contemptuous.

'Morale's low. You can hardly blame folk.'

She sighed. 'That you can't. At least he's not in pub.'

'Where he usually is.' I wiped the condensation from the window and stared out as the grey buildings turned to green fields.

Ethel and the team were peeling the tatties when we arrived at the soup kitchen. The bus ran late because it had been diverted from its usual route. The police had set up a road block on the main drag down to the pit. Scab labour was being shipped in and they were trying to stop pickets and protestors clashing with them.

'You've never seen so many police. Looked like pictures on news in summer,' Ann said.

Ethel threw an apron at her. 'Get a chuffing move on then. We'll be busy today and men'll be hungry. Mandy, you want me to start choppin' tails up?' She picked up a kitchen axe, her other hand resting on her expansive hip. Although I was used to Ethel, and nowhere near as terrified of her as I had been, every now and then she still gave me the willies. I imagined a gaggle of Ethels on the picket front line, all brandishing kitchen knives. The coppers wouldn't stand a chance, riot shields or not. She was a fearsome woman, no mistaking, and I never wanted to cross her.

Just as Ethel had warned we were especially busy and time whizzed by. I was scrubbing the pots when Ann came over with a tea towel. Ethel was marching about giving orders. As always, Ann had spent most of the time gossiping with the other women as she served, but she was a committee member, her husband was big in the union, and so it was hard to tell her to pull her finger out. Whenever Ethel was about she worked faster, looked busier, and that's why she was offering to help with the dishes. Ethel was on the warpath.

Ann chattered away as she dried, about everything

and nothing, mostly nonsense and I was barely listening, enjoying instead the warmth and comfort of the soapy water on my hands and arms. I spent so much of the time feeling cold. It was only when I heard her repeat my name, a spot of annoyance in her tone, that I stopped wiping the Brillo pad against the bottom of the metal tray and looked up at her.

'So now your Rob's back on board, will he be coming to Notts at the weekend?'

'Back on board?' Out of the water my fingers were throbbing, scratched raw by the scrubbing pads. I knew I should wear rubber gloves but they were so difficult to pull on and they pinched my arms below the elbow. I inspected my nails. Never a strong point, they were soft and chipped with sores round the cuticles. The back of my left hand bore the mark of a burn from one of the ovens some months ago. There was another on my right forearm. Battle scars I called them. My head was spinning; there'd not been quite enough grub, so women helpers had gone without. I'd chewed on a slice of stale bread at Ethel's say-so as I'd not had breakfast either. I felt light-headed and disconnected from my surroundings.

'Back on board picketing,' Ann said. She spoke to me like I was an idiot. 'So is he coming at weekend?'

I vaguely remembered Rob saying something about not being around this weekend. He'd done more and more duty at the weekends lately, taking time off during the week. It was nice that he was able to meet the boys from school some days, take them to the park. Knock a ball about.

I nodded and drifted back into my own world, plunging my arms into the water. The suds had all but disappeared and the water was only luke-warm. Ann talked on. I looked forward to the end of the day.

Ethel appeared by my other side and tipped her head at Ann, who put down her tea towel and turned to face me. I knew it was serious when she folded her arms, and I felt guilty even though there was absolutely nothing I'd said or done that I could possibly feel guilty about. Ann had that effect on people; it was why she was so powerful in the local politics.

'I've been speaking with our MP, Member of Parliament . . .' she started.

'I know what MP stands for.'

'Right. He thinks it would help our cause no end if someone from mining community, specific-ally a woman, a miner's wife, were to speak to GLC. That's the Greater London Council.'

I knew what she, and Ethel, were gunning for immediately and my stomach turned over. It wasn't entirely nerves, there was genuine excitement too. My confidence had grown. I'd given more and more speeches, at student meetings throughout the north and Labour Party gatherings. I'd even taken part in a radio debate.

'Now we know that addressing a group of

important London people, councillors no less, is entirely different to speaking with a bunch of students,' Ethel butted in. Her contempt for such la-di-da types evident in the stress on the 'st' and 'd'.

'I'd love to do it,' I said.

'Are you sure now?' Ann spoke slowly and deliberately, as if to a child. 'You can take your time to think about it.'

'I've thought about it. I'd love to,' I repeated.

'Settled then.' Ethel slapped me on the back so hard it hurt. 'Knew we could rely on you. Unlike some people I could mention. Flibberty-gibbets.' A loud tut and a shake of her head acted as full stop.

She was referring to her daughter-in-law. Ruth had pulled back on her FAG duties. School commitments had made dedicating such a large chunk of her time to the cause simply impossible, and it was with the deepest regret that she resigned as chairperson. As a member of the Braithwaite family Ruth's decision had been accepted, if not respected, by an embarrassed and obviously furious Ethel, who made it clear that while Ruth was a Braithwaite she was only so in law, and this act of weakness was proof, should any proof be required, that her blood was inferior to pure Braithwaite blood.

Publicly I'd defended Ruth. After all she was the provider of our children's education, such an important role, but though I felt disloyal even entertaining such thoughts I had speculated privately whether this decision to resign had been prompted by my accidental seizing of her role as chief FAG spokesperson. I'd not seen her in ages. In the end I dismissed such thoughts as petty and small-minded.

Ann chirped up again. 'Marvellous. You'll raise a packet for us, Mandy. I know it.'

'Perhaps we could use the extra cash to do more for the families?' I said.

It was getting harder and harder. Benefits had been slashed by the DHSS months ago, savings had run out. My children were hungry all the time, and they weren't the only ones. We were cold and getting sick.

'Oh, I don't know. There's so little in pot,' Ann said.

'But I'm going to raise shed loads of money, you said.' I could hardly believe it was me, standing up to Ann Landers, with Ethel standing next to her. It was impossible to read anything into Ethel's expression. If she was with me, or against. 'I already have,' I added.

'You've not done it single-handed, Mandy Walker,' Ann spluttered.

'She didn't mean that, you bloody fool.'

We turned to Ethel, both gobsmacked. Me because I couldn't believe she was defending me, and Ann because Ethel had been so rude to her.

Ethel continued unabashed. 'Christmas isn't so very far away, no one's got bugger all money, there'll be few presents for kids, least we can do is give them a decent party. Get one of lads to dress up as Santa. We can brew our own beer . . .' Ethel was getting carried away. But they were great ideas and I was enthusiastic.

'If we go round a few more places while in London we could raise enough to give kiddies a little gift. Brilliant idea, Ethel. Brilliant,' I said. Ethel merely turned the corners of her mouth downwards and nodded; she didn't need mine or anyone else's approval, but there was joy in her eyes.

'We'll do silent collection,' she said, pursing her lips; her red lipstick had seeped into the deep lines fanning her mouth.

I shook my head; I didn't know what she meant.

'Heard about it from another group. None of that few coppers nonsense. They're loaded down south. Notes in bucket only. We'll be minted,' Ethel said, running a hand over her hair; she'd had a new perm recently.

'Let's not get carried away,' Ann said. 'We still have small problem of space. We can't feed everyone here.' The way she said 'small' made it clear she considered it anything but a small problem.

'We'll use Institute in Fenley, as kids is used to it.' Ethel's hands had made their way back to her hips, signalling that the conversation was as good as over. 'Your man can arrange it,' she finished, tipping her head at Ann. She picked up the sopping wet tea towel and tossed it into the nearby dirties bucket. Ann had no option but to agree and bobbed out of the kitchen, in that peckerty manner of hers.

'Mean old bitch,' Ethel snorted.

'She's not got kids, doesn't understand what it's like to see them go without. Funds are blimmin' low too.' I looked at the kitchen clock. 'Speaking of which, I've got to fly. Bus is leaving in five minutes.' I tore off my apron and went to fetch my coat. Ethel called after me.

'That were a good shift. Thank you.'

I stopped and stared at her; she'd never thanked me before. 'Thanks,' I stammered, unsure how to respond.

'Skedaddle. You'll miss that bus,' she said.

CHAPTER 18

The bus took ages again, another diversion, and it was gone half past six when I got to Mum's. The lights were out. I hammered on the front door though it was obvious there was no one home. She must have taken them back to mine so I pelted down the hill. As I skittered past the school I noticed there was a light on in one of the upstairs classrooms – Ruth's – and it crossed my mind that she worked too hard. My legs were like blancmange by the time I pushed the key into the front door and I was so famished I could have eaten the kitchen table.

As soon as I came into the hall I knew something wasn't right; it was so still, the air leaden. Our house was never that quiet. I walked into the kitchen to find Doug sitting at the table with Mark and Johnnie who were pushing shredded wheat around their bowls. Doug pushed himself out of his chair as I entered.

'Doreen didn't know what else to do,' he said.

I shook my head, uncomprehending. 'Where's Becky? David?'

'With your mum. She didn't want to leave baby.

Boys and me, we've been alright, haven't we lads?' The boys nodded, mute. Doug pointed at their bowls and said, 'Thought they'd need something to eat. Couldn't find much, Mrs Walker. You must always ask. If you need help.' He was a good man. A miserable old bugger sometimes, but a decent man.

'Where are they?' The words came out as a whisper; my legs trembled and it wasn't hunger or the fast walk this time.

'Sit down, please.'

'Where are they, Doug?'

'David wasn't so good. Your mum and him and baby have gone to the hospital.'

'Hospital?' David had been coughing for weeks, but he wasn't really sick. I'd taken his temperature regularly. I desperately tried to recall the last time I'd taken it, the last time I'd asked him how he felt. I couldn't. 'What happened?' I asked, gripping the table edge.

Perhaps there's been an accident.

But deep inside I knew that there hadn't been. That cough hadn't shifted; I'd ignored it for too long. I should have been more vigilant. The hairs on my arms stood on end.

'He was hot, right hot. Your mum stripped him right down, wet rags, but we couldn't get lad to cool down. I phoned for ambulance when it looked like he might fit.'

'Might fit?' The words came out as a scream. 'Get your coats, boys.' They scurried down from the table and raced to the hall. I picked up their bowls, desperate to be doing something, anything. I threw them on the side. Milk slopped over the edges and into the stainless steel gullies of the draining board. What a bloody waste, I wanted to scream, you think we've got enough to be chucking food in bin? My hands shook. 'Why didn't anyone call the kitchen?' I asked, as Doug helped Johnnie on with his anorak. I stood by, useless. 'I should have been told.'

'Your mum said that you were needed, vital like. That there was nothing you could do that she couldn't. Not to worry you.'

'I'm his mother.' My breathing was shallow. 'What the bloody hell were you all thinking?' My voice had risen to a reedy, high-pitched shriek; I sounded hysterical. I needed to get a grip. I closed my eyes, took a deep breath and as calmly as I could asked Doug if I might use his telephone to call a taxi.

'Of course, lass. Sit still, I'll do it. I'll be back in a jiffy.' And with that he was gone, eager to get away from my rage, guilt and fear.

All three of us were sitting in the back of the mini-cab before I wondered where Rob was. He wasn't on picket duty this evening; he should have been back around the same time as me, if not before. Had I misunderstood, or got the days wrong? It was a possibility. Perhaps there'd been some kind of an emergency, or someone else had let the union down at the last minute? We were

231

both so busy, wrapped up in our own schedules, little time for each other, or the kids. God, the poor little mites. We'd let them down. I'd let them down. My stomach turned over and I felt like retching, but I forced myself to hold it together. The cabbie would throw us out at the first sign of anyone being sick.

The journey seemed to go on for ever and a day. The cabbie drove like an OAP out for a Sunday jaunt; the sort of driver Rob used to holler at in the days when we could afford a car with room for us all. The boys were silent until we reached the outskirts of the town when they pointed out of the windows at all sorts of exotic places: late night shops, Indian take-aways, the greyhound track that I'd gone to with Rob only weeks before Mark had been born. I'd won ten quid after a salmon-coloured dog called Ginger ran in second.

Outside the hospital the meter on the cab read seven pounds forty. I didn't have anywhere near that amount in my purse, but went through the charade of opening it up and looking. My giro was due to arrive the following day.

'Clock's still ticking, love,' the driver muttered.

I ushered the boys outside onto the pavement and leaned in towards the driver's window. 'I've not got enough. I'm so sorry, in the rush to get here I forgot to pick up tenner on the side board. I'll drop it round to offices tomorrow. Give me your number and I'll make sure it gets to you.'

Without looking at me the driver started to curse.

I continued to grovel, promising to get the money to him, all the while thinking that I needed to get off the pavement and into the hospital. Without warning he pushed open the door, nearly knocking me over and stepped out of the cab; I wanted to run. He brought his face right close to mine, so close I could see the blackheads on his nose. 'Miner's wife, aren't you?' I nodded, hoping he was softening, knowing deep inside he wasn't. 'Dinosaurs, the lot of you. Good riddance to bad rubbish. Mrs T, she's got the right idea.' His hatred was so powerful, so real, it felt like something I could touch, like something sitting on his shoulder. He jabbed a finger at my face and hissed, 'I know where you live.' Then he climbed back into the car and slammed the door.

Shaking, I watched him pull away then yelled, 'You sad bastard! Bet you cart scab scum into pits! Hope you rot in hell, you miserable, miserable bastard!' I stuck two fingers up at him, with both hands, and Johnnie followed suit, enjoying the opportunity to be obscene without reproach. Tears stumbled down Mark's cheeks.

The brakes lights came on; the cab screeched to a standstill. I grabbed the boys' arms and yelled, 'Leg it!' We ran across the forecourt and into the hospital reception without looking back.

In a private room off a long corridor of a closed ward David lay on his back, fast asleep, a tube snaking from his wrist to a bag of colourless liquid dangling from a wheeled trolley. A see-through mask covered his little face and a monitor bleeped above his head. He looked small and peaceful and more beautiful than ever. I burst into noisy tears, quickly followed by Mark who'd never stopped sobbing. Johnnie climbed onto Mum's lap and sucked his thumb.

'What did doctors say?' I asked, wiping the tears away with the back of my hand before stroking David's forehead.

'Pneumonia. A severe lung infection. Few more days and it could have turned into pleurisy. He's been lucky,' Mum replied.

I continued to stroke his forehead. 'He's not been lucky, Mum. I should have known things weren't right. Oh, little man, can you ever forgive your great stupid mum?'

He opened his eyes, slowly, like a mole emerging from his tunnel, and through more tears I smiled down at him. 'Hello, chum.'

I forgot to be angry with Mum for not calling me; I was grateful David was alive, being cared for.

It wasn't long before a doctor pitched up and filled me in on what was up with David, what they were doing for him, how long he'd be in here. Most of it went right over my head. The doctor made it clear there were too many people in the room, it wasn't good for David or other patients on the ward. 'There are some very sick children here, Mrs Walker, we have to be vigilant about infection. You are welcome to stay, we can fix up a bed, but everyone else must leave. Two guests at a time, during visitors hours only. I'm sorry. And do not worry, we will have this young man back on his feet in no time.' His teeth gleamed white against the chocolate brown of his smooth cheeks. He looked so young, maybe only a handful of years older than me.

'Will you make sure Rob is told?' I said, as Mum gathered up the children, 'I've no idea where he is. But he'd want to know as soon as.'

'I'll stop at yours. Best they're in their own beds,' she said.

'Mum?' She stopped in the doorway and turned.

'Once he's back on his feet and we're back to normal I'll be stopping at home more. There'll be no more of this FAG stuff. The kids need me.'

She looked tired. I noticed dark circles under her eyes, the lines across her forehead, a glint of grey at her crown. She smiled and said, 'They're not the only ones, love.' And then they were gone.

The room was well heated; I was warmer than I'd been in weeks. I slumped in the low armchair next to the bed, suddenly exhausted, hand in hand with David, the steady bleeping of the monitor a comfort.

In the middle of the night another doctor came in and checked on David, and though I tried I couldn't get back to sleep. In the morning a nurse brought me breakfast, the first meal I'd had in over twenty-four hours, and insisted that I go outside for a breath of fresh air. When I returned less than ten minutes later Rob was at David's side.

'You look like shit.' Given that he'd barely looked at me, I was surprised he noticed.

'What do you expect? I've been at his side all night.'

'Mand, I'm so sorry. I've been worried sick.'

I took hold of his hand. It felt softer than I'd ever felt it. 'He's going to be fine. Three days, maybe four and he'll be out of here. Mind you, food's not bad and it's like Jamaica in here. Wouldn't mind staying a while longer meself.' I smiled.

'Doctor's a Paki.'

'Wrong side of the world. He's from the West Indies. Besides, they're not all foreign, and it's Pakistani. Paki is offensive.'

'Only joking. Cool your boots.'

Six months ago Rob's casual racism wouldn't have bothered me so much; I might not have even noticed, but now, I bristled. I'd seen the posters, read the leaflets in the students' unions and women's groups.

I leaned into him and he slung an arm over my shoulder. 'Sorry.' Nestling my head against his chest I breathed in his smell. Something was different. At first I wondered if he was using a new aftershave. He'd always been a Brut man; his mother bought it for him without fail every Christmas. But it wasn't that. It was the smell of his shirt, a floral smell, as if he'd used a fabric softener or something. I meant to ask, but then David woke up and all was forgotten.

'Daddy!'

'Hey up, soldier. Been in wars?'

Rob scooped him up, drawing him into his chest. I slipped my arm round Rob's waist. This was no time for fretting about small stuff; my boys needed me.

CHAPTER 19

'What the hell are you doing?' Rob stomped across the yard towards the lawn.

'What's it look like?'

'Have you gone mad, you stupid mare? What'll we eat off?' he shouted above the sound of splintering wood.

I stood upright and looked over at him. He sucked on the cigarette hanging from his mouth, pulled it away and picked a string of tobacco from his top lip.

'We've got laps, haven't we? What use is a table when there's nowt to put on it?' I said. The fold-out lips of the table were already off. I turned it on its side, picked up the saw and began to attack a leg. 'You never liked it anyway.'

'Mum gave it to us, as a wedding present.' He sounded pathetic, like a sulking child who'd given away a neglected toy and seeing another enjoy it, regretted the decision and wanted it back. 'What'll I tell her?'

'The truth? That it's freezing and we've nothing to burn. They're threatening to switch leccy off. Burnt magazines and old hutch yesterday. This'll keep us going a while.' The guinea pigs Penny and Frank had gnawed their way through the wood to freedom a couple of months earlier, fed up of the poor food and freezing conditions at our house. Just like everyone else.

'There's still plenty of coal on muckstack.'

'Says who?' The saw jammed. I rattled it.

'Mates.'

I tugged the saw free, turned the table over, and came at the leg from the other side. I held the saw handle with both hands.

'What? Those down pub? How'd they know, never get off their backsides.' A chunk of pine fell to the hard grass. My shoulders ached. 'It's getting more and more dangerous.'

'Not if you're careful. Got to be worth a go?'

I threw the saw to the ground. 'Get the kids, we'll have a family outing.'

'I've a meeting.'

'Typical.' I pushed past him and into the house. My breath formed clouds of steam in the kitchen air as I shouted for the kids to get their coats. They were already wearing them.

Although we'd not seen much rain that autumn, the spoil was wet and sludgy, like a rancid sponge mix, shifting beneath my feet as I made my way further up the heap. In my leaking wellies my toes were unable to feel, let alone grip, and I slid backwards again and again, falling to my knees, my hands grabbing at the filthy pit waste. With only a few lumps of coal stuffed in my bag I staggered back down. At the bottom Mark was sitting with Becky on carrier bags – their only protection against the rising damp. David and Johnnie scrabbled in the dirt nearby. Our bucket wasn't even half full; after two hours we'd collected enough fuel to feed a fire for an evening. Maximum. And our clothes were so dirty that it'd cost a fortune to get them clean. Not to mention the cost of heating the water for the bath. I'd taken to sending the older lads swimming with Mum at the flash sports centre in a nearby town to save on bath water. I ran one bath a week. Becky and Johnnie went in together, followed by me, then Rob when he was around, which seemed to be less and less, though it could have been that I noticed his absence more since I was tied to the home again.

There was so much time to plug; the days were long and hard. And it had only been two weeks since David had been discharged from hospital. I wondered how I ever managed to fill the time before I started working with the action group and the kitchen and the fundraising and all that. Perhaps I baked all day, did the housework, the shopping. Nowadays there was precious little money for shopping, the food parcels when they came were like gold dust, and vacuuming and ironing and cooking all used up energy we couldn't afford. There was no money for luxuries like cake baking. Occasionally, and when I was so bored I wanted to cry, I brushed the carpets with a broom, much to Johnnie's and Becky's amusement.

I wiped the coal dust from my knees, noticing my chapped and cracked knuckles, and told the children that I'd have one more go and then we were off.

'Enough's enough,' I said, pulling my bobble hat further down over my ears.

'I like it here,' Johnnie said, face smudged with dust, nose cherry red.

'You would,' said Mark.

'I'm coming up,' piped David.

'You are not. Collect down here. We'll have a competition. Who gets more. Me or you.'

'What's prize?' he said.

'A kick up the bum.'

'Oh yeah!'

Laughing and rubbing my lower back, I surveyed the scene and wondered if the other gatherers were managing to smile despite the miserable conditions we found ourselves in. There must have been half a dozen clusters, mostly families, most of them on their hands and knees at the base of the muck-stack. I recognised some of them and remembered that we were all in this together. I felt comforted by the thought. As I stared I became aware of two figures striding across the field towards the spoil heap; the bearing of one was so familiar but I couldn't place it initially. I squinted into the setting sun. Ethel. Which meant the other figure must be Ann. They were heading my way. I put down the bucket.

Ethel wore a camel coat – pure wool I'd have said, it was probably new in the 1960s – and a red silk scarf tied round her head like the queen. A metal clasp handbag hung across a bent arm. Ann was similarly dressed; though two large curlers poked out from the front of her head scarf, like crocodile eyes. The children fell silent, even Becky. Ethel had that effect on everyone. I raised my arm in greeting.

Ethel didn't smile; she meant business, no mistaking. She held her left hand over her right, resting them on the bulge of her stomach. Ann spoke first. Gesturing to David she forced her face into the likeness of a smile and said, 'Little fella looks well, doesn't he, Ethel?'

Ignoring her, Ethel said, 'I'll not waste time. I'm sure you'd rather be making your way home, just like rest of us.'

I nodded.

'Thing is, we were wondering if you'll still be coming down to London to do talk to men at GLC. They're expecting you Wednesday, and we've all sorts of folk lined up. We've been onto Miners' offices and there are all manner of groups ready to meet, share ideas and what-not. Some of lads are going down too, collecting in different parts of city. My Dan's heading up fundraising for union now; he's clever, brains and brawn, and he's full of good ideas.'

'I'm sure he is,' I said.

'It's a vital time for us; public support is wavering,

Thatcher's rags are turning people against us and collections are dropping off.' Her voice rose higher and higher as she spoke. It was rare for Ethel to talk for so long; she was a woman of few words, one who used silence as a form of intimidation. A slight raising of an eyebrow, a narrowing of her left eye was usually enough to get what she wanted.

At the mention of the capital my heart fluttered; I'd been looking forward to the trip, at the chance to meet new people, see new sights again. Johnnie pulled at my jacket, wrapped his skinny arms round my thighs. Guilt quashed my eagerness to go. I glanced down at Johnnie and then at David, Mark, and Becky.

Ethel took a deep breath, her chest rising, like a bird pluming her feathers, ready to fight. I thought she might think I was using a weapon from her arsenal, that of remaining quiet, forcing the opposition to show their hand. But my silence wasn't a deliberate tactic; I was torn. I wanted to go, but I couldn't break a promise. Not to my kids.

Ethel spoke again, addressing the children this time. 'Are you having fun here, children?'

Ever the good boy, wanting to please his mum, Mark nodded. David stared, mouth tight, but Johnnie piped up, 'It's boring.'

Little traitor, said he liked it while back.

'I'll bet it is, lad. I'll bet it is. Would you like your Aunty Ethel to fetch you some proper coal, like? Save you scrimping here?'

Johnnie looked confused by the use of the word 'aunty'. Not half as daft as he looked, he knew full well that Ethel was no aunty, but he also knew what proper coal meant: a fire, no collecting twigs from the woods, or coal dust from muck-stacks. He jumped to his feet and yelled, 'Yes! Yes!'

'Where'll you get it from?' David said, hands on hips.

Ethel tapped the side of her nose. 'Ways and means, lad.' Turning to me, she added, 'One good turn and all that.'

I bit my lip. God, how I wanted to go to London. And coal! Real coal. 'I made them a promise.'

'Kids are resilient.'

'And what about Rob?'

'Leave that useless lump to me.' She waved a finger in Ann's direction. 'Ann, give these kids a humbug.'

I'd not seen Dan since that night on the moor when he'd accused me of having a big mouth. Ruth sent a handmade card signed by all David's classmates along with a box of chocolates to the hospital, with a note to me and Rob from her and Dan wishing us all the best, saying that they were 'praying for little David'. I thought it was overblown; he had pneumonia, not cancer, and it was 1984 not 1884. She made it sound like he was about to peg it. I said as much to Rob. I was tired and miserable, having had only a couple of hours' sleep for the second night running. 'And

244

I had no idea she was religious. I bet Dan's not. None of Braithwaites have set foot in church for generations!'

'What would you know about Dan Braithwaite?'

'Nothing.'

'Then shut it. You know nothing about their business.' Rob said.

'Everyone knows that. Vince had a run in with last but one vicar. Ethel's dad nearly burnt church down.'

'That were a rumour.'

'And how come you're defending them? Thought you hated them?'

'I do.' And with that he'd swanned out of the room, muttering something about needing to fetch the kids from his mum's. She'd been looking after them for all of a couple of hours. Thank God for my mum, we'd have been right stuck without her help. Then I felt bad because there I was thanking a god I didn't believe in and slagging off Ruth for saying she was going to pray for David.

There was a sentence scratched in a different ink on the note. At the bottom, a P.S. From Dan. Saying that he hoped I was taking good care of myself as well as David, and 'sorry for everything that's happened.' Was he talking about David or the row we'd had? I wasn't sure, but that line cheered me up no end when I read it again later. It was definitely a make-up line. I hated falling out with people and the argument with Dan had unsettled me more than most. We were going to London together.

Three of us travelled down the M1 in a tatty VW camper van: Roger, who I'd met at the Notting Hill Carnival, me, and Dan. And although I was stuck in the middle of the two men for the better part of five hours Dan and I managed barely a dozen words to each other. I tried to make conversation, but he seemed distracted, uninterested in what I had to say. Admittedly most of it was trivial, and Roger talked ten to the dozen so it was difficult to get a word in edgeways, and after a while I gave up and pretended to sleep. Dan and I were like strangers.

Given that I couldn't sleep in the van with the men overnight, alternative accommodation had been found. I didn't know a soul in London; I didn't know anyone outside of Fenley, but Ruth's university friend, Jane, had offered a bed – 'insisted', Ethel said. The men turfed me out of the van with my small suitcase before heading off towards Hammersmith and the river. Easy to park the van up for the night, without getting a ticket and being harassed to move on by the police, according to Roger, who claimed to be something of an expert in these matters having spent time in the city on more than seven occasions since the strike began.

I'd asked if Dan wanted to say hello to Jane, only to be told that he hardly knew the woman; she was Ruth's friend, not his. They left me on the pavement outside, staring into the empty front room. The light was on and they didn't have nets. 'No shame, these London types,' Roger had commented, as if leaving your curtains open was a crime. I waited until the van turned the corner before walking up the tiled pathway to the wide front door with its stained glass windows. I pressed on the intercom button until a robotic-sounding voice barked, 'Yes?' The voice, male, didn't sound like he was expecting anyone. My stomach flipped; perhaps they'd forgotten.

'Graeme?'

'Yes.'

'It's Mandy Walker. Ruth's friend.' I felt like a fool, standing there shouting into a box on a wall. I glanced around to check that no one was watching.

'Oh God, yes. Hello. Hello. Welcome. Come in. Give the door a good shove. It's a bugger for jamming.' He sounded friendly now; he had the trace of an accent. He wasn't from the south, I was sure of it, but I noticed how inoffensive 'bugger' sounded when he said it. Not like swearing at all.

Apologetic that Jane wasn't there to greet me – an impromptu staff meeting had been called – he took my case through to the bedroom, scurried around the living room, brushing imaginary crumbs from the settee, plumping the cushions before offering me a seat. I didn't want to sit down, I'd been on my backside all day, but didn't know what else to do. I perched on the edge. Standing before me in corduroy trousers, checked shirt, and an off-white apron, he clapped his hands together and asked if I'd like a cup of something.

'I can tell you're a teacher,' I said.

His brows furrowed. 'Really?'

'English teacher at my old school used to clap his hands together like that before starting a lesson. Wake us all up.' There was a beat or two of silence. Me and my big mouth. I'd managed to ignore his question and insult him. Then a deep guffaw filled the room.

'It'd take more than a clap to wake those I try to teach. An exploding Bunsen burner more like!' he laughed.

I remembered he was a chemistry teacher and pointing to the apron I said, 'Are you doing an experiment now?'

'Good Lord, no. I'm cooking supper. My turn on the rota tonight. Hope you like quiche Lorraine.'

I'd never tasted quiche Lorraine, so merely nodded.

'Ruth tells us you're something of a chef yourself.'

'I wouldn't say that exactly. I cook a few meals for pickets and the families, that's all.'

'Nothing "that's all" about it. It's marvellous what you're doing. All of you. We have so much respect for you. Showing Thatcher what's what, socialism's alive and well, thank you very much. Now, Mandy, will you please excuse me. Otherwise the quiche will spoil and Jane'll have my guts for garters. Make yourself at home.'

'I could help you in the kitchen,' I said, feeling uneasy about sitting around doing nothing while he rushed about making tea.

'That'd be fantastic. You can teach me some tricks of the trade. My pastry's very hit and miss.'

He wasn't what I expected, Graeme. He had that confidence that the university types I'd met over the past months had. That sense of ease with themselves and the world. A sense of entitlement. But he wasn't arrogant, and he was self-effacing and modest. He talked to me as if we'd known each other for years rather than having met only a few minutes ago. As I crumbled the butter into the flour I watched him scrubbing the potatoes, preparing them for the oven. It was such a strange sight: a man at the sink, in a pinny, no less. I tried to imagine Rob doing the same thing.

By the time we heard Jane pushing the key in the lock, the food was almost done and conversation had turned to family and background. He was the son of a bus driver and dinner lady from Buckley in north Wales. A clever lad, he'd got lots of O levels and teachers encouraged him to study for A levels and apply to university. 'My mam was clever, you see, but she never had the opportunities I had. She wanted better for me,' he said.

Just like Dad. A clever man wanting more for himself and me.

'Not that there's anything wrong with driving a

bus. It's about choice. And opportunity. Everyone has the right to fulfil their potential.'

'My dad used to say that.'

'Then he's a wise man. Glass of vino?' he said, lifting a bottle of Blue Nun.

I didn't tell him Dad was dead.

We ate at a table which folded out from the kitchen wall. Quiche (looked like a flan to me), baked potatoes, a green salad, water in a jug on the table, alongside the wine.

'Graeme! This quiche is amazing. Best yet,' Jane said, helping herself to another slice.

'Much as I'd like to, I can't take the credit. The pastry's Mandy's, and that's the difference. Beautiful, isn't it? Just perfect,' Graeme said.

I beamed with pride and took another sip of the wine. I was light-headed already, unused to alcohol, and drinking too quickly to quell my nerves. Jane wasn't at all as I'd imagined her from Ruth's description, but she had quite a presence. Small and stick-insect thin, with tightly curled ginger hair, she wore a knee-length Laura Ashley dress in a floral print. Pinned to her breast was a selection of badges: Rock Against Racism, CND, Che Guevara, Reclaim the Night, *Spare Rib*. There was no sign of the glasses Ruth had made fun of.

'Cooking's not your only talent, though, is it? You're a formidable speaker, according to Ruth's mother-in-law,' Jane said.

Bashful, I could only shrug. My mind drifted to

the conversation between Jane and Ethel; I couldn't imagine it, and, not for the first time, I wondered why Ruth hadn't made the call herself. I heard my name and snapped back into the present.

'Could I persuade you to find time to come and speak to my sixth-formers while you're here? We're studying Lawrence and we could weave in some political education alongside an insight into a mining community. Naughty, I know, but the head need never know.'

Flattered, I smiled. 'Ever so nice of you to ask, but it depends when. There's my children, see.'

'You've a husband at home, haven't you?' she said, tucking into yet another slice of flan. I wondered if she had worms.

'Well, yes, but he's busy. What with picket duty—'

'You're busy too, aren't you?' she said, eyes boring into me. For a moment I thought she could read my thoughts and blushed to think of her listening to the excuses stuttering around my head.

Graeme came to my rescue. 'Leave the poor woman alone.'

'Do you have any idea how patronising that sounds? Honestly, you think you're a new man, but you've a long way to go. Ignore that comment please, Mandy.' She shook her head, like one might at a child, and I wanted to say that I thought she was being pretty patronising now too, but I didn't.

Graeme placed his hand over Jane's. 'Centuries of patriarchy can't be undone in decade or so. The battle's only just begun. I'm on your side, don't forget.'

Her eyes softened as he spoke and I saw the love and respect between the two of them, and a kind of envy pricked at my heart. They kissed and I stared at the empty glass in my hand, wanting to disappear. To allow them this moment of intimacy in private.

There was a clap of hands and Graeme said, 'I'll clear up and be off. I'll see you two later.' My heart sank. I had nothing in common with Jane.

Jane asked if I'd like to go to the pub – the same one I went to with Ruth. The only decent one in the area, according to Jane, but I was tired from the journey and the wine. While Jane made a phone call, I wandered into the living room and flicked through a magazine I'd picked up from the coffee table. Glossy and full of pictures of expensive clothes, it was very different from the weeklies I'd treated myself to before the strike. It spoke about smashing the glass ceiling (whatever that was), and how to have multiple orgasms. Reading through the orgasm article I wondered if I'd ever experienced one. The feelings roused in me during sex with Rob were nothing like those described. It wasn't that I didn't enjoy it, I did, but I blushed to read some of the ideas the author suggested women demand of their partners.

When Jane came into the room I threw the magazine down. She was holding another bottle of wine in one hand and two glasses in the other.

'May I join you? Or do you want some time to yourself? The bedroom's all yours; there's a TV in there too.'

I shook my head; I couldn't take their bedroom. But Jane was insistent. I would need the personal space; I was here on important business.

'I've been looking at them with my sixth-formers,' she said, tipping her head at the magazine by my side. 'On the one hand they sell an idea of equality, on the other they brainwash us into thinking that the only way to happiness and success is to look like that,' she flicked a fragile wrist at the cover model, 'be a superstar in the kitchen and an athlete in the bedroom. No wonder we're all so messed up.'

I laughed. Partly because I knew she was right and partly from a nervousness that she was going to talk sexual politics all night. 'Let's get pissed,' she added, slamming the bottle on the table. 'I had a shit day at school.'

For such a small woman her capacity for alcohol was impressive; she held it well, unlike me. The alcohol freed me from my usual constraints of social awkwardness with strangers and self-consciousness, and my nosiness ran wild. The conversation turned to Ruth, and Dan. In a way this was natural. After all, Ruth was the connection. She told me stories of their student days, the parties and gigs, the marches they took part in.

'So Ruth was always interested in politics and that?' I said.

'Not really. I think she enjoyed being part of the gang, didn't want to miss out on anything.' There was no malice in Jane's voice. 'All that had to change when she met Dan, of course. Being an army man. If I'm honest I think she was relieved. And we were in our final year.'

Noticing again her CND badge I asked if it was difficult for her when her best friend took up with a squaddie. 'I'm not a pacifist. How is Dan these days?' she said. I detected a hint of pity in her tone.

'OK. I don't know him all that well. But he seems happy enough.' Even as I said the words I realised it was a lie. Dan was one of the saddest people I'd ever met.

'I'm glad. It must have been so hard for him. And then having to go back. That was the last thing he wanted. And Ruth. It was hard on them both.'

Hard for him? What was so hard about being a hero? The questions burnt at my throat. 'Did they have to come back to Fenley?' I said at last.

'Didn't have much of a choice, did they? Things are on the up down here, but jobs are still hard to come by, especially for those without skills. And then Ethel mentioned the vacancy at the local school and it seemed there was no choice. That's certainly the way Ruth presented it. I'm so glad it's worked out for them though.'

And I wondered how, exactly, it had worked out for them. Ruth had married a soldier with prospects, and now she was married to a miner, a striking miner who was more than likely going to lose his job. Maybe not this year, maybe not next. But in ten years' time would there be a deep pit in Fenley? For the first time I admitted that although I believed we would win this battle – how could I carry on without believing this – deep inside I knew that the war was lost. Thatcher was no ordinary Tory, no ordinary woman. She and MacGregor had finished off the steel industry and coal was next on their list. What was to become of us? Me, Rob, Dan, the children?

I cried myself to sleep that night, pushing my face into the pillow so that my sobs wouldn't be heard by my hosts. My lovely, caring middle-class hosts who had no idea how it felt to be cast aside like a worn out rag. Written off. Stuck.

CHAPTER 20

I woke with a renewed sense of purpose, sure that the previous evening's gloomy thoughts were the result of too much booze. After showering I stared into the dressing table mirror and thought about helping myself to a dab or two of the expensive-looking face creams – Estee Lauder no less – before admitting that a good night's sleep and a vat of tea would work more wonders than any amount of fancy moisturiser. I smiled.

You're wrong, Mandy Walker. We will win. We bloomin' will. We've never lost yet.

Water dripped from my hair, soaking my T-shirt. Picking up my hairbrush and a blow dryer borrowed from Jane I began the attack, pulling the brush away from my scalp, holding it taut, and running the dryer over and over my strained locks, torturing them into a semblance of style. It wouldn't last, but I wanted it to be straight for the meeting. It was a well-known fact that no man took a woman with unruly hair seriously. In the autumn a Greenham woman had told me that out of control, naturally wavy hair suggested wantonness, a quality most men were afraid of. She'd meant it as a compliment; she'd ordered me to relish and enjoy my 'natural, unrestrained feminine power', but I erred on the side of caution. I needed to be taken seriously. I emptied almost half a can of hairspray into the air, almost choking and blinding myself in the process.

In the kitchen I studied the scraps on which I'd written the speech to be delivered later that morning. Jane offered good advice: bullet points on cards – index box cards, easier to hold and use than A4 sheets of paper – a glass of water to keep my mouth well lubricated, look people in the eye as I talk, address the whole room, sweep my gaze from left to right periodically. My stomach churned regardless.

'You look tired. Feeling alright?' Dan said, as I clambered into the van, struggling in my slim-fitting skirt. I was terrified of laddering my tights; no spare pair.

'Too much wine, that's all,' I said, surprised he noticed.

'Then serves you bloody right!' quipped Roger as he crunched the gear stick into first and kangaroo leaped from the kerb almost colliding with a red Audi Quattro.

'Southerners!' Roger yelled, shaking a fist. 'Look where you're going.' The driver responded with a raised middle finger before speeding away through an amber light. 'Good mind to report him,' Roger said.

'If you don't feel sick now, you will soon,' Dan said, winking at me. The conspiratorial nature of the gesture felt good, like we'd made up, were friends again.

The traffic was terrifying: horns honked, engines revved; the noise deafening; cyclists weaved in and out of cars and buses, and pedestrians trotted into the road, eyes fixed determinedly ahead. The moment we got going, Roger had to slam on the brakes to avoid another jay walker. We crawled through west London and into the centre, where I finally relaxed and took in the sights. Attractions I'd missed because Ruth and I had travelled underground. Everything felt familiar and strange: Big Ben, the Houses of Parliament, the wide, dirty river; I'd seen them all on the telly but in life everything felt larger, louder, more vital. It was exhilarating, to feel part of something so exciting and dynamic.

Outside City Hall we were ushered to a reserved parking space and, feeling like royalty, we made our way into the building, almost strutting, heads high. The feeling soon altered. At Reception our bags were searched and the men were frisked. 'Security,' said an unapologetic official. Thatcher was Falklands War-popular again after the bombing in Brighton. I shivered, daunted by the tasks that lay ahead. The immediate one: the delivery of a speech to the GLC; and the greater one: winning the strike. Taking my nervousness as a sign of guilt the security guard called a female colleague and I was promptly frisked too.

The suggestion that I was an enemy of the state no longer hurt, but that I could be suspected of terrorism offended me more than I'd have thought possible. I kept my dignity, nose poked at the ceiling while this stranger ran her hands up and down the contours of my body. I hoped she wasn't going to attempt to run her fingers through my hair – it was as stiff as a motorbike helmet. She touched the top of my 'do' lightly, rubbing her fingers against each other afterwards, as if contaminated. In a way, she was. That spray was toxic.

The heavy doors to the council chamber opened. A surge of adrenaline rushed through my veins as I regarded the sea of suits sitting in the wooden panel-clad room. I paused, resisting the urge to turn around and run out. I felt a hand on my shoulder and glanced over, half expecting it to be Dan, offering support and reassurance. It was Roger. Next to him stood a grey-haired man, whispering that he would introduce me once the current speaker had finished.

The applause began before I'd reached the podium. A steady clap rose to a crescendo of cheers, stamping of feet and whistles. I looked out at the mass of faces and raised my hand. Silence descended. I coughed and looked down at my notes. The letters were blurred and incomprehensible. I looked again at the men before me, wetted my lips, and lifted the cards, hand trembling.

'I can't read the words written here. The words I spent hours and hours putting together, trying to make sure they said what I wanted them to say. To be honest, I'm not sure they achieved that anyway, so perhaps it's for the best.' At this point I tore the cards in half and threw the pieces into the air and watched them tumbling down like oversized confetti. 'I'll not talk to you about the picketing, the way the police treat us like we're scum, the soup kitchens, or the marches and the demos. No doubt you've heard all that before. If you'll listen, I'll tell you about my home town, Fenley Down, and what it were like growing up there, with a miner for a father, and friends who were all connected in one way or the other with pits. About the community and its way of life and how all that will go. And if that is to be our future, I'll ask you to think long and hard about what will replace it. What will be lost. For ever.'

I burbled on, my cheeks growing hotter, but those grey faces were rapt. There was no coughing or shuffling in seats. The only thing I heard other than the sound of my own voice was the jangling of keys and wallets as Dan and Roger made their way through the throngs with their red buckets covered in stickers.

Afterwards, I bent down to collect the rubbish strewn on the floor at my feet, only to be told not to worry, that someone else would clear up. No one had ever cleared up after me before. The buckets were awash with notes and outside the chamber Roger slapped me so hard on the back I almost fell over.

'By the bloody 'eck, full of surprises, you is,' he said, stuffing the notes into a canvas money bag. 'Keep this safe. Robbing gits round here. Now let's get some dinner. I'm famished.' He waltzed off.

Dan lingered, watching Roger moving towards the exit.

'Was it alright?' I asked, suddenly unsure.

'Brilliant. You made me proud to be a miner, to be a miner's son.'

'And that's good, is it?'

'I was always ashamed. Didn't seem good enough, not for—'

'Will you two get a bloody move on,' Roger shouted, and we raced to the door. I never did get to hear who thought being a miner wasn't good enough. Dan. Ruth. Vince. Ethel.

'I know of a brilliant place to get dinner,' Dan said, holding the door for me. 'We'll leave van here and take tube to Soho.'

'Soho? Full of sex shops ain't it? Dirty place,' Roger said, rubbing his hands together, as if they were cold. 'What are we waiting for!'

I raised my eyebrows and he added, 'Sorry, Mrs Walker.'

'No need to apologise. I'm interested as it happens. Never seen anything like that. New experiences and all,' I replied.

Both Roger and Dan looked embarrassed; they didn't have a clue what to say, and I enjoyed the feeling that I'd wrong-footed them, surprised them.

But we didn't see any sex shops before we got the café. At least I didn't, and if Roger, or Dan, saw any then they kept their mouths shut. From the tube Dan lead us through a maze of streets littered with rubbish and vegetable skins. Red and gold painted restaurants, supermarkets, and chemists selling herbs lined the way. Skewered poultry turned in shop windows, dripping fat, oozing a pungent aroma. It smelt nothing like the take-away in our neighbouring town; the air choked with the aroma.

Within minutes the streets opened up and we left the Chinese quarter, stepping into the Italian section. Red, green, and white dominated the colour schemes of the restaurants and pizzerias, the smell alone almost satiating my hunger. Almost, it was nearly two o'clock.

Dan paused outside a poky café and checked the menu displayed on the wall.

'This is it. Great grub and dirt cheap, for London. Came here with Ruth and some of her university friends a while back. Wasn't sure I'd find it again.' He looked pleased with himself.

Roger looked unsure. 'Is it all foreign? I don't like that pasta stuff, all slimy.'

'Have you ever tried it?' I sounded as if I was talking to a child, but I longed to try a genuine Italian pizza or a plate of pasta. Roger pursed his lips. 'Look. You like cheese and tomato sandwiches, yes?' I knew he did; he'd scoffed loads on the journey down. 'Well, pizza is like that. 'Cept the bread's warm. Come on, don't be such a nancy.'

Roger was cornered, it had begun to rain, the wind had picked up, so in we went.

Dimly lit and crowded there were no free tables in sight. My heart sank; we'd have to go elsewhere. We hovered by the till.

'No worries, there's a downstairs,' whispered Dan, and sure enough a dark-haired waiter led us down some narrow steps and into a windowless room. Formica-topped tables were laid with stainless steel cutlery and the sort of glasses you get in fish and chip shops stood in haphazard formation. Almost all the tables were occupied. In a way I was disappointed with the place; I'd wanted something different, swankier, but at under three quid for a main course what had I expected?

We stared at the menu for ages. I'd never seen such a selection of pastas and sauces, pizzas and toppings; we didn't look at the meat and fish dishes as these were way out of our price range. In heavily accented English the waiter took us through the dishes of the day, and assuming none of us had a clue took us through the more straightforward dishes available: spaghetti bolognese, margherita pizza, carbonara.

'I'd like a Rigatoni Alfredo, please,' I said, 'and sorry if I pronounced it all wrong.'

'It was perfecto, Signorina.' And he winked before jotting down the rest of the order and sailing off.

Roger and Dan gawped at me.

'What?' I said.

'They're very forward, the Italians. Mind he sees your ring next time. Pour water would you, love?' Roger nodded at the jug the waiter had placed on the table along with a basket of bread. 'And if pizza's like a butty, why do they put bread on table as well? No wonder they're all fat.'

I glanced around. No one was fat; customers, staff. I poured the drinks. Dan still stared. 'What?' I repeated.

'Where did you try alfredo?' he said.

Roger was shovelling bread into his face.

'I've not. First time. Can't wait.'

He raised his eyebrows. I continued. 'I've read books. Looking for recipes. Not that kitchen can afford the ingredients, assuming we could get hold of them half the time. Never seen parmesan in Spar, have you?'

'Parm what?' He smiled.

'See, not as daft as I look,' I said.

'Never said you were.'

'By the 'eck, this bread's blooming gorgeous.' Roger held out the basket and when neither Dan nor I responded he shook it and said, 'Go on, try a bit. You won't regret it.'

'Not worried about getting fat, Roger?' I said. He put the basket down.

The meal was delicious – everything I'd hoped for and some – no doubt helped by the fact that I'd not had to prepare it and there was no washing up to be done.

Outside we lingered on the pavement, watching people go about their business, collars upturned, heads down against the wind and rain, before we headed down the street towards the underground station. We'd only walked a couple of hundred yards when Dan stopped abruptly and turned. Behind him was a window full of exquisite cakes. Strawberries dipped in white chocolate sat on top of twirls of cream, white butter icing had been stroked into spikes and dusted with nibbed almonds, exotic fruits circled a marbled sponge walled with dark chocolate. My mouth fizzed as I speculated on the ingredients, the taste.

'Patisserie Valerie. Best cakes in all London,' Dan said. 'Maybe the world.'

I laughed at that and, peering beyond the cakes into the café, said, 'Looks pricey.'

'My treat.'

'I'm stuffed,' Roger said, rubbing his extended belly.

'What do you say?' Dan said, looking at me. Turning to Roger he added, 'We'll meet you later at . . . where is it tonight? Swiss Cottage?'

'Euston. I'll get van and banners.' Roger pointed at me and said, 'You only live once, Mrs Walker, and I know how you like your cakes.'

I sucked in my stomach and, unable to resist, nodded. Roger tipped his finger to his forehead, and said his goodbyes.

Dan led me into the café; it was warm and woody. The scent of freshly ground coffee beans stung my nostrils, the low hum of conversation and the noisy hissing of the coffee machine drifted on the air. It was another world, and I loved it. The café was based on the continental model, Dan told me, as a tall, angular waitress led us to a round table. The waitress took our coats: Dan's heavy, black donkey jacket, my cheap mac. He held out the chair for me, and I wondered if this was something he learned in the army. He was all set to be an officer, or so I'd been told, and I imagined him practising small acts of chivalry in the barracks, unaware that opportunities to use them would be limited in civilian life. The waitress returned with a pencil and pad and we ordered cappuccinos before drooling over a trolley laden with sump-tuous treats. I wanted to try them all.

'Let's order something different from each other and then we get to try two,' Dan said, excited, like a boy. Dan had a sweet tooth. I remembered the way he'd savoured my sponge at the spring fair, hunched over it, unlike his usual rigid, straight-backed stance. He opted for a slice of black forest gâteau while I dithered, my eyes darting from pastry to cake and back again. Seeking guidance, I wafted my hand at a moist sponge that might have been a carrot cake, though I wasn't sure. 'What's this?'

'Passion cake,' said the waitress, 'great choice.'

'Right. Thanks,' I said, retreating into my chair. I caught sight of myself in one of the many mirrors; the rain had played havoc with my hair, all trace of the morning's work gone. I touched it, flattening it in an attempt to restrain my curls. It had grown long; past my shoulders for the first time since I was in infant school. I'd had neither time nor money to visit a hairdresser.

'Why do you do that?' Dan asked.

'What?' I said, pretending I didn't know what he meant.

'Push your hair down.'

'Not a clue; I'm fighting a losing battle with this mop whatever I do!'

'You've lovely hair. Like a pre-Raphaelite model.'

I'd no idea what he was talking about and told myself he was probably taking the mick. I scrambled for a witty reply but no words came. Instead, I threw a lock of hair over my shoulder in an extravagant gesture, picked up a fork, holding it as if it were a trident, and turned my face in profile, staring resolutely ahead. Regal, like Britannia on the back of the copper coins when I was a kid. Dan laughed and I relaxed. A little.

We made small talk until our order arrived; the cups steaming with frothy milk sprinkled with chocolate, the cakes reclining on the plates, side on, their moist interiors exposed. Cherries and cream and seeds oozed onto the napkins, the heady smell of the liqueur that laced the sponge of Dan's gâteau rising between us. Dan pierced a fruit with his fork; purple-red juice spilt across the white ceramic, and he admired it a moment before slipping it into his mouth. His back curved as he gave in to the pleasure of the cake. His eyes were downcast and I watched as he chewed.

'Real cherries. Soaked in brandy,' he said, thrusting his fork back into the sponge. It won't be brandy, I thought. Kirsch, more like, though I didn't correct him. I noticed a smattering of freckles across his nose and cheeks, the lily-white skin of the back of his hands. They were as they'd appeared in the photograph on the sideboard, when he wore a uniform and a shaved head.

I took a mouthful of the passion cake, the texture soft, melting on my tongue, expecting my senses to be heightened. But I tasted little.

Perhaps I'm just too full to enjoy it. That's what comes of being plain greedy.

I took another mouthful, eyes down, unable to look at Dan as we ate. I could feel the metal of the fork cold on my lips. I gulped the cake down. I looked up. There was a dab of cream in the corner of Dan's mouth; I wanted to tell him, but for some stupid reason, couldn't. I wiped the corner of my own mouth, hoping he would mirror me. He did not, and took another forkful instead. I watched his mouth moving, his lips rolling and swelling as he chewed, slowly, silently; the light catching a glint of stubble on his chin and upper lip. He was usually so clean shaven. I wondered what it might be like to kiss those generous lips, if the bristles would tickle. The only man I'd ever kissed was Rob. How many girls had Rob kissed before me? Loads. I wondered if he'd kissed anyone since.

'Not enjoying that,' he said, awaking me from my daydream, flicking his fork towards my plate. Glad he couldn't read my mind, I nodded vigorously.

He's Ruth's feller for god's sake!

The cream remained in the corner of his mouth; I pointed to the corner of my lips and mouthed 'here'. He smiled and wiped it away, licking his finger with the tip of a crimson tongue.

'Gorgeous. Absolutely gorgeous,' he said, looking straight at me. 'You want some?' He pushed his plate towards the middle of the table; I pushed mine forward. The plates sat beside each other.

'But you've not had half of this,' he said.

Brushing a crumb from the tablecloth I dismissed his concern for equality, conscious of my thighs, breasts, stomach, the enormous lunch we'd devoured and said, 'It's enough.'

'Never.'

'It is. I'm ever so full after all that pasta.'

'Go on!'

I reached over, pulling the plate, and stabbed at the cake.

'That's more like it. I like a woman who enjoys her food.'

'That's me,' I mumbled, covering my mouth with my hand as I spoke and thinking about Ruth, and how I rarely saw her eat. Perhaps he was saying that to make me feel OK about stuffing my face.

'How is Ruth?' I asked, dropping two lumps of

sugar into my coffee, stirring hard, the spoon noisy against the cup.

Dan straightened his back; he looked very serious. 'Fine. Though I might have asked you that. You see more of her than I do. And what with her job and all that . . .'

I didn't know how to respond. She was no longer a FAG member; according to Ethel she was extremely busy at the school, but she'd not popped round to mine in weeks and weeks. I'd called a few times, but she wasn't at home. I'd pushed a note through the door a while back and she'd telephoned Mum, ours had been cut off months ago, to say that it would be lovely to get together, but somehow it had never happened.

After what seemed like ages, I made light of it and said, 'It's a job and a half, that one. Looking after all them kids.'

'Not the same as your own though, is it? Now *that* must be hard work. How'd you manage?'

'Much the same as your mum I'd imagine.' I tried to picture Ethel as a young woman, cuddling one of her seven boys as babies. 'You'll have children, you and Ruth?' He looked surprised at my boldness. 'Sorry, that were very personal.'

His right hand gripped the edge of the table. 'No. It's alright; I don't mind you asking. Everyone else does. All the bloody time.' His lips tightened as he spoke and a faint colour rose on his cheek. 'Sorry for swearing.'

'Oh, it's not like I'm not used to it,' I snorted,

glad the conversation was drifting away from sensitive areas. I took another bite of gâteau, the syrupy kirsch awakening my sense of taste. I was diving into the third mouthful when Dan broke the silence.

'Ruth can't fall.'

I was about to say how sorry I was, but he continued, the words tripping over each other as they fell from his lips, his eyes stuck on the table-cloth. 'We tried and tried, for ages, when we first came back to Fenley. Seemed no reason not to start straight away, what with family being around to help, me . . . you know. But it never happened, and then the strike, and Ruth's breadwinner now . . .'

In my head I was doing the maths, working out that they couldn't have been trying for all that long if they'd only started when they returned to the village, but there was plenty of time; they were young and healthy. 'Sometimes it takes a little longer. Have you had a chat with doctor?'

'There's nothing wrong with us.'

My throat tightened; I'd offended him and began to say that wasn't what I meant when he blurted, 'Ruth was pregnant, when we got wed.'

'Oh. I'm so sorry.'

We were silent a moment or two, and then I reached over and put my hand across his. It was as soft as I'd expected. 'But this means that you can do it; you'll do it again. You're going to be a lovely dad, I know it.'

'We'll need to spend more—' He stopped abruptly,

pulled his hand from under mine. 'Thank you. I appreciate your kindness.' He sounded very formal, clipped, all warmth had disappeared; I removed my hands from the table. He looked at my plate and said, 'You not going to finish that?'

'I've had enough,' I said, and took a sip of my coffee. It was too sweet and almost cold. He finished the cake and we said no more about babies.

CHAPTER 21

It was almost dark when we emerged from the patisserie. Rain continued to fall and the temperature had dropped; the wind nipped under my coat, my collar, and I tightened my belt in a knot. The buckle was broken. The streets glittered with the promise of adventure, but despite this, and the highs of the early part of the day, I felt tired and flat. Ready for my bed; my own bed. I didn't want to have to make polite conversation with Jane and Graeme, lovely as they were. And there was collecting to do before that.

On the underground, commuters' damp clothing steamed on the underground as the train rattled and shook its way north. The conversation in the café echoed round my head. I couldn't imagine what it must be like to really want, to crave, children and not be able to have them. Why hadn't Ruth shared her fears, and disappointment, with me? We were best friends, weren't we? Friends share everything. I admitted it must have been hard for her at first. I was visibly pregnant for the fourth time within weeks of our reunion. And I'd not planned any of mine. And she knew this. They just happened; they came along as part of the course of life, and I couldn't imagine what my life would be without them. The driver braked suddenly and I was thrown into Dan's chest. He caught me by the elbows and pushed me upright again, away from him, as if he'd been scalded. I could sense his regret at sharing their secret.

At Swiss Cottage Roger was waiting for us, stall set up, buckets ready, van parked a short distance away. Most people were friendly enough, but pickings were slim. No one wanted to stop in the awful weather and fiddle with purses and wallets for loose change for a cause that had lost its potency months ago. Christmas was fast approaching; there was famine in Africa; no one was interested in a bunch of miners, reminders of a bygone era. A new epoch was almost upon us: materialism, services, leisure. It was evident, here in the capital. I was relieved when after only an hour and a bit Roger announced that we might as well pack up for the night.

'No need to flog it. Plenty raised from this morning.'

As we fought our way back to Hammersmith I got to thinking about my friendship with Ruth again. She was the only close friend I'd had, so in truth I had little to compare our relationship with. But I watched the telly, read a few books, magazines. I knew what girlfriends were supposed to do. I questioned how close we were. Yes, we talked about clothes and make-up and our men a bit, but we didn't share our secrets, doubts, innermost hopes and fears. We didn't even see each other all that often. Get-togethers had centred on FAG meetings and events, community gatherings like the Institute Christmas dinner-dance and school occasions like sports day (a disaster for Mark and David). What had we in common, aside from our husbands' jobs and our shared history?

'Not far now. Soon have you back in the dry,' Roger interrupted my thoughts. The heating in the van was faulty.

As girls we spent almost every waking moment together. We sat next to each other in primary school, Ruth telling me how to write my stories, colour my pictures. In the playground I carried her on my back, her: the little princess; me: her trusty steed. As teenagers she plucked my eyebrows and tonged my hair, singeing my left ear in the process. I shared dinner money when she spent all hers on eye-shadow and lip gloss from the chemist on the corner of Russell Street. I sat outside the changing rooms in Chelsea Girl for hours while she paraded one fashionable outfit after another. She lent me her favourite platform shoes for the school disco, painted my nails. The object of my affections, a lad in the year above, didn't look at me twice, and when the slow dance came on at the end of the evening Ruth and I danced together like an old married couple.

During long, hot summers we lay in the long grass beyond the rec planning our futures; the

275

same patch of earth where I conceived my first child a few years later. 'When I die I'll have a plaque set into the ground: In remembrance of Mandy Walker, who loved to lie in this spot,' I'd said.

'I shall be a dancer and travel the world. Marry someone rich, drive a sports car, and live in a mansion,' Ruth'd sighed, nibbling on a piece of grass.

'What about me?' I'd asked.

'Oh, you can come too.'

She'd confided in me then, why not now? I was hurt, and questioning if I even had the right to be. Were we friends, really?

The van screeched to a halt. We were outside Jane's flat. I peeled my damp thighs from the seat and said my goodbyes.

'No boozing tonight, missy. Early start,' Roger said as I clambered onto the pavement, stiff and aching.

'Message received and understood.'

Dan said nothing, but turned his head.

'Over and out,' I said, reaching for my handbag.

Dan went to touch my hand, then stopped himself. 'Thanks for coming to Patisserie Valerie. It was good to talk with you.'

'Thanks for paying,' I said, smiling, and understanding that he meant me to keep our conversation to myself. 'See you both in the morning. Ta-ra.' I bolted up the path.

★   ★   ★

276

Graeme was cooking when Jane ushered me in.

'I bet you're starving,' he said, waving with a wooden spoon.

'Well . . .'

'Coq au vin with creamy mash potatoes, mange tout on the side.'

'Sounds delicious.'

Jane grabbed a chair and levered down the table. 'Take a seat. Your feet must be killing. Now, what can I get you to drink? I've opened some Californian white. De-licous.'

It struck me that the middle-classes put it away as greedily as the rest of us, only difference being that aside from the occasional visit to a wine bar, they did it in the confines of their own home, whereas the likes of Rob and the Braithwaites did it down the pub, and it was the brawling on the streets afterwards that led to the bad reputation. 'No, thanks, I won't. Need to be with-it for the kids tomorrow.'

'Cup of tea, then?' Graeme said, as Jane topped up a glass that looked as if it was made for brandy rather than wine.

'Marvellous.'

'You must have missed them?' Jane said.

'Not half. But it's been a good trip. Be the last for a while I'd say.'

'With any luck there'll be a settlement before Christmas,' Graeme said, coughing amid a rush of steam as he opened the oven door.

'I wouldn't bank on it, sweetheart. The old bitch

is as stubborn as the proverbial mule,' Jane said, taking another swig.

'Let's not talk like that. You'll depress Mandy here.'

'Don't worry about me. I think you're right, Jane. I can't see an end to it . . . we've got to hang on in there. Front her out.' I stared at my tea, watching the bubbles swirling round and round, slowing, settling. 'What are your plans for Christmas?' I said, wanting to change the subject. I was fed up of politics.

Graeme guffawed and emptied a pan of mange tout into a colander. 'I'm off up to Buckley to see my folks; Jane's going to Surrey to see hers. We'll hook up again for New Year. Supper's up.'

'You don't spend it together?' I said, astonished.

'No. Pathetic, isn't it? We're twenty-four and twenty-five respectively; we live together; a mortgage no less, and yet neither of us feels that we can say to our parents that we'd like to spend Christmas together, in our own home. Now if we were married . . .' Graeme said, putting the plates in front of us. 'Jane. You've not even laid the table.'

I leaped up and took some cutlery from the draining board. Ignoring Graeme's reprimand, Jane said, 'Marriage is an institute I wholeheartedly disapprove of. It enslaves women and nothing will persuade me it can be of any benefit to me. Not even the prospect of not having to sit through yet another arse-achingly boring Christmas lunch with my mother and her God-awful toyboy.' She sounded slightly pissed.

Placing the salt and pepper cellars down and taking his knife and fork, Graeme laughed. 'I agree that marriage is an out-dated institution – sorry, Mandy – and I'm not suggesting it. Heaven forbid! There must be easier ways of getting out of spending the holidays with your mother–'

'Dysentery, perhaps?' Jane said, and I laughed out loud. I could imagine how awful it must be. The regulation Sunday afternoon visits to Rob's mum and dad were painful enough without having to spend holidays with them, let alone Christmas.

'Kids'd do it,' I said. 'This looks delicious, Graeme. Thank you.' The smell of the chicken and herbs had sparked an appetite after all. 'You'd have to spend it here if you had kids of your own.'

Jane stood up. 'That reminds me. We've something for you. I'll get the bag.'

'Eat first,' Graeme said.

'I'll forget if I don't do now. Only take a minute,' she said, disappearing out of the kitchen. 'She'll not eat it now. It'll go cold.'

Sure enough, Jane was gone ages. Mine and Graeme's plates were almost empty by the time she returned.

'For your little ones. For Christmas. Some chocolates and a toy each,' she said, placing a Woolworth's bag on the side.

I was so touched by their kindness I couldn't

speak at first. My throat contracted. 'You shouldn't have . . .'

'We wanted to. There's a little something for you too. Caught you going through the book shelf. Jane thinks you'll enjoy it. But no opening them till Christmas day,' Graeme said, wagging a finger at me.

'Yes, sir. Will you give me the cane if I disobey?' I said.

'No one canes anymore.' Jane said dismissively and sat back down as Graeme cleared away the dishes.

'You're right, of course. Kids would solve our problem,' Graeme said to me.

'Do you want them?' I said, unsure if a feminist like Jane agreed with having children.

She surprised me with a definite, 'We want children. It's one of the reasons why I chose to teach.'

'The holidays?' I offered.

'Not entirely. More that women seem to be punished less when they become mothers than in other professions,' she said.

'You don't see too many headmistresses, mind you,' I said.

'You're not wrong there. Sharp as a razor, this one,' Graeme said, looking at Jane and nodding towards me.

'Plenty of deputies, though,' Jane added.

I nodded. 'Reckon you're bright enough to go right to the top.'

She laughed. 'Reckon you are too.'

Her faith in me, a relative stranger, was refreshing and moving. Like a friend. I thought about Ruth again, and what Dan had told me. I wasn't meant to talk about it, but Dan didn't know these people, what difference would it make?

'Is that why Ruth became a teacher too? Because of kids? She's ambitious, like you.'

'Is she?' Graeme said, returning to the table and pouring himself a glass of a wine. He threw the empty bottle into the bin.

'Well, she definitely wants kids,' I said.

'What now?' Jane said. 'Graeme, grab another bottle from the fridge. Has she said something?'

'Errrmmm . . .' I didn't know what to say. Whether to lie, or break Dan's confidence. But it wouldn't be breaking a confidence to say that they wanted children soon. Only that they were finding it difficult to conceive. 'Dan. He said.'

'Oh.' Jane looked uncomfortable; she lowered her eyes. 'I'm pretty sure she wouldn't want children just yet. When we were training she often spoke about waiting till she was in her thirties to have kids.'

I jumped in. 'Said same to me.'

Jane continued as if I'd not spoken. 'But before that, she wanted to have fun, develop her career, travel, she said.'

'How could she travel as a teacher?' I said, wondering if I was being stupid.

'Of course, she had to do her NQT year, but it's such a transferable skill . . . what with Dan being in the army, the chances of him rising up the ranks, joining the regimental band, maybe even making it to officer,' Graeme said.

Jane snorted. 'Wives don't travel with the bands. Typical Ruth.' She laughed affectionately. 'Didn't do her research.'

None of it made sense. Dan had said they married because she was pregnant, but then she lost the baby. They'd been trying ever since. I was bursting to ask about Ruth's pregnancy; she must have fallen while she was in her final year at college, but couldn't see a way to enquire without looking like a gossip-mongering fishwife.

All sense of weariness had vanished so when Jane suggested we retire to the living room with the second bottle of wine I agreed readily. Graeme was off out to his regular pub-quiz night.

Much to my disappointment she asked if I wanted to watch television. 'I'm bushed. Expect you are too,' she said.

We watched the news, commenting idly on the various depressing items. There was no mention of the strike. She drank steadily, while I held onto my single glass.

'Do you think people can really change?' I ventured.

'Yes, I do.'

'Then maybe Ruth has.'

'Yeah. Maybe.'

'She was pregnant when she married.'

'She wasn't.'

282

'Sorry?' I nearly spilt my wine.

'She lost the baby before the wedding. Months before.'

'How dreadful. Poor Ruth.' Poor Dan too. Perhaps that's what Dan meant. She didn't have trouble conceiving; she had trouble holding onto her babies; she was bulimic. I wondered which had come first: the bulimia or the inability to carry to term. Did Dan know? Bulimics were masters at hiding their problem. 'She must have been in a terrible state.'

'She seemed OK. I mean, she cried a bit and all that. But she recovered pretty quickly.'

I couldn't believe what I was hearing. How could a so-called friend be so heartless? Ruth would have been devastated. 'She can't have been,' I said.

'She wasn't that far gone, apparently,' Jane leaned forward, conspiratorially, drunk. 'I'm not convinced there was any baby. Graeme thinks I'm being a total bitch. That Ruth wouldn't go that far. But I tell you, she wanted that man. She liked the glamour of the uniform, the lifestyle. She liked the idea of being a future officer's wife.' She sat back. 'And now, I've said too much. You think I'm a cow.'

I shook my head.

'I like Ruth. I really do. Perhaps it was a genuine mistake; her period was late; she told Dan; it would have been embarrassing to say she'd made a mistake. All I'm saying is – watch her.'

If Jane was right – and I couldn't believe she

was, there must be an explanation – how must Ruth have been feeling? Shattered dreams. She was a miner's wife. In a small town in the north of England, surrounded by mothers and their children. With a husband who desperately wanted kids.

Poor Ruth.

CHAPTER 22

'Are you sure there are enough crackers? One each, mind, I'll not have 'em sharing.' Ethel stood in the kitchen doorway, looking at the stack of boxes leaning up against the back wall. I understood her concern; it looked paltry, and in less than an hour we were expecting almost three hundred children under ten.

'Twenty-four to a box; thirteen boxes . . .' I scribbled on a scrap of paper, working it out for the third time. No way did I want to get it wrong. '. . . will cover us and leave a few spare.'

'Then let's get on with setting tables.'

Ann scurried out of the kitchen, leaving me to finish off the jam sandwiches. There were six of us cutting and chopping, arranging and garnishing; a team of twelve in total, all gathered to give the children one very special day in what was going to be a pretty miserable Christmas. Not all were members of FAG; they were wives and mothers, and Ruth.

I'd not seen her since my return from London, not to talk to at any rate. Naturally, she was there at the school concert, smiling across the hall, as

Mark pretended to sing in the back row, and David bashed at a large triangle, missing every single beat. The percussion section of the school orchestra was notorious for harbouring the village's most unmusical children, but David managed to stand out even amongst this tone deaf, rhythmless bunch. I might have imagined it, but Ruth's smiles and occasional waves had a ring of insincerity; they were over-enthusiastic. Like she was making up for something. Jane's warning came back to me.

Ethel appeared in the doorway again. 'Will you come and look at this.' It wasn't a question, more of an order. I walked towards her. As I stepped out of the kitchen and into the bar which over looked the main hall of the Institute she placed her left arm across my shoulders and swept her right arm in front of her, almost knocking over a couple of glasses of Britvic. 'What do you think?'

I gasped. The hall was barely recognisable; it looked magnificent: like an elves' grotto. Lights twinkled from the rafters, round the windows. Tinsel dangled from the ceiling and imitation snow dusted the windows, chair tops, and tree. Oh, the tree! It was beautiful. Floor to ceiling, and decorated with red, gold, and green baubles. On top the fairy's sequinned skirt caught the light, sending silver moonbeams across the air.

Ruth was standing by the tree, putting on the finishing touches. It was her imagination and flair that had transformed the place, and a box of decorations she'd borrowed from the school.

'It'll do,' I said to Ethel, before collapsing into a squeal. 'It's flipping great! Kids are going to go wild.'

'They'd better bloody not,' Ethel said, but smiled as she did so. 'Let's have a drink to celebrate.' She'd turned to a vodka optic and helped herself to a large measure. 'Pass us the cordial, will you?'

'Orange or lime?'

'Orange. Can't stand lime. Sets me teeth on edge.'

I wondered how cordial could have such an effect on dentures.

'What you having, ducks?' she said, taking a slurp. 'Champion.'

I shook my head. Someone fiddled with the stereo and the first bars of Slade's 'Merry Xmas Everybody' rang out. Ruth trotted over to where we stood, ribbons of tinsel clutched in one hand. 'I'm so glad you like it.'

Throwing my arms around her, I shouted, 'I love it,' ignoring the flinch of her shoulders as I did so. I took her empty hand. 'Remember how we danced to this at the school disco? You were in love with Dave what's-his-face!'

'I didn't fancy yours much,' she laughed.

'Who was that?' I screamed over the din.

'Noddy!' We both pulled a face and shrieked like teenagers. She threw one strand of golden tinsel round my neck; the other she draped over herself. Spirits souring, we danced round the tables as we laid a cracker beside each and every paper plate.

Once done we surveyed our handy work, enjoying the moment.

'Right. Best get back in the kitchen. They'll be here soon,' I said.

'What a shame they'll mess it all up. Can't be precious though.'

Ignoring her, I glanced down at my shabby shirt and old jeans. Perfect for work; not-so-perfect for a party. 'I'd best get something decent on,' I said.

I had a dress hanging on the back of the toilet door: two years old and only worn once, it'd been bought for the wedding of a distant cousin of Rob's. Mum had made a few alterations on her sewing machine, 'to make it more individual,' she'd said.

'Me too,' said Ruth. 'Let's get ready together. I'll do your make-up; it'll be just like old times!'

'So long as you don't still have that blue frosted shadow!' I said as we raced into the toilets.

When I emerged from the cubicle, Ruth was already at the mirror, mascara wand in hand. Seeing my reflection she stopped applying the mascara and spun on her heels.

'What do you think?' I said, brushing my hands over the rise of my full-skirted dress.

'Wow. It's very glamorous for a kid's party,' she said, adding, 'you look a-maz-ing!'

'Is it the bare shoulders? It had puff sleeves, but Mum cut them off, added the halter strap. I have a cardie,' I said, turning back to the cubicle to retrieve it.

'No. No. Your breasts are incredible. I'm jealous.'

I held my cardigan in my fist; I could throw it over my shoulders. 'The skirt? I could take the petticoats off?'

'I love them. Gives it a fifties feel. Honestly, you look dynamite.' She turned back to the mirror, shoved the brush back in the tube and out again and began reapplying mascara. Seconds later she swung round again. 'And your hair is beautiful. So much better long. You know people pay a small fortune to get their hair to look like yours.'

'People pay for this?' I laughed, though I knew they did.

'Yours is a million times better than any dodgy home perm.'

I was learning to love my hair, and I knew the dress suited me; I felt good in it, but feelings of guilt, like I'd deliberately tried to outdo Ruth, which I hadn't, swept over me. I'd had no idea what she planned to wear; it wasn't like when we were teenagers and regularly conferred over outfits for this and that social occasion. Ruth wore a loose jacket with padded shoulders, a T-shirt, and a short skirt with thick tights; she looked lovely, but was distinctly more casual than me.

I stepped towards the mirror. 'Make-up then?'

Ruth threw a hairband at me, and licking her finger and swiping it over her brows said, 'Right, think I'm done. Turn to face me.'

When she turned me back to the mirror I had the strongest feeling of *deja vu*. One of the reasons

I wore little make-up as an adult was the damaging effects of Ruth's make-overs during our teenage years. Armed with enough cosmetics to stock a small chemist thirteen-year-old Ruth was lavish in her application, and because the products had been bought for her, they did little for someone with entirely different colouring. Secretly, I'd thought the 'after' was considerably worse than the 'before', but, afraid of seeming ungrateful, I'd left her artwork untouched. Not this time; I was older and wiser. Thanking Ruth politely I fussed about, wasting time, until she gave up waiting for me.

The moment she was gone I grabbed squares of toilet paper and dabbed away at my face until there was barely a trace of purple blusher, metallic lipstick, and black eyeliner. And once it was all toned down, I was pleased with the results. Checking my watch I bombed back into the kitchen, relieved that I'd avoided Ruth on the way.

The squeals and shrieks of the children tore me from the kitchen. The hall was brimming with shiny faces, hand-knitted jumpers and wide-awake, delighted eyes. Outstretched hands clamoured for the balloons Ruth was giving out. I scanned their faces for my own brood. There they were, thumping and punching a balloon across the space. Rob stood in the doorway clutching Becky. I waved, but he didn't see me, which was odd because I was standing in his favourite place: the bar. He raised his hand and I raised mine again, then stopped. He wasn't greeting me; he wasn't even looking in my direction. He was waving at Ruth. I looked at her, standing in front of the tree; she was smiling at him, eyes gleaming, a shot of natural colour across her cheeks. She couldn't wave back, her hands were full, but her face said it all. I looked back at Rob, his expression familiar; it reminded me of the day he asked me to meet him down the rec; our first official date. Hopeful, filled with anticipation. I went cold.

Ethel appeared behind me, helping herself to another vodka. 'Can I tempt you now? Go on, love. You've earned it.'

'I will, thanks, Mrs Braithwaite.' My voice sounded so alien it was as if someone else had answered.

'Will you call me Ethel. God knows how many times I've told you. Now, what's your poison?'

'Anything.' I watched Rob. He was gazing at Ruth again, but then Becky kicked her legs – she probably wanted to get down and run about – catching him in the groin. He winced and as he turned to her, noticed me. He smiled and waved. 'I'll have whatever you're having,' I said to Ethel.

'Double vodka and orange it is!'

She offered the glass. I reached out and took a slug. The alcohol hit the back of my throat, I gasped, suppressed a cough and took another gulp.

'Steady on, girl. You've almost finished that,' Ethel said.

I had. I felt the effects instantly. I closed my

eyes, the image of Rob and Ruth's faces seared on my retina.

They were only being friendly.

I opened my eyes and felt dizzy; I clutched the bar, dropping my head and when I lifted it Rob was right in front of me.

'Pint of lager, Mand. Didn't know you were behind bar. Thought kitchen was your place.'

'It is.' I paused. He looked perplexed. 'But I can get you one,' I said, reaching for a glass beneath the counter, the smell of the slops tray pungent. It hadn't been cleaned from the night before.

'Put it on tab. You look right nice.'

I thanked him as I pushed the pot over the polished wood and watched as a third of a pint slipped down his throat. Ann's words about the flying pickets and needing support came back to me in a rush: 'So now that your Rob's back on board, will he be coming to Notts at the weekend?' I'd not been aware that he'd dropped off the board. Was it possible that he and Ruth . . . I stopped myself. It wasn't possible. When would they have had the opportunity? Her job, the kids. It was impossible.

That look, though.

Rob put the glass back on the bar without releasing his grasp, turned slightly, and surveyed the hall. I stared at the back of his head, his hair falling below his collar, the contrast between his blue-black hair and the white shirt acute. My mum had the kids most of the time, Ruth had stopped

FAG duties, she'd distanced herself from me, she was never in when I called round; I'd been away quite a bit, Manchester, Leeds, Liverpool, London. London. Dan and I had both been away. I felt sick.

Jane warned me.

'Mandy?'

I jumped. Ruth was staring at me. 'Time to get the food out.'

'Right. Yes,' I said, trying to control the wobble in my voice.

'What happened to your make-up?' Ruth said, before turning to Rob and adding, 'I made your lovely wife look even more beautiful earlier. Didn't you like it?' she said to me.

'No, no. It was lovely. Kitchen. It's boiling in there. Must have melted.' I walked away.

The kitchen was packed with women peeling cling film off silver trays before racing into the hall to feed the masses. I snatched two bowls of crisps and set about serving.

The afternoon passed in a blur. Ethel brought me another vodka. I drank without tasting it; I felt nothing as children pushed and pulled and snatched and grabbed at me. There was music and laughter and crying all around, though it was as if I was swimming under water, with everyone else at the surface. As the party drew to a close and Santa, aka Roger, dished out gifts donated by one of the unions to all the children, I sat down, bent legs tucked under my skirts, all prim and proper, on the far side of the hall, next to the fire exit. I needed to be within close proximity of an escape route.

Rob wavered across the room. 'Little ones are tired. I'll take 'em back. See you later.' He touched my shoulder with his hand, and I prayed he wasn't going to lean down and kiss me on the cheek like he sometimes did when he'd had a few too many jars.

I watched his tall figure grow smaller as he loped to the double doors and the way out; his shoulders curved over as if he had his hands permanently wedged in his pockets. He was the only man I'd known, and when the vicar had said, 'till death do you part' I'd said 'I will' and I'd meant it. I dropped my head and stared at my lap, the lush green of my dress sickening.

I saw a pair of boots, dried mud on the stitching between the soles and the uppers. I recognised them; I looked up. Dan. He'd arrived earlier, after the children had eaten, organised games with Ruth: musical chairs, musical statues, sleeping lions, the usual. I'd not had chance to say hello.

'You OK?'

'Yes,' I swallowed the word, a knot the size of a football rising up my throat. I took a deep breath, counted to five. I noticed the way Dan waited; sensing there was more, but he waited patiently, when so many others would push for an answer, push for more information, whether it was ready to be given or not. It wasn't just me; I noticed he afforded others the same respect, the same space. He didn't crowd. 'Tired, that's all,' I said.

'Would you like a lift home once you're done; I'm taking Mam, so it'd be no bother.'

'Thank you, that's very kind.'

Home. The last place I wanted to go; I didn't want to see Rob; I wasn't sure how I'd react. I didn't know what to do. 'But I'd like to walk, thanks all the same.'

'It was a great party. The kids had a ball.'

I stared into his steel-grey eyes. He was attractive, not in that poster boy way of Rob's, but handsome all the same. How could Ruth desire another, let alone her best friend's man? But hadn't I thought about what it might be like to kiss Dan? I'd not done anything though.

You're being ridiculous. It was just a look. Nothing.

'If you're sure,' he said.

'I am.' I forced a smile.

'Take care then.' He turned and walked away, back straight, shoulders square, and I watched, wondering if he'd turn round. He didn't.

CHAPTER 23

The effects of the vodka had worn off by the time I reached the turning into Mum's road, blisters were forming on my toes, making it difficult to walk with ease and I was cold. That morning Ethel had given me a lift to the Institute so I'd no coat, and my cardigan offered scant protection against a north-easterly wind. I considered abandoning my plan to walk on the moor and debated whether or not to call in on Mum instead. There'd be a fire, a cup of tea, and a biscuit, but there'd also be a torrent of questions and she knew me too well for me to disguise my feelings. I couldn't tell her. She'd go mad and all that ill-feeling about Rob would resurface; she'd bang on about how I should never have married him. I couldn't bear it. And who was to say she'd be in? She might be down The Boar's Head helping Dean out behind the bar, something she did more and more. I turned round.

I'd only gone a few paces when I heard the sound of a car engine behind me, growing louder. As it approached, the engine slowed and I speculated which house it would pull up in front of. I didn't know anyone well from this side of the village. I kept on walking, expecting to see the mystery car pull in front of me, but instead it drove alongside me for a few yards. My feet throbbed with every step; I could feel the top skin of the blisters tearing. At first, I figured that the driver must be looking for house numbers, an infrequent visitor who'd forgotten exactly where number forty-eight was perhaps. But as the car continued to trail me my pulse increased and I upped my pace, hobbling along in a pair of shoes I'd thought elegant and dainty only hours ago. I was planning to kick them off and leg it when the car pulled up ahead of me. It came to a standstill. The engine chugged, steam pouring out of the exhaust.

Still walking, I turned my head ninety degrees to catch a glimpse of my potential assailant – it would be useful for the police statement I reasoned – and almost crashed into a lamppost when I recognised the figure stretching over the passenger seat as Dan. I stopped dead: furious, embarrassed.

I slapped my chest. 'Christ almighty! You nearly gave me a heart attack.'

The door swung open.

'I'm sorry. I didn't mean to frighten you. You were moving so fast. You've no idea how difficult it is to wind down a window while driving and keep car straight.' He had the nerve to smile.

'No, I bloody haven't any idea. And I can't have been moving that fast in these chuffing shoes.'

'You were moving fast enough.'

'You're just bloody slow.'

'Car's a right old shed, but heater works.'

I struggled to find a retort.

'Will you get in? I'll take you home. You look cold,' he said.

I paused, considering his offer. My feet were on fire. I climbed in, slammed the door, kicked off my shoes, and sighed. He repeated how sorry he was and asked if I wanted to sling the jacket lying on the back seat over my shoulders. I shook my head.

'What are you doing round these parts anyway?' I said. It was the opposite end of town to Vince and Ethel's, and though it was possible to come past on route to his house it was certainly not the most direct way.

'Looking for you.'

His candour wrong-footed me. I shifted in my seat to face him. 'Why?' I said.

'You didn't seem right.'

'Where's Ruth?'

'She went to pub, The White Lion, with Ann and Jean and some of the others. Said you'd been asked.'

I didn't remember, but it was possible. The entire afternoon was a fuzz.

It was difficult to see him clearly in the dim glow of the street lamp. He was facing me, one hand on the wheel, the other resting on his lap, his wedding band clear. It was thick and flat and silver-grey, like his eyes, rather than the usual gold. Rob had never worn a ring; he was allergic to the metal, he'd said. I wondered if Dan suspected anything about Rob and Ruth.

'I thought you might go for a wander, on moor,' he continued. 'Might welcome a bit of company. Or a coat.'

I furrowed my brow; what did he mean 'coat'?

'Mam couldn't believe it when I told her you'd gone and you were walking. She had your clothes. Found them in toilets. Said you'd not got a coat and you'd catch your death. They're in boot.'

He'd not got a clue about Ruth, I was sure of it.

'Well, it's very nice of you. To go to all this bother.'

'What are friends for?'

'Are we friends?'

'I like to think so.'

'Oh.' I turned and reached for the seatbelt. Dan revved the engine, released the handbrake, and the car slipped away.

Perhaps Ruth and Rob are just friends? After all how does it look now: me and Dan, in his car?

We rumbled past the school towards town, bouncing up and down in Dan's old wreck. As we rattled along, the only car in sight, anxiety stole into my bones; I wasn't ready to go back; I needed more time. Seconds before the turning to our road I blurted, 'Can we drive a while? I don't want to go home yet.'

'Sure,' he said, and we sailed right by my street,

through town to the open road. He didn't ask why I didn't want to go home and I never said.

We'd been driving along country lanes for about fifteen minutes when Dan pulled into a layby. I wondered if he'd heard something in the engine, if we were about to break down.

'I love this spot. The view's incredible. Warm enough to get out and take a look?' he said.

'It's dark.'

He craned his neck and pointed through the windscreen. 'Full moon. Come on. Just for a minute.' He reached for the jacket and slung it at me.

I shrugged, and released my seat belt. It was agony pushing my feet back into those shoes.

Outside the air was sharp, but what struck me was the sound of the night: the rustling in the undergrowth, the screams of foxes, the wind whistling through bare branches. A cloud stole across the moon; dulling the light. Dan marched in front of the car and beckoned. I followed. The ground fell away, suddenly and steeply, he reached out his arm to halt me. We were at the edge of an abyss. The cloud drifted away and moonlight flooded a valley, a canopy of stars overhead.

'I love this view,' Dan said.

'There's the big dipper.' I pointed at the sky.

'It's what I missed most: the landscape. How it changes. Turn a corner and bosh. You've moved from moor to hills. What do you miss most?'

'Never been away. Not for long enough to miss it at any rate.'

'When you were in London then. What'd you miss? What do you think you'd miss?'

'My kids.'

'Other than the obvious.'

'The people. Places are nothing without people. They're what makes it. For better or worse.'

He laughed, and I detected a hint of bitterness. But he'd alluded to his time away, and his return, and I forgot about my aching feet and Rob and Ruth. 'What do you miss about the south?' I said.

'The anonymity.'

I didn't know what to say to that but I knew what he meant. In London, travelling on the underground, I'd had a powerful feeling that had taken me a long time to articulate: a sense that anything was possible there. I wasn't saddled with any reputation. No one knew Mandy Walker, the girl that was a bit hopeless after her dad died; the girl that got into trouble with the truant officer and the police for shoplifting in Woolies, Mandy the miner's wife, the mother. I was free to lose myself, to be reborn.

Dad was older than Mum by ten years and at eighteen he'd been called up for National Service. He'd spent time in Aden; he'd shown me photographs of the desert, him looking hot and uncomfortable in his uniform, stroking the nose of a camel so grumpy it would spit on a whim, covering those nearby in a thick, rancid spittle. He'd enjoyed the camaraderie of the army – made easier by the lack of actual fighting – and the travelling, the 'getting away' as he called it. 'It broadens the mind, Mandy, love. Broadens the mind. The next best thing to an education.' Sitting at the dining table, helping me with my geography homework, he'd looked into my eyes and said, 'You could do both: university in Oxford, Bristol, Exeter. A good degree and plenty of job offers. The world'd be your oyster.'

'But what about you and Mum and home?'

'You can always come back,' he'd said, placing his hand over mine, squeezing gently.

Dan broke my thoughts. 'Did you hear that?'

I'd heard nothing; I'd been caught up in memories. The desire to know more about Dan returned. Where he had been. 'What about the other exotic locations you've been to?'

He turned to me, confused.

I made myself clear: 'The Falklands?'

'Did you read the papers? See the pictures?'

I nodded. The cold bit at my legs, nose, fingers. 'Didn't look up to much. Not like my idea of South America.'

'Nor mine.'

I hoped he was about to talk more about his time there, what, specifically, he was awarded the medal for, why he left, when he lifted his hand to his ear and said, 'There it is again! Listen.'

'It's an owl. Owls. There's more than one. Out early tonight,' I said.

'What'd you call a group of them? Ruth tells me you were good on collective nouns, when you were a lass. That and stars.'

So Ruth talked about me; about our friendship. She valued it. I began to think that perhaps I'd over-reacted. What had I seen, in truth? A smile, a blush. Nothing more.

'A parliament. I've been looking them up again lately.'

'How peculiar,' he almost laughed.

'Not as funny as a rabble.'

'What's that one for?'

'Butterflies!'

He belly-laughed, and I joined in. It was funny; delicate, graceful creatures, it didn't fit. Before their transformation, maybe, but after?

'What about caterpillars?' he said.

'An army.'

He turned back to the view. I shivered and pulled his jacket round me further.

'I'd better get you home. Rob'll be worried.'

He drove faster on the way back, barely said a word, and I longed for the intimacy we'd shared outside, gazing over the valley.

He stopped a few doors away from the house; I saw Doug's curtains twitching. Nosy old devil. I held my shoes in my hand; the thought of forcing my battered feet into them again unbearable.

I held the door open. The icy pavement was a balm on my feet. 'Thanks for the lift.'

'You're welcome. If ever you need . . .'

'What?'

'Nothing. Merry Christmas, Mandy.'

'And you. Happy Christmas, I mean.'

I watched him turn the car around and waited until the red brake lights disappeared into the black, before realising that I still had his jacket on and that the bag of my scruffy clothes remained in the boot of his car.

CHAPTER 24

The digital clock radio read 03:07 before I fell asleep. My eyes were stinging, but I couldn't stop fretting about Dan's jacket and the bag of clothes in his boot. And the seconds when Rob and Ruth smiled at each other played over and over in my head. In the morning I woke with a scream: Johnnie had pressed his face right up against mine. Once he'd learned how to open our bedroom door without making a sound it became a common trick, one that made him howl with infectious laughter. So infectious I couldn't stay angry with him for long. But that morning I shouted at the poor lad with such ferocity he began to cry.

Nauseous with sleep deprivation, I threw on my dressing gown and headed downstairs. I resolved to call on Ruth as soon as possible. I couldn't have this hanging over me. And anyway, what was I fussing about? Dan had given me a lift; lent me a jacket. End of. She probably had nowhere near as suspicious a mind as me. Dan had no doubt told her to expect me. He might be at home himself; picketing had slowed right down for the Christmas break.

I made a batch of mince pies while the children wrestled in the front room. The pastry was yellowish – the margarine was a cheap blend – and great lumps of suet laced the mince, reminding me of the maggots the boys used to frighten the girls with down by the stream. I pricked the pie tops with a fork, forming a cross, and lamented the fact that I'd no spare egg for glazing. Instead I dusted them with icing sugar and when I laid them in the tissue-lined tin I was pleased with the result. They smelt gorgeous, but then mince pies always do.

There was a wreath of holly on Ruth's front door, the berries were red and fat, and tree lights shone in the window even though it wasn't dark outside. The sun was trying to force its way out from behind a cloud. It was just after eleven. There was no sign of the car, though it might have been parked in the garage. I was about to press the bell when the door flew open. I jumped.

'Didn't mean to frighten you!' Ruth said. She was skittish and jumpy. 'Saw you coming. Watched you walking up the close.' She was undressed, and her hair was lank and dull and looked as if it'd not seen a hairbrush in a good while.

I smiled, hoping that it would disguise my disappointment. If she'd been out, shopping perhaps, and Dan had been home alone, it would have made life a whole lot simpler.

'You were ever so slow, darling. Have you hurt your leg or something?'

I looked down at my wellies; they were the colour of the berries and the only thing I could bear to put on. 'Blisters. No plasters at home.'

'Oh, you poor love. And you walked all the way over here. Must be important!' She pulled a funny face and laughed again, high-pitched, nervy.

Has she always been patronising?

I admitted she had; I'd been blind, but I reined in my annoyance. I was on the defensive.

So Dan hadn't mentioned that I might call for my clothes, to return his jacket. 'But look at me. How rude. Come in.' She waved me forward. I stepped out of the wellington boots, and left them standing on the doorstep. Inside the hall carpet felt like velvet, the air warm and inviting. I couldn't tell if Dan was out or not. 'Shall I take your coat? Staying for a cup of tea? Or coffee?' Ruth's skin was paler than usual and there were dark circles round her eyes. She looked as if she had last night's make-up on. I found it difficult to look her in the eye.

'That'd be lovely. Nice to get out of the house. Kids are driving me mad; they're so excited.' I pulled out the tin and offered it.

'Shortbread. How lovely.' She drifted into the kitchen. I followed.

'It's mince pies, the tin's an old one, from last year.'

'Dan'll be pleased. More for him.'

I must have looked confused because she poured cold water into the coffee machine and added,

'I'm veggie now. Been reading all about the benefits of a meat-free diet.' I wondered if this accounted for her drawn cheeks and lacklustre complexion. 'Do you remember that woman we met in London? From Greenham Common? She got me onto it. I ordered a recipe book too. You can borrow it if you like? There are some simply fabulous dishes.' She pointed to a stack of books on the window ledge. I relaxed a little; everything was normal.

'That'd be great. I'd like to try more vegetarian food,' I said.

'More?' She rubbed her forehead. It was her turn to be puzzled.

'When I did that talk in Manchester, the students took me to a café by the union, all veggie it was. Vegan. That's no animal products at all. No eggs, no milk, no cheese, nothing. Well, I thought it couldn't be done; thought it'd be all beans and lettuce and other tasteless slop. But you know what, Ruth? It was fantastic. Carrot and carob cake. Chuffing marvellous. I had two pieces.' I was excited; it was good to share this. I'd brought some muesli home to try and had encouraged Rob to give it a go, but he'd dismissed it as 'rabbit food', unfit for human consumption. 'I wouldn't serve that shit up to a gerbil.' I didn't much like it either, but I didn't tell Rob that. I wasn't going to let it put me off trying other healthy stuff when we had the cash.

'Marvellous,' Ruth replied, though her tone suggested something different. 'I could do with a sugar fix now. I've got a raging hangover. My head feels like it's about to rip apart.'

'Sorry about the pies.'

'Don't be a ninny.' She reached into a cupboard. 'You'll have coffee?'

I nodded; I needed a shot of caffeine too.

'I'll put sugar in mine, and milk. What the hell! I'm not vegan, unlike your friends.'

'They're not my friends. Look, let me finish the coffee. I can work this machine out, I'm sure. You look terrible. Go and sit down, I'll bring it through. We don't need to stand on ceremony.'

While the filter machine coughed and spluttered, I gathered a tray, two mugs, poured sugar into a bowl and milk into a jug. The cupboards were almost bare and the fridge was empty bar half a pint of milk, a chunk of mouldy cheese, and a jar of mint jelly. The machine continued to spit out drips of brown liquid; I stared at the garden. It was neat and tidy, formal, with low lying bedding plants. It didn't have much in the way of personality. I decided I preferred our garden, with its ramshackle fence, sprawling rose bushes, patchy lawn, and out-of-control weeds. At least it looked lived-in, enjoyed.

When the coffee pot was over half full, fed up of waiting, I placed it on the tray. Another drop of liquid fell from the machine and hissed as it hit the hot plate; I flicked the off button and went through to the lounge.

Ruth was slouched on the settee; curled up in

her pink, fluffy dressing gown with matching slippers. She looked like a bundle of candy floss. The television was on, the volume turned down low. I poured the coffees and stirred in two heaped spoonfuls of brown sugar. Ruth sat up when I offered her the drink. She took a few sips, and so did I. I didn't like the coffee; I preferred instant. Camp was my favourite.

'You had a good time then?' I said.

'Too good!'

'You do look a bit worse for wear.'

She groaned and said, 'To put it mildly. I look like death.'

'Sexy in a rock-star-groupie, heroin-addict kind of way.'

She laughed. 'But not as sexy as you yesterday, you saucy little minx! Golly, the men's eyes were on stalks every time you leant over. Did you see Vince's face?' I shook my head; I'd noticed nothing. She chuckled, deep and throaty; it turned into a cough and she thumped her chest. 'God, I smoked so much too. I'm sure that's what's given me the hangover. Nothing to do with ten Malibus!'

I didn't realise Ruth smoked.

'You smoke much?' I asked.

'Hardly ever. Dan doesn't approve; the hypocrite!'

'He's right.' I thought of Dad and his cough; his waxy skin the colour of putty.

She heaved herself off the settee. 'What time is it? I really, really must get dressed. Have a shower.

Dan's going to be mad as hell when he gets back if I'm not. Look, Mand, I don't mean to be rude, but . . .'

'Don't worry. You go and sort yourself. I'll see myself out.' It struck me as odd that she called me 'Mand'. It was a new affectation. She'd always called me Mandy. Even when I went through a phase of wanting people to call me Amanda. I was twelve years old. No one did.

I couldn't tell if Dan had told her about our evening drive, about me forgetting my clothes. She'd talked as if she'd not seen him since last night. It was clear she'd got back late, drunk, and that he'd left earlier this morning. There was nothing for it, I had to ask, return the jacket.

I was about to open my mouth when Ruth stopped in the doorway and said, 'Did you call for anything in particular? You never said?'

In the hall, I took Dan's jacket from my carrier bag and explained that he'd given me a lift home. I didn't mention the jaunt to the valley.

She threw it on the coat stand. 'Oh, your clothes are probably still in the boot. He's gone shopping; I was supposed to be going with him, to get Christmas presents. He's going to be so cross with me.' Her voice had that edge of vulnerability we all get when we're sick, hung-over, emotionally fragile.

'Look, don't you worry. Go and spruce yourself up. I'll call again, and I'll clear up before I go. Make sure you have something to eat.'

'Oh, thank you. You're a brick. Don't know what I'd do without you sometimes.' She didn't look at me as she spoke. A flash of pink behind the bannisters and she was gone.

I returned the tray to the kitchen, swilled through the mugs. I'd pulled the front door shut when Dan rolled into the drive. My head was swimming and I'd not heard an engine, let alone recognised the sound.

He stepped out of the car. 'Hi.'

'Hi.'

We stood there, like we were super-glued to the ground.

'I like your wellies.'

'Style's my middle name.'

He shook his head.

'I brought your jacket back.'

He walked round the car and opened the boot. We peered in, our shoulders almost touching, his physical presence overwhelming. My hand brushed his as we rummaged amongst the Morrisons bags packed with food. The hairs on his fingers flickered in the light; I could see the curve of his ear in my peripheral vision, his delicate, almost non-existent lobe. I pulled back abruptly, banging my head. 'Ouch!'

'You OK?'

'Fine.' Though I wasn't; my skull throbbed. 'Ruth said you'd gone Christmas shopping. For presents. Not food.'

'She's up then?'

I nodded, hoping that she'd heard the car above the sound of the shower, was out and dry and throwing some clothes on. I didn't want him to find her undressed, to see her slender limbs and flat stomach.

'Couldn't face city and we need to eat. Here you go.' He handed me the bag.

'I explained that you gave me a lift.'

'Would you like a lift home now? Ruth can put shopping away. It's no bother.' He rubbed his foot on the ground, as if he were stubbing out a cigarette.

'Best not. Anyway, it's nice now. I'll enjoy the walk.' I felt strangely guilty; we were complicit in . . . what, exactly? Neither of us had lied, but nor had we told the whole truth. And what was the truth? He glanced up and we stared at each other. His face was expressionless and my stomach clenched. The coffee had made me feel sick, I reasoned, but my insides were melting.

'See you then. Enjoy your walk,' he said.

I turned and sauntered down the close, conscious of every step. I held my back straight and tried to picture what I looked like from behind. I wished I was in my green dress, with my hair freshly washed, teetering in uncomfortable shoes that made me feel as if I walked like a pop star, or an actress in a film.

CHAPTER 25

Christmas came and went. It wasn't as miserable as we'd expected – they didn't disconnect the leccy (my greatest fear) and we didn't miss out on the basics: a small bird, trimmings, pudding, cake, and a cheap bottle of scotch (Rob's greatest fear). I even made brandy snaps and babas for Christmas Eve. During Christmas dinner Mark reminded us of the starving children in Africa and I, for one, lost my appetite, so there were plenty of leftovers for Boxing Day.

A swap party at the Institute provided most of the children's gifts. Mark and David got almost-new bikes; Johnnie got a set of plastic animals, Hot Wheels cars, and *Star Wars* action figures; and though she was too young to understand Becky seemed delighted with her rag doll and tea set. The swap party was my idea.

'Bloody inspired, yet again. Is there no end to your talents,' Ethel had said.

Rob gave me a necklace; I gave him a lighter: a Zippo. Ann's husband had been trying to give up smoking for years and the donation of the lighter was another grand – ultimately doomed – gesture. The necklace was beautiful: a single pearl hanging from a delicate silver chain. 'It'll look alright with that green dress, Mand.' I was touched, though I found it hard to believe that Rob had chosen this himself. Was it guilt? It was very un-Rob. Past birthday and Christmas presents had included an electric whisk, a rake, and a deep fat fryer, and I'd been happy with most of them, though the rake came as an unwelcome surprise.

The days of the holiday passed in slow motion; I felt disengaged and rootless, stuck in the home, playing happy families. I'd shrugged off my suspicions about Ruth; Rob was so normal, I couldn't believe he was that good an actor, but we were distant from each other. In a polite, on our best behaviour kind of way. We were more like strangers than husband and wife, and I shuddered to think that we might end up like his parents: stuck in the same easy chairs, night after night, watching the same old tripe on the telly, tolerating each other, but with barely concealed disgust. Like sewer rats, living in shit, unaware there was a better life above ground.

Mum called round, but didn't stay long. She spent most of Christmas at The Boar's Head with Dean and seemed happy. Really happy. Our evenings were spent sitting in front of the telly. I played with the pearl on my necklace, worrying its hard, smooth surface between my thumb and index finger. I thought about Dan and Ruth and what they might have given each other. Sexy lingerie? Body oils? Aftershave or books?

The electricity board cut us off on New Year's Eve, at about four o'clock in the afternoon. We'd not long put a light on and had settled down to watch an episode of *'Allo, 'Allo* when we were plunged into a silent, grey murkiness. Rob jumped up from his chair and thumped the side of the telly as if it was being temperamental, but I knew straight away. He started swearing, Mark started crying, and I walked into the kitchen to get the candles I'd kept stored in the drawer since the first threatening letter had arrived almost five months ago.

Once there were candles dotted around, throwing off a soft, yellow glow, the children become squeaky-voiced excited at the prospect of an evening in near darkness. I remembered power cuts when I was a child; I was just like my children were: fed up and a little frightened at first; the power had gone part way through an episode of my favourite TV show, then thrilled by the strangeness of it all.

'Like camping,' said Mark.

'Let's tell ghost stories,' whispered David.

'There is something romantic about it,' I said, grinning over at Rob, squeezing his hand. A peace offering for unknown offences I wasn't even sure we'd committed.

'Won't be so sodding romantic when tea time comes,' he grunted, though he sniggered as he said it. We'd bought an electric cooker not long before the strike began.

'A cold buffet,' I said in a mock posh voice, and he smiled.

'Least heating's gas. Let's treat ourselves and put it on now,' he said. 'Right, who's for a board game?'

It was amazing how quickly the candles burnt down. Two hours later it became apparent that we'd all have to be in bed by 8.30 p.m. if we didn't get some help.

I knocked on Doug's door.

'Candles?' he said, narrowing his eyes and sticking his chin out, like he was addressing a Jehovah Witness rather than me, his neighbour of almost eight years.

'Just a few. I'll pay you back day after tomorrow.'

He craned forward, peering to his right, staring at our house. 'They've cut you off, haven't they?'

There was no answer to that; it was blindingly obvious they had. I don't know why I didn't tell him straight away. Misplaced pride.

'New Year's Eve 'n' all. Bastards. Hang on a minute, duck.' He disappeared back inside and reappeared two or three minutes later armed with three head torches, and a lamp, the sort you'd take camping. 'From my garage,' he said, 'don't have much in the way of candles.'

I stared at the head lamps.

'Nicked 'em from coal board during my time. Hope your Rob don't mind, reminder and all.'

'He won't have to,' I said, taking the torches. 'Thanks, Doug. I really appreciate this.'

'Don't mention it. What about kiddies? What'll you feed them?'

'We'll manage.' I waved goodbye, walked down the path and as I closed his gate, he said, 'Pop in for drink at midnight if you're still up.'

'That'd be nice. Will do.'

'No need to bring owt. I've plenty in.'

I waved again and raced up our path.

The boys were in bed by nine, Becky earlier, bored after a game of Cluedo and an abandoned game of Monopoly. Johnnie was too young for the games anyway. I wondered why Monopoly was so popular; everyone owned a copy, but as games went, I thought it was pretty poor. I'd managed to acquire Park Lane and Mayfair, much to Rob's annoyance; I usually ended up with Whitechapel and the Old Kent Road, the Angel Islington if I was lucky. I'd just built a couple of hotels when Johnnie – our banker – started throwing money, houses, chance cards. He was hungry. We all were. There hadn't been much in the fridge, and cold beans on bread didn't appeal to anyone. We'd eaten the last of the pickled onions, with some crackers, toast, and hard cheese.

By ten o'clock Rob was increasingly edgy; he wanted to go down the pub, I knew it, but he'd promised to spend the evening at home, rather than leaving me to see in the new year alone.

'How about a game of cards?' I ventured, sipping on a shandy.

He shrugged, but opened the cupboard and dragged out a pack. 'What do you want to play?'

'Depends what I can remember. Been a long time since I had a game.'

'Poker? We could bet with matchsticks?'

'Best keep them for candles! Strip poker?'

'You what?' Even in the low light I could see he was taken aback.

'Come on. We used to play. You taught me.'

'That were ages ago.' He hesitated, tempted. He took a gulp from the can. 'Go on then. Why not?'

We laughed and laughed. More than we'd done in, oh, such a long time. And I'd not lost my touch; I was as mean a player as I'd been at sixteen. Rob was sitting in his briefs, socks, and Doug's miner's hat when we heard the knock. I still had my dress on, though no shoes, tights, or jewellery bar the pearl necklace and my wedding ring. We froze and stared at each other, wondering who on earth it could be. We weren't expecting anyone and from the outside the house must have looked empty, all shut up, owners out on the town.

The knock came again. More insistent this time. 'It must be Doug,' I whispered, remembering his generous invitation. 'He doesn't want to spend this evening alone.'

'Did he say as much?' Rob hissed, groping about in the near-darkness for his clothes.

'No. But I can tell.' I stood up. 'I'll keep him on the doorstep for a few minutes while you sort yourself out.'

'You're not letting the old bugger in.'

'He's got loads of booze.'

'Give me two minutes.' Rob near enough jumped up.

'Hello, D—'

'Happy New Year!'

I stared at a gaggle of rosy-cheeked, pinched-nosed faces, all brandishing bottles of one description or another. The jammy lips and kohl-rimmed eyes leapt out at me as in a nightmare.

'Bit early, but not far off. 'Bout an hour to go!' I recognised this voice: Mum. I picked her out of the crowd. 'You're not going to invite us in then? Fine welcome this is!'

Stunned, I stepped aside and they trooped past: Mum and her cronies, some people whose faces I recognised but couldn't name, and a couple of the Braithwaite boys. As they rolled in I realised that not only did they all bear gifts – bottles of booze, bags of crisps and nuts – but many of them clutched a candle, or a torch.

How did they know?

I was about to ask Mum when I realised, with horror, that Rob might not have had time to dress.

From the shrieks of laughter coming from the lounge, it seemed I was too late.

There were smutty comments about Rob's chest from Mum's friends (he'd managed to get his trousers on, thank goodness). Phil and Michael Braithwaite, the two oldest brothers stood, backs pressed against the far wall, embarrassed, their flushed cheeks clear even in the dim light.

Rob responded by prancing about like one of those Chippendale blokes, much to the merriment of the older women. I thought for one horrible moment he might remove his trousers again, though I was fairly sure he'd not had enough to drink for that.

I turned to Mum and asked why she wasn't down The Boar's Head with Dean. It hadn't struck me as odd that people had brought candles at that point. She explained that Dean had taken a call from Doug, who'd explained our situation, and said we might welcome a few guests, to lift our spirits and help bring the new year in.

'We were going to wait till midnight, do first footing, but were frightened you might have gone to bed so we came straight away. Well, once we'd finished drinks. Shame to waste. I'll go back to pub once clock's struck. You don't think noise'll wake the lassie?'

'You know they're all heavy sleepers.'

Bless Doug. He was a perfect neighbour despite our grumblings, and he cared. I felt bad; we were neglectful. He was old and lonely. Who could blame him for being miserable? I hurried next door to invite him to the party he'd created.

He didn't put up a fight. He'd three large bottles of spirits in a carrier bag by the door, and he'd changed his shirt and wore a red and yellow striped tie. He kept his slippers on. 'Corns,' he said, when he caught me staring as he pulled his front door to. 'Blinking chiropodist's useless. Our Jeannie used to sort 'em out, but now she's gone . . .' I touched his shoulder. Jeannie, Doug's wife, died six years ago, shortly before David was born. They were four months short of their golden wedding, and after he'd told me that she'd died all he said was that Jeannie was proper fed up not to have been able to hang on long enough to meet the new arrival. 'Loved babies, she did,' he'd said. Doug and Jeannie were like my mum and dad: doves. They'd mated for life.

There was music when I returned with Doug; Phil had a beat box, and some of the women were dancing. Rob was standing next to Michael, though neither was speaking. It occurred to me how odd it was that the Braithwaite boys had come. They disliked Rob as much as he did them, and though they tolerated each other, even working together on the picket lines, after the fight with Dan relations had sunk to an all-time low. I crossed my fingers that none of them would pick a fight.

At ten to twelve the front doorbell rang again. This time Ann and other members of the FAG team trooped in along with Vince and Ethel. I was grateful the twins hadn't pitched up.

There'd be trouble for sure if they did.

'Doug said you might need cheering up. Brought some sausage rolls and leftover mince pies. Still hot,' Ethel said, tapping a foil-covered tray, heading towards the kitchen.

I'd barely closed the door when there was another knock. Dan and Ruth stood on the doorstep. Ruth beamed, waving a bottle of Asti Spumante in one hand. Dan looked as if he'd rather be anywhere but here.

'A little bird told me there was a party here tonight! Happy New Year, darling. Golly, here's hoping it's a better one than the last,' she said, plonking a cold kiss on my cheek.

'You're just in time. Countdown's about to begin.' I waved them in. Dan didn't meet my eyes.

As we stepped into the living room someone turned the music off; switching the beat box from stereo to radio mode. Silence descended as everyone listened to the commentator's voice, struggling to be heard above the roar of the crowd in Trafalgar Square. 'Ten, nine, eight, seven, six . . .'

'Three, two, one!' We joined in.

The first chime from Big Ben rang out. 'Happy New Year!' we all screamed. People turned to the person closest to them, hugging them, kissing them on the cheek, wishing them a victorious 1985. I was wedged between Ruth and Dan. Ruth flung her arms around her husband, nudging me out of the way. Stepping back I fell into Doug, who steadied me before taking my hand, and lifting it to his mouth.

'Come here, you silly old bugger. Happy New Year,' I said, pulling him towards me in an embrace.

Spinning round the room, from one person to the next, I was acutely conscious of Dan's absence from my path. Waxy lipstick kisses were deposited on my face from Mum, Ethel, Ann, and friends. Rib-crushing embraces from the men folk. Every time I turned to look for Dan he was locked in an embrace with someone else, stiff and uncomfortable looking. But he seemed unaware of my presence. Finally, Rob and I crashed into each other. I went to kiss him, properly, but as I did so Ruth called his name and he turned. My kiss caught his ear.

'Rob. You have any glasses?' she said, lifting the wine bottle.

He tapped me on the bottom, winked and said, 'Get Ruth a glass, Mand.'

In the kitchen only two candles remained alight; the others had burnt out long ago. I took a tumbler from the cupboard; we had no wine glasses, never had done; and returned to the party. 'Auld Lang Syne' filled the smoky air. I pushed my way into the circle of interlocked arms and joined in. Mum and I caught each others' eyes; we were both thinking of Dad. There was no sign of Dan.

Afterwards, when the music went back on and the dancing started I made my way upstairs, to check on the children. I held a torch, the battery was running low; it grew dim and died as I climbed the stairs, only to be resuscitated with a bang against the wall. I was unsteady from a mixture of shandy, vodka, and cider.

The boys' bedroom was thick with the feral smell of children, the sound of their rattling chests rising and falling in the cool air. I pulled their duvets up, wobbling on the bunk bed steps, and made my way to the box room where Becky slept. She lay on her back, arms outstretched, clutching a pink dummy in one hand, her yellow curls stuck to her forehead. Her hair was the colour of Dad's. I watched her sleep a while and wondered what she might grow up to be. A nurse? A doctor? A world leader? How I hoped she'd aim for the top. Anything was possible nowadays, wasn't it?

Torch dangling at my side, on its last legs, I made my way along the narrow landing. As I negotiated the small steps to the bathroom, before the main flight down to the hall, a figure emerged from the gloaming. I gasped as the figure took hold of my shoulders, turned me and pushed me into the darkest corner. The grasp was firm but gentle; there was nothing threatening about the action. I knew it was Dan.

'It's a new year. I hope it brings you everything

you wish.' His breath was hot. I lifted my face upwards. He leaned in further, his lips almost touching mine, his smooth chin brushing mine, caressing it. Our lips touched; we trembled. We pressed ourselves against each other. I was ready to explode, my desire like lava, simmering beneath the surface. His hand brushed my cheek; I could sense his longing, and fear. I wanted to speak, to say something, anything, but couldn't. I would reveal too much. He spoke again, forming his words on my lips, words I held captive in my mouth, imprisoning them. I wanted him to kiss me so badly I thought I might cry. I wanted him to explore me; I wanted to explore him, to know what he felt like. To have his tongue encircling mine, his fingers caressing my nipples. To hold his cock in my palm. To feel those slender fingers pressing at me with the same tenderness and skill he showed his flugelhorn.

'You . . . you're . . . beautiful,' he said.

I fell into him, pressing my lips against his, cupping his face with one hand. I waited for the touch of his tongue.

I don't know if it was the thud of the torch hitting the carpet, or my jolt at the sound, but he pushed away from me, still holding onto my shoulders, and whispered, 'I can't do this. It's wrong. I'm wrong. I've let too many people down already.' His voice shook. Then he turned and raced down the stairs.

Shaking, I dived into the bathroom.

What are you doing? You're a wife, a mother. His wife's best friend. A few drinks and you lose your head.

Bent over, gripping the edge of the hand basin, I sobbed. Great, thundering, snot-laden sobs. If I could have seen my face in the mirror it would have been pink and blotchy, my eyes red like a rabbit's. But it wasn't guilt that brought on my tears, they came because of the engulfing, crushing disappointment. I hurt; I physically hurt.

CHAPTER 26

Downstairs, it appeared that I'd not been missed. I'd no idea how long I'd been gone; time had melted away. I fumbled my way through to the kitchen and grabbed a half-empty bottle of vodka, before putting it back down. I'd feel terrible enough without a hangover from hell. A headache was already forming at the base of my skull. I wanted everyone to leave, but judging by the merriment there was no chance of that. I filled the kettle before remembering there was no electricity.

Instead, I took a glass of lemonade outside with me, throwing on a jacket of Rob's hanging on the back of the door. I wandered up the narrow passage, past the kitchen, to the front wall of the larder – the section of building that jutted out from the kitchen – and sat down, my back resting against the wall, the concrete patio cold against my bottom. I curled my bare legs under the skirt of my dress and pulled them up to my chest. I stared into the garden and wished that I smoked; I needed an activity.

The garden, scrappy as it was, always lifted my

spirits. It reminded me of the children; the games they played, the joy they brought. Without any overspill of light from the kitchen it was dark and shadowy. The old pear tree loomed in the near distance; its branches bare and spiky. It looked dead, but it'd recover. Bloom again.

I was about to push myself to my feet when I heard the door opening, then slamming. I heard a match being struck; the smell of tobacco hovered on the icy air. I remained seated, still. I didn't want to have to explain myself. The door opened again. Then, a voice. A controlled but hostile tone; violence, or the threat of it, just below the surface. It was Phil Braithwaite.

'You've bin sniffing around. There's talk.'

'Talk is talk.' It was Rob, and though he was trying to sound casual, confident, I knew him well enough to hear the tremor in his reply. He had good cause to be scared. I heard one of them take a long slurp of a drink. 'Want one?' He was offering a beer, or a cigarette.

'I'm not your mate, Walker.'

'Then what you doing in my house?' The beer had made him bold, or foolish. I feared for him.

'Came to tell you to stay away.'

'From what?'

Shut up, Rob. Shut up.

'You know damn well what.' I heard the shuffle of staggering feet. Rob had been pushed. 'You've been warned. You go near her again, and you're dead. You get me?'

So it was true; I'd been right. Phil was protecting his baby brother, defending Dan's honour. With no idea what he'd been up to with me only minutes ago.

'Sent you to do his dirty work, has he? I know things about your family. Your brother; your dad. The accident—'

'You can't prove anything.'

'You're all cowards,' Rob slurred.

Jesus Christ, belt up.

What'd happened to the fear I'd heard? Had he lost his marbles?

Pushing myself up, I listened for the reply, or the sound of knuckle against bone, but none came.

Rob spoke again. 'Like father, like son. Soldier boy's a bastard coward. Not man enough for army, not man enough for—'

I kicked over the empty glass as I jumped out from my hiding place and flung myself in front of Phil, grabbing him by the wrist, mid-air; his clenched fist inches from my face, the skin of his hand grey in the subdued light. There was a howl – mine I realised later – and the rattle of the glass spinning on the concrete.

'Don't you dare! Not in my house,' I hissed through clenched teeth, straining to hold Phil's rage at bay. I held on, his arm pushing against mine, both shaking, as in an arm wrestling contest. Just at the point when I thought I could bear it no longer, when the ache became a searing pain,

Phil relaxed and I let go; his arm dropped to his side.

I began to tremble, and then to cry. It was relief; relief that Phil hadn't walloped me. But he wasn't to know that.

'I swear I didn't know you were there, Mandy. You were never meant to find out. We were going to sort it. Man to man,' Phil said, rubbing his fist as if he'd actually thumped someone.

'Can you leave us? Please?' I said, wiping away my tears.

He scowled at Rob, jabbing an index fingers at his face. 'Watching you,' he said. Then he turned and walked down the side of the house, disappearing through the kitchen door.

When the door slammed behind Phil, Rob began to speak. His voice shook, his bravado all used up. He lifted his fingers to his temples, head down, and walked in small circles. 'Jesus, thank Christ you were there, Mand. Thank Christ.'

Still in shock after confronting Phil, I watched Rob as I might a dog chasing its tail, with a kind of bewildered amusement, waiting for the grovelling apologies, the denials. They never came; he burbled on and on about how mental the Braithwaites were, all of them. 'The mad bastard. They're all mad. Psychos.' How he was going to show them what for, show the lot of them up, especially 'that fucking pansy, Dan.'

I thought about what had happened on the landing; it was Dan who'd stopped it. I thought about how much I'd wanted him, and regret and anger rose from my gut. I started to hyperventilate. Rob stopped pacing. He turned to me, the garden behind him.

'What?' he said.

I lunged at him, fist clenched so tight I broke the skin on my palm, though I didn't realise some of the blood on my hand was my own until much, much later.

'You bastard!'

He staggered to the side, falling against the pebbledashed wall, sliding down it as he held onto his chin. I was glad I was left handed; had I hit him with my right he'd have fallen against the boundary fence and that would have been something else to pay for and fix.

I don't know if he went down easily because he'd had a few, or whether I was stronger than I realised, but I wished I'd knocked him out, because as I turned to leave he said, 'I love her.'

The pain in my hand, which seconds ago had felt so great I was sure I'd broken bones, disappeared. Instead an agony so intense I lost my footing seized me. It hadn't been hard to imagine Rob finding Ruth attractive; she was beautiful; most men would. And, at the kids' Christmas party, though I was shocked, it hadn't been difficult to believe that they might be having an affair. I had believed it, at first. But I'd never considered that he might love her.

Why not? I'd loved her when we were kids. I'd

idolised her as an adult. Why wouldn't he? Ruth's treachery was complete, and it felt worse than Rob's betrayal. She'd deceived her husband and her best friend. Was she my friend? Was I hers?

You've desired her husband. You are one and the same. As bad as each other. But Dan and I stopped; ours is a smaller betrayal. Or is it? What is it you really want? What do you really feel?

Agony coursed through me. Not because Rob didn't love me; it was the agony of realisation: I no longer loved him. Had I ever? Infatuated; yes. But love? I wasn't sure I'd known what it meant until recently.

I am in love with Dan.

Numbness stole through me. Steading myself against the wall, I took a deep breath and continued into the house.

In the kitchen I held my hand under a cold tap and washed the blood away. I winced as I dried it with the tea towel hanging by the sink. I dabbed the cloth under my eyes, across my cheeks, afraid there was evidence of tears. I ran my fingers from the back of my neck over my scalp, pulling my hair upwards, and as I pulled I caught the chain of my necklace. I touched the pearl, aware how odd it felt to do so with my right hand. I tore it from my neck and slung it across the work surface; protecting my damaged hand I walked back into the living room.

There was no sign of Phil or Michael, but as I scanned the room Ethel waved and strutted over, wiggling her hips in time to the music. I wondered how long the batteries in the stereo would last, unsure if I wanted the party to go on all night (no danger of having to talk to Rob, or Ruth, then) or finish immediately. But whether or not there was ample booze would be the deciding factor, and there was plenty. I resigned myself to a long night.

'Eh up, duck. How you doing? Not boogying?' Ethel flung out her right arm in imitation of John Travolta in *Saturday Night Fever;* it was quite a sight.

'Staying alive! Staying alive!' I sang back at her.

She tapped her collarbone and mouthed something I didn't catch.

'Your necklace? Where is it?' she shouted. 'You had it on earlier.'

'Took it off; the silver is irritating my skin,' I said.

'Shame. Gorgeous, isn't it?'

I nodded.

'Dan said you'd like it.'

I screwed up my face. 'Dan?'

'Bugger. Was meant to be a secret. It's the booze,' she said, lifting a plastic cup and taking a swig.

'How would he know?'

'Haven't got a clue, duck. But he saw it, at swap party, and said he knew it was perfect for you, and I was to plant the idea in Rob's head. Those two might not see eye to eye over much . . . but they care about you. Everyone does.' She swayed into me as she spoke, draping an arm round my neck.

You're wrong. Not everyone cares.

Johnnie appeared in the doorway as I swept plastic cups, paper plates, and half-eaten sausage rolls into a bin liner. It was shortly after six o'clock.

I'd not seen Rob, or Ruth, or Dan for the rest of the evening. Dan and Ruth must have sloped off home; Rob I didn't know or care about. No doubt he was spread-eagled on our bed, sleeping off a hangover. I hoped his jaw hurt when he woke.

After the last guest had left, over an hour ago, I'd not known what to do with myself. I'd collapsed on the living room floor with the remains of a bottle of Malibu after helping myself to a cigarette from a discarded packet on the mantelpiece. I was a hopeless smoker; it was only about the fourth I'd ever had in my life and the other three had been with Ruth at school, trying to get in with the rough, popular girls. But I persisted, enjoying the sensation of feeling light-headed and sick, enjoying the knowledge that I was poisoning myself. I drank and drank, without effect; with no idea what I was going to do, other than I couldn't stay. I'd rarely been more certain of anything in my life.

In the near darkness, sucking his thumb, Johnnie picked his way through the debris as if he woke to such a sight every morning. I remained sitting on the floor, resting against the settee, legs outstretched. He dropped onto my lap and leaned into my chest. I put my arms round him and stared at my feet. Chipped red varnish on my toenails, black smears between my toes. I'd always liked my feet, but they weren't at their best. I stroked Johnnie's hair.

'No dummy?'

'Lost.'

The candles were almost gone – all that remained were waxy mountains on side plates; there was no television or radio, little food. I rocked Johnnie back and forth, humming songs until the dawn broke and the rest of the household awoke.

CHAPTER 27

'You can't stay holed up here forever, love.' I turned off the electric whisk and picked up the spatula, turning the mixture over and over. Smacking it really. It was so white; pure and virginal and innocent.

'You'll ruin it doing that.'

'I'll buy you more eggs.'

Mum came over. She took the spatula out of my hands and put her arms around me. She felt so thin-boned, frail, but she wasn't. Tough as cheap meat, that one. 'I don't give a bugger about the eggs; I do give a bugger about you. It's not healthy.'

'Who knows?'

She relaxed her grip, sighed, took the bowl and began to pour the mixture into the bin. 'Difficult to tell. Rob's not been in pub a lot, of course. Worried I'll knock his block off. Dean's been sniffing around, trying to get lowdown on his movements. He's drinking in The Dolphin, apparently.'

'Still same old Rob then.' I stuffed a peach slice in my mouth, the syrup dribbled down my chin. 'You want some? May as well finish the tin.'

'Don't be daft. We'll make more meringue.

There's another half dozen eggs in fridge. So stop scoffing the fruit.'

'So you've no idea who knows?'

'Not really. A few have asked after you. Said you were poorly – bad bout of 'flu, but it's been nearly three weeks. It won't wash any longer. People'll be asking questions. Go and pick kids up from school.' She pointed at me as if she was telling me off; she meant business this time.

'Ruth'll be there!'

'She's not been out on playground. Scared, I reckon. And so she should be.' Her voice rose as she spoke, ending in a shout. She slammed the egg box on the counter.

Probably all smashed.

I had no idea if Ruth knew I knew. If Dan did, or Ethel, or Vince or Ann or any manner of people. The only people I could be sure knew about the affair were Rob and Ruth, naturally, Mum, Dean, and Phil and Michael Braithwaite. We were approaching the last week of January, and since I'd dragged myself, the children and two suitcases into the taxi and ordered the driver to take us across town, I'd barely stepped outside Mum's front door.

I'd half expected Rob to pitch up, begging forgiveness, but he never did. He'd not even come round asking to see his children. They were confused and upset, and even Mum's constant spoiling couldn't lift their spirits. It couldn't go on. Something had to give.

*   *   *

Mark and David were delighted to see me, with Johnnie and Becky, standing at the school gates at three o'clock. Mum had shoved a fiver in my hand before we left, telling the little ones that it was for Mum to take them all for a hot chocolate at The Cupcake on the high street before coming home. She was a cunning one. Her house to the school was no distance at all; a few of hundred yards down a couple of residential streets, I wasn't likely to bump into another human being, let alone a friend or someone who knew me. She was forcing me into town.

The street was quiet; it was drizzling and getting dark. Stomach somersaulting, I held my head high, just in case the entire population of Fenley did know. There was no way I wanted to be seen as hapless victim. Deep inside, I was hurting, wondering if in some small way I had contributed to this. Was it my fault? The strike and my involvement in it, the work it brought in its wake, had meant I'd neglected my family, spent time away from them. But I did it for family, didn't I? I acknowledged that I also did it for me. I enjoyed it; it had enriched my life, but there was a price to pay. Was I deficient in some way for failing to keep hold of my man? Shouldn't I have been able to keep house and a job? Thousands of other women did.

This is not my fault; I'll front it out.

The Cupcake was empty so we parked ourselves in the far corner and ordered from a waitress so young she must have only left school six months ago. She had just placed four steaming mugs and one plastic beaker of hot chocolate on the table when a shrill, 'You-hoo!' filled the room.

The voice was unmistakable, and it belonged to the fourth-to-last person I wanted to bump into: Ethel.

She dragged over a chair and plonked herself down next to me. 'Ey, they look right good, kids,' she said, nodding at the drinks. 'You lucky beggars.'

Not at all lucky. She can't know.

'And how are you, Mandy? Heard you weren't so good.' She lit a cigarette, turning her head and blowing the smoke out behind her, the one concession to the children's presence.

'Not bad,' I whispered, hoping the kids, especially David, wouldn't grass me up.

The waitress materialised at Ethel's side and my heart sank as she ordered a pot of tea. She was in no hurry to leave. The conversation took another turn as she asked the kids about Christmas, what they got from Santa and so on. Her tea arrived.

'Been trying to get hold of you for weeks,' she said, tipping a third spoonful of sugar into her drink and stirring vigorously. 'Pushed notes through your door and everything. Holiday's over. Back to work for us. Battle's not over yet. There's men drifting back to work. Fucking scabs.' She looked at the children, all of whom bar Becky were giggling, and said, 'Excuse my language.' Turning back to me, she continued, 'Work to be done,

Mandy. In the end, Ann asked at Boar's Head and Dean said you were staying at your Doreen's for a while.' She poured some tea into the saucer and took a slurp. 'Excuse me again, kids. I'm gasping. Too hot in cup.'

I was about to offer an excuse for my departure from the marital home when Ethel spoke again. 'Who can blame you?'

I nearly choked on my chocolate.

So she does know.

'What with the leccy off. Bloody miserable. With little 'uns and all.' She squeezed Becky's cheek. 'Is it back on now?'

'I'm . . .' I couldn't think what to say. It should have been easy to lie, to say, 'Yes. Everything's fine, thanks.' But I dried up. And then Mark spoke.

'Mum's left Dad. She told Nana there were things to sort out.'

I began to cry, unsure if it was Mark's pain and confusion that tipped me over, or hearing the words spoken by another, the finality of it all. Now everyone would know, and Rob's safety could be jeopardised. Had he heeded Phil's advice; had he stayed away from Ruth? I was sure I no longer loved him, but I didn't want to see him beaten to a pulp. No one deserved that. Not even Rob. My hands were shaking.

Ethel rested her hand on Mark's and said, 'Now sometimes grown-ups fall out, just like you kids do. Your mam and dad will sort it out, mark my words.' She took a slow draw on her cigarette. I marvelled at the length of ash balancing precariously from the tip of the filter. 'It's a difficult time, love. The strain on everyone is immense. You and Rob, you'll be all right. You've a life together, children. You think me and Vince have never had cross words? Been together getting on for forty year. But by God, we've had some barneys. Left him myself once. Taught the old man a lesson.' She squeezed my hand, the smell of tobacco hovering between us. I smiled. She didn't know after all. Not yet.

CHAPTER 28

Four days passed; life settled into a skewed normality. I took the boys to school; I attended a FAG meeting. There was still no sign of Rob, or that anyone knew why I'd left. The days were spent in a state of high anxiety; I fluctuated between thinking I ought to make the first move, to stop being so selfish, go to Rob, try to patch things up for the sake of the children, and between wanting to rush out onto the moor, find Dan, and tell him that I loved him. But that was crazy. A pipe dream.

Ethel called an emergency FAG meeting. The date of a court case of a miner arrested during a mass picket had been brought forward. The meeting was to be held at her house. She rallied the troops; those who attended regularly, those whose attendance was sporadic, and those who'd not attended for ages. I dreaded Ruth turning up. She fell into the 'not active for months' category, but there was the possibility she might have been bullied into coming. I had no idea how I'd react upon seeing her. One thing was certain: if she didn't know already that I knew about her and

Rob, she soon would. I wouldn't be able to disguise my feelings of betrayal, guilt, and envy. No longer my friend, she was my enemy, my rival. Perhaps she always had been and I'd been too blinkered to notice.

Frightened I'd either cry or thump her, for the first fifteen minutes I was so preoccupied nothing that was said sank in. Eventually, I relaxed, confident Ruth would not turn up. Morale was very low. Public support was dwindling, a steady trickle of men returned to work, others were banged up in gaol. I shut out the low rumble of defeat and tried to throw myself into the work with gusto, an attempt to stop my busy head whirring with thoughts of Dan, Ruth, Rob, New Year's Eve. Ethel was organising transport to the court house for the hearing, Ann was sorting out the banners and there was little for me to do. I offered to make tea.

As the kettle boiled, I stared out at the bleak garden. The windows misted over. Thinking, thinking, thinking: Dan, Ruth, Rob. What was I to do? What did I want? I was pouring the water into the teapots when I heard the creak of the gatefold kitchen door. I turned my head and almost scalded myself. It was Dan, looking almost as shocked as I felt, standing there, holding onto the doorframe. He was pale, more so than usual. He'd had his hair cut. Short, really short.

'I'm looking for my mam,' he said, staring straight at me. 'I've a key,' he added, holding it up. As if he needed to explain himself.

'She's in front room. It's a bit busy in there.' I couldn't take my eyes from his. Did he know about Rob and Ruth? Had he guessed how I felt about him? Was it obvious? I felt transparent.

'How've you been?' he said.

'OK.'

'I'm glad.'

The world around us fell away, like snow slipping from the mountainside, an avalanche. We were left, the two of us, standing on a ledge, staring into a precipice, the mountain path growing narrower and narrower. The silence grew; I waited for the sound of ice cracking.

'Rob told me.' His voice didn't shake, his eyes were dry. They were soft, warm, smiling almost, and gazing right at me. Inside me.

I gasped; I couldn't help myself. Dan was bound to find out eventually. But from Rob? What possessed him? He didn't like Dan, never had, but to be so malicious? He would ruin everything, for everyone. Not content with ruining our relationship, Rob wanted to do the same to Dan and Ruth's. Was he mad? Wasn't he afraid?

And then it struck me: Rob does love Ruth, or believes he does. And he must believe that she loves him, to risk everything. His physical safety, for pity's sake. One of the Braithwaites would kill him.

I heard a voice, a distant voice, as if from a pot hole or cave. 'What's taking so long? We're parched in here.'

Ethel peered through the dumbwaiter; I wasn't sure if she could see Dan. Without turning I said, 'Coming right up.'

'Hello, love. Come and join us for a minute, will you?' she said to Dan, before disappearing. She didn't close the hatch doors. I picked up the first tray and Dan stepped aside to let me pass. He followed me into the meeting with the second tray of tea and biscuits.

The women on the settee shuffled along to make space for him. He waved a 'don't bother', but they ignored him and he sat down after Ann patted the empty space beside her several times. Her eyes glittered.

I poured the tea and offered the custard creams round, aware that Dan watched my every move, as I did his. When everyone was sorted, I sat down on the only available seat – a straight-backed dining chair with a raffia seat. It was positioned directly opposite Dan. I didn't know what to do with my legs. If I crossed them there was a danger the clipboard with my paperwork on it wouldn't balance on my knee; with no surface nearby to rest things on I had a cup and saucer to negotiate as well. But uncrossed my splayed thighs looked expansive. I left the clipboard on the floor and swung one leg over the other, brushing my hand down my thigh, as if to flatten creases. I wore a dark skirt and the pearl necklace which I'd retrieved from the kitchen before I left mine and Rob's house.

The meeting droned on; I tried to concentrate on what was being said, I really did. Dan and I were the central images in a photograph where everyone else was out of focus. As in a photograph the moment was frozen, moving neither forwards nor backwards, and I didn't want it to end. We stole furtive glances. The settee was deep and low. He rested his elbows on his knees, legs bent. There was an exposed section of leg where his sock finished, before the hem of his jeans. The skin was white, covered in light brown hair. I wondered if he had hair on his chest, if it snaked down his torso, below the line of his underwear. Was his skin soft or rough? Cool to the touch, or warm? I remembered the sensation of his lips hovering over mine, the promise of the kiss that never quite came.

'More tea?'

'Huh?' I jumped and tea from my cup spilt onto my skirt. It was cold. Ann began to fuss.

'It's nothing, don't worry. Look, I'd best be off. Mum's got kids and she'll need to be off to The Boar's Head in a bit.'

'Her and Dean getting very close, aren't they?' Ann said, conspiratorially, though it was common knowledge.

'Looks like love to me,' a woman in a thick turtleneck said. There were clucks of approval all round.

'She deserves to be happy, does Doreen,' Ethel said.

'Doesn't everyone?' I said, meeting Dan's eyes.

They all stopped and looked at me; heat rose up my chest and neck. I looked at the floor. I had to get out of there; it had become unbearable.

''Course we all do. Now off you pop, or your mum'll not thank you.'

Snow continued to fall; the landscape took on a new form. I ambled down the cul-de-sac and onto the high street, enjoying the sensation of crunching beneath my feet, the spoiling of something pure. Mum wasn't going down to the Boar's Head. The assistant manager was running the evening shift; there was no need to rush. Dean was coming to Mum's; he was great with the children.

A brisk wind blew snowflakes into my face; they landed on my eyelashes, nose, and lips. I relished their icy kisses, the relief they offered my flaming cheeks. I tipped my head to the sky; a few people stared through their fringes and pulled hats down over their ears.

I was walking past the Boar's Head when I noticed a group of people gathered outside the Spar, shouting, waving their arms about. I couldn't make out the words; I was about a hundred yards away. Wanting to avoid whatever little drama was taking place, I stopped and looked up the road left and right, checking for traffic. As I stepped into the sludgy gutter the wind blew words down the street: 'Scum', 'pasting'. Mouth dry, I stepped back onto the pavement as a car flew past.

Lowering my head I crossed the road and continued my journey, hoping no one would notice me, hoping to dissolve against the brightly lit shop windows like a snowflake. But curiosity is a powerful emotion, as is the instinct to stare at a violent scene, like an accident or the aftermath of a fight. As I neared, the crowd dispersed and, unable to resist, I turned. A figure lay curled on the floor, foetus-like, its back to me. It was unmistakable in form and shape. With wobbly legs, I reeled across the road, not thinking to look. A car braked; the driver honked the horn, yelled. I muttered my apologies, heart racing. Calling Rob's name I slid onto the pavement behind him, almost falling over. He was pushing himself up, head lolling between his arms, flesh exposed as his thin jacket rode up his back. I whispered his name.

'Rob?'

He staggered backwards, spun around, flinging droplets of blood from his mouth and nose as he did so, staining the virgin snow. His nose was broken, spread across his cheeks like a beaten steak. Blood poured from his lips; they were either split or he'd lost a few teeth. His right eye was closed, swollen and shiny. He clutched his ribs with his left hand as he stumbled towards me, groaning, mumbling something indecipherable.

'Oh my God,' I screamed, rushing at him, before stopping abruptly, afraid to touch. 'What have they done to you?'

I'd imagined beating Rob to a pulp myself on

more than one occasion in the past weeks, but the reality was heart-wrenching and sickening. It seemed I didn't hate him as much as I thought.

'Who was it? Phil, Michael?'

He shook his head.

'Sweet Jesus, not the twins.' My hands covered the lower part of my face.

If it had been the twins he'd be unconscious.

He shook his head again.

'Which one of them was it? We've got to report this, Rob. This is assault. It's serious.' Anger built in me; this was no way to treat someone, no matter what. It would kill the children to see their father like this. I dragged a hankie out of my pocket, pulling half a cream cracker out with it, and went to dab at Rob's lip. He jerked away from my touch, wincing.

'It wasn't Braithwaites.'

'What?' It was difficult to make out what he was saying; his words were like porridge: sloppy, grey and sludgy. I thought I'd misheard.

'Not Braithwaites,' he slurred, blood running down his chin.

'Then who?' I was shouting again, confused. 'We need to get you to hospital.'

None of this makes sense.

Another small crowd had gathered, on the opposite side of the road this time.

Why isn't anyone helping? Why are they standing there, watching?

I shouted across. 'Has anyone got a car? We need to get to hospital.'

No reply. Rob was staggering up the street, bent double into an L shape. He skidded and fell on his side.

'Help me, please,' I cried.

The crowd turned and continued on their way.

What the hell was happening?

I'd been so focussed on the crowd opposite I'd not noticed a woman approaching. She was upon us before I recognised her as Ann's eldest daughter. She was in the year below me at school; pretty at fourteen, plain by twenty.

'No one'll help a scab.' She spat where Rob lay, a gob of white spittle landed on the shoulder of his jacket, like a large, wet snowflake. It dribbled down his back; he barely noticed.

A scab?

'You didn't know?'

I shook my head, unable to speak.

'He was seen, coming out of pit after morning shift. Slipped by pickets on way in, thought he'd got away with it. Fucking chicken, scab,' she directed these words at Rob who still lay, groaning, 'sneaking in like a thief. Scum.' She spat again, hitting him on the cheek this time; he wouldn't have felt it. But I did.

'Sorry you found out like this, Mandy. You deserve better, you really do.' She kicked snow in Rob's face and walked off.

I leaned against the Spar window and slithered down it, till I rested on my haunches, next to Rob who was whimpering like an animal caught in a trap.

'Why? Why? After everything we've been through. After all this time?' I pitied him; how had he fallen so low? What drove him to this terrible act of betrayal? Not just of me, but of the whole community?

'There are things she wants, things she deserves. Man with a wage, backbone. Not some coward . . .' He swallowed his words; it was an effort to talk.

'You're the coward, Rob. You.' I looked at the ground beside me. A dog had urinated against the wall; the snow was yellow. Tears built behind my eyes but I held them back. He'd done this out of some misguided sense of loyalty to her, some misguided sense of what she deserved. And now I'd lose my place in FAG; I'd lose the friendship of people like Ethel, Ann; my role in the campaign, my sense of purpose. Shaking with a cocktail of rage and despair, I pushed myself up and headed towards the phone box, praying I had ten pence on me.

Dean pulled up in the Beetle and we bundled Rob into the back. At A&E we pulled up behind an ambulance and pushed him out.

'You sure you don't want me to go and park?' Dean said.

'He's on his own. I've done my bit.' I turned to Rob, who stood there, shoulders hunched, clutching his ribs, head hung low. 'If you were ever thinking of visiting your kids, don't bother until your face is fixed. You'll give them nightmares.'

We got back in the car and Dean drove off. I didn't look back.

Mum was playing Twister with the children when we got back. After hugs and kisses and stories and coming down stairs four times (Johnnie) they were finally quiet and us three adults sat in the lounge in front of *World in Action*. The reporter was interviewing some veterans of the Falklands conflict, Welsh Guards judging by their accents.

'Must have been horrific on that boat. Difficult to comprehend, isn't it?' Dean said.

'Poor lad looks like a shell,' Mum said. 'Can I get anyone a cup of tea?'

I stared at the television; the reporter spoke about trauma and stress and how scant the support was that the pilots and sailors received. And soldiers I assumed, though he didn't mention them.

'Look, I'll go and read in bed or something, give you two some peace,' I said, standing up, unable to watch any more. Though they didn't mean to, I felt like a gooseberry, and the love between them was so clear it served to highlight the lack of it in my life.

The image of Dan's face as he sat opposite me at Ethel's flashed before me over and over. The longing in his eyes, had I imagined that? In my mind's eye I saw the dip of flesh at the base of his neck, along his collarbone, and longed to stroke it with my index finger, to feel its softness and vulnerability.

'There's a great book waiting for me on my bedside table,' I said.

I'd joined the library after I'd devoured the book Graeme and Jane had bought me for Christmas. I found the novel a bit odd at first; all about this ugly woman whose husband called her a she-devil, but after a while I was hooked and finished it in days. There'd been a note inside the book, a 'required reading list for an intelligent woman' and desperate to stop thinking about Dan, the affair between Rob and Ruth, I'd gone to the library, loaned the first on the list, and made a start. *Woman on the Edge of Time*.

'Don't go up just yet,' Dean said, glancing over at Mum.

'What?' Was there something else I didn't know?

'We've . . .' Mum's voice trailed away.

'We've something to tell you,' Dean said, before clearing his throat.

I sat back down again.

He coughed, like on some cheap sitcom. 'I've asked your mum to marry me, and I'm delighted to say she's agreed.' He didn't look at me as he spoke; he stared straight at Mum. Their smiling faces shone with love and happiness, bulging cheeks red and shiny. Mum had never looked prettier.

The tears were falling before I got the words out. 'That's fantastic. Blinking fantastic. I'm so pleased for you both.' I threw my arms round Mum, who hugged me so tight I nearly passed out.

'Timing's rubbish,' she said. 'What with everything that's going on . . .'

I looked over her shoulder at Dean. 'When did you propose?'

He pulled a face, all apologetic. 'New Year's Eve.'

We laughed; we couldn't help it. 'Out with the old . . .'

'I brought some bubbly, from the pub . . .' Dean said.

'Get it out, then! I'll get glasses!' And I raced to the kitchen.

Tonight we were going to celebrate.

CHAPTER 29

Love brings with it a certain freedom, as well as responsibility. Freedom to view the world afresh, with eyes that find the best in everything. Freedom to not hold back, to let loose and enjoy, secure in the knowledge that if all else fails there's always loving and being loved.

Dad always said the greatest honour Mum could pay him, and their marriage, was to do it all again after he was gone. Naturally, she swore that she wouldn't; she couldn't love anyone as much as she loved him, and she kept that promise for far longer than she should have. But, at last, Mum was free of the grief that had hijacked her for ten years, and she was free of guilt. Guilt that she had carried on without him, even though she had no choice; there was a child to look after.

I hadn't made it easy for her. After a couple of years she should have moved away, a new start in a new town. I was sixteen, getting married, an adult. She stayed because of me, because she felt guilty about me. Guilty that had she not been so devoured by sorrow she might have noticed her daughter going off the rails, making the wrong choices, making a bit of a mess of things. So she put her life on hold to help out with mine. It was time for her to take flight.

In the mid-morning February light Ruth's house looked oh-so-ordinary. How could I ever have thought it something to aspire to? With its bland pebbledash front, concrete paved driveway, and heavily draped curtains. It was what Jane might have mockingly called bourgeois, and it was so much less desirable to me now than my shabby council house with its coal hole, outside toilet, and corporation front door. And I didn't much like that house either. What kind of a home did I aspire to, want? I wasn't sure.

The ding-dong of the bell echoed. I heard footsteps, the click of the lock, and Dan stood before me. He didn't seem surprised to find me on his doorstep but there was something missing in his eyes, as if a part of him had shut down.

'We need to talk,' I said.

Without replying he stepped aside to let me pass. I wiped my feet thoroughly on the coconut hair mat and stepped into the hall.

'Can I get you a brew?' he said.

'That'd be smashing, thanks.'

'Go through; take a seat,' he said, gesturing to the lounge.

I parked myself on the settee, noticing a stain on one of the cushions. A stale, artificial floral scent hung in the air. There was an air freshener on the window ledge; the gel-like substance that gave off the smell had shrivelled to the size of a grape. It was quiet; a crushing kind of silence. From the kitchen there came the occasional tinkle of tea-making, though it seemed to me Dan was creeping around, trying to be inconspicuous, trying to disappear.

I longed for the thrum of a radio, a noisy carriage clock, anything. I was acutely aware of my own presence, in this house that belonged to Ruth. To relieve the waiting I drummed my fingers on my thighs and stared at the picture frames opposite. They were all back on display: wedding, party, holiday. And then I noticed a new one: taken this Christmas. I stood up and crossed the room, catching my calf on the edge of the glass coffee table in my haste.

I rubbed my leg it as I hobbled over to the photograph. I could feel the tear in my nylons.

Damn, now I look a right mess too.

The picture had been taken at Ethel's; I recognised the wallpaper. A snapshot really, except that they were formally posed. Ruth was leaning into Dan, her left hand positioned flat against his chest, ring gleaming, cheek resting against his shoulder. She was all teeth and hair; Dan stared straight into the camera, smiling only with his mouth. I tried to imagine what he was feeling. Hearing the creak of the kitchen door I raced round the table, jumped back onto the settee, and tried to appear serene.

He placed the tray down on the table's edge, slipping his fingers from underneath it, pushing it to the centre, with those elegant hands. Then he sat on an easy chair, directly opposite, and said, 'Sugar?'

'I'm trying to give up.' My leg throbbed. All that waiting had crushed my early confidence, my resolve to say what needed to be said. The time had been filled with nerves and doubt.

I should have refused the tea. Remained on the doorstep. What a fool.

He handed me the drink, handle out. 'So how've you been?'

I shrugged. 'You know.'

'Mam says you're not to worry about yourself, or the children. That if anyone gives you any trouble, she'll sort them out.'

The sound of his voice made my heart beat faster; I stared at the tea, the mug resting on my knee, feeling the heat penetrating the outer layers of my skin.

'Who knows?'

'You don't need to worry about that. You're protected, safe.'

I wanted to feel his arms around me, his body pressing into mine.

I'd feel safe with you.

'You know. I see it in your eyes,' I said, looking up.

It was his turn to stare at the carpet and as he dropped his gaze I realised he'd been watching me all along. He was the most beautiful man I'd ever seen.

Does he know, really know, how much I want him?

'Is this what you wanted to say?' he said.

No. No. No. The very worst thing that could happen would be to walk away without having spoken the truth.

'Do you still love Ruth?'

'Still?'

'Do you love her?'

He stared at me, and I watched those steel grey eyes grow darker. 'I don't love Rob. We're through, him and me.' This was true. There was no turning back for me.

'I'm not who you think I am.'

'Do you have any feelings for me?' I wanted to hear him say the words. I'd felt his desire, his concern. I needed to hear the words. Nothing else.

'I can't rescue you.' His eyes flickered. 'I'm no hero.'

There's something else; what is it you're not telling me?

'You think I didn't work that out? "The only heroes are dead ones," my dad used to say, and he was right. No one's ever seen the medal. No stories or battlefield anecdotes? I could have believed that you mightn't brag, but your dad? Your mum? Lovely though she is. 'Course they would. Wouldn't have been able to help themselves. Something terrible happened to you. I've seen the way your hands tremble; the dark circles under your eyes, that shut-down look you get.' My voice was shaking, growing higher and higher. I stood up, spilling my tea. I went to grab a serviette from the tray.

He stretched forward, put his hand over mine, stopping me. 'Leave it,' he said. 'It doesn't matter.' He held his hand there, those long fingers, bony knuckles covering mine completely. 'Mandy—'

'We could leave together.' The words fell from my mouth.

'We're tied to this place, these people.' His voice was steady, calm.

'We'll take the children.'

He pulled away. There was sweat on his brow, even though the room was cool. 'I'm not strong, like you.' His voice fractured. He rubbed his forehead with his index and middle fingers, from his brows to his hairline. I longed to reach over and kiss him there, to ease his pain.

'What happened out there?'

His hands fell away, his head stayed low. Then he told me.

It was the first time he'd shared his experience of war, the experience that haunted him, tortured him, drove him back down the mine and into the cloying bosom of his family here in Fenley Down. The bare bones he'd told to Vince, and Ruth, I guessed, but the detail he kept to himself, reliving it time and time again in his dreams and waking nightmares. But it was the experience that tied him, shackled him. It put an end to his freedom, his ambition, his health. He did as they wished, not as he wished, because they protected him; they kept his appalling secret. They'd given him another chance to prove himself a man.

He never once looked at me as he spoke. 'The army was a way out; travel; meet people. I thought if I did it for a while, maybe even rise up the ranks, lance corporal or something, I'd have proved myself and then I could do what the hell I wanted. Dad could be proud whatever I did, because I'd been a soldier once. A fighter. A hero. There would have been option to move across, to join regimental band. I had the skills.' He pushed his thumb across the flat nails of his left hand.

'What went wrong?'

'Nothing. At first. I liked it. It was exciting, challenging. And when we were told we were going to the Falklands, to defend our countrymen, unlike most others, I was over the moon. This was it; no one could touch me after this. None of us thought there'd be any actual fighting, or not much. Thought we'd walk in there with our superior equipment, superior skills, and Argentines would capitulate, wave the white flag, before we'd fired a single shot.

'It was so cold. And wet and dark. There was no light. Cold like I'd never known, trudging for miles and miles across those bleak islands, through boggy, frost-dusted ground, wind tears freezing on your cheeks, rain lashing against your forehead, eyes, ears. Snow stole into your boots, numbing so deep you longed for the sting of the ice because at least it meant you still had your toes. And when we neared the battlefield mud became wetter, warmer, and this felt good till I realised that it was sodden with blood, human blood. The blood of men I called my colleagues and those I was supposed to call the enemy. But I didn't see them that way. Not really. We'd captured prisoners, before that horrific march. They weren't evil, invading killers. They were boys: sixteen, seventeen years old. Thin and scared with crappy guns and cheap uniforms, soaked in their own piss and shit. No one tells you about that in training: pissing yourself at sound of the guns, of the dying.

'After that walk we had to fight, in black, smoke-filled air. Close combat, the closest we'd been to them, the so-called enemy. And Frank Campbell, a private from Aberdeen I knew only vaguely, was bayoneted, in the stomach, and I shot the guy who did it, just like that: bang!' At this point Dan held his arms like boys do when they're playing soldiers, and he jerked his arms up when he shouted, 'bang!' like it was really happening, as if he was killing that Argentinian soldier again. Dan's face was wet with tears though I don't suppose he felt them.

'I bent to help Frank. There was blood all over his hands and mine, and I could hear the other guy moaning. He wasn't dead. I pushed myself up and went over to where he lay. He had a pistol and with a hand shaking with fear, or shock, he lifted it towards me. I raised my rifle to finish him off. But I looked into his eyes as he looked into mine and realised that I did not hate this boy; I could not kill him, not now, not like this, just as I knew he could not, would not, shoot me. Neither of us were to die that miserable June evening. He lowered his pistol. Above the noise and chaos of battle I heard the clunk of a magazine being loaded; the boy's eyes flicked to my right, there was someone there, outside my peripheral vision. He hadn't lowered his pistol because he did not want to kill me, he'd lowered his pistol because a comrade had approached. His ally, my enemy. I spun and fired. A body flew through the air. I ran to where it lay. There was no shoulder or left arm and half of his chest had been blown away.' Dan was hyperventilating, reliving the scene as he spoke and I wondered how many times these minutes, seconds, had been played over and over and over in his mind.

'And this shuddering body, in the paroxysm of death, that had once been a son, a husband, a father, a brother, wore a British uniform. He hadn't been trying to kill me, he'd been protecting me.'

'Friendly fire, they call it,' he said, 'Blue on blue. I killed a man. A friend. There was an inquiry. I had to leave. Every time I heard a gunshot I was sick; I couldn't hold a rifle without trembling. How could I stay? I requested a PVR. My officer-in-command couldn't refuse. What was I to do? I had no choice; I had to come home.'

'You need help – professional help. Not to keep all this in. War is terrible; terrible things happen. You're not alone. You are not a bad person; stop punishing yourself,' I said. Ruth and Vince and Ethel and all the brothers, they were his gaolers, not his liberators.

'I owe them. What would have become of me without them?'

'You owe them nothing. You didn't even want to be a soldier, it was an escape. You want to play music, jazz, in a band. You let them bully you. You don't have to stay here. You're not going to be happy spending your life down the pit. Your first loyalty is to yourself. What do you want, Dan? Really want.'

How I ached for him to say: 'You. I really want you, Mandy.' But he was silent, and I had the strongest feeling there was something else; something else tying him to Fenley, to the pit, to Ruth.

He remained silent. And it no longer mattered that Dan's dreams didn't include me. It hurt that they didn't. Of course it did; the pain was so great I wanted to lie on the floor and howl, as I did in childbirth, but I loved him enough to want him to fulfil his ambition, not to be held back by a misguided sense of loyalty, a debt to be honoured. To be tied to a woman who didn't love him, to a job he hated.

I turned and grabbed my scarf – I'd slung it on the settee beside me – and made my way out. He came after me and stopped in the doorway.

Outside I paused and, wrapping my scarf round my neck, said, 'Follow your dreams. Even if they don't include me.' As I walked down the drive, I heard him mutter, swallowing the words, as if he was talking to himself rather than me. 'I didn't say they didn't include you.'

I turned around but the door was closed.

CHAPTER 30

As the month drizzled out Rob was well enough to see the children; it had been so long since he'd visited. We'd agreed to blame the broken nose and black eye on a picket line scuffle with the police, the irony not lost on either of us. Mum was at home when he came to collect them; I was buying stock for the soup kitchen. Funds were so low I was struggling to feed people anything other than bread and water. Because of their father's wages my lot ate decent meals, and I was grateful, though the guilt was terrible. I could barely eat food bought with his dirty money.

I was first to arrive at the kitchen. A Saturday morning, others were taking it easy. As I hung my coat on the peg, I noticed how worn it was below the belt. The fabric was so thin you could see the lining. Leaning against the door, I surveyed the space: sharp angles, stainless steel, utensil pots standing to attention, counter top surfaces reflecting the gleam of the halogen strip lights. An empty hive, still before the oncoming activity, the only sounds the thrum of the fridge and the muffled rumble of distant traffic. This was my kingdom; the place where I was undisputed queen.

I swept my hair to my crown and secured it with a scrunchie; tied my apron, and opened the fridge. It was almost empty: milk, margarine, the usual assortment of half-empty condiment jars in the door, four eggs. How much longer could we go on? More and more FAG members stayed away, feigning illness or other commitments; we'd not seen Paula for weeks. Despair sidled in the wings waiting to make an entrance. I hogged centre stage, desperate to carry on fighting; it was how I got out of bed most mornings, that and Johnnie wailing for his Weetabix.

From the larder I dragged out the vegetables. Throwing tatties onto the countertop I began to chop leeks. The arduous task of peeling the potatoes would have to wait. An oniony tang filled the room and reminded me that spring wasn't so very far away. The daffodils would be budding soon; the evenings were growing lighter. Lost in thought I didn't hear the footsteps crossing the hall or the click of the door handle being turned.

'Can I have word?'

Startled mid-cut, I missed the leek and sliced the blade through my flesh. Swivelling to face the speaker, I raised my hand, finger stinging, a trickle of blood running down my palm, following the groove made by my lifeline.

Ruth.

She'd had her hair permed and it stuck out either

side of her head as if she was wearing bunches. With her narrow frame and skinny limbs her head seemed enormous. She reminded me of Looby Lou, and I glanced at the ceiling half expecting to see a puppet master up there. But no one controlled Ruth; she pulled others' strings. 'You made me jump.' I made light of my surprise, and crossed the space towards the sink, biting on my bottom lip.

Does she know I went to see Dan? Has he said anything?

'That looks bad; you need a bandage,' she said, looking at the floor.

Drops of blood spotted the tiles, tracking my movements.

I held my hand under cold running water and remembered how I'd done the same on New Year's Eve. She handed me a tea towel, the corner of which I wound so tightly about my finger I couldn't tell if it throbbed because of the cut or because the blood supply was so restricted. Neither of us spoke.

My head whirred with the reasons why she might be here: to apologise for sleeping with Rob; ruining my marriage; to warn me off Dan; to hit me for wanting him to kiss me; to beg me not to tell anyone his, their, secret.

How much, how little, does she know? What a mess.

'This is my fault. I'm sorry,' she said.

The cut? My marriage? She knew I've left Rob. Everybody knew that.

'It takes two,' I said, heart throbbing as much as my hand.

Stay calm. Stay casual.

Shrugging, I picked up a potato with my bandaged hand and began to peel it. Dried mud caked in clods at the top and bottom. Blood seeped through the tea towel as I pulled the blade through the dry potato skin to expose the slippery yellow flesh below.

'I thought you'd hit me.'

I blew air out of my nose. Did she really know me so little? Streaks of mud decorated the potato; I tossed it into the colander sitting in the sink.

She continued, 'It's over. We've not seen each other for weeks. You have to believe me. It's over.'

She must know Rob went back to work. The sacrifice he made. For her.

'I believe you. Does he?' I wrapped the rest of the rag round my hand, binding all of my fingers together as boxers do before the gloves go on. 'He says he loves you.' I picked up another potato.

She laughed, high-pitched, nervy. It had shocked her – that he'd told me, not that he loved her; he'd have told her a thousand times, over and over. I could hear him saying it. 'How is he?' she said.

Does she know he got beat up?

'Bruises are healing. He'll survive.'

'What about you? You'll have him back?'

'Back?' I put the potato down and looked at her, really looked at her.

She had no idea. Not the foggiest.

'Everyone makes mistakes. Does silly things, things they regret in the cold light of day.' She smiled, chin down, lips held together, eyebrows slightly raised.

Who are you talking about? Rob? Yourself? Dan?

My stomach lurched, and I picked up another potato.

Did Dan regret what passed between us? Is that what he'd told her?

'Rob's betrayed so many people, not just me,' I said evenly, amazed how composed I sounded, and felt, about the disintegration of my marriage. Slice, slice, slice. Another potato done, tossed into the colander. I gripped the knife.

Perhaps it's the blood loss. Making me so calm.

'We're going to make a go of things. Me and Dan.'

'He's forgiven you?'

'We're having a baby.' She held her hand to her board-flat stomach.

I clenched tighter still. How can she get pregnant when she doesn't eat? Anorexics stop ovulating; bulimics too. I'd done some reading about Ruth's problem.

'Nothing's going to come between us. Nothing,' she said.

She meant no one. She meant me. This was a warning, not a statement. And she knew I understood. I hated her then. Glancing at the blade I considered how much damage it might inflict on pale, thin skin.

I wanted to scream: You better not be lying about the baby this time, you bitch. You better not be.

Inside I dissolved. Placing the knife on the counter edge I stared at my hands. There were livid ridges on my palm where the handle had pressed into my flesh. The physical pain that Ruth's words inflicted reminded me of when Mum told me Dad was dead. Sharp, like a needle prick, followed by a steady, radiating iciness. So debilitating I was unable to speak.

The door swung open and Ethel burst into the kitchen, whistling the title tune from *Oh What a Lovely War!* I jumped, knocking the knife, which clattered onto the floor. Ethel swept it up and slammed it on the countertop.

'Morning, ladies.' She threw her coat over mine. 'And to what do we owe the honour?' she said, addressing Ruth as she unfastened her headscarf and folded it into a pocket. From a drawer she pulled out a paper bonnet and pulled it over a head full of rollers.

'Right. Let's to it. Don't just stand there, pass us a bag of spuds, Ruth.'

'I'm not stopping, I'm afraid. I've too much on today,' Ruth said.

'There'll be no avoiding cooking once the kiddie arrives. You've got to get used to it sooner or later. Get your precious mitts mucky,' Ethel said.

So it's official then: the baby.

Ethel thrashed away at the potatoes, a mound

of peel building. 'Smashing news, isn't it? Made my day. Even Vince was pleased, though he didn't like to show it.' She looked at Ruth, and then widened her eyes in mock horror. 'Flipping 'eck. I've not gone and put my foot in it, have I? You've told Mandy, surely to God?'

'Of course I have. We're best friends.' She walked over to where I leaned against the sink and lifted my bandaged hand. 'Mandy cut herself,' she said, showing Ethel.

'Occupational hazard,' Ethel replied, dicing potatoes and hurling them into an enormous tureen. 'You put stock in yet?' she said to me.

I shook my head.

'You should be more careful. You might get really hurt next time,' Ruth said.

I pulled my hand away. 'There won't be a next time.'

'You make sure of that.' She turned and walked towards the door, side stepping the blood in her path. She stopped. 'Probably the last time you'll be doing this,' she said, nodding at the ovens, her eyes darting round the kitchen.

I shook my head, not understanding her meaning.

'Word is it'll all be over within days. Fifty per cent of the men are back already. Your Rob's not alone.' She emphasised the 'your'.

Ethel stopped chopping. 'We don't know that for certain. It ain't over yet.'

'Oh, I think we do.' Ruth slammed the door behind her.

'Is this true?' I said to Ethel, feeling like I'd taken another punch.

'She's a mare sometimes, that one. Take no notice, love. We fight on regardless. Until we're ordered to stop, we fight on.'

I listened to Ruth's heels clickety-clacking across the hall and knew the end was near, no matter what Ethel said.

She turned on the radio; the relentlessly cheerful voice of the DJ filled the air. 'Just nipping to the lav,' I said, scooting out of the kitchen, desperate to be alone.

Inside the cubicle I bolted the door, lowered the toilet seat, sat down, and wept.

Take good care of him, Ruth. Take good care of him.

AFTER

Passion cake

Originally made for weddings as an inexpensive alternative to the traditional wedding cake, which requires large amounts of dried fruits and spices, its name reflects the love and commitment of the nuptial couple.

CHAPTER 31

The sombre crowd lined the pavement of the high street, as if awaiting a funeral cortege. In a way, we were. We felt them coming before we heard them. The ground seemed to tremble as if they were coming from below, cracking their way through the unyielding earth to the surface. Seconds later the boom of the drum reverberated through the gusty air followed by the deep cry of the tubas.

'Dum.'

I turned to Becky who sat astride my waist clutching my shoulder with one hand. 'What did you say?'

'Dum. Dum.' She wacked my back to the beat of the drum with the rattle held in her right hand.

'Drum! Drum! Boom, boom, boom! Did you hear that boys? She said "drum". Drum.'

Mum butted in. 'What a clever girl.'

Becky responded appropriately, grinning widely, four pearly teeth in a wet, pink mouth. It was all a game to her, a lovely morning out.

'Mama. Mama.' She pointed down the street.

The red and yellow colliery banner fluttered into

view, held aloft by Vince and Phil; heads held high. Behind them, silhouetted like matchstick figures, the men of Fenley Down, the miners of Fenley Down, marched, like victors, ready to claim the spoils of war. Those of us on the pavement clapped, some cheered, others wiped tears from their cheeks. We'd never thought it would come to this, not until the dying days of February, and even then many denied the end was near. I was one of them.

Dry-eyed, I forced a smile as the marchers edged closer; men nodded in our direction – the members of Fenley Action Group huddled together for warmth and moral support – thanking us as they filed past. I thought about Vince and Ann's husband, men of an age who would, undoubtedly, be thinking of redundancy, wondering how to fill the days of their forthcoming early retirement. I thought of the younger men, and how much longer they would wear the helmets worn by their fathers and their father's fathers. What they might do to support their families, for the days of the pit were numbered. I thought of how the community might alter, for change it would. Dad always said change was good; it was progress, and not to be resisted for the sake of it, though it was hard to agree, looking at the men. Proud, working men; the industrial working class.

Dinosaurs. Perhaps that vile cabbie had been right.

Then came the band, striking the first bars of

'Abide With Me'. The brass cheerful and defiant against the slate coloured clouds. We waved furiously. And there he was, sandwiched between the cornets and the trombones: Dan.

Ann turned to Ethel. 'Good Lord. I didn't know Dan still played trumpet. Must be years.'

'Flugelhorn,' I whispered. 'It's a flugelhorn.'

Ethel said something about being surprised herself, but I stopped listening. The tears came. For the men, for all our hard work, for the inevitable loss of a way of life, a community. But mostly, I cried for me. I'd lost everything. There'd be no call for soup kitchens, fundraising events, speakers, and marches. And love. I'd lost my love.

Not Rob; our marriage wouldn't have stood the test of time. Had it not been for the strike who knows how long we might have lasted. Five, ten years? Till the last of the children left home? It didn't matter. What mattered was I'd lost Dan, not that I'd ever truly had him, but he was the real thing; I knew that.

He didn't tilt his head as he passed; he kept his eyes fixed on the music sheet pinned to his instrument. I clung onto Becky even tighter and pulled Mark nearer with my free arm, and my sadness and self-pity was tinged with joy. Dan was playing in public, and I wondered if I'd had any part in his decision to do so. I hoped that I had.

Back at Mum's, the boys dropped at school, late, like most of their classmates, I put Becky in her playpen, filled the kettle, and wondered how I was to fill the hours between now and home time. I made shortbread, with real butter, and Becky and I scoffed the lot.

The days dragged on and spring arrived. The FAG team met up occasionally, for old time's sake, and to help families as they tried to get back on their feet, pay off the debts, rebuild their lives. We distributed chocolate eggs to the children at Easter; organised a Bring and Buy for summer wardrobes. Members continued to drop off, and when Ethel got a job in a call centre the group all but disbanded.

Rob and I settled into a rhythm all broken families must find: negotiating formal maintenance payments, visiting rights, and times. Money was never a problem; he paid regularly and in full. Visiting was trickier, neither of us prepared to spend time in the others' company with the children, despite their pleas. It was too soon.

We moved out of Mum's as soon as the electricity went back on; Rob went to his mother's, a nightmare for all concerned. I tried not to think of all six feet of him curled up on their two-seater settee in that cramped living room; it wasn't my problem and Mum needed her space back, though she never said.

It was hard, being in the house Rob and I had shared. All those memories. The double bed, half-empty wardrobe.

One day, Becky at Mum's, so chuffing bored

and with a cupboard full of home baked cakes, I had yet another sort out. It was a struggle to find anything to chuck. In the bathroom I came across a razor at the back of the cabinet, short black whiskers stuck to the rusting blades. It must have been the last of Rob's possessions in the house, but I felt his presence everywhere. I wandered through the rooms searching for evidence of him, but found none. Sitting on the settee I stared at the picture hanging above the mantelpiece: a drawing of a woman with cropped spiky hair, bright pink lipstick, and sunglasses half way down her nose, winking at the viewer. We'd bought it from Athena a couple of years ago in an attempt to add a dash of modernity to our outdated front room. I'd chosen it, but had grown to hate it. She reminded me of Ruth; not so much in her appearance as her attitude: her false chumminess, her 'hey, we're all equal and having fun' wink, rebellious haircut for the girls; her jammy lips and cleavage for the boys. I took it off the wall to reveal a brown outline where the frame had rested.

I should decorate. Brighten the place up.

Two hours later I stood in the front room in an old shirt, brandishing a sponge roller caked in a paint described on the tin as Peach Melba. The assistant in the ironmongers had reliably informed me that pastels were all the rage, and that it would look less sickly on the walls. I hoped he was right as I couldn't afford to paint them again. The furniture was covered in the only spare sheets I had

– my clear-outs having been so ruthless as to leave minimal bedding.

Tentatively, I placed the roller on the chipboard wall and pushed upwards. The sponge squeaked and slurped; the peach looked rancid against the old mustard yellow. I rolled and dipped, rolled and dipped, and within minutes, or so it seemed, the chimney breast was almost covered. I crouched to refill the tray and was easing the metal lid off the pot with a screwdriver when the doorbell rang. Groaning, I went to answer it, wiping my paint covered hands across the front of my shirt.

Rob stood before me. His jet hair curling outwards at the collar of a white shirt, voluminous and ruffled, like one worn by highwayman Dick Turpin, according to a picture book Mark borrowed from school. Rob looked thinner, diminished, but still handsome.

'Decorating?' he said, smiling, pushing his thumbs into the front pockets of his jeans, dropping his gaze to the floor. I noticed that he wore fashionable suede pixie boots. Something else that was new. He looked like someone dressed to impress.

'I fancied a change.'

'Is this a bad time?' he said, rocking back on his heels.

'Well, it's not what you'd call ideal.' I brushed my forehead, catching some hair. There was still some paint on my hands, and now there were strands of hair covered in it too. I sighed.

'I'll call back another time. It's just that you're alone, your mum's got Becky . . .' He smiled again and looked at me with those blue, blue eyes.

'It's alright. Do you want to come in?' I stepped aside to show him I meant it.

Inside I offered him coffee and he refused. He hovered by the table.

'Sit down, will you,' I said, surprised and touched that he'd waited to be asked. It was still his home too; he paid the rent for it at least. He went to sit in his usual place at the head of the table, then stopped and sat in the chair usually reserved for David. I waited to hear what he'd come to say.

'How've you been?' he said, resting his elbows on the table, fingers interlaced. He was wearing his wedding ring.

'Fine.'

'Smashing.'

'What about you?'

'Fine.'

'Good.'

He looked at the ceiling, cast his eyes about the room. 'You going to decorate in here too?'

'I might. Depends.'

'On what?'

Puzzled, I said, 'I'm not sure. Look, Rob, did you call to ask about home decoration, or was there something in particular?'

It crossed my mind that he might have heard about Mum and wanted to see if the children and I would be moving back into her house once she'd gone. The Boar's Head was going to close; the brewery had offered Dean another pub, on the coast, a bigger one that had live music and served food at lunchtime. Mum was going to keep the cottage. A 'nest egg' she'd said, and a bolt hole if either she or I ever needed it.

What he said next shocked me; I'd not seen it coming.

'I miss you, Mand. You and the kids; the life we had. Wasn't so bad, was it?'

'You love Ruth. You don't love me.'

It was as if I'd not spoken; as if he had a script and would say it no matter what. 'Would you have me back? We could start again.' I felt as if I were in a soap opera, *Dallas* or something, just without the gigantic houses, shoulder pads, and Pammie's tiny waist.

Momentarily, I was tempted – aside from the children my life was devastatingly empty. Accepting Rob's offer would make the children happy, life would be easier; I'd have someone to care for and care for me; life would return to a comfortable, safe normality. I stared at the table top, at my paint-encrusted fingernails, before lifting my eyes to meet his. His face crumpled, the tears welling. He knew there was no going back; it must have been written all over my face. I wanted more; more than he could ever give me.

He rested his head in his hands, the sobbing noisy and unrestrained. I let him cry. Did he still love me after all? Was the news of Ruth's pregnancy enough to finally convince him that he'd been a plaything, a distraction? That he'd risked everything: his wife, his children, his reputation, for a woman who cared nothing for him. Who'd had no intention of spending the rest of her life with him. Had he wondered if the child was his? I had.

After a while he rubbed his eyes with the heels of his hands and said, 'Is there someone else?'

'No.' It was true, though it pained me to say it. 'It's not all your fault. You must know that.' I reached out my hands and touched his. 'I am as much to blame as you.'

'What will you do?' he said.

'I'm not sure. But I will do something.'

'I know you will. You were always the clever one, even though you tried to hide it most of time. That's what I liked about you. Your spark. "She's like her dad," my old man used to say. You just needed igniting. Funny it were something as bloody awful as strike.'

I nodded, knowing it wasn't only the dispute. Ruth. Dan. 'What about you? What will you do?'

'Oh, I don't know. Work at pit till they kick us out. I'd leave village if it weren't for my mum and dad. I'm Most Hated now. Be sure you do something brilliant, Mand. Make kids proud.'

'I will. Don't you worry. Just got to work out what.'

We shared a pot of tea, talked about the children, about what to do with the house; we agreed I should apply to the council for a transfer – somewhere close enough for Rob to visit, far enough away to make a fresh start. We were almost like an old married couple.

After he'd gone, I walked back into the living room and sealed the paint pot. The rest of the room never did get finished. At least not while I was there.

CHAPTER 32

The council had offered me a transfer when I received Mum's letter. I was undecided whether or not to accept. I'd declined their first offer, but this was more promising. It was for a three-bedroomed house (tick) with a garden (another tick) in the next village, where we ran the soup kitchen (no tick, too close to Fenley). If I turned it down, the council were obliged to make one more offer only. I'd applied for a few jobs: one I'd seen at the job centre, another in the local paper, though neither was ideal. Not what you'd call challenging. And I was up for a challenge, craving it. One was a position as dinner lady at a primary school in the next village; the other a data entry operator for the local council. Rob's mum had agreed to have the little ones; her decision prompted by guilt, no doubt, though perhaps it was unkind of me to think this. Although the pay for both positions was rubbish, at least the office job offered training in computers, and the man at the Job Centre had assured me they were the future, once he finished questioning my decision to work in the first place.

'But you're receiving support from your estranged husband, Mrs Walker? There's no necessity to work?'

I nodded.

'You understand that any monies earned will result in a reduction in payments from your husband?'

I nodded again, tempted to ask if he was against women working in principle or just in my particular case, and to ask how come one so young (he looked about seventeen; probably on a YTS programme) was so well-versed in the ins and outs of divorce settlements.

Over the weeks and months my life had contracted, shrunk to its pre-strike smallness, though I was less invisible. People in the village seemed to make more of an effort to engage with me, seeking my opinion on everything from whether or not the SDP-Liberal Alliance was a viable alternative to Kinnock's Labour Party (I'd not the faintest idea) to how to stop a soufflé sinking (lots of tips here). Women asked about my 'secret recipes' for cottage pie, summer pudding, and even toad in the hole which I thought practically impossible to mess up.

'My Terry bangs on and on about your sponge, Mrs W.'

'I tell you, the next time he complains about my Yorkshire puds, I'll ram bloody things down his cake hole!'

I'd tap my nose and state that the recipes were my grandmother's (mostly true) and I owed it to her memory not to share these time-honoured family secrets.

Day in, day out, I got up; took the kids to school, washed, cleaned, baked, and played with Becky. After Mum left for Whitby I'd spend hours at the kitchen table writing her letters filled with our news. News . . . huh. Sitting in my empty house with my empty life. I bought magazines like those Ruth and Jane read, devouring articles about the glass ceiling and how hard it is for career women to give it all up and go back into the home when children come along, how it is even harder to resume a career – 'Why shouldn't we have it all?' the headlines screamed. Why, indeed. I hadn't understood before, but I did now.

Summer stole in, dry and dusty, and thoughts of holidays and long, long days occupied my thoughts. The kettle had just boiled when the first post dropped onto the mat. Shuffling through the pile, brown envelopes to the back, my spirits lifted the moment I saw Mum's handwriting; it was unmistakable. Schooled in the days when beautiful handwriting was considered important, the perfectly formed letters were rounded and neat, the loops of the 'y's and 'g's generous without encroaching on the letters below. Chucking the bills and official-looking letters onto the sideboard, I made a cup of tea, plonked Becky in her playpen, and sat down to read. Sun poured in through the windows catching the dust motes in the air.

I pointed. 'See the fairies, Becky? See the fairies? There's magic in the air!' It was what Dad used to say.

Only one sheet of rose decorated notelet paper this time. It was an invitation.

Once school has broken up for the summer, why not come and spend a few weeks here with us? The council won't do much in August anyway – slack so and sos – let fate take its course. You'll get the transfer you want; it just might take a while as so much council stock has been sold off. That blinking woman!

I'd not told her about the council's latest offer.

It's even more gorgeous here, now the sunshine's arrived. There's lots to do and Scarborough's less than twenty mile away. Dean will let us take car and we can go on one of our famous jaunts. How about it, love? It'd do you and the children world of good, and I'm missing the little beggars like crazy. You too. Dean says if you're short of cash he's more than happy to pay train fare. Hope that cheating bugger is paying you what's due, mind! Telephone to sort out dates.

I almost raced to the telephone box at the end of our road.

The day we arrived was overcast, and by evening the town was shrouded in a fine mist. After tea we walked round the harbour, watching the yachts and fishing boats bobbing on the evening tide, the sound of the mast bells eerie and comforting.

'Storm's due,' Mum said, looking out to sea like a weathered old sea dog, rather than a coastal inhabitant of less than three months. 'It'll clear the air. Going to be beautiful tomorrow.'

'And this was really, really where Dracula landed?' David shrieked. Mark's grasp on my hand became a little tighter.

'So the story goes,' Mum said, shaking her head and smiling. 'Not that I've read book, mind.' She turned to me. 'Sort of thing your dad might have liked. I prefer a good romance.' Her bedside table was always stacked with pocket-sized paperbacks featuring cover illustrations of big-breasted swooning women and dashing blokes.

My reading taste had continued to develop, and when I'd visited the library to borrow some books about Whitby and the surrounding area I'd picked up a copy of Bram Stoker's novel. I'd childhood memories crammed full of Christopher Lee's glaring red eyes, his fangs poised, ready to sink into the milky flesh of some unsuspecting maiden. The illicit thrill of watching such films powerful even in reminiscence. But the book was hard going and I'd abandoned it, reckoning Victorian literature was beyond me, at least for the time being.

From the harbour we wandered through the narrow streets and alleyways of the town, stopping at a rock shop for the children. There were barely any others open, most were closing for the night. The shop was cramped, narrow aisles flanked by raked counters stacked with pink and pastel sticks, over-sized transparent red dummies, lollipops swirling with candy pink, green, and yellow, like optical illusions. Becky reached up from her buggy, snatching at temptation and when the second pile of rock sticks hurtled towards the floor, I wheeled her out of the shop.

I walked further up the main street, hoping the motion would lull her to sleep. At the top I stopped, and gazed down. That's when I saw it, on the opposite side of the street: an empty shop, the facia battered by the north easterly winds, the lettering faded and chipped. At first I couldn't make out the name. Then it came into focus: *Flo's Place*. There was a sign in the window, obscuring the view in. I crossed the street, snapped on the buggy brake, and using my hands like half open shutters, pressed my face against the glass. It had been a café.

There were Formica tables and hard-backed chairs with steel legs scattered about. On the tables were red and brown plastic sauce bottles, salt cellars made of thick glass with screw on tops, like the sort you might see on a chip-shop counter. An empty glass display cabinet at the back, like those in a butcher's or baker's, and an open door leading to what I assumed must be a kitchen.

What happened here? Why was the business abandoned? What kind of food or light refreshments were served here?

I imagined cheese and ham sandwiches made with white bread, Chelsea buns with maraschino cherries on top, thick pastry pasties, and cheese swirls. I don't know why I thought of such plain fare; it must have been the salt cellar. Stepping back, I read the notice stuck to the glass. Written in blue biro, the writing looked hurried, or written with the shaking hand of the elderly. *Family tragedy. Gone away. Back in a fortnight. Flo.* But Flo had never made it back.

A loud bang made me jump. It came from above. In the gathering wind a board flapped against the first floor of the shop. An estate agent's sign. It read: Leasehold Available.

CHAPTER 33

Mum was right, the storm did clear the air, and our holiday was filled with sand-castles and wave jumping, ghost stories and walks up to the ruined abbey. The night before we were to travel home I went to bed early, but couldn't sleep. I sat at the bedroom window staring out to sea, elbows resting on the window ledge, chin in my palms, the noise from the pub below rising in gusts. Dean was having a lock-in.

I didn't want to leave, and neither did the children. My head was full of crazy ideas. A cloud passed over the moon; the moon was silvery and fuzzy. Dan rose in my thoughts, and my chest contracted, halting my breathing, the pain acute; I remembered our trip to the valley on that moonlit night, and my stomach tightened. I'd seen him only once, from a distance, since the miners' march back to the pit. Catching me in an off-guard moment as I staggered out of the supermarket with four full bags of groceries, he was crossing the road, hands at his side, back stiff, head up. I saw the tilt of his nose, his unshaved chin, and fled back through the automatic doors to the tills and grouchy shoppers where I promptly fainted, coming round in a sea of smashed eggs and broken biscuits.

What he was doing right now? Was he lying in bed, stroking Ruth's swelling belly, waiting for movement, an elbow or foot kicking at the womb wall? Was she far enough gone for that? I couldn't remember. I recalled the embrace on the landing, the touch of his hand against my cheek and ached to reach out and caress him. I closed my eyes and listened to the sounds of Miles Davis, Dizzy Gillespie, and others whirling in my head. Like a masochist I'd bought all the tapes and listened to them over and over. Was he practising his flugelhorn on the moor? Did he still do that, now that he played often and openly, or so I'd heard? And was this because of me, because of my encouragement?

A car horn jolted me from my maudlin reverie.

You should take your own advice, Mandy Walker. Follow your dreams, you said.

Throwing on jeans, a T-shirt, and flip-flops I headed downstairs, sneaking out of the back exit. As I opened the door the catch clicked; the noise echoing through the pub. I heard footsteps and stopped, holding my breath, frightened of being seen by Mum or Dean, wanting to avoid questions about where I was going, what I was doing. I needed to be alone. The footsteps fell away; I breathed and stepped out into the night.

Waves slopped against the harbour wall. Sitting there, legs dangling towards the slimy green bricks of the high tide mark, I focussed on the rhythm of the sea, the sharp slap of the breeze against my forearms, ears, and nose. It was the closest I'd ever come to meditating. An American accent jolted me from my near transcendental state. They were behind me, the soft soles of their trainers squeaking on the cobbles. I kept very still; I did not want to engage in conversation.

'Gee, it is *so* quaint. This place is hundreds of years old. Hundreds. Feels like going back in time. All this history.'

'Urg-huh.' A bored reply; like she'd heard it a hundred times already.

'And don'tcha love the way they drink so much tea?'

'Sure do, honey-pie. Sure do . . .'

The alien tones faded into the background, as the sound of the sea dominated once more. I waited until I was sure they had gone, heaved myself up and raced, as fast as my flip-flops would allow, up the main street.

56874. 56874. 56874. Got to remember the number. Got to remember the number.

A group of blokes staggered out of the pub three doors along; they headed my way, dropping from the pavement and into the road. Considerate. Didn't want me to feel threatened, I supposed.

'You've not got a pen on you, by any chance?' I asked.

Two of them patted their chests, near the breast pockets, and then down at their hips. They shook their heads. I was about to thank them for looking when another stopped and opened his jacket. He handed me a biro. Weighty, with a gilt clip and fine nib, it was good quality, a Parker.

'Oh, thank you. Thank you,' I said, scribbling the number on the back of my hand.

'Interested, are you?' the pen owner said, nodding at the empty shop.

Articulating what I'd not even been sure of myself a minute ago was both terrifying and exhilarating. 'I'm going to take over.'

'Good luck, missus. Had three owners in as many years. Times is tough round here, though judging by your accent, you'd know that already.'

'I do. And I'm not frightened by a challenge. In fact, I like 'em.'

He laughed, kindly, and said, 'I bet you do. Best of.' He trotted up to his mates who had walked on ahead.

'I'll give you a discount, when you come in. Be my first customer!' I shouted after him.

'You're on!' He waved, turned and disappeared round a corner.

I tumbled back to the sea and the now quiet pub, my head bursting with ideas.

Why not? Why not? The kids love it here. It's not too far from their dad. Mum'll be close by to help out. Stuff the banks if they won't give you a loan. There's the cottage to borrow against; Mum will support me, I know it. Enterprise Allowance, training courses, book-keeping . . . the baking'll be the easy part . . .

The sun was rising before I fell asleep, but when Johnnie woke me a few hours later, I didn't feel in the least bit tired. Quite the reverse – I felt more alive than I'd done in months. I remembered Dad's words: You can do just about anything. Anything. Dreams can come true, if you pursue them.

CHAPTER 34

The boxes towered like obelisks; one pile marked for storage, the other for Mum's. I was sitting on the floor between them, drinking a glass of water, mouth parched from lugging boxes down the stairs to the front room. The majority were crammed with children's toys and clothes. Once the flotsam and jetsam of my married life had been divided with Rob little remained. I was travelling light to my new life.

Everything had moved very quickly after that late evening dash up to Flo's Place, and here I was, six weeks later, ready to leave Fenley and begin again. As the leaves were turning brown, ready to fall, I was ready to bud. Dean subbed me the initial fees and renovation costs on the premises, until the loan secured against the cottage came through. As expected, a number of financial institutions had 'declined to offer' me a loan, but the process had been vital. I had a business plan, and though the banks thought my venture risky, I knew the idea was solid; I could make a success of it. My debt to Mum would be repaid within five years; I'd made a promise. We were to stay with Dean and Mum till the flat above the shop was habitable; a process that would take only a few weeks according to the builder. The boys had places at a local school and while Mark was nervous about the prospect of being the new boy, David relished the prospect of being the centre of attention; Mum would care for Johnnie and Becky while I worked.

I checked my watch: an hour until the man with the van arrived; nearly four hours before my train. Mum had collected the children first thing, piling them into Dean's rickety Beetle, before chugging off down the road, three little faces pressed against the back window, waving furiously, as if they'd never see me again.

It was the kind of dead time that would have driven me into the kitchen to bake, but with nothing to work with I picked up the paperback I was enjoying instead. I'd read only four pages when the doorbell went.

Ruth.

In a short dress and denim jacket she looked as pretty as she ever had. And as thin. Her cheeks were flushed, as if she'd been running. Though I tried to disguise it, she must have seen my eyes stray to her flat belly.

'Thought I'd missed you,' she said, breathless. 'They said you were leaving this morning.'

I wondered who the 'they' were; probably Ethel and Ann, or some mums from the school, though I'd heard Ruth had stopped working months ago, before the summer holidays.

'I wanted to catch you, before you left. To see you, to explain. If I can.' She laughed as she said this, high-pitched, nervy, just as she always had.

Where's the baby? Was there ever a baby? Did you really stoop so low?

Uncharitable thoughts bounced around my mind; I remembered Jane's suspicions about the first baby, and later my own, and recoiled at the notion that Ruth could do such a despicable thing to Dan, not once, but twice.

I went to speak but she got there first. 'May I come in? Please? I won't take much of your time. There's something important I have to say.' There was a tremor in her voice.

I stepped aside and waved her in. 'Go to front room; there's something to sit on in there.'

She perched on the chair in front of the window; I hung back by the door. 'I've nothing to offer, only a glass of water if you're thirsty.' Ever the hostess.

'I'm fine. Thank you.' She pressed her thumb into the palm of her hand.

'What happened?'

She clutched her belly. 'I lost it.'

'No one said.' As soon as I'd opened my mouth, I realised it was a stupid thing to say. Who would tell me about her baby? I'd kept myself to myself since spring, and people in the village knew exactly what had happened. No one said anything, fearful of what Ethel or Vince might do to them if they were seen to be gossip-mongering, but word got round. How could it not? With Rob moping about the place, spilling his guts to whoever would listen. And while there weren't many, there were always some ready to lend an ear for a free pint, even if it did come from scab-scum.

'She was stillborn. A little girl. But all wrong; she wouldn't have survived if she'd been . . .' Her bottom lip quivered, then tightened, as she struggled to regain her composure. 'She looked like her father.' She pressed her index fingers into the corners of her eyes, to stop the tears. The pain of such a loss must have been excruciating.

My stomach clenched.

She chewed on her bottom lip, tears welling now. I thought of Dan, and how cruel it was he should have had to endure this on top of everything else. The weight of a sadness so heavy I believed I might fall bore down on me; I stumbled into the empty chair opposite her.

'Why?' I whispered.

'No one knows,' she said.

'Why did you do it?' I wanted to understand. She didn't love Rob, she never had. Did she love Dan, the way I did? She couldn't do, could she?

'It wasn't supposed to be this way. For me,' she chewed at a hang nail on her thumb. I waited for her to continue, to explain.

'We needed you.'

I shook my head, uncomprehending.

'In the support group. It was my idea to ask you to join. I wanted you there, at first. I needed a friend. What with all those hard, embittered women. I felt out of place. And I knew you'd be brilliant in the kitchens. I remembered the rock cakes you'd made in cookery like it was yesterday. But then there was all that other stuff . . .' she trailed off and looked at me imploringly, as if I should fill in the gaps. I remained quiet.

'. . . That was meant to be my role, not yours. I watched you grow as I shrank, stuck here in this God-forsaken town, in a school full of old maids going nowhere. And I didn't like it. It was like being thirteen again. I thought I'd escaped all that when I left this place.' Her arms moved as she became more animated, more agitated.

'What?' I said. I really didn't understand.

'You were always bursting with ideas, with confidence—'

'At thirteen?'

She nodded.

'I was fat, clumsy—'

'No, you weren't.' She raised her voice, rancour surfacing. 'You were unconcerned what others thought. You might not have been the skinniest or the prettiest, but you were true to yourself. That takes a special kind of self-belief. I envied you.'

There was nothing I could say. It was true. I'd forgotten about that Mandy. Mandy Williams. She got buried when Dad died and Mum's grief ate her up, leaving only a shadow. She was buried further still when Ruth left.

Powerful Mandy was back. I had the strike, and Ruth, and Dan, to thank.

'You never gave that impression,' I said, at last. 'That you were jealous.'

'Good at pretending. Mum always said I should have gone onto the stage.' She smiled, half-heartedly, almost catching my eye as she did so.

'After your dad . . . the tables were turned.' Ruth looked at me properly, green eyes glistening; they were the saddest eyes I'd ever seen. Sadder even than Dan's. 'I'm sorry, Mandy. Truly sorry.'

This wasn't a performance; she meant it. I didn't hate her; I pitied her. I was so much richer than she was. I always had been; I'd simply lost sight of it.

'Don't think we'd have made the course, anyway,' I said. 'Me and Rob.'

She looked confused. 'I didn't mean that. You're worth so much more than him. Than both of them.'

I didn't know what to say.

'I'm leaving. Going back down south.'

'And Dan?'

'It's over for us. He won't leave; can't leave.'

The edges of my vision were blurring, my mind swirled, black and silver stars gathered on the outskirts of images . . .

Dan: sitting eating my cake, head bowed, shoulders hunched, vulnerable; Dan: playing the golden flugelhorn, strong, concentration etched into his furrowed brow, creating a sound so pure and beautiful and lovely it made me cry; Dan: the smell and sight and taste of him; the tiny scar threading through his left eyebrow, the ivory-white skin of his shins, the broad, flat fingernails; his touch: long, gentle fingers on my cheeks, in my hair, on my neck, my waist.

Dan: damaged, fearful, stuck. Unable to follow to dreams, his heart. A man whose life was unravelling, who needed help.

Darkness claimed me.

When I opened my eyes I didn't know where I was at first; I was staring at a white artexed ceiling.

My ceiling, my house.

No.

A house where another life had been and gone, in a town where I no longer belonged, which held no future for me. Green eyes came into view. Ruth.

'What happened?' I said.

She helped me into a sitting position. 'You fainted. Only out for a few seconds. Can I get you anything? Help in any way?' She held onto my hand.

'I can manage. Thank you.'

'Goodbye, Mandy,' she said, letting go of my hand, standing, ready to leave. There was nothing left to say. 'Good luck.'

THREE YEARS LATER

Sepia pictures of horse-drawn carriages and clippers floating in the harbour adorned the walls, interspersed with framed pages torn from *Mrs Beeton's Book of Household Management*. Teaspoons chinked against floral china cups on white tablecloths draped over round tables; the air thick with the hum of convivial chatter.

'And what can I get my favourite customer today?' I said to the man sitting at the table in front of me. He was an oddity; a breeze of faded denim and designer stubble amongst the beige slacks, loud shirts, and loafers of the American tourists, the rouged cheeks and tight perms of the elderly ladies who made up the bulk of my clientele on weekday lunchtimes.

'You know, I fancy Welsh Rarebit, followed by a slab of that delicious carrot cake of yours, and a pot of Earl Grey tea.' As he spoke he folded his newspaper – the crossword half complete – and clicked the top of an expensive ball point before slipping it into the pocket of the jacket slung over the back of the chair.

I began to make a note on my pad, but my yellow

Bic faded to nothing, the nib tearing at the paper. 'Can I borrow your pen, Nigel?'

'You ever going to invest in a decent biro? It's not like you can't afford it anymore.' He smiled, reaching for his jacket.

'I find it's a great way to meet people,' I smirked, holding out my hand, flicking my fingers towards my palm. 'C'mon. Hand it over.'

'Seriously, though. Buy a decent pen. And congratulations. Saw the piece in the paper last week. Businesswoman of the year, no less.'

Taking hold of my skirt, I bobbed a strange little curtsey, because I was embarrassed and didn't know how else to respond. It had been such a shock. A delightful, amazing, fantastic shock.

'It's not all been plain sailing,' I said.

In a month's time I was opening another café, down the coast. Similar in style and concept: old-fashioned, home-made staples your granny might have cooked, served in a cosy, Victorian-styled parlour. The new place had a shop front too, where bread, cakes, and pastries baked daily would be on sale to take away. The banks had been falling over themselves to invest, though I'd told them to go whistle. Mine was a community affair, with friends, old and new, the main stakeholders in my growing empire.

Nigel laughed, the air swimming with his warmth. 'Steady on. It's not an OBE. No need to be practising your curtsey, madam. And I know it's not been easy. You've worked bloody hard. Just buy a decent pen, will you?' He stretched out his hand, waiting for his pen to be returned. 'Thought any more about my kind offer?' he continued, a flicker of uncertainty in his eyes. And desire.

I still thought about Dan, occasionally, and the strike and FAG and Ruth, though there was no longer any pain; only bittersweet memories and the hope that Dan was working towards a kind of contentment, peace even. Had it been true love? At the time, I was so sure. But now I was only sure that he'd been the catalyst, as had Ruth, and the strike and my part in it, that set me on this path, and that I had no regrets. Would I have taken the same route, knowing the eventual, agonising, outcome? Yes, a thousand times, yes.

'Kind offer? I'm not a blinking charity,' I said, still holding onto Nigel's biro.

'You're certainly not.'

'I've thought about it.'

'And?'

'Maybe.'

'Doesn't have to be anything. A drink. With a friend.' He smiled, brown eyes warm, uncomplicated.

'I'm thinking about it.'

I like him, I really do. Before he leaves I'm going to say: 'Yes. Let's go out. I'd like that. Ta very much.'